The Chronicles

Of Hausse

Book One:

The Trouble with Dragons

By

Debbye Graafsma

Awakened to Grow Ministries
P.O. Box 546
Indian Trail, NC 28079
Find us on the web at awakenedtogrow.com

This book is dedicated

to the child-like

heart in each of us

and

to Ellie and Caedmon

The Trouble with Dragons

Table of Contents

Part Three

Part One

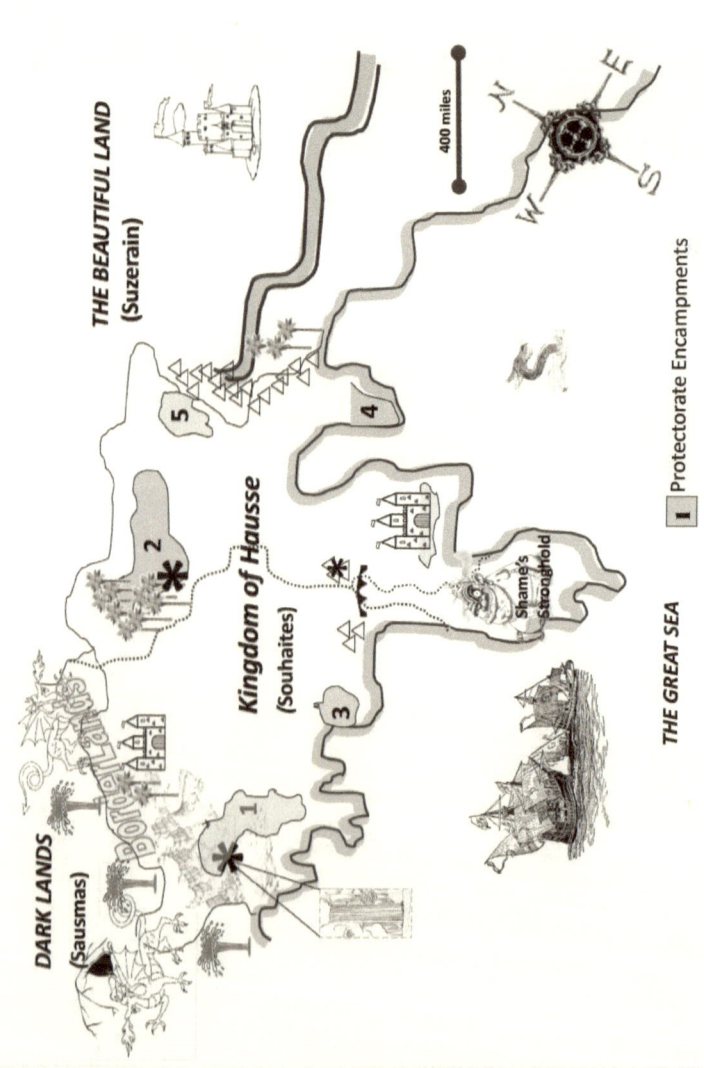

THE BEAUTIFUL LAND
(Suzerain)

DARK LANDS
(Sausmas)

Kingdom of Hausse
(Souhaites)

Shame's
Stronghold

THE GREAT SEA

400 miles

Protectorate Encampments

Chapter One
"Five Years before It All Began"

"There's the signal!"

Startled by the hand shaking his arm, as well as by his friend's loud whisper, Peyton looked up quickly.

"Are you sure it wasn't more lightning?" he asked.

"No, look!" Jaret pointed towards the castle window. "The lantern went back and forth three times. You'd better get a move on."

Jaret let out a low whistle. In response, a horse's snort was heard from further in, behind the trees.

Stepping out from under the cover of branches, Peyton grimly assessed the rain which continued to fall. "Hope I can get there through the mud," he muttered.

"You *cannot* fail," Jaret spoke with determination, handing his partner a bow and quiver of arrows. "Here; just in case."

Peyton stroked his horse before he took the reins, swinging up into the mount. After checking to be sure his rapier was still in its sheath at his belt, he took the additional weapons. "Thank you," he said. "Now, remember, if I'm not back before daybreak...."

"I know what to do. Don't worry." Jaret gave the hind quarters of his friend's horse an encouraging whack. "Good speed. Be careful."

Lurching just a little in the saddle as he began to move forward, Peyton looked back over his shoulder. "You as well," he replied.

Watching his friend ride away, Jaret spoke quietly, more to himself than to anyone. "Without help, we will all be dead by morning."

Slipping quiver and bow over his shoulder, Peyton put his attention forward. He pulled the thick black hood of his cloak over his head, to further hide himself in the darkness. Perhaps the rain was a good thing, he considered. No one would be walking the castle walls tonight. More likely, they would be inside warming by a fire.

Nearing the castle, he noticed the drawbridge had not yet been drawn up for the evening, and the gate was still open. He breathed a sigh of relief. The informer *had* been genuine after all; they had kept their side of the bargain.

Just before reaching the drawbridge, Peyton dismounted and tied his horse loosely to a nearby tree. He took off his cloak. As he wrapped up his sword and quiver in the cloak, he spoke gently into his horse's ear.

"Stay here, Goliath. Wait. I'll be back, and I'll need you."

He then made his way into the cold water of the moat, holding his cloak and weapons over his head, to keep them from soaking. Arriving at the gate, he silently slipped through, staying against the walls and in the shadows.

Once through the gate, he looked for the…. What had the informant said? Oh yes, the second door

to the left. *Look for the burning torch mounted on the wall.*
He was to go through that door, and wait in the
darkness for his contact to come. Strange, he reasoned.
He still had no idea what the purpose of his mission
was. It was better that way, he decided. If he was
caught, there would be nothing to deny. He could not
endanger the rest of the Protectorate – or, as the Queen
referred to them, "The Rebels."

Shutting the door of the little room, Peyton took
a quick breath, double-checking his movements. Was
this mission going too easily? Could a trap be waiting
for him? *Well, it was too late to worry about it now.*
Hurriedly, he stepped away from the grate-covered
window-opening in the door, and leaned against the
cold stone of the castle wall. Just as he did so, two of
the Queen's Guard walked by on patrol.

Had they seen him? No, apparently not. He was
safe for now.

After what seemed like an eternity of waiting,
Peyton slid down against the wall, into a sitting
position. After a few moments more, he caught himself
nodding off into sleep. He shook himself awake. No,
this would not be the time or place to take a nap, he
thought.

Suddenly, there was a noise at the door. Peyton
reached for his rapier, and slid up the wall to stand on
his feet once more. As the door opened, he readied
himself to run the intruder through.

A girl's voice spoke softly and carefully. "Is
anyone in here?"

Startled, Peyton remained silent, not sure whether this was his contact.

The girl spoke again into the inky darkness. "If you are here, the Prince will come."

Relieved to hear the code words he had been waiting for, Peyton replied. "And the King will rule forever."

"Oh good," the girl replied. "This is my second time to come since the signal was sent, and I wasn't sure how I would explain another absence to my mistress."

"What is my mission?" Peyton asked her.

"Here," she whispered in reply, lifting the rather large bundle she had been holding close to her chest. "You must take special care of this package. Don't let anything happen to it. Strap it to yourself if you must. But hold it lightly. It can be easily broken. Don't undo the wrappings until you are sure you are back in a place of safety."

"What *is* the package?" Peyton's curiosity posed the inquiry before he realized his question placed both the girl and himself in grave danger.

"I cannot tell you," she replied. "But you will find out soon enough. Seeing that you were the one trusted for this task, you must know that to succeed you will have to move with great speed and speak to no one. The Sausmas has his spies everywhere. The entire future of the Protectorate Cause might rest on what you do tonight."

Peyton stuttered. "I –I wasn't told. I'm sorry."

The girl lowered the shawl she had pulled up over her head, smiling. "Don't worry. I am sure there are Light-Bearers all around us. Do you know the way out?"

"I came by way of the moat and inner gate."

"Oh, no," she whispered. "You cannot go out that way. We met in this room, because there is a tunnel entrance which begins here and lets you out in the trees. There is a small cottage there, where you will find provisions to accompany your package. Here; let me get a little light to show you. Hide behind the door. Crouch under the window."

From her cloak, the girl drew a candle. Opening the door, she looked carefully to and fro to be sure she wasn't observed. Then, she reached up to the burning torch and lit her candle. Cupping her hand around the flame, she pulled carefully back into the dark room. From there, she moved to the corner of the room and lifted an escape hatch hinged in the floor boards.

"Come!" she urged. "Quickly!"

Peyton clutched the package tightly, and prepared to go down the short stairs into the tunnel.

"Here," the girl said, "take the candle. You will need it down there."

As the candle passed between them, Peyton caught a glimpse of the girl's face. She couldn't be much older than I am, he thought. "What is your name?" he asked as he took the candle from her.

"Elda," she replied. "Yours?"

"Peyton." He paused. "How old are you?"

"I am the Queen's third handmaid. I am nine years," she whispered, motioning for him to hurry.

"I'm ten years a week last," he whispered back.

"Good to meet you," she said. "Now get out of here before you get us all killed. Remember the instructions I gave you about the package. Don't open it until you are sure you are in a place of safety."

Waiting until she saw the candle's glimmer fade into the tunnel, Elda lowered the escape hatch door once again, and stepped back into the center of the room. Closing her eyes, she took a deep breath.

"Please, *please* surround him with safety," she whispered.

Then, pulling her shawl back over her head, she stepped out of the room into the castle courtyard, and pulled the door shut behind her. Hastily, she made her way back to the Queen's bedchambers, hoping her absence had not been noticed. Even one hint of a doubt, or shadow of a question would endanger the plan they had all worked towards for months now.

Exiting the tunnel in the woods, Peyton was thankful for the candle Elda had given him. He blew it out and decided it would be wiser to place it in his pocket and take it with him, than it would be to leave a trace of his presence behind. Taking in his surroundings, he discovered Goliath no more than ten feet away.

Now, where was the cottage she had mentioned? Looking around, he saw an abandoned guard house. It probably hadn't been used since the drawbridge had been built, he supposed. No need for a guard or a guard house when one added a moat to a castle.

Stepping into the guard house, Peyton saw a rather large basket on a table. Next to the basket was a wooden crate, filled with various containers and scrolls.

How would he get all of this onto the back of his horse, he wondered? After some consideration, the boy decided to place the package inside the basket and then surround and cover the package with as much as would fit from what was in the crate. Then, he realized, it would be easy to travel, with the basket held in front of him as he rode Goliath back to the Protectorate Encampment.

As he completed the task at hand, Peyton's thoughts turned philosophical. Funny how even what they called themselves came down to the side someone was on. The King, Suzerain, *(Soo- zee- rayn)* had decreed that those who stood against the Queen and Sausmas *(Sawz-mahs)* were to be given honor and respect. He had even issued orders to his Light-Bearers and all those in His Realm were to offer assistance to the Cause in any method necessary. In fact, the title "Protectorate" had been his creation. But to Queen Souhaites *(Soo-hay-teez)*, and to everyone else under Sausmas' controlling influence, they were considered Rebels.

Preparing to mount his horse again, Peyton remembered Elda's words. "Hold the package lightly. It can be easily broken." Sighing, he readjusted the items in the basket, placing the package on top.

Riding stealthfully back to meet Jaret and the others, and then to the Encampment, Peyton once more found himself thankful for the rain. He wondered just why the mission had gone so easily. Upon his arrival, the sentries wasted no time ushering him to Commander Carel's Pavilion.

The Commander was pacing back and forth, anxious for news of Peyton's mission. "How did it go, boy? Were you discovered?"

Peyton placed the basket on the floor by the door. "No, sir. Everything went as you had said. In fact, I am troubled it went so easily."

Chuckling, Carel patted the boy's shoulder. "It went as the Light-Bearers told us it would. Suzerain prepared the path for you. That is why we sent you, as one so young."

"But I thought...." Peyton's voice trailed off.

"That it was a dangerous mission? That it was." The Commander nodded, stroking his beard. "That you were chosen because you gained your Rapier Status at such a young age? Well, perhaps." He lowered his voice and spoke conspiratorially. "But you and I both know the Dark Arts of Sausmas and the Queen extend into crafts that are best left alone. We cannot fight them on their terms, nor with our own skills. We must depend upon the king, and his timing. This mission was his direct command."

As though prodded by an inner sense, the Commander changed the direction of the conversation. "Where is the package?"

Peyton moved back to the tent door. "Here, sir. I still don't know what it is. Can I see it?"

"Certainly. Certainly." He raised voice once again. "Roberts? Where 'ere ye?"

Commander Carel's subordinate immediately appeared at the tent entrance. "Yes sir?"

"Go and fetch the young woman. It's time." He once again turned his attention to the package. "Now, let's see what we have here." Carefully, Carel lifted the package and laid it on the table. Gently, he began to untie the strings securing the heavy cloth. These had hidden its contents.

Watching him, Peyton remembered his unaware, clumsy attempts when first loading the basket, and how remembering Elda's words of instruction had caused him to rearrange it. He held his breath, hoping his first efforts had not damaged the highly breakable object inside.

Carel worked carefully as he untied the last of the cords, and pulled the heavy grey flannel apart, revealing a second layer of much thinner cloth within. Peyton instinctively reached to touch it. It was the softest substance he had ever seen.

"What...." he began.

The Commander raised his finger to his lips. "Shh, now, boy," he urged gently. "We must speak softly now, and dinna' wake the wee lad." He removed two more layers of the gossamer cloth to reveal a sleeping baby boy. "Today is his birthday!"

"Who's baby *is* he?" Peyton stood transfixed, considering all he had witnessed that day.

"That is a secret to be discussed at a future time, son. For now, just suffice it to say that the future of our Cause just might rest here in this wee lad."

At that moment, Roberts returned with a woman from Protectorate Area One. Carel quickly covered the baby. "No one is to know the service you have rendered today, or the outcome of your mission, Peyton. Do you understand?"

"Yes, sir."

"I'm sure you will discover the facts at some point in the future." He turned his attention to his assistant. "Roberts, see this young man is given some food and a bath. He may rest tomorrow."

"At once, Commander." As Peyton moved to exit the Pavilion with Roberts, the woman moved further in. She smiled at Peyton as they passed.

Carel greeted her. "Come in, good woman! Thank you for being willing to help us." He waited until Roberts and Peyton had left. Picking up the baby boy, he transferred the child to her arms. "This child was born earlier today. His mother cannot care for him any longer. I'm sure it has been a while since he has been fed."

The woman instinctively drew the child close to her. "What a Providence that our own baby girl was delivered just two days ago! This poor little one will need a family."

The Commander spoke with determination. "Yes, that is probably truer than you realize. Now, your husband has been in the Coastal Encampment for the past six months, and your baby daughter is still in the

Time of Seclusion. Is that true? Good. Good ….. And because of that, no one has heard of your delivery, or seen your daughter other than your mother who served as your midwife. Is that so? Good. Good….. So, I must ask you a favor."

"Yes?" her eyebrows rose inquisitively. "Am I not supposed to be in seclusion with the child as well?"

"That is why I called for you at night. Captain Roberts is a good man. He and the boy who just left are the only ones who know of our meeting. Roberts is trustworthy, so don't worry. I would trust him with my life." Carel continued. "That being said, as far as anyone is to know, you have given birth to twins. Even your husband is to believe this to be so. I myself will explain the situation to your mother. You will receive the awards and honors that accompany such an omen. You are to raise this boy as your own, and never speak of what has transpired tonight to anyone. If you have a problem or a question arising because of the child, speak of it to no one but myself, in person. At some future date, Suzerain may expect more of you in regard to this child. The King will let you know what you are to tell your husband."

As she contemplated Carel's words, the woman nodded. "I think I understand. I will do as you ask." She looked up. "Thank you for trusting me Commander." Reaching for the heavy flannel covering on the table, she wrapped the baby once more, and then moved to exit the Pavilion. As she reached the tent door, she stopped. "Does the child have a name?" she asked.

Commander Carel had already moved on to his next task. He had begun to assess the containers and scrolls within the basket, accompanying the child. When he replied, he did not look up.

"You will have to give him a name."

 **Chapter Two**

How the Trouble Started

"If you ever *kill* a dragon, don't assume doing so will make it easy to complete the task again. Be careful you don't allow yourself think because you defeat *one* dragon with *one* strategy, that *all* dragons will be conquered with the same methods. You will need a fresh and unique tactic each time."

The Tutor stopped and looked over his spectacles at his students, allowing time for his words to be understood. He had already repeated the statement once. When he was sure he had the attention of the entire class, he continued.

"And not *all* dragons are *bad* dragons."

This last statement caused a murmuring among some of the boys in the back of the room. Ignoring the noise, he raised his voice and continued. "Some dragons would gladly go back to change the path they took to get them where they are. Believe me, life imprisonment under Sausmas is a terrifying predicament."

It was almost the end of Discovery Season One. Elder Tallis had served as the Instructor for Protectorate Area One for more years than anyone could remember. He had seen hundreds of students come and go. And yet, for some reason, the first part of this school year had seemed different to him, as it also had to several of the younger instructors. They *all* sensed it. There was something unusual......different... *special* about this particular group.

Tallis considered the collection of this year's fresh recruits. As with all students, each one had grown up in Protectorate Area One from infancy, and was now in year fifteen of living. While in childhood, each one had been trained in the academics of reading, writing, mathematics, history and geography. Each had spent hours training in the Arts and Sciences. They had learned Elements of Life from the Crown Prince, Kyriel. They had encountered the Essence of Suzerain's Power on many levels, experiencing his nature and the atmosphere of his Realm – or, rather, as much as was possible while living in Protectorate Area One...

And now, they were close to completing their initial Discovery Season. One Discovery Season would be completed and nine more would follow; two Seasons in each of the Five Protectorate Areas. Still, the Tutor was thankful he was not forced to say "good-bye" to any of them just yet. One more Discovery Season would follow before they departed for Area Two some two thousand miles northeast of Area One.

Area One had been the first of the five secret Protectorate Encampments, or Area Communities, to be developed within the borders of the Kingdom of Hausse.

It was a story still remembered; written down for generations to come. In the days before the Ancients, the first mortals and their descendants had first sought King Suzerain for protection from Sausmas, and the Queen. It had been the Crown Prince who brought them to these cliffs in the desert. Yes, Kyriel himself had personally opened the Great Stone Door behind the waterfall. And hadn't he been the one to introduce the first mortals to King's Suzerain's Light-Bearers? Come to think of it, Tallis considered, it had been Prince Kyriel who had designed the Plan.

And still, even as High Ruler, Kyriel continued to pour out of his resources to help them. What a generous heart the Crown Prince possessed!

Elder Tallis' thoughts came back to the task at hand. He sighed.

Yes, he would miss this class; especially its potential leaders.

Several hands were up in the back of the room.

"Yes?" he responded.

"Elder Tallis, I have some questions," one boy in the middle of the group stated.

"Say on, Peyton."

"Why do you say that… 'not *all* dragons are bad dragons?' What does that mean? Why do you speak of life imprisonment to Sausmas? Why do you say *that*? And, I've been wondering…. where do the dragons *come* from? Why do they keep coming back after so many die each summer? And why don't we ever see *baby* dragons?"

Elder Tallis smiled. "Those are perceptive questions, my boy. They show that you have been using that brain of yours." He pulled up a stool and put his pointer down on the desk. "I'm glad you asked. Perhaps today *would* be the day for us to cover that subject. We can always come back to what I was discussing later." He chuckled to himself, anticipating the predictable responses of his students to the question he was getting ready to ask. Taking a seat on the stool, he rubbed his hands together in delight.

"Let's see…. Does anyone *else* have questions about *dragons*?"

Suddenly the room was almost electric with a unified excitement.

You would think I lit a fuse! Tallis thought to himself with a smile. Hands shot up all over the room.

"Oh my! This *must* be the subject we need to discuss today! Let me hear some of your questions. So…. What do you what to know?"

"Why do they breathe out fire?"

"Where did they come from?"

"Did Sausmas create them?"

"How can you tell a good one from a bad one?"

"How do you fight one?"

"Why are they only in the West Country?"

Elder Tallis put up his hands in mock surrender. "Oh my, I wonder if we can cover all of this today! Perhaps I will need a week or two!" He paused for a moment to look around the room, winking at the front row of students, his eyes coming to rest on one particular young woman. "Elizabeth, how shall we cover this material?"

The quiet, blonde-headed, young woman to whom the Tutor had spoken blushed just a little. Looking up, she realized her hand was still raised. Pulling down her hand, and a little embarrassed, she looked around at her classmates, who hadn't seemed to notice. In a shy, quiet voice, she responded. "Could you tell us a *story* about the dragons, Elder Tallis? Something that really happened to *real* people?"

Tallis beamed at her. "What an excellent idea! An *intelligent* idea! That way you can ask me questions as we walk through the story!" He paused. "Why don't you all put your supplies away, so you are prepared to leave for Vespers, while I try to remember a proper account of a dragon to help you to learn? That way we can talk about these things just as long as physically possible before we all must part ways for the day."

Immediately, the room was filled with bustling activity. Books were replaced in the class library shelves, study satchels were filled with scrolls and tablets, inkwells were refilled and put on the supply shelves, making workspaces ready for the next day. Several of the students, whose assigned turn it was to sweep the floor, did so. Several set to work tidying the laboratory counters and the fencing drill area. Within ten minutes, the room was immaculate. Much sooner than Elder Tallis anticipated, I'm sure, thirty-five eager faces were once again in their seats, impatiently anticipating the Tutor's storytelling.

It only took a few moments for the older boys to realize the instructor had momentarily left the room. Zyniker, the student who usually sat next to Peyton, leaned over towards his friend. "Hey 'Tiny,'" he said, "You got anything we can throw at the girls?" *(Zyniker called Peyton 'Tiny' not only because everyone else did, but mostly because already at fifteen years, Peyton was six feet tall; taller than any of the other Initiates in the class).*

Peyton looked over at his friend. "Not now, Spider. We're so close to the last week of the Season. I don't feel like repeating, do you?" *(Peyton called Zyniker "Spider," not only because he had black curly hair that looked like a big ball on top of his head, but because Zyniker had taken a dare to eat a red spider on the first day of classes.)*

"Hey, Tiny," Jaret called to Peyton. "Do you know where Lord Tallis went?"

"No," Peyton replied. "I...

Just at that moment, Elder Tallis backed into the room, pulling a wheeled cart behind him. Resting in the cart was a huge painting on its side.

"Is that the painting from the hallway, Elder?" a girl named Lisette asked. She and two other girls rose to help steady the picture as the cart moved into the room.

"That it is, that it is," the Tutor responded. "Would a couple of you boys come and help us to turn this frame right side up?"

Jaret and Zyniker were the first to jump up. They all worked as a team to upright the very old, very heavy, ornate frame. As they did so, Peyton made an observation. He had walked by the painting for years, and had never really looked at it. And now, it apparently would be the centerpiece in the most interesting lesson of the entire semester!

How could he have been so unaware of how important it was? Why hadn't he seen it until now?

Elder Tallis had resumed his perch on the stool. "All right, children," he said, once more picking up his pointer. "Take a good look at this painting and tell me what you see."

He pointed to the image before them. The artist's design showed a silver clothed warrior, with arms raised, holding an immense shield in his right hand. In bright colors, painted on the shield, were four images; a lion, a man, an ox and an eagle. In the center of the shield, were two wheels, one inside the other, with eyes encircling the outer wheel. Six feathery wings moved out from the center.

In the soldier's left hand was a rapier, drawn at the ready, and enveloped in fire. The silver warrior stood before an immense winged and scaled reptile. Its feet had long claws like a bear, and its massive bat-like wings overshadowed the man, dwarfing him in a cloud of smoke and cinders. From the dragon's mouth a stream of fire shot out, exploding into sparks as it struck the shield. The creature was covered with scales appearing like armor in the firelight. It had fangs like a giant wolf, dripping blood.

Destruction surrounded it. The sky was filled with black clouds, as though lightning might strike at any moment.

Behind the knight was a woman dressed in rags, huddling forward to protect two small children, who were also dressed in rags. Was the warrior standing between the dragon and the children, he wondered?

What were the ruins around them? Where were they standing? Was this a real place?

Peyton was fascinated by the images. As he gazed, the faces of the two small children somehow looked familiar to him. But where had he seen them? And what did the look on their faces mean?

To the left of the warrior, were four figures, also with wings, who were dressed in Fire and Light. Each one wore a golden belt, and carried a flaming sword. What or better said, *who* were they, he wondered? He had never seen anything so brilliant!

Then the boy noticed something else. The figures dressed in light, held much larger versions of the silver knight's sword, each of them filled with fire of the same color. But then Peyton noticed something. The fire coming from the dragon's mouth was darker somehow, tinged with a color diluting its brightness. What did *that* mean, he wondered?

Elder Tallis broke through his reverie with a hand clap.

"All right!" the Teacher announced. "Let's begin! Have each of you had enough time to absorb the images in front of you?" He waited for responses. "Good. Good.

"Now, I want you to observe the warrior dressed in silver. Those of you who complete all Ten Discovery Seasons will have the opportunity to *become like* this warrior. This is the king's purpose in creating the Protectorate and the Protectorate Areas. In fact, if and when you choose to remain in classes, you will receive your first armaments in Area Three....."

Glancing around the room, he paused.

"Now...... for our *story.*" He surveyed his students, confirming he had their full attention. "Are you comfortable? Good. Good."

"As you remember.....Before the Beginning and continuing into Forever, King Suzerain is the Sovereign Ruler of everything seen and unseen. Alone, and without help from anyone, he created everything, even the concepts we mortals hold in our minds. He is good, and kind. He is always safe.

"Now, before the Dawn of Time, just after Light began, Suzerain created the first mortals, Hekastos and Khavvah. These were the parents of the Ancients, whose children we are. Even the King's name tells us about his intentions toward us. Although he holds the power to rule absolutely, he refuses to control. Even the substance we breathe in and out is part of his Essence. Without him, we would cease to exist. But, even though he knows we are dependent upon him, it is his wish we each be free to govern our own Inner Realm. For that reason, everyone who serves him, from the youngest initiate, to the most highly distinguished Knight of the Dragon's Cross, does so out of love for him. Now, this applies to .... *Everyone* in Suzerain's

Realm – whether a person, or a family, or even a government. No one who is truly part of his Realm does *anything* for him because they have been forced to do so.

"Well, the first Mortals were generously given a large portion of 'The Beautiful Land.' That was originally the name given to all the lands Suzerain developed." The Tutor's eyes misted. "That was in the "Before." Everything was *filled* with Light then…."

Watching his Instructor, Peyton found himself wondering how Lord Tallis knew such a thing.

The Teacher continued. "The first mortals were very close friends with Suzerain. They walked together and talked together every day. Suzerain shared with them the secrets of Fire and Light. Things went along very well for a time.

"Then, a Light-Bearer who stood in the King's Court, whom Suzerain loved very deeply, decided he wanted more. He became discontent with Suzerain's Kingdom. He chose to betray the king. He wanted the Suzerain's Power for himself.

"He began with whispers. First, he cast doubt on Suzerain, and suggested to other Light-Bearers near to him, that *he* would be a better ruler than the king. I have to tell you he was very convincing. In fact, many of Suzerain's Light-Bearers believed his lies and followed him into a battle for the throne.

"Now, if you remember, when we studied this last month, I told you the king won that battle easily. All those who joined with the betrayer were exiled from Suzerain's Realm along with him. I'm sure they didn't realize what would happen. They lost everything they held which had represented the King. For example, they no longer had Light, or Life, or Joy, or Community. Instead, the absence of Suzerain filled them. They learned to breathe another substance than the King's Essence. Everything within them became black and twisted.

"That Light-Bearer is now called 'Sausmas.' His name means 'The Terror.' He currently calls himself, 'The Dark Prince,' although he hasn't one ounce of royal blood in his being.

"He charmed the first mortals, and stole their trust away from Suzerain. Then, just as he had done with the Light-Bearers who had followed him, he convinced those mortals to give him the right to rule over them instead of Suzerain. He convinced them the king was evil and was hiding Truth from them. Over time, he eroded away their trust in Suzerain, by casting doubt. He convinced them if they trusted the king, their lives would be controlled, limited and miserable. Then, in contrast, he offered to give them freedom to do as they pleased.

"Do you remember I told you the first mortals were generously given dominion over the entire visible realm? This is what they traded away. Sadly, they believed Sausmas, and gave him the legal authority to rule their portion of 'The Beautiful Land.' We now call that territory 'The Kingdom of Hausse.'

"Of course, after he seized power, Sausmas went back on all of the promises made to the first mortals. In addition, the Light-Bearers who had been exiled from

Suzerain's Realm *with* Sausmas now had no sense of loyalty, or order. Each *one* wanted to rule, to control.

"Enki, the Terrible, is part of this group. So are the Shades, the Weavers and the Muddlers. In Discovery Season Two we will learn how to recognize these entities, and their methods of operation. For now, let me just tell you that when a mortal lives outside of Suzerain's Realm, it is impossible for him or her to recognize them. It is easy to become deceived.

"Now, when Sausmas gained the power over them he sought, he betrayed the first mortals. All ability to rule was stolen from them, and they were reduced to slavery. It didn't take long for Hekastos and Khavvah to discover what had happened, but by then it was too late. They had already lost everything."

He paused and looked around the room. "Since the moment the hoax was made known, Sausmas has continually worked to destroy *all* mortals in the Kingdom of Hausse."

From the middle of the group of students, a hand raised. It was the youngest member, who had found a place of favor with the instructor.

"Yes, Anna?"

"What does all of this have to do with *dragons?*" she asked.

Tallis smiled at her. "I'm coming to that, my dear. Don't despair." He took a deep breath before he continued.

"You know how the Protectorate Area Encampments began, don't you?"

There were many differing responses among the students, so Tallis continued.

"When Sausmas' deception was exposed, Crown Prince Kyriel removed those descendants of the first mortals who were, in their hearts, still loyal to Suzerain, and travelled by night to the desert, where we are now. These are the mortals we refer to as 'the Ancients.' It was Kyriel, who opened the Great Stone Door behind the waterfall, and showed the hidden passageway into this cove where we have lived for more than a thousand years.

"It was Kyriel who provided the water we so freely enjoy."

Jaret spoke up at this point. "My father's family had to *pay* for *their* water."

The Tutor nodded. "Yes Jaret, that's true. Those mortals who enter the Protectorates as adults come into one of the other Area Encampments. From the time they enter onward, they receive *free* water from the Suzerain. However, those who remain outside must *purchase* water from the Queen." He paused. "All of you have lived in the Protectorate Areas since your childhood. However, your Moment of Choosing will arrive during your Fourth Season, while you are assigned to Area Two. At that time you will be find it necessary to ask the Suzerain where he desires to place you for the furthering of his Plan. Many of you will choose to marry, and either live in an Area Encampment, or work as agents for the Protectorate in the Kingdom of Hausse. Incidentally, we have many who have joined the Cause and live outside the Area Encampments, with those mortals yet ungathered.

"That being said, most mortals who live in the Kingdom of Hausse have believed Sausmas and the Queen, when they lie about King Suzerain. There are some who even refuse to believe he exists at all."

Anna sighed; "But Elder Tallis, what about the *dragons?*"

Her obvious excitement, mixed with impatience over the lesson, ignited a ripple of laughter among her classmates. Glancing at Anna's face, Elder Tallis couldn't help but smile.

He continued. "Take a look at the dragon in this painting, and tell me what you see."

"Fire."

"He's awfully big, and scary."

"He has fangs."

"How would an arrow get through those scales?"

"Very good…. What else do you see? The Tutor wanted his students to look deeper than the obvious. He wanted to see how insightful they were. The more perceptive ones would carry the most potential as the class moved forward in the development of Inner Life.

"He's mean," Anna offered.

"The knight is standing between the dragon and the woman with the children," David offered from the back of the room.

Peyton spoke up. "Elder, may I ask a question?"

Tallis nodded.

"Are *all* dragons fire-breathers?"

Tallis was surprised by the question. He stopped and looked at Peyton. "Very good question, Tiny. No, not *all* dragons breathe fire. At least not at first."

Peyton's curiosity was stirred. "What do you mean, *at first?* What happens?"

The Tutor looked over his spectacles at his listeners. "Before, someone asked whether Sausmas *creates* dragons. The firm answer to *that* question would be a resounding 'NO.' Sausmas does not have power to *create anything*, nor is it his nature to do so. He is a destroyer, plain and simple. In the case of dragons, it would be more precise to say he *develops* them. Now, who asked me why we don't see *baby* dragons?"

Lisette's hand went up.

"What made you think of that question, my dear?"

She spoke shyly. "I don't know exactly. I know they fly. Are they like birds that lay eggs?"

Elder Tallis smiled. "No, they don't lay eggs, and no, there are no such things as baby dragons, at least not in the sense *you* mean."

He stood up and began to move about as he spoke. "Several moments ago, I explained to you what happened to the Light Bearers who chose to trust Sausmas in his rebellion against the King. After the battle, those beings turned bitter and dark. They became the Shades and Weavers and Muddlers. If you remember, I also mentioned Sausmas' seconds-in-command. They are the Pythons. The most powerful of these is Enki, and he is very skilled in his trickery.

These dark beings all work together to deceive all Mortals – even you…."

At this point, he paused, and looked intently from face to face to increase the impact of his words.

"….*even you* could bc lost to the Cause, if you do not learn to guard your soul."

Sitting down on the stool once more, he turned his attention to the painting. "I want you to look carefully at the dragon's eyes. What do you see?"

There was a moment of silence.

It was Anna who spoke up first. "He looks sad…. and really angry too."

"Yes, very good. *Very* good!" was the reply. "Anna, what do you think is the story behind this painting?"

Anna looked at the picture judiciously, as did the rest of the class. All were intrigued and looking for the answer to Elder's question. Finally, she spoke. "I think he's trying to get to the woman and the children. I understand that the knight is protecting them." She paused, and looked at Tallis. "Is the dragon *trying* to destroy them?"

"Good question. Does anyone have an idea about that?"

Elizabeth said, "Maybe he's just mad, and doesn't know what he's doing."

"Excellent thought, Elizabeth," the Tutor responded. "Any other thoughts?" He looked around the room, waiting.

Peyton spoke up. "Well, *you* said, there are no *baby* dragons, which makes me think that *this* dragon must have been *something else* before it became a dragon. Is that right?"

Tallis paused. "Go on."

Peyton continued. "Well, if that's *true*, and the silver warrior is protecting the woman and her children *from* the dragon ....." He stopped mid-sentence.

At this point, Jaret picked up the train of thought, and said, "Elder, you also said that dragons are *developed*, and you warned each of us to guard our souls from Sausmas' deceptions..."

Peyton interrupted. "*And* at the beginning of our class today, you told us that not all dragons are bad dragons. You said life imprisonment under Sausmas is terrifying."

"He also said if a dragon could go back and change their choices, they would," Zyniker interjected. "What does that prove?"

Peyton continued. "No, Spider, think about it.... If we put *all* the statements Elder Tallis has made today *together*, we already have a good idea of the story told by the painting!"

Peyton looked at his Tutor, whose eyes were twinkling in delight. "Elder Tallis, is the dragon in the picture actually a *person*? A person who didn't guard their soul?"

Chapter Three

*"The Truth About
How Dragons Are
Made"*

    Elder Tallis paused for a moment before
answering the question posed, allowing the significance
of Peyton's words to sink in. When he was satisfied the
children had gained the next step towards the Lesson he
was leading them into, he spoke once more.

    "*Now* we are ready for a story."

    The Instructor rose to his feet. "This painting
tells us many stories. It is a combination of many of the
accounts of those who have escaped or been rescued
from the Queen's Kingdom. As a Protectorate Initiate,
you are in a very privileged position, one you will not
realize until you experience more Life Encounters.
Perhaps, however, your parents, or even grandparents,
have told you their own stories, all of which are on
record, and might be somehow represented by this
illustration. Now, each of *you* were born into a
Protectorate Area, and you have had the benefit of
learning of the Suzerain in this environment.

    "Notice the woman and children huddling here."
Tallis pointed to the figures dressed in rags on the
canvas. "This is a mother and her children. In the

beginning, they were part of a family who had great potential to become strong and healthy. The mother and the father both had hope of a future that would last.

"In the beginning, they did very well together. They expressed love to each other, and chose to marry. They made plans for the future. That's when the trouble began."

He paused, as though consider his next statements. Then he went on.

"If we were to make comparisons: For each *one* of *you*, there are *thousands* born into the Kingdom of Hausse, who experience untold Pain and Difficulty without ever knowing of the king. For many, their Moment of Choosing has been delayed because of Sausmas and Enki. Still others, for many different reasons, put off their Moment of Choosing until their Exchange Day approaches. Confidentially, those are the mortals for whom I myself grieve. Those mortals miss entirely the adventure the Suzerain has waiting for them.

"How many of you know the stories of how your family came to be part of the Protectorate?"

Hands went up all over the room. Tallis continued. "If your parents have *not* told you the story, it is important you come to know what life was like for them…. *before*…. for those who lived outside of this Area Community. Each story is different, but, in some ways all stories are the same. Knowing the history of your own generations is a large part of your preparation and effectiveness in becoming a part in the Plan."

He looked to the boys in the second row. "Jaret, you mentioned your father's family had to purchase water from the Queen."

Jaret nodded.

"Have your grandparents, or your father ever told you what their lives were like when they lived in Hausse?"

Jaret paused and then spoke slowly. "They told me some of the story. My grandparents told me it was hard to come up with the money for water. They worked all the time. The cost of the water kept going up and up. My father's two sisters were born before my father was. Each time a baby was born, Queen Souhaites would send a Regent to the house. When my aunts were born, the Queen gave my grandparents gifts and promotions. They even received extra horses and a larger house. But my grandmother said those things didn't make up for the extra hours grandfather had to work to earn money for the water."

Zyniker chuckled. "Why didn't they just sell some of the stuff the Queen gave them to pay for it?"

Jaret looked at Elder Tallis. The Instructor spoke. "Do *you* know why they didn't do that, Jaret?"

The boy looked down at his hands. "Because… It is an action punishable by imprisonment or death to reject gifts given by the Queen. My father told me that one of their neighbors had tried to do that, and the father was taken away to serve as a slave in the palace. That family was left abandoned, and had no money at all."

The room was quiet. Gently, Tallis prodded him to continue. "What happened when your father was born?"

"My grandfather told me the week after my father was born, the Queen's Regent came to the door. Since the baby was a boy, his orders from the Queen were to take my father away to execute him, if his parents couldn't pay the extra tax it would cost to keep him. Most baby boys are marked for death in Hausse. So, my grandparents had a choice. They could pay the extra tax, and keep my father to raise him; or, they could give him to the Queen and receive more gifts and honors."

"What did they do, Jaret?" Anna asked sympathetically.

Jaret looked around at his classmates. "A lot of families in Hausse just give their boy babies to the Queen. The ones who *do* manage to pay the tax, and are allowed to raise their sons, end up having them taken into the Queens control anyway when they become older. In Hausse, sons are made to work hard even when they are small. When the Regent came, my grandfather lied and told him the baby had died in childbirth. It was a dangerous thing to do, but they loved my father."

"What happened?" Peyton wanted to know.

"Well," Jaret answered, "at first, they tried to hide him, but then he got too big. It was hard to hide him when he would cry. Soon they couldn't hide him anymore. My grandmother used to dress him up like a little girl, and they let his hair grow. But he got old enough that the neighbors were suspicious, and someone reported them. When the Queen found out, her Regent came back and gave my grandparents a tax bill, with interest added. My grandmother said that the interest addcd was a penalty for lying to the Queen. As punishment, the soldiers forced my grandfather to drink a little bottle of some black liquid. Grandmother thought it was poison, but grandfather didn't die. He said it was very bitter tasting, and he wanted to run away."

"Did your family leave, and come into the Protectorate then?" Anna asked.

Jaret shook his head. "No, they thought they would just work harder and harder to fix it. They tried to gain the Queen's approval once more, and regain her favor. But the Queen's Regents made my grandfather work hours and hours just to buy water. Grandmother said they were always hungry. Sometimes, even all of the hours Grandfather worked, the tax bill had to be paid first; and they only had enough money for water or for food. Many times, they had to choose between the two."

"What happened? How *did* they come to the Protectorate?" Peyton asked.

"Well, my grandfather thought he would get ahead of the tax bill. He worked long days, and was always gone from home. But over time, my grandmother told me something changed in his heart. He started acting differently; he was selfish. He and my grandmother started fighting… all the time. My aunts, at ten and twelve years, even began to work for other people – they would take care of children, or clean – anything to help buy food. I'm not sure how it started exactly, but my grandfather told me that one day he looked in the mirror when he was getting ready for bed, and noticed that the skin across his chest was changing color."

Elder Tallis interrupted him. "Did he tell you about anything he felt before that night?"

"Not that I remember," Jaret replied, "except, my grandmother told me that they had stopped talking. He said he just seemed to go numb inside. The family stopped having fun; or even being together. He was always angry, and she never knew when he was going to yell at her. She said it was like he was alone and she was alone, but they were living in the same house. She did remember that he talked about being afraid all the time during those days. She also said that my aunts were afraid of him. Everyone tried to avoid making him angry. They just stayed out of his way.

"Anyway, that night he noticed a change in his chest. When he woke up the next morning, there were scales growing on his back. His nails had become very thick. When he looked in the mirror, his teeth had changed. They were turning yellow, and growing longer."

"Jaret!" David called out. "Are you kidding? Are you trying to tell us that your *grandfather* turned into a *dragon?*"

Jaret looked at him. "He said it didn't happen all at once. But after that, he began to wear long sleeves to hide what was happening. He began to think only about himself. All he could think about was finding a way to be comfortable and happy. He kept thinking that other people were out to hurt him. He stopped trusting my grandmother. He made lots of rules for my aunts and my father. He started hitting them, and getting angry all the time. I don't know how long it was, but one day, when he was angry, he noticed he felt really hot. His head hurt terribly. He stayed in bed after that, and stopped going to work."

"Was he sick?" Anna asked.

"That's what my grandmother thought. She said he had a fever, and tried to help him. But he wouldn't talk to her. Then, one day, she went to take him some water, thinking he must be thirsty. The bedchamber door was locked. She heard voices on the other side of the door, and didn't recognize them. She was afraid to go in. The next day, he didn't answer her when she called for him to open the door. She waited until after he had been in the bedchamber with the door locked for several days. She was afraid he was dead. A neighbor helped her break the door down."

Jaret paused, thinking about the story in light of the painting in front of the class.

"*Was* he dead?" David wanted to know.

"No," Jaret replied. "He wasn't *dead*. He just wasn't *there*. Instead, there was a huge dragon in the room. It was as though the dragon had grown inside the room and had been stuffed into it like it was a big box. When the door opened, the dragon bit the door in half. Grandmother said it tried to turn around, apparently looking for the window. Its tail tore through the wall, as

41

it tried to escape. Then, suddenly, it was in the yard. My aunts and my father, the children, heard the noise and went outside to see what was going on.

"My grandmother saw the children go outside, and called for them to get away from the dragon. It was then that the dragon looked at her. She said its eyes were blue, just like my grandfather's. So, she realized what had happened, and tried to talk to it. When she did, it growled at her and fire came out of its mouth. It burned the house down."

"Can you tell us how things ended, Jaret?" The Instructor asked.

"Well, the Queen sent her Regent and they poked him with sticks until he flew into the sky. They chased him away to the West Country. I'm not sure what happened in his heart that caused him to be trapped that way, but the Queen said he would have to live forever in Sausmas' territory, because he was unsafe for mortals in Hausse to be around. She allowed my grandmother and the children to travel with him, but refused to provide for them. They ended up living in the caves not far from here, in the desert. Grandmother was afraid they were going to die.

"One day, my grandfather said two silver knights came to see my grandmother. They brought her water and some food. He doesn't remember much after that, except that he became very angry at her."

"What happened when he came to his senses?" Elder Tallis asked.

"I'm not sure," Jaret responded. "I just know my grandmother said that there were two silver knights, and Crown Prince Kyriel was involved somehow. She says all the time that he has never been the same since that day. All I know is they came into Area Two when my father was twelve. They went through the Stages of Repair. Then, they moved to Area One, just before my father began Discovery Season training."

"That is an amazing story, Jaret," Elder Tallis said. "Thank you for sharing it. I would love to have your grandparents come and finish telling the story, and add details from their point of view."

At this suggestion, there was a murmur of agreement that spread through the students.

From the back of the classroom, David raised his hand. "Lord Tallis, are you telling me there really *are* such things as dragons?"

Several students turned to look at David in surprise.

"Don't *you* believe in dragons?"

Staring back at his classmates blankly, David sputtered. "It's just that I've only *heard* about them, and never really seen one, or known anyone who knows about them, except the people here. My family has always lived inside Area One. My parents were assigned here by the king before I was born."

Elder Tallis smiled. "Ah yes. It is difficult to appreciate what we have when we have always had it, isn't it? Don't fear, David. Your strengths lie in other areas. You have learned to trust the king with all of your heart from an early age. That awareness is a great gift. But…. with great gifts, come great responsibility."

"Yeah, Dave," Zyniker spoke with conviction. "You can't let anything steal that from you."

The Teacher nodded. "That's true, Spider."

Zyniker continued. "I mean, after all, if you don't let yourself *believe* in this stuff, it can't really hurt you. Use your mind."

A murmur of agreement rippled through the room.

The Teacher smiled. "Really?" he asked. Tallis turned to look at the speaker. "Spider, do you believe in gravity?"

"What?" Zyniker questioned.

"I said, 'do you believe in gravity?'" the Tutor repeated. "The law of gravity; do you believe in it?"

Zyniker snorted. "Well, that's a dumb question. Of course I do. Anyone who doesn't is just plain stupid!"

"Why would they be stupid?" Tallis asked.

"Because," the boy sputtered. "It's obvious! Just by looking you can tell that *some kind* of force is holding things down on the ground!" He looked around the room. "What? Could things fall UP?" Zyniker pointed to the ceiling with both forefingers. Then he pulled out a pencil and tossed it in the air in front of him. He watched as it landed on his desk. As it clattered on the surface, Zyniker winked at one of the girls sitting close by, and pointed down and shrugged. He then proceeded to repeat the action, and looking at another student sitting near him. He was the center of attention, and he knew it. Playing the class clown was something he really enjoyed doing.

Slowly, a wave of mirth filtered through the class. Elder Tallis smiled lightly. "So Spider; if I choose not to believe in the Law of Gravity; does that Law continue to affect my day-to-day actions? *Could* I fly if I decided I wanted to hard enough?"

The laughter died down quickly.

"No," Zyniker responded quietly. "You can't."

All eyes were riveted on the Instructor, who continued to speak. "Can I make something so just by *thinking* about it?" He waited for an answer.

Zyniker looked his Teacher in the eye. "I don't know," he replied. "All my life I have heard I must guard my soul. I'm not sure exactly what that means. So, I try not to think about things that scare me. If I don't look at those things, they can't make me afraid. I try to block that stuff out."

"I see," replied Tallis softly. He looked from one face to another, speaking intently to the students entrusted to his care. "Class, if you take only one lesson home from our time together today, let it be this: You cannot make something that is real and true, into something *un*real and *un*true just because it makes you uncomfortable to believe it happens. Truth and Reality do *not* change or go away just because we don't like what they represent, any more than something could 'fly UP!'"

The Teacher's eyes twinkled at Zyniker, as he continued.

"The Law of Gravity continues to operate in spite of whether we consider it or not. Trying to convince oneself Evil does not exist will not make that

Evil go away, nor will it take away Evil's ability to influence the world we live in. In actuality, the opposite is true.

"You see, when a person refuses to concede there are influences of Evil, that person is essentially giving into Sausmas' main strategy against mortals. Ignoring an enemy's influence does not hamper that enemy. Rather, it provides that enemy with room to do his dirty work. That enemy then continues… unopposed.

"But….a *mature* and *ready* warrior not only *believes* in Sausmas, but is *educated in the knowledge* of his strategies and powers. He, or she, is then able to be on guard, and at the ready. He, or she, is conscious of the personal danger produced by giving that enemy ground…."

Lord Tallis paused, and raised his pointer to touch the image of the silver knight's shield in the painting. He looked around the room. "*That warrior* will not give away as much as an *inch* of his soul. *That warrior* holds to, and stays within King Suzerain's Realm. *That warrior* does not place undue confidence in himself, or believe he can control anything other than his own Personhood. In fact, he, or she, grasps that Character and Courage are the elements that tool us for further effectiveness in the King's Realm."

"Now, I think we have had enough instruction for now. I hope we have answered some of your questions today. Hopefully, some of the pieces are coming together for you. And, if you don't understand, or get the meaning right away, don't worry. Some lessons take longer to learn. Sometimes, I gain understanding long after the story-teller is finished; when I am alone, considering what I have heard."

Clapping his hands, Elder Tallis spoke in a little louder voice, "Lisette, would you please ring the bell? Class is over for today. Enjoy your family time. Please think about what we have learned this afternoon."

For a few moments, the room was filled with students hurrying to gather their belongings, readying to leave. Less than 10 minutes later, Lord Tallis stood at the wall of windows overlooking the garden, watching his charges scatter to their homes. In the midst of the dispersion, Peyton stopped. Looking over his shoulder, up to the windows, he waved at his Instructor.

"Thank you, Elder Tallis," the boy murmured under his breath. "I can't wait for tomorrow."

Later that evening, the plates and cups were put away. Peyton sat on the long bench at the wide table in the center of the family's community room. The area was simple, with a table with benches, two rockers next to the fireplace, and several cabinets for storage along the walls. Under the window, by the outside door, stood a bookshelf filled with books and scrolls.

The table doubled as a workspace for many tasks when it wasn't family meal time. Tonight, Peyton sat at the table to read, but was finding it difficult to immerse himself in his studies. Perhaps, it hadn't been a good idea to sit so close to the fire, he concluded.

Anbeter, Peyton's mother, sat across from him, making a list of what she would need to purchase in the open market the next day. Peyton's younger brother and sister were sitting on the floor near the fire. They were playing a game with stones and cups, called "Capture the Peasants." His father, Tvirtas, was across the room, working with a small knife and a three-inch block of wood. He was carving chess pieces to go with the inlaid wooden board he had just completed. This was the fourth set he had carved this year. Hopefully, he and Peyton would have the opportunity to pay at least one game before this one would sell.

In the corner, on a small table, lay Tvirtas' violin, where he had placed it when he joined the family for dinner. Leaning against the table, was a rather large hand drum. Peyton had finished its construction three days ago, and had been experimenting with creating a variety of sounds and rhythms.

The boy had been quiet all evening, his mind absorbed with lessons covered during the day. Tonight his bright mind was filled with images of knights and dragons.

Anbeter put away her scroll and quill, and reached for the mending basket. She touched his arm.

"Peyton, what *are* you thinking about? You were quiet all through dinner this evening. You only ate one serving! Do you feel all right?" She had moved next to him as she was speaking. She felt his forehead with her fingertips. "You don't seem to have a fever...."

Still somewhat distracted, Peyton responded, using his pet name for her. "I'm fine, Miemi. I was just thinking that's all."

"What did Elder Tallis teach you today, Peyton?" Tvirtas asked off-handedly.

"It was really good," Peyton answered. "He started teaching us about dragons today."

"He did?" Anbeter spoke. "What did you learn?"

Peyton spoke distractedly, still looking into the fire. "That dragons are not *born*; they are *made*. Elder Tallis said I must guard my soul to prevent from *becoming* one."

Hearing his son's words, Tvirtas stopped working. He laid aside his carving and moved across the room to sit on the table bench next to his wife. Anbeter stood up to get a pitcher of water, and some cups for the three of them. She spoke to the younger children. "Louise, Tycho, it is time for you to get ready for bed now. Gather your game and go up to your rooms. It's getting later than your bedtime."

Nine year-old Tycho responded. "Okay. We just finished the game anyway, and I won."

Ever perceptive beyond her years, seven-year old, Louise looked at her father. "Father why can't *we* hear about the dragons?"

Tvirtas chuckled and picked her up off the floor. "So!" he teased. "You were listening! You will never beat Tycho if you don't put all your attention in one place!"

He tweaked her nose. "You cannot listen because it's bedtime. We will tell you *all* about them sometime;

when it is light outside and it won't give you bad dreams!"

"*Please*, can't we listen, Papa? We won't say a thing!"

"Not tonight, little one. I think Peyton needs to ask us some questions alone. And you know, the questions *you* ask us are not family discussions, unless you want them to be." He glanced towards Peyton. Placing Louise back on her footing, he patted her behind. "Now off you go, both of you. You may read for a little while. Your mother and I will be up to tuck you in soon." Her lower lip protruding just a little, Louise looked up at her father. "I love you, Papa," she said.

Tvirtas smiled at her. "I love you too, little one. See if you can change into your nightdress, and wash your face before I come to tuck you in."

"Okay, Papa," Louise replied, nodding. "But you will tell me about the dragons sometime?"

Raising his eyebrows, her father nodded, and looked towards the wide-stepped ladder in the corner, which led to a hinged door in the ceiling.

Little Louise followed his silent direction, somewhat disappointed.

Lifting the pitcher, Anbeter poured three glasses of water, and sat down across from her son once more. Pushing aside the mending basket, she looked at her son. "Did the lesson today trouble you?"

"Did you know that a *person* can become a *dragon*?" Peyton looked at his parents, who then looked at each other. "And how did our family come to the

Protectorate? How is it, Father that you are so well versed in the use of a rapier and in battle strategy, but I have *never* seen your *armor*? What happened in our family *before*, making you able to teach me so much before I ever attended my first Discovery Season? Did you know the other boys in my class don't have swords at all? We won't be allowed to receive our first foils until next Season…. But *I* have a *rapier*…. *and* I know how to use it."

He looked at his parents. "Why is that?"

Tvirtas repeated himself. "You *have* been deep in thought! What did Elder Tallis teach you today, son?"

Peyton looked at his father. "It was just as I said, Papa. We learned about dragons; what they are and where they come from."

His father spoke slowly. "What stories did you hear?"

"There was only time for one story today. Jaret told us how his grandparents came into the Protectorate because they had been homeless. His *grandfather* was a dragon. I had never heard the things he told us about the Queen." Peyton looked from one parent to another. "Does *our family* know anyone who has been a dragon?

Anbeter and Tvirtas looked at each other once more. "It's time to tell him, I think, my love," Tvirtas said to his wife, gently.

She smiled at her husband. "Yes, I think you must be right." She looked at Peyton, and took both of his hands in her own. "My *mother* was a dragon," she said simply.

Peyton wasn't sure he had heard correctly. "What?" he asked.

His mother's voice lowered as she gazed intently into her son's eyes. "Your Bibi turned into a dragon when I was a little girl."

Stunned, Peyton tried to absorb his mother's words. Bibi, his grandmother, was his favorite person in the entire world. It was Bibi who had read him stories as a toddler; who had comforted and cuddled him when he fell. She was the one who had made him hungry to learn at an early age. A short woman, no more than five feet tall, she was round and soft. Her soft, gentle laugh was musical and gentle. As Peyton had grown in years, the boy had developed a special place in his heart for his grandmother. He had made an inner vow to himself years ago to become her defender as he became older. It was his plan to become her provider and protector should circumstances ever change in his family.

Not only was it difficult to believe what he was hearing, but he was finding it impossible to imagine how drastic a change must have taken place. It was difficult to believe. His Bibi was gracious and kind. Everyone said so. Didn't she serve in the King's Court on occasion? At seventy, she divided her time between serving in Suzerain's Court, and training warriors in Areas Four and Five. He usually saw her on her monthly visits to Area One. If what his mother was saying was true, how had Bibi's name become a legend among the entire Realm?

Peyton's mouth dropped open, as he returned his mother's gaze. "Really?" was all he could say. "How? When?"

"It's a long story," Tvartis answered, "one that will most probably take us into the wee hours of the morning. Let me tuck in your brother and sister." He patted his son's shoulder. "I'll be right back."

Peyton brightened. "I'm not tired. I'd like to hear a story."

Anbeter laughed lightly. "All right then. I will make us something to snack on while we talk." She rose and took some apples from a basket on the counter. As she worked to create a platter of cheese, bread and apples slices, she looked at Peyton. "Besides, it will be easier for me to speak of some of these things, if my hands are busy."

Peyton had never heard his mother speak this way. She had always seemed so strong to him.

"Did you live outside? I mean, when you were little."

Anbeter began slicing cheese. "You mean, 'outside the Protectorates?'"

"Y-yes," Peyton replied, realizing he wasn't really sure what he meant. "What was it like?"

His mother stopped working to look at him. "Different. I don't remember much about Hausse when I was a toddler. I remember we lived in a large stone house, and I had my own room. My mother used to sing to me when it was time to go to bed. I had an older sister, but I don't remember her name."

"You don't remember her name?" Peyton repeated.

"She died when I was three. My parents never spoke of her again."

"Oh," was all he could say.

Anbeter touched his arm, and smiled. "It is all right, Peyton." She went back to preparing their platter, and continued. "I remember my father being kind. He always made me laugh, and I always felt safe with him. I remember he used to give me hummingbird kisses with his eyelashes, and tickle me. He held me up over his head, and let me touch the ceiling. Sometimes, he threw me up into the air, and would catch me. I would laugh so hard."

"Father used to do that with me, too!" Peyton replied.

"I remember," his mother replied.

Pulling bread from the breadbox, she continued.

"After my sister died, the Queen offered my mother a title. She was called a "Lady Regent in charge of Family Safety." It was her job to travel through our particular province, and gain the loyalty of the women. The Queen was afraid of the rumors she had heard from a few of her chambermaids. There were stories that Suzerain was mounting a Plan; a Plan to destroy her Kingdom.

"You have to know; Queen Souhaites has laws about everything – who may work, who may not work, how many children a family may have, what gender they are allowed to be, even what colors are acceptable to be shown, or painted on the walls of a home. To keep her subjects under her control, she makes them dependent upon her for water. They must buy water, or they cannot live. So, she makes the water expensive, and regulates it so each person receives just enough to stay alive, but not enough to quench their thirst."

Peyton thought for a moment. "Does that mean everyone in the Kingdom of Hausse is thirsty all the time?"

His mother nodded. "Well, most of the people are, Peyton. So many have just learned to live with it; and many, especially in those homes where the Queen's rule is obeyed without question, have more than enough of everything. Those are the people in the kingdom who laugh at Suzerain, and defy His Light-Bearers. They refuse to admit they have any need...."

Her voiced went quiet for a moment. She shook her head. The platter was completed. She carried it to the table. Peyton followed her and they sat once more on the benches.

"What was *your* family like, Miemi?" It was the name he had called her since he had first learned to speak.

"Well, I remember things changing after my mother received her title. Because I was so young, I didn't realize it at first, but my father became less and less like he had been before. He became quiet, and grumpy. The Queen called him to serve in her Court. When he came back, he was still nice to me, but we didn't talk anymore. I know now he must have been very unhappy."

"How did your mother turn into a dragon?" Peyton had been holding the question, hoping Anbeter would come to the subject presently.

"Well, my mother stopped relating to me much at all. By the time I was thirteen years, she had become very powerful in Hausse. She advised the Queen, and was given the responsibility of choosing which baby boys born to families were allowed to stay with their parents, and which were to be executed."

"Why does the Queen hate boys the way she does?" Peyton asked.

"I don't know all of the reasons, son. I do know she is afraid of Rebellion. She fears losing the control she carries. I know this because of what happened to Bibi. During the time my mother was a Lady Regent, she began to believe she could do things without the Queen's knowledge. She either forgot, or refused to ask permission for decisions she made. She was very controlling. She used her influence with the Queen to advance her own interests. She stopped caring about the people in her province, and became cruel in some ways. I still remember the first time I saw a certain look in her eye. I was terrified of her."

As she had been sharing, Tvirtas had rejoined them. With an apple slice in his hand, he interjected at this point. "I was a Company Commander at that time. The King had ordered me to deliver supplies to the Hidden Well Community in that particular province. We knew we were going into dangerous territory, so we went well-armed."

Anbeter spoke again. "I'm not sure of the sequence of events, because many things happened so quickly. I remember my mother beginning to have nightmares. There were strange things happening in our house then as well. I remember coming downstairs one morning and seeing a man in a black robe, holding a clear glass ball in his hand. Next to him was a lizard standing as tall as his elbow, but with a man's head. They looked at me with such evil red eyes. I looked upstairs and called for my mother, but she didn't answer. I looked back and the two had vanished. Another time, I heard voices behind a door, when no one was home but me.

"One day, my mother met a man who said he was a Conjurer in the Queen's service. My mother asked him how she could become more influential, and perhaps even draw on the dark powers of Sausmas. She had been using spells and hexes for some time. I always saw books near her bed with words like "Deep Magic" and "Black Arts" printed on them. This man gave my mother a potion, and told her if she would drink it, she would receive ultimate power in her province. No one would dare to defy her.

"I remember standing in the kitchen the day she drank it. She was so excited. She giggled like a little girl, and told me that someday we might even have our *own* kingdom. She talked about raising an army and moving against the Queen.

"I have heard some say that the Alteration happens over time; but for my mother, it began immediately. At that time, I didn't know what was happening, but I knew it was evil. Her nails began to grow out. Her teeth and face began to change. The skin on her arms began to change color. I screamed for her, and she reached for me. Her nails dug deep into my chest, and I almost didn't get away. She growled like a lion. I was frightened and bleeding badly. I ran from the house, without anything but the clothes on my back. One of my friends lived a less than a mile away, and I ran to her home. I didn't know it, but they were part of the Hidden Well Community."

Tvirtas spoke up. "I was standing in that family's gathering room, when Anbeter burst through the door. I had never seen anyone so beautiful."

His wife blushed slightly at the compliment. He continued. "She was so upset, and obviously in mortal danger. She just blurted out the entire story, and said she didn't know what to do."

"Your father was in full battle armor," Anbeter interjected. He ran to his horse, and called for two of his trusted men to join him. They rode to my house and found what was left. The dragon, who had been my mother, had flown away, and my father was lying in the yard, badly burned."

Tvirtas stopped her, touching her arm. "He should know how Prince Kyriel helped us." He looked at his son. "Your mother's father was so badly burned; he found it difficult to breathe. He was able to tell us the dragon had attacked him. I had no medical supplies with me, and even if I had, I had never been a Curative Officer. Suddenly, Crown Prince Kyriel was kneeling next to me. He placed his hand on your grandfather's heart, and the charred parts of his body began to regenerate. The Prince Himself poured medicine into the wounds and bandaged them. Kyriel used His own horse and carried your grandfather to the Protectorate."

"Where does he live now?" Peyton wanted to know.

"Oh, he had his Exchange Day several years ago," his mother replied. "I still miss him, but we will see each other again someday."

Tvirtas spoke. "Should we stop there for tonight, Peyton? Or, do you want to hear what happened to Bibi?"

"You can't stop now, Papa! What happened?" he asked.

Tvirtas grinned. "A boy after my own heart!" He rubbed his hands together. "All right then. The dragon had flown away, but it is the priority of all knights to rescue those who are trapped by the Dragon's Lair. If you can catch a dragon just after the Alteration had taken place; before it reaches the BorderLands; you have a better chance of Generating Redemption. Once a dragon reaches Sausmas' Territory, the very substance *breathed* there will cause the Imprisonment to deepen.

"The very old dragons are hardest to rescue. Some knights have died trying.

"With this particular rescue, my men and I followed the dragon on horseback, watching the smoke trail in the sky. You see, young dragons try to breathe fire, but the best they can do at first is shoot sparks and little flames. And this was Bibi's first flight."

"Why is that fire a different color than the Light Bearers?" Peyton wanted to know.

"Where did you see that?" Tvirtas was surprised.

"In the painting in Initiate Hall. Elder Tallis explained it to us today. I noticed a difference in the fire colors during our observation time."

"Very good, Peyton," his father encouraged. "There is a black liquid that spews from the ground in Sausmas' Territory. It looks like black lava. Simply put, it is the DNA of Evil. Whenever someone tastes it, it goes inside of them. It has a life of its own. It changes them into an embodiment of Sausmas' nature.

"Now, the Light and Fire from Suzerain's Realm are pure and unfiltered. The problem is, if a person has never seen Suzerain's Light, they could be fooled by Sausmas and the Queen's imitation. Additionally, the black liquid changes the appetites of whomever it touches. For instance, after a dragon has been drinking that substance for a while, they aren't thirsty for water any longer. It becomes the only thing they want to drink."

"So, you and your men had to get to Bibi before she drank more of the black liquid!" Peyton exclaimed in discovery. "Jaret said the Queen's officers forced his grandfather to drink a black liquid. Is that what *that* was?"

"I think so," Tvirtas responded. "There have been many stories about Souhaites using the black liquid for her own purposes. Some have suggested she even treats the water she sells in Hausse. That way, when her people purchase it, they are trapped into remaining loyal to her. Those in our Hidden Well Communities, who receive Suzerain's Water on a regular basis, tell us it tastes sweeter somehow than the Queen's water.

"To continue with the story, Bibi had fallen from the sky, crashing into the trees. She had broken a wing. You see, the problem with dragons is Rage. It drives them to do things beyond their capabilities, and they become wounded. Many die, because there are no provisions for healing in the Queen's kingdom. She just discards the damaged and looks for the new. You will learn more about these things in your future Discovery Seasons, but know this:

"There is no more loyal or determined knight in the King's Realm, than a Rescued Dragon.

"When we reached Bibi, she was bleeding badly, and had no strength left to fight us. And, as he always does at a Dragon Rescue, Prince Kyriel came. He spoke with Bibi privately for some time, and then he touched her. Suddenly, there were bright lights all around her, which moved into her being and lifted her from the ground. As she rose, her shape was transformed. When she was lowered to the ground once more, she was naked and ashamed. The Prince took a white cloak, edged with red and gold, and wrapped her up in it. She went with him into seclusion in the King's Court for a time, and then she came to Area Two."

"I had thought I would never see her again," Anbeter's eyes were moist. "She was so different. She was so sorry for all the pain she had caused me. I had already been reunited with my father in Area Two. It didn't take long for my parents to be reconciled. We all lived together until my father died.

"Then," she took her husband's hand, "Tvirtas came to Area Two. I had completed my Third Discovery Season, and he asked whether I would consider marrying him. I knew he was the one I wanted. He was always such a gentleman. After we married, the king asked my mother to help in Training, Rescue and Restoration. She has been busy ever since."

The room was quiet. Tvirtas stood and stretched. "I should put another log on the fire, to keep us warm until morning. And, if you can sleep now, Peyton, you really should go to bed. The dawn will not delay itself."

"But I have so many more questions, Papa!" Peyton protested.

"Yes, I know," his father put his arm around him and gave him a squeeze. "But this old brain has no more answers for tonight. It is almost time for the third night watch to begin."

"Good night then," Peyton replied. After giving each of his parents a hug, he moved towards the ladder in the corner. "I can't wait until the next time we can talk like this."

A soft laugh emanated without warning from his mother. "I'm sure it will happen sooner than we expect it," she murmured.

It was a statement which would prove to be more foretelling than Anbeter would have ever considered it to be.

Chapter Four
First Encounters

Peyton had not realized how tired he really was, until his head finally hit his pillow. Almost immediately, he fell into a deep sleep. Then, nearly as quickly as sleep had come upon him, he began to dream.

He was standing in a field. The sky was dark, and he could not tell whether it was day or night. Somehow, he knew he had just stepped into a clearing from the cover of a small group of trees. He could sense the Queen's winter castle was close by. In the distance, an eerie auburn glow emanated from the ground.

Where am I, he wondered?

Suddenly, someone touched his right foot. Looking down, he noticed he had on silver boots reaching above his knees. On the ground, were three small children, dressed in rags, like those he had seen in the painting with Elder Tallis. All three were wide-eyed with fear. Somehow, Peyton wanted to help them, but felt transfixed in his position. He couldn't move.

Then, around his head a cloud whirled; or *was* it a cloud? *Was it speaking to him?* Looking down once more, he realized the children had disappeared into the cloud; or had they *become the cloud?* He stretched out to touch them, but was disappointed. His hand reached *through* them.

"*He-e-e-lp us!*" their voices spoke in an unnatural, other-worldly refrain which stemmed from the ground where they had been. It felt as though it progressed through Peyton's entire being.

Then, out of nowhere, two arms lifted the boy under his arms, off the ground, and into the air. As he flew, Peyton looked down, and realized he was being relocated from the field. He could see the layout of the land below, and recognized several landmarks, including Protectorate Area One.

As his feet hit the earth, a volley of fire shot over his shoulder from behind. A hot wind exploded behind him. Wondering where the heat and wind were coming from the boy turned around. Without warning he found his face just inches from the head of an evil looking dragon. Startled, he realized he was looking at the animal eye-to-eye.

Was just the head of this beast as tall as he was?

The dragon growled, the sound building from under the earth, up into its nostrils. For a moment, the two observed each other. Peyton could feel the creature's hot breath, and the stench it contained.

What is that smell? He wondered.

It spoke, guttural and hostile. "What are *you* doing here, boy?"

Abruptly, Peyton was observing the interaction from another angle. He was seeing himself from *outside* himself, *watching* the dragon as it threatened him. With interest, the boy saw, that the area where he stood contained more light than the rest of the canyon. *Where was it coming from?* Then, he looked at his hands. His rapier was *on fire!* Yet, it gave off no heat to burn him! How was that possible?

Then, without warning, the dragon stretched out its massive wings, and rose into the air. Kicking and squirming in its claws was a child; a little girl. She was screaming, and reaching out to him.

"Don't leave me here! Help me!"

As the creature ascended, it looked back at Peyton with an evil laugh. The boy watched in horror, as the dragon pulled the girl into two pieces and consumed her. With blood dripping from its jaws, it moved once more towards the ground, where it selected another child. This one, it threw up into the air and caught, ripping into its flesh with its talons. Then, blasting out fire and smoke it moved towards a mountain which suddenly appeared from the ground.

As the boy watched, it seemed the ground opened up. He noticed a small cave entrance at the base of the mountain. Then, the cave's entrance unexpectedly expanded. It was like a wide, yawning mouth, filled with the auburn glow Peyton had seen from afar.

Playing with the child like a ragdoll, the dragon hurled it into the cave. *What was inside that cave? Were they dead or alive?*

Then, he was back inside his skin.

A voice spoke. Looking to his right, Peyton saw a tall, well-built man. He had his hand on the boy's shoulder. "These are the BorderLands," the man said.

As Peyton continued to take notice of the man, he realized there were wings reaching from his back into the heavens. A bright, white light, without auburn tint, glowed from him. Around his waist was a golden belt, and in his free hand, he held the largest sword Peyton had ever seen. It was also on fire. The man used it to make a sweeping motion, indicating everything their view could see.

"All along the edge of the line between Hausse and the Dark Lands, this territory continues," he told Peyton. It is the last area where Suzerain's created Light can be seen."

"But I don't understand," the boy responded. "It even *feels* dark here."

The Light-Bearer smiled grimly at him. "Yes, that's true. But the Darkness becomes even deeper than this; much, *much* deeper. Where Sausmas dwells, there is no Light at all. In fact, those who live in the Dark Lands have become used to the blackness. Those are the ones who make their way entirely by feel, and not by sight. When Light shines, they are so used to the Darkness, it hurts their eyes." He paused and looked at Peyton carefully.

"I am Uriel, and I bring you a message from the king."

Peyton stared blankly at him. "Are you a Light-Bearer?"

Uriel let out a kind chuckle. "Isn't it obvious?"

The boy pointed to the immense wings growing from the Light-Bearer's upper back. "Are those heavy? Can you fly?"

Uriel smiled. "That is like me asking you if your arms are heavy! I have always had them, since my Formation Moment." He paused, and then added, "Who do you think carried you to this canyon ridge?"

Slowly, Peyton's mind began to take hold of the information he was receiving. *"You?"*

"Yes, Peyton," Uriel responded. "Now, we have a little more training to attend to, before I can give you the king's message. Are you ready?"

Not knowing what to say, and a little overwhelmed, the boy nodded eagerly.

"All right, then," the Light-Bearer continued. Taking Peyton's hand, his wings began to move back and forth. Together, the two lifted from the earth.

Amazed, the boy realized they were heading towards the cave entrance in the ground.

I wonder why I'm not afraid.

"Because you are covered in the king's Light," Uriel responded.

"Did I say that *out loud*?"

"No, but my home is the Suzerain's Realm. I am a messenger sent from that Realm. Everything you can see and *not* see is visible to him."

Peyton was puzzled. "What do you mean? You can *see* my thoughts?"

Uriel laughed. "Not all the time, no; nor can I see *all of them*. It's not like *that*." He shook his head. "I am not the *King*. He is the only one who sees *everything*. There was once another Light-Bearer who thought he *could* take the King's place. He caused all of the trouble we see here."

Peyton understood. "Sausmas?"

"Yes, Sausmas," the messenger replied. "In fact, I can only see what I *need* to see in order to accomplish the mission the king has given me."

"How is it you can see my thoughts *now*?" the boy asked.

Coming close to their destination, Uriel responded. "It is my mission to instruct you, and to provide you with protection for your next Season."

"You mean at Initiate Hall? In my classes with Elder Tallis?"

Uriel set their feet on grounds near the mouth of the cave entrance. Peyton could feel heat rushing outward. The Light-Bearer smiled once more. "No, I mean for your next *Season of Living*. Let me help you to understand. It is important from this point forward…. When you receive instruction, try to consider the Jurisdiction you are standing in at that particular moment. For example, in the Realm where I serve, we consider the *larger* sphere before we discuss the *practical* matters. If you agree to what the king is suggesting; then, for this next Season, your abilities and gifts will be utilized for a greater good than the limited existence you know day to day. There will always be a higher meaning."

He led Peyton toward the cave entrance.

"Look down into the opening, Peyton," he said. "What do you see?"

"The fire does not fill the entire entrance like I thought it did," the boy responded. "The flames seem to hold to the roof of the cave." He paused.

"What else do you see?" Uriel prodded.

"There are steps leading downward into lower regions below us. Are there rooms below where we are standing?"

The Light-Bearer nodded. "In some places; whenever you are below, remember that. Those who are imprisoned below cannot even consider breaking through from their prisons because the fire would consume them. So, they hope for Sausmas to release them. Most are in chains."

"How?" Peyton wanted to know. "*Does* he release them?"

"Never; we are their only hope."

Suddenly, the two were below the earth. Peyton looked around. They were standing in a large room with stone walls. The only light in the room came from the flames which travelled along the ceiling, making the entire cavern unbearably hot. To make matters worse, there did not appear to be a water pot anywhere in sight.

Along the walls were iron rings, attached to tall, upright posts, about six feet apart. Chained to each ring, were childlike figures, similar to the three children who had appeared at the beginning of the boy's visit to this place. Many were weeping. Some were silent. Still others were begging for water.

As he continued to watch, Peyton became aware of Monstrous Beings moving about the cavern. The creatures took differing forms, and each was covered in a sort of ooze or slime. Some had two or three heads. Some were covered with mouths that tried to devour the prisoners. Many carried whips, or other implements of torture. It seemed to Peyton they moved from one captive to another, inflicting pain, for no apparent reason at all.

When he looked to the far corners of the cavern he saw still more captives, also in chains. However, these captives stood on their own feet. Each one was silent, walking in circles with eyes closed. Each one held a weapon in their hand, and continuously used the weapon upon themselves.

"Why don't they just leave?" he wondered.

Then, Peyton noticed several of the Monstrous Beings moving among the standing captives. As he observed, his vision focused on one particular little girl, who had stopped using the whip in her hand upon herself. Standing still, her eyes fluttered, beginning to open. She began to pull against her chains. At that moment, a three headed being with tentacle-like arms drew near to her. Wrapping her in its many suction-cup covered arms, it began to squeeze, while simultaneously using two of its heads to whisper in both ears. Its third head blew hot breath on her eyes, causing them to close tightly once more in reaction. When the being was satisfied her eyes were closed once more, its arms released her, and placed the whip back into her hands. As the being moved on to the next captive, the girl began to weep. She picked up her whip once more and began to use it.

Understandably, the cavern was filled with screams; screams which reverberated and echoed, increasing in volume, recirculating and never leaving the cave.

Looking down at his feet, the boy realized he was standing in the blood of the captives. It was then that the smell of the place reached his senses. How would he describe it? He pondered….. Like rotting garbage, and the odor of a dead animal mixed together. But there was something else…. Sickeningly sweet; as though someone had sliced a million apples and hung them to mask the stench. It was the same odor he had sensed coming from the dragon's mouth in the confrontation above ground.

"What is that *smell?*" he asked.

"Death," Uriel answered.

"What *is* this place?" Peyton asked, horrified.

"This is the Hollow of Tortured Souls. It is the tormentors' playground," Uriel answered. "The soul dies slowly here." He pointed to the chained captives. "These are the souls of those who have ceased to experience living. They have been snared by Sausmas in one manner or another. They have also been unwilling to accept King Suzerain's provision of Restoration. Their bodies still exist and breathe above, in the Kingdom of Hausse."

Peyton was dumbfounded. *Why would anyone choose this place instead of living under King Suzerain?* Aloud, all he said was, "But, w-why?"

"Many of these have believed the lies the Queen and Enki have told them about Suzerain. Some even believe they are experiencing Suzerain's Realm in their present state. And some of them are those who just refuse to trust anyone but themselves."

The boy wanted to grasp all Uriel was telling him. "You mean these are the souls of mortals who are still *living?*"

The Light-Bearer nodded. "Yes, that is what I am telling you. Those who *refused* to trust the king, whose bodies have expired, cannot join the multitude of The Waiting, who stand before him. Those are the Phantoms of the Night, whose spirits roam the visible realm; who have no home."

"Are they *all children?*" Peyton asked.

"No," Uriel answered. "They are of many different ages. But the soul of man does not age in the same way his body does. The soul of man is *always* that of a child."

"But I thought we became *older* as we grew up...."

Uriel spoke slowly. "*Maturity* has nothing to do with physical age, Peyton. *Maturity* has to do with choosing to *trust* the King. It also means not being afraid to show who you are; *to be known.*"

Suddenly, the boy's eyes began to burn. Distractedly, he spoke. "My eyes hurt," he said, rubbing his eyes, blinking continually, seeking to allow his tears to wash the smoke from his vision. As he did so, he sank down to the ground. Keeping his eyes closed, he waited to hear the next sentence the Light-Bearer would speak.

"Now that you have *seen....*" Uriel continued. "I must tell you why the king sent me."

Peyton opened his eyes. He was surprised by what he saw. He was no longer in a cavern under the earth. Gone were the Monstrous Beings, and the captives. Gone were the dragons. Gone was the fire. Instead, he was in his own bedchamber, sitting up in his own bed. Through the doorway in the next room, his younger brother slept soundly.

Standing by his bedside, with his glowing wings extending through the ceiling, was Uriel.

"Have I been in my bed the entire time?" Peyton wanted to know.

"What do you think?" the Light-Bearer smiled at him.

"I don't know," the boy replied.

"Look to your heart," came the answer. "What does it tell you?"

Peyton considered. Something deep inside told him it had *not* all been a dream. "Were we really there?" he asked.

"Absolutely," came the answer. "You will need the lessons you learned this night, in the days to come."

Uriel paused. "Now," he continued, "to the mission. It is the desire of the king to involve you in a rescue operation in the BorderLands. There are several others who will go with you, but you will be one of the youngest in company. There will be several younger. You will receive instructions as you go. If you choose to *go*, you will receive intensive training, which will equip you for future missions. If you decide *not* to go, the Suzerain understands. You will remain in your

Discovery Season group, and move ahead with your classmates at the normal pace."

The boy didn't even stop to consider his options. "I want to *go!*" he whispered excitedly. "But how will I tell my parents?"

"We will discuss that in the morning," Uriel chuckled. "Sleep now."

Without a word, Peyton lay down once more and slept until morning.

Sunlight was streaming through the window, when the boy finally awoke the next day. Startled, he bounded out of bed onto his feet. "I'm going to be late to classes," he muttered to himself. "I wonder why they didn't wake me?"

Still in his nightclothes, Peyton hurried down the ladder to the family living space. His mother was putting a log on the fire when she heard him.

"Well, good morning, Sleepyhead!" Anbeter greeted him.

"Good morning, Miemi," he replied. He looked around the room. "Where *is* everyone?"

His mother smiled. "Your brother and sister are at the neighbor's house, playing. Your father and Uriel are gathering training supplies."

Peyton was dumbfounded. "Uriel?" he repeated. "You mean, he..." his voice trailed off.

"What is it son?" she asked.

"Uriel," Peyton said once more.

"The Light-Bearer who came last evening, you mean," Anbeter responded, confirming her son's unspoken question.

"Yes," came his answer. "How did you....what's going on?"

"Well, your father has been asked to go on the rescue mission as well. That is all I know," she said simply.

"Do you know where we are going?" her son wanted to know.

Anbeter paused, looking at him. "Peyton," she began, "do you know what your name means?"

"Yes," he replied. "It means 'farm boy who is a warrior.'"

"Do you not think your father and I named you such a name for a reason? Do you not think we are versed in the King's methods of battle?"

This concept was new to Peyton. "I guess I never thought about it until now," he answered honestly.

Anbeter smiled. "I went on missions like yours before you were born. I have seen. Days will come when I see more. My current mission is to make sure *you* are aimed into *your* generation to hit the king's mark for you." Suddenly Peyton remembered his mother teaching him skills with bow and quiver.

Watching him, she read his thoughts on his face. "Don't worry, son. In this season, I am learning as well. Believe me, it is no easy task to train children! I will have even more adventures; probably when Tycho and

Louise are older. Look at my mother! She never stops!"

"So you are *all right* with us going?" Peyton inquired, concerned.

Anbeter smiled, her face aglow. "I really am. In fact, I'm excited for you, Peyton. I cannot wait to see what you learn!"

"And you're not afraid for us?" he worried.

"No, why? Should I be?" she asked.

"It just seems natural that you would be," he replied.

She shrugged, looking at her son. "It's simple. I trust the king."

Just after lunch time, Tvirtas and Uriel returned. It was Tvirtas who greeted Peyton as they came through the door.

"Well, son," his energy giving a clue to his excitement, "are you ready for an adventure?"

"Yes, sir!" Peyton responded.

"Are you packed yet?" his father wanted to know.

"No, not yet. I didn't know where we were going," came the reply.

Tvirtas patted his son's shoulders. "Good man. *Good* man." He laughed and looked at Uriel. "I told you. The boy doesn't make assumptions, and he waits for instruction."

Peyton looked at the man who had entered the house with his father. "Uriel?" he asked.

The Light-Bearer returned Peyton's gaze. "Yes? Something wrong?" There was a slight twinkle in his eyes as he observed the boy's discovery.

"You don't look like you did last night," Peyton told him. "Where are your wings? And don't Light-Bearers... well... you know.... *have to glow?*"

Uriel chuckled. "And how would it be if I walked down your street with my wings extending above the rooftops? Do you think we could keep our mission a secret then?"

Peyton pictured the scene Uriel was describing for a moment. He joined the laughter. "I guess not" He thought for a moment. "Do other Light-Bearers disguise themselves this way as well?"

Uriel smiled. "We all have the *ability* to do so. In fact, many times, our assignments from the king to his subjects in this territory *require* we take on the appearance of mortals. Even the fallen Light-Bearers in league with Sausmas have that ability, although their changes are much more devious and sinister. I will tell you more in the days to come." He looked at Tvirtas and Anbeter.

"We will need to leave in the morning, in order to have enough time to complete our preparations. Could we plan to eat a meal as a group this evening, so we can discuss the next steps we must walk together in the king's strategy?"

77

Anbeter nodded. "I have some stew simmering, and I was just about to make bread. It will be ready in a couple of hours."

Tvirtas rubbed his hands together. "That sounds really good."

"If we are leaving in the morning," Peyton asked, "what *will* I need to pack?"

Uriel smiled. "It is good to consider using your time well, Peyton. You will need enough clothing to keep you warm in the cold; and yet little enough to carry when you are in the heat. You will need a blanket for sleeping, a towel for washing, and a good pair of shoes. You will need a light and all of the weapons you know how to use well. Oh, and any scrolls you read to find comfort when you are sad." He paused. "I think that list will give you a good beginning. Please pack it all in such a way you can walk with it on your back."

Peyton brightened. "I have a leather knapsack that fits on my shoulders! I usually take it when we go to the woods on hunting trips for food. Will that work?"

Uriel nodded. "That would be perfect."

Anbeter laughed. "Who knew when we purchased that particular knapsack for you earlier this year; it would be just what you needed for this adventure?"

Tvirtas moved towards his wife. "Who knew indeed? *Nothing* happens by accident when our hearts are listening." He kissed her cheek lightly.

About an hour later, Peyton was adding the final items to his knapsack, when he heard voices downstairs. A man's voice was speaking.....

"Anbeter! Is Tvirtas here? It has been a long time!"

Peyton could hear his mother's soft reply, but could not distinguish one word from another.

"I wanted to wait until after the Encounter had taken place, before I came to see you," the man said.

Again his mother responded.

Curious, Peyton left his knapsack and made his way down the ladder, just in time to hear the next statement made by the visitor.

"I wanted to bring these items to Peyton," he said. "I know he'll need them."

At the foot of the ladder, the boy turned around, and came face-to-face with Elder Tallis, who was dressed differently than his classroom attire. The Instructor was still wearing his outer cloak. It was deep purple, a color revealing his kingly station. The cloak was actually a cape, trimmed in white, reaching to the floor. In his hand, extending through a slit in the side of the mantle, he still held his walking staff. Peyton had never seen him like this.

"Lord Tallis!" he said with surprise. "I'm sorry I missed class today. I wanted to hear more."

Looking over his spectacles, the Instructor appraised the teenager from head to toe. "Oh," he said, "but haven't you had a *real* Encounter?"

Surprised, Peyton looked at his mother, and then back at his Teacher. "How did you know? Did father tell you?"

Lord Tallis smiled. "I have known.....for some time," he replied. "It is important to the king, and to

Kyriel, I tell you they view your participation in this mission as vital. I also came to give you tools for your journey. You will find you have room in the side pocket of that leather knapsack you are packing upstairs."

Surprised, Peyton's mouth dropped open. "But," he said, "my knapsack doesn't *have* a side pocket, Elder."

Tallis looked over his spectacles once more. "Are you *sure*, son?" he asked.

I'm pretty sure, Peyton thought to himself. *After all, its my knapsack, and I use it every day.*

Aloud he said, "Let me go and check." Turning on his heels, he once more climbed the ladder to his room, and retrieved the knapsack. Returning downstairs once more, he set it on the table.

Lord Tallis pointed to the side of the bag. "What's that?" he asked.

Peyton looked. Suddenly, as he watched, his bag grew a pocket. Then, it grew a strap and buckle, both apparently for securing items to the outside of the bag. Peyton was dumbfounded. He looked at his Instructor. "How did you do that?" he asked.

"Do *what*?" his Teacher chuckled. "Listen. When the King is directing your steps, you will always have what you need. At that moment, you needed a greater capacity for what I am about to give you."

From his own satchel, he began to draw five items. "I think you will need these almost every day, in order to succeed in your mission. These items have come from Suzerain himself, and they are his own design."

Tallis drew the first item from his bag. "This is a map of all lands, seen and unseen. It shows the locations of the Queen's summer and winter castles, and each of the Protectorate Areas. It also holds many other clues you will need as your journey progresses, so *don't lose it.* If you are disoriented, you can find your bearings by laying out the map on the ground, near a visible landmark. Stand on the map, and Inner Sight will reveal your location and what you are to do next. It is leather, so even if it gets wet, it cannot be destroyed."

He reached into his bag once more. "If you are not near a landmark, use the other tools to help yourself to discover your way. The second item is a compass. Whenever you look at it, it will point due north, toward King Suzerain's Realm. If you walk in that direction, you will find safety, and people to help you on the way."

Pulling out the third item, Lord Tallis continued. "This is a quadrant. When it is night and you have no light to see your compass, use this. In the desert, or the wilderness, when you do not know where you are; or how to return here, use this. Just look for the North Star; it stands over Suzerain's Palace. Then, look at the reflection, in the quadrant. Follow the direction it leads you.

"The last two items are the most important, because they came directly from the king just *for you.* The first is a letter, defining your part in the expedition. There are parts of it you will understand right away, and others which will elude your understanding until you are ready to grasp their meaning." He handed the scroll to Peyton. "Read it. Write the words on your heart and mind. They will keep you in the king's Light."

Slowly, Lord Tallis drew the fifth item from his satchel. It was a small bottle, about five inches tall, with a cork stopper closing the top opening. "This," he said in awe, "is my favorite of the King's many provisions. It is a King's Water Flask. It will never run dry, nor will you ever need to refill it. The water it pours comes directly from the river flowing from the king's throne-room. Whenever you drink it, you will be refreshed, reinvigorated, renewed and restored. Whenever you pour water out, it will provide a cure to anyone who tastes it."

Tallis lowered his voice, and continued. "This is *your* flask. It is only for *you* to use. All those who are truly in the King's Realm receive their *own*. Understand now, there are those who want the King's Water, without stepping into the King's Light. These are not to drink from your well. You may pour out the water, and *serve* it *to* them, but if you allow them to take from it from you, or add their own flavor, the color of the fire on your rapier will change. Also, Sausmas and his alliance would love to steal this from you. If they do, they will taint the water, or even dilute it. If they do, you will lose connection with the King's Realm, and with me. You will do well to hide this flask on your person at all times, and do *not* neglect it, or put it in your knapsack."

With that instruction, he lifted up the little flask. Peyton was surprised to see a silken cord attached to it. When Lord Tallis placed it around his neck, the length was just right. Peyton tucked the flask inside his shirt.

"One more thing," his Instructor warned. "If you ever disregard the King's purpose for the water in the flask, and take it for granted, or choose to use it to make a name for yourself, *the water will cease to flow.* Do you understand what I am telling you?"

"Yes, sir," Peyton responded, aware he felt just a little taller and a little stronger since his Teacher had arrived.

"All right, then," Lord Tallis said with finality. "I must be on my way home. Blessings on your journey, Peyton." He looked at Anbeter. "Please tell Tvartis I will stop by in the morning to see him before they leave."

Anbeter smiled. "I will, Lord Tallis," she replied. "Thank you for your gifts to Peyton."

Realizing he had been distracted, missing their conversation, investigating his gifts, Peyton looked up at his Instructor. "Yes, thank you, Lord Tallis."

The Teacher grabbed Peyton's hand, and pulled him in to hug him. "Keep your heart open," he whispered. Releasing the boy, he hugged Anbeter. "All will be well," he told her.

Moving toward the door, Elder Tallis pulled the hood of his cape up over his head. As he opened the door, he turned, looking at Peyton with a clear gaze. "Stay in the King's Light…. always."

"I will sir," Peyton replied. "And you as well."

Part Two

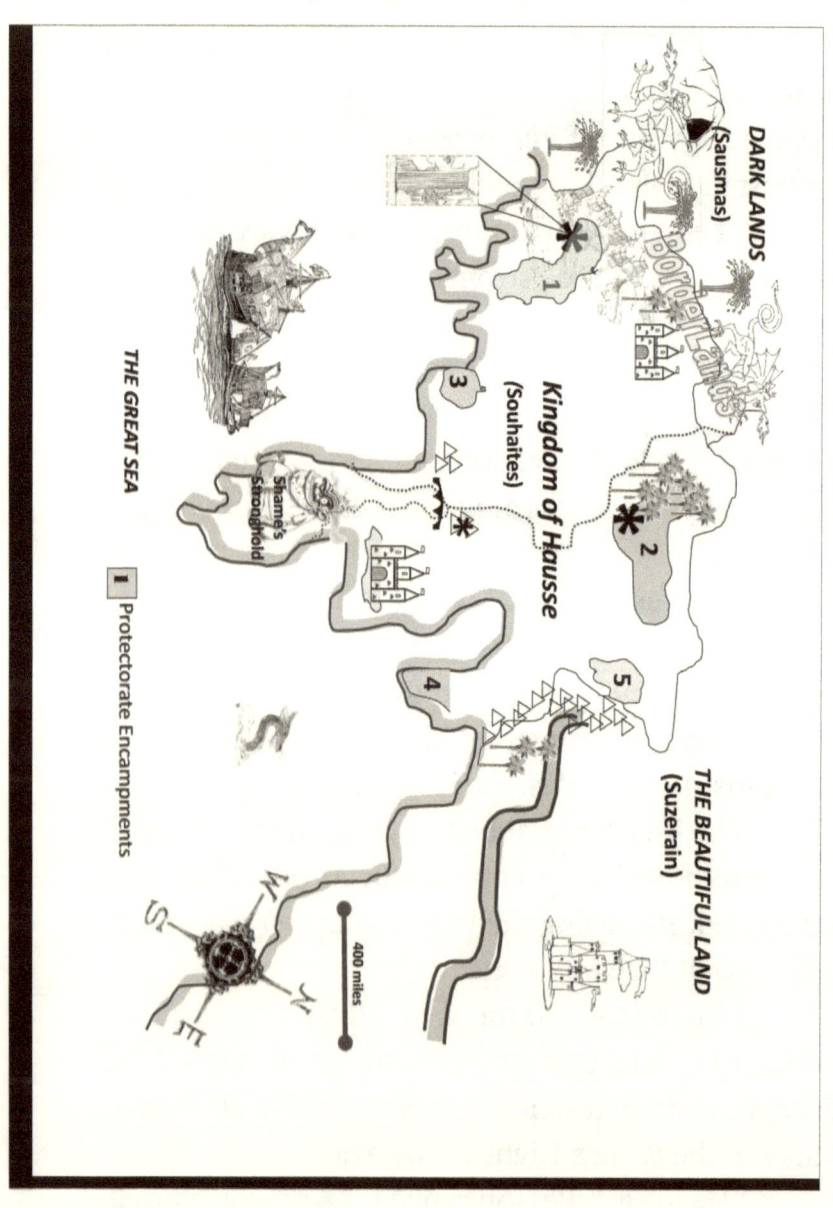

Chapter Five
Daydreams

Princess Karaliene sat on the floor in the Nursery of the Queen's summer castle. Nearby, her nursemaid and lady-in-waiting worked by the window opening, a needlepoint stand stationed in front of her. Against the curved wall, candlesticks shed light to dispel dark shadows, next to tapestries of fields and flowers, which brightened the environment considerably compared to the cold, gray stone.

"I want *my* daughter to have a *happy* childhood," Queen Souhaites had told everyone when Karaliene was born, "and I want her to be protected inside these walls. You never know when an intruder might break in."

The servants had never understood the reasons for her fears. After all, she hadn't taken as many precautions in building the winter castle. Of course, they reasoned, the winter castle was closer to the Borderlands. Perhaps the western kingdom was too remote of a region for such carefulness.

In contrast, this castle; the summer castle; was built on its own island. At every change in the angle of the castle walls, a tower had been constructed. Within each tower, groups of six guards served continually, in four-hour shifts, rotating day and night. Between the towers, additional guards were stationed on the top of the four-foot thick curtain walls built in the event of siege or battle. Four-foot wide pathways ran along the tops of the curtain walls. For further security, height extensions, or battlements, had been added to the outside walls next to the pathways. Some were as high as five feet; with soldiering provided for complete protection should warfare ever occur.

Moreover, the castle had two lower levels, with expansive rooms underground. These luxurious spaces had been carved out of the rock for retreat, as well as for storage. It was rumored the Queen could live forever within the castle walls and never need anything, including water.

Added to the castle's daunting fortifications, had been the construction of a moat fifteen feet deep. It was stocked with flesh-eating fish, said to swarm like bees upon any creature brave enough, or unfortunate enough, to enter the water. One witness reported having watched a calf as it was fed to the fish. According to the story, the fish had reduced the animal to mere bones in the space of an hour, devouring it alive in a feeding frenzy. A few of the fish had even jumped out of the water to get a first bite, as the animal had been lowered into the water.

Based upon the accounts of those who knew, the only safe method by which to cross the moat was by lowered drawbridge. And the drawbridge was only lowered when the Queen gave a direct command for it to be so. In fact, no one knew of a time the bridge had been lowered and left open all day, since the day the

Queen had brought Princess Karaliene to live in the castle. That had been five years ago, next week.

No one living in the eastern Kingdom could remember when the castle had been originally constructed. It had just always been there, as had the Queen. It was said the Principal tower had been constructed when the first mortals had roamed the land; that the Queen had added to the structure year by year; but no one knew for certain.

In the top room of the Principal tower, the princess stood, and moved to look out the window at the steadily falling rain.

"Ellie," she said, "isn't there *anything* we can *do* today?

Her companion stopped her needlework. "You can always work on a pillow cover. I have some new stitches I can show you," she offered.

"I don't *like* needlework," the princess pouted. "It hurts my fingers." She climbed up into the seat next to her nursemaid friend, swinging her feet from the chair as she sat. She sighed. "Has my mother sent word what we will be doing tomorrow?"

Ellie stopped her needlepoint. Slipping the needle through the fabric to keep it from falling, she looked at Karaliene with a knowing smile.

"Are you excited about your birthday, Kara?" Using the nickname she had given the child as an infant, she smoothed the child's tight curls out of her eyes.

"I *want* to be," the little girl answered. "My mother hasn't said *anything* about it *this* year. Last year, there were visitors coming, and presents came for *weeks* before. *Last* year, there was a big party, and the grown-ups had a fancy ball....." her voice trailed off. A quiet tear forged a path down her cheek to her chin. "I just thought there would be *something.* "

Ellie picked the little girl up and held her on her lap. She spoke softly, "Last year, the Queen was receiving guests for political reasons as well. Those guests brought presents for you *with* them when they came for her meetings."

Karaliene took in what her nursemaid was telling her. As she thought about it, her eyes welled up. "Does that mean they didn't come *just* for me and my party?" she asked.

"I'm sad to tell you that's true, dearest," Ellie replied. "Yes, that *is* what I mean. Don't you remember? She came back from the winter castle early last year."

There was silence in the Nursery for several moments. The only sound heard was the creaking of the lady-in-waiting's chair as she slowly rocked the five-year old little girl back and forth, holding her on her lap.

It was a dejected Karaliene who broke the silence. "Why doesn't she come to see me?" she murmured. "And why can't I ever go *with* her when she goes to the winter castle?"

"I don't know," Ellie whispered gently, "but I'm certain it isn't because of anything *you* did."

The princess shook her head slowly. "I'm sure there's something *wrong* with me," Karaliene responded. "Why doesn't she want to be *with* me?"

Holding the little girl in a comforting embrace, Ellie said nothing. Each fall season since the child's birth, it had been the nursemaid's station to care for her through the winter. Queen Souhaites had made it her custom to spend fall and winter months in the western Kingdom, since the years before Ellie had been drafted into her service. In fact, the girl considered, hadn't she originally *served* in the winter castle? Ellie still remembered the night the Queen had ordered her to assume responsibility of Karaliene's care. She had left everything she knew behind her to care for the child. They had moved to the summer castle the very next week. She had barely been able to say goodbye to her family.

Ellie smiled, looking back. How had she done it? She had been a child *herself* at the time. Of course, the summer castle's servants had taken pity on her; or had they been hoping for favors from the Queen? Her own parents had expressed concern, but there had been nothing they could do to change the Queen's command. Such was the way of life in the Kingdom of Hausse.

"Why did we ever allow you to respond to the Court's invitation to work there?" her mother had wept. "We thought it would help the family......now I will never see you again."

She hadn't known what to say at the time. She hadn't expected the circumstances either.

From what she could remember, Karrem, the Queen's cook in the winter castle had been a family friend of her father's since before she was born. Apparently, he had needed an extra set of hands in the kitchen, during the Queen's yearly stay.

For the first several months she had been at the castle, Ellie had worked at menial tasks, peeling potatoes and doing dishes. At first, working in the castle had been fun for her. She had enjoyed the expensive clothes she was given. She loved spending time in the afternoons with Karrem, learning to cook and being treated much older than her years. Most importantly, she had taken food home for her family each night, after a day's work. She was sure now the Queen had never been aware of what the kitchen workers did to help them.

One day, the Queen had sent a request to the kitchen for help. It seemed she was sick that day, and wanted someone to sit with her. Ellie had sat quietly, and cooled the woman's forehead with cold rags.

"Who are you?" the Queen had inquired, upon emerging from her fever.

"My friends call me 'Ellie'," she had responded. "I am helping Karrem in the kitchen. Would your Majesty like to eat something?"

Somehow, that moment had elevated her in the monarch's favor. From that time forward, she had been requested in the Queen's presence. Strange, she thought, how quickly her life had changed....

Who would have been here for Karaliene had she not been serving in the castle the week the baby was born?

The child in her lap stirred. Then, a princess' words broke into her reverie. "The last time she was mad, I asked her if we could have cupcakes. I *thought* I had waited 'til she wasn't busy to ask her... she yelled at me, and said she didn't know why she had me at all," Karaliene confided tearfully. "I don't know *why* she doesn't like me."

Ellie stroked the girl's hair, and continued to hold her close. "Sometimes grown-ups say things they don't mean when they are angry. When they are finished with the anger, they think the words they said are finished too."

Karaliene nodded. "But *her* words *don't* go away. I keep thinking about them. I haven't talked to her since she was mad that day. I haven't even *seen* her, except through the window when she was leaving us."

Sniffing, and seeking to wipe her tears away, the child pulled her knees up, closer to her chest. She tried to snuggle in closer to her companion. With a sad sigh, the child put her head against Ellie's chest, sitting quietly for a moment. After a few minutes passed, she spoke once more. "I can hear your heart beating."

"You should be a doctor when you grow up," Ellie giggled.

A whimper was part of the child's response. "But I have to be a *princess*," Karaliene reminded her.

"Oh, that's right," Ellie answered. "*I* remember now." She began to hum a song as she continued to sway back and forth, holding the little girl. Before long, little Karaliene's tense arms had relaxed, and her breathing became deep and even. She was fast asleep.

Ellie spent the next little while thinking about her conversation with Princess Karaliene. There were only a few weeks remaining before Queen Souhaites returned to the eastern Kingdom for the spring and summer seasons. She had been at the winter castle for a little over four months now. Looking down, she absent-mindedly played with Kara's long black curls.

Unexpectedly, a dream she had experienced two nights prior flashed across her mind. It seemed a lifetime away. What had the voice said? She strained to recall. Closing her eyes, she rested her head against the high-backed rocker in which she sat, trying to picture the images in her memory.

Had it only been two nights ago? Everything seemed to run together. Focusing her energies, she gathered her will up from its hiding place.

I cannot let this place defeat me, she decided.

Suddenly, as though flood-gates had opened, her memory re-engaged. She had tried to forget it; it had so shaken her.

The vivid images within her dream replayed once more. She was in her family home in the western Kingdom, seated at the long table in the common living area. Across the table from her were both of her parents. Their eyes were blindfolded, and yet they were reaching out to her. She could almost smell her mother's biscuits. Her mouth watered. It had been five long years. What she would give to have one *taste* of her mother's strawberry jam again! She looked around for her brother and sisters. They were not in the room.

As she remembered, the images moved across her heart once more. Out of nowhere, misty smoke began to fill the house. It was as though she was floating in a cloud. Then, from the ceiling, a giant dagger had come crashing down, splitting the table between her and her parents in two. They were drawn through the walls, and she was left alone. Looking down, she saw a baby in her arms, and recognized Princess Karaliene. The baby in the dream had been sleeping as well, unaware of anything but being safe in her arms.

Without warning, the roof above her was ripped away. Ellie looked up in time to see a dragon's claw reaching into the house; as though it were digging. Then, the room filled with fire, and a dragon's head lowered to fill the room. Ellie remembered shielding Karaliene in her arms, and turning her back to the dragon. Fire had then surrounded her with an intensity she knew she would not survive.

A voice spoke. "There isn't much time."

She had awakened in a full sweat. What did the dream mean?

What was she supposed to do?

The dream's images had greatly puzzled and frustrated her for most of that day. Then, last evening, she had decided; it was all just too mysterious and silly. Perhaps she had just eaten too many cakes that day; or perhaps it was the books she had been reading from the Queen's library….

The voice spoke again. But this time it filled the room she was sitting in. Was she sleeping?

"There isn't much time, Ellie."

Ellie opened her eyes. Blinking, she realized; the large, gray room was now filled with light, brighter than any candlestick flames. Unconsciously, she lifted one hand to shield her eyes. As she grew accustomed to the surrounding brilliance, she saw the form of a man standing in front of her. He seemed to be completely made of the white light. He was in a long robe, and wore a golden belt, from which hung the biggest sword she had ever seen. From his back, immense radiant wings reached through and above the ceiling, into the heavens.

"Who are you?" she asked.

"I am Jophiel," the brilliant specter responded. "The king has asked me to make myself known to you, and to bring you a message."

Ellie was surprised. "Are you a Light-Bearer?" she asked.

Jophiel smiled. "Yes, Ellie," he answered. "I serve in the position of Serving Messenger. I have been assigned to you for this season of your life. You also have another, like me, who has been guarding your soul since the days before you were born."

With wide-eyed wonder, she gazed at him. "My mother used to tell me about them... I mean ... about you. But I have never seen one of you until now." She paused. "You're *bigger* than I imagined."

Jophiel chuckled. "And I am one of the King's *smaller* creations," he told her. "You should see Fire-Bearers and The Four. Just *one* of them is bigger than this entire room!"

94

"The Four?" she inquired.

"They are amazing Creatures, who describe the ever-present, all-seeing, far reaching, and unlimited nature of the Suzerain. Each one has four faces; a mortal, a lion, an ox, and an eagle. Each face looks in a different direction. In the center, they burn with fire. Each creature has wings which cover his body, and arms which extend out from under the wings. Under each creature is a wheel, attached to the creature, which spins as he flies. Each wheel is filled all around with eyes which observe everything taking place in every part of the King's Realm."

"They sound scary," Ellie replied.

Jophiel nodded. "In some other setting they might be, but there is no Fear in the Suzerain's Court..... Ever."

"Ever?" she wondered.

"Ever. There is no need for Fear, where there is love," Jophiel continued. "And wherever the king is, love is."

"Love is what?" she asked

"Love just *is*..." he gazed at her clearly. "Love will never share its space with Fear. They cannot exist in the same place at the same time."

Ellie looked at Jophiel, confused. "I will have to think about that one," she answered.

The Messenger continued. "The king has asked me to make myself known to you, and to deliver his communication once more: 'there isn't much time left.'"

Ellie responded, frustration showing in her voice. "I did hear you when you told me the first time. I really did. I just don't know what the message means." She stopped, realizing the manner in which she was talking to this magnificent creature from another Realm. "I'm sorry," she said.

"If you want to know an answer, you must ask a question," Jophiel told her.

"How do I know what questions to ask?" the girl inquired.

Jophiel smiled. "Just start with the one on top," he said. "No matter what it is, the answer will begin you on the king's journey."

"All right, then," Ellie answered. "May I ask a question?"

The Light-Bearer nodded.

"Why did *I have to be the one* who had to leave their home and family, and be locked in a tower with a small child; when I haven't even had a chance to be a child myself?"

Jophiel looked at her with compassion. "Is that *really* the question you wanted to ask?" he said.

Ellie felt her cheeks turn hot. She hesitated. "Not really, no. I'm sorry. It just came out, I guess. I had a dream about my parents and my home...." Her voice trailed off.

"I saw it too," the Light-Bearer reminded her. "It was my voice you heard as you slept."

"What does the dream mean?" she continued. "Why does it keep coming back to me? What do the words mean.....What *time*? Time left for what?"

Jophiel regarded her for a moment before he responded to her questions. "Suzerain only repeats himself when something is important. He will continue to speak until you have understood his meaning.

"The dream is warning you of things to come, and preparing you for your part in the king's Plan. In the future, the dream will take on a different meaning, and become deeper in your understanding.

"For now, its meaning has to do with the child you are holding. The time is nearing when the Queen will reach out for her; to shape her for destructive purposes. In small ways, she has already begun to do so. Your care for this little one is of great importance; more than you can possibly realize at this moment. Use this time to create memories to give her hope in dark days.

"Tomorrow, when you both are on horseback, ride into the town. Go to the Bakery on Third Street, and ask for a man named Nathan. He will be waiting for you, and will tell you what to do."

Just as quickly as he had appeared, Jophiel disappeared from her sight. As he did, a warm, gentle breeze blew across her skin. What was that wonderful aroma, she wondered?

And then it was gone.

Shifting in her chair, Ellie realized the sun had set outside. How long had she slept, she wondered? Was the room was darker than she remembered? On her lap, Princess Karaliene began to stir.

It would be time for dinner soon.

Perhaps she should go to the kitchen and speak with the cook.

On the outskirts of Protectorate Area One, just inside the edge of the Great Canyon, a small party of travelers had set up camp for the night under the trees. There were twelve of them now accompanying the Light-Bearer, ranging in age from five years to…. well, Uriel's age, which no one knew.

Today marked five months since Tvirtas, Peyton and Uriel had parted from Tvirtas and Anbeter's home. As the training had deepened, Uriel had gathered seven more into the circle.

This morning, Peyton sat near the fire-pit, and found himself considering those who had become as close to him as his own family over the past few weeks.

Tividar had come from Area Five, where he stayed after completing Discovery Season Ten. Dark headed, with piercing black eyes, Tividar had completed his fourth order of chivalry. This was impressive, Peyton considered; as in all, there were seven orders of Chivalry. Every student who completed all ten of the Discovery Seasons was automatically installed into the King's Service. Tividar was a Knight second class, in the Order of the Dragon's Cross. Watching him, Peyton realized the twenty-year old must have worked extremely hard to get to such a high level at his age. He smiled, considering. Yet, no one would ever know Tividar had achieved such high honors. He conducted himself like a humbly born farming pcasant. He had no airs of superiority or self-importance. Peyton had liked him as soon as they met.

Two sisters had been recruited from Area Four; Pythia and Panna. Both were expertly skilled in throwing knives, and in acrobatic arts. Whenever they worked on their tumbling moves, the entire company stopped to watch them in fascination. Peyton had been paired with Panna in sword-fighting drills several times, and had found her a challenging opponent. Both girls were pleasant enough, he thought, but it would help if he had an easier time telling them apart. It had been two months since they had joined the company. He still had difficulty telling which one was which.

Three months ago, a married couple and their two children had joined the group. Ramon and Shyla were from Protectorate Area One. Their children; a son, Jayden and a daughter, Damara, were both five years old; paternal twins. Peyton wasn't sure about each of their roles in Uriel's plan, but he enjoyed spending time with the entire family. Shyla carried a leather satchel, in which she carried a variety of flutes and pipes. Whenever time allowed, she would pull one or another out and play. Tonight, she was blowing gently over the tops of her smallest set of panpipes, creating a captivating tune. Peyton closed his eyes. The sound was soothing.

Having lived in the same Protectorate Area; Area One, Tvirtas and Ramon had struck up a friendship. As a result, Ramon's son, Jayden, had become Peyton's shadow. Tonight, the lad was leaning his head against Peyton's leg, close to sleep, his day's energy spent. In contrast, Jayden's sister, Damara, quiet and creative in nature, was holding one of her mother's small flutes, blowing across the opening to evoke a sound, but without success.

The same week Ramon and Shyla had joined them, Uriel had returned within a few days from Area One with Jaret, Peyton's classmate and childhood friend. It was good to have someone he knew besides his father in the midst of training. It would be good to work with his friend again, Peyton considered. He had thought many times about their mission for Commander Carel five years prior.

Had that been preparation for this, he asked himself?

He and Jaret had spent almost every evening since by the fire, retelling stories and dreaming about the future.

The most unusual members of the group were the last two to join them. It had been almost two months ago. Just after dawn one morning, an old woman from Area Two, named Galen, had arrived. She was bent over, and walked very slowly with a walking stick. Her ragged cloak barely reached the ground, and her hands were wrapped in strips of wool to protect them from the cold. Peyton smiled as he remembered Jaret's whispered assessment of Galen: "she must have been born *before time began*."

Poor Galen's entire face was a mass of lines and wrinkles. When she smiled, it was evident where the creases had begun, and the ancient woman smiled continually. Her smiles also released a view of missing teeth. How did she eat anything, Peyton wondered? If the old woman had been concerned about not being accepted in the group, she hadn't needed to be. She had been immediately accepted and given room by everyone in the camp. Galen had brought her own wagon, filled with bottles of essential oils, and hanging herbs. It was somewhat humorous to watch her drive her wagon. Instead of one or two horses to draw it, a small burro was hitched to its front. She had named him Harry.

"I can ride him when I need to," she had confided in Peyton while setting up her station in the camp. "A burro's back is low enough for this old woman to still reach."

Concerned for her health, and the safety of the company, Peyton and Jaret went to Uriel. "Why do we need the old woman, Uriel? Won't she slow us down?"

Uriel answered them with a laugh. "Everyone needs a medical officer, boys. Besides, her gifts will be of use in our mission."

It was then Peyton had thought the company was complete. But the Light-Bearer had added one more. Just after the midday sword fighting drills, on a day some eight weeks ago, Uriel had returned to camp, with a little girl. She was deaf and mute, and had to communicate with her hands, in a language only Uriel and Galen seemed to understand. Since Galen knew her hand language, Uriel had assigned her to sleep in the old woman's care.

The first three months had been filled with training. Along with the entire company, Peyton had been trained in weaponry and survival. He had been taught strategy and logic. He could now hit the middle of the target with his arrow from three hundred feet. He had found a style of arrow he liked, and had perfected its design. He had learned to strike a spark to flame with flint and steel. He had learned to wield and sharpen a broad-sword. He could hold his own battling with staves, as well as with axes.

Moreover, Peyton was decidedly the quickest in rapier skills in the entire camp. Additionally, in archery practice, his arrow design had proven more accurate than most. Yet, in the midst of these accomplishments, Peyton did not feel Pride. He was thankful to be included on the mission, and still desired to learn more.

Sitting around the fire tonight, he found himself deep in thought. In coming to this place; in joining Uriel; hadn't each of them discovered a portion of what it meant to live the life of a soldier?

In the midst of the group, Uriel stood to address them. The glow of the campfire highlighted his face. Watching him, Peyton remembered how the Light-Bearer had looked when he had first appeared in Peyton's dream. Now, he looked just like one of them. How long would the boy be able to continue to learn like this? He wondered. How amazing it was to live day to day in the presence of a Light-Bearer!

Uriel raised his voice.

"I am so grateful that our company is complete. All members have settled in nicely. As you know, for the first twelve weeks of our time together, you were in training. Each of you has been diligent to improve your skills. I am thankful for the character qualities I have observed in each of you. Each day I receive more understanding for the king's choices and instructions for our mission.

"For the past eight weeks, we have worked on our undercover training. It has been demanding, and you have done well. I must say, you have learned to portray a convincing representation of a gypsy family. The combinations of your gifts have provided an amazing cover for our activities. Tomorrow, we will begin our journey, stopping in villages as time allows. We are seeking to build our reputation within the region as entertainment for hire. I'm sure we will be able to offer a believable program wherever we go. From this point forward, we will call ourselves 'the Romani family.'

"If you haven't had time to get to know Galen, our medical officer, it is vital to the mission that you do so. She has been in the king's Service for a long, long time. She is an alchemist, as well as a physician." He paused and looked at Galen directly. The old woman met his gaze and smiled her somewhat toothless grin. His hand made a sweeping motion and ended as an indicator of Galen's wagon. "She is also a very accomplished concertina player."

Peyton had never heard of a concertina.

What was a concertina?

"Our newest and youngest member is Lysandra. She is seven years old. She is also deaf and cannot speak. We use a language written with hands to communicate with Lysandra. If you don't know the language, please learn it. Galen or I can teach you." He bent down to pick up the little girl, holding her in his arms as he continued. "Do not let the problem of her deafness get in your way when it comes to seeing her as a vital part of our company. Her handicaps have caused her other senses to become truly profound. She wouldn't be here if she didn't have skills we need to make this mission complete."

"What skills does she have, Uriel?" Jaret asked. "I would love to know what she is experienced in, and how we are to utilize one so young. Is she well-versed in warfare, or the sword?" It was an honest question, asked without rancor. Nevertheless, at this statement, a ripple of laughter was heard on the side of the fire where Jaret was sitting. Peyton smiled. It was good to have his friend's company once more.

Across from him, Tividar smiled.

Uriel looked around the circle, and then at little Lysandra. "Before our mission is complete, each of you will have given thanks to this little one for your very life. She has a gift of Divine Sight."

Involuntarily, Peyton let out a low whistle. "Wow," he said out loud. Although he had heard the term before, he had always thought the gift belonged in legends and folklore. "I didn't know it was a *real* gift," he said. "I thought it was just a fable."

"All folktales have their basis in a grain of Truth," Uriel responded kindly. "Many times, this little one can see what most mortals cannot, *and* sense the presence of evil before it arrives. Get to know her language over the next few days. Allow her get to know each of you." He put Lysandra back on the ground. "Now, let's all try to get some sleep. Tomorrow will be a busy day."

With that comment, the company began to break up for the night. Each member moved towards their assigned wagon. Observing the camp, and how it had been arranged, Peyton now understood. Gypsies lived in wagons, and traveled from place to place, bartering for goods, entertaining, making repairs, and generally providing diversion for the local citizens of any town or village. He now understood Galen's role. She would be a purveyor of cures for townspeople's various ailments. He found himself wondering what else she could do, and what else was hidden inside her wagon.

Thinking each person's role in the mission through, with the limited knowledge he had to date, he began to realize the answer to a problem he had perceived...... Now, it would be easy to hide the horses....

...*Hidden in plain sight!*

 **Chapter Six**
The Edge of Darkness

In the kitchen of the summer castle, Princess Karaliene sat on the massive hearth rug near the stone fireplace. In the brick oven built into its side, a flatbread smothered in garlic and cheeses sent out stimulated anticipation of its flavor. Ellie sat tailor-legged on the same rug, not far from Karaliene. Between them, a small, square, wooden board showed a game in mid-progression.

Over time, Ellie had discovered it was good to venture out of the tower at least a little each day; otherwise their existence became too depressing for words. Accordingly, when the Queen was away, she and Karaliene made it a habit to eat in the castle kitchen. For some reason, that particular room seemed to hold more light that any other room in the castle. Not only that; but being in close proximity to food held a great lure for both of them. When the Queen was in the western kingdom, at her winter castle, the atmosphere within the summer castle's stone walls was more relaxed. Half of the staff travelled with the Queen. Those who served on staff, staying behind, lived in the town nearby, and did not reside on the grounds. Other than the gate sentries, tower guards, housekeeping staff, and the gardeners, the castle was virtually empty. Most days, it was Ellie's responsibility to find some method of entertaining the child.

"Oh goody! Three!" Karaliene declared. Giggling in delight, she moved her game piece to the base of a painted ladder on the wooden board. "One, two, three!" she cried. Tapping the steps on the ladder, she moved her piece to its top on the board. "There! Now *I'm* ahead!"

Ellie laughed with her. "Yes, once again, you have risen to the top first!!" She shook the cup filled with counters, and poured it out again. Reading the marks, the nursemaid moved her piece on the board.

"Oh *no!*" she sighed with an exaggerated sound. Counting, she feigned dejection as the count landed her piece at the top of a large dragon painted on the board. Placing her piece at the tip of the dragon's tail, she slid down to the bottom. "Whoo-oo-sh! And it appears I must begin *again*! Why do you *always win?*"

"Because I'm *good* at this game!" Karaliene declared.

"Yes, you are!" Ellie told her, taking her own go at the game.

As little Karaliene shook the counters for her next turn, Ellie looked up at the woman across the room. She had come to work at the castle during the Queen's absence this winter. She was quiet most of the time, and Ellie had had few opportunities to know her, even though she and the princess ate in the castle kitchen most evenings.

"Myra, what are you making now?" she asked.

Her back leaning against the counter along the long castle wall, the large woman in a castle uniform cradled a huge mixing bowl. Her right hand held a wooden spoon. She was furiously stirring something in the bowl that Ellie couldn't see. "One minute, child," Myra responded. "You'll see." As she watched, Myra pulled a shallow stone dish from a shelf, and filled it with the batter she had been mixing.

Moving to the oven, the cook lifted a pole. At its one end was attached a large, flat wooden paddle. Maneuvering the paddle under the flatbread, she slid it out of the oven, and placed it on a tabletop tray nearby, next to a bowl of cored apple slices. Laying down the paddle, she then placed the shallow stone pan in the oven. She then looked down at Karaliene, who had also paused in play to watch her activities.

"I thought a cake might be nice for tomorrow," Myra said, bending down to pat the little girl's hair. "Isn't it your birthday? How old will you be?"

"I'm going to be five years old tomorrow!" the princess announced. She jumped up and hugged Myra's legs. "I can't wait! What kind of cake is it? Will it have sugar frosting too?"

"Well," the cook answered with eyes twinkling, "I'm sure it will have frosting… What kind I don't know yet. Let's see… I'm not sure what flavor of cake I made. It might change in the oven. We'll have to wait and see."

"Is it chocolate?" the little girl asked.

Firmly, Myra shook her head. "Not telling," she replied. "But if you eat your cheesy flatbread, you can lick the batter from the spoon and bowl. Then you will find out."

Forgetting all about her unfinished game, the princess moved to the table. "I will eat the whole flatbread!" she declared. "All by myself!"

"I don't think so!" Ellie interjected with faked indignation. "There might be two *other* people in this room who are hungry too!"

"*I'd* eat flatbread," Myra interjected, taking off her apron. She gathered three mugs and plates from the shelf, and moved to sit at the table. "Ellie, would you get the pitcher? I filled it with milk earlier and put it outside to cool."

Ellie opened the back door. A blast of frigid air blew into the room. "Brrr!" she muttered, rubbing her arms. Reaching into the storage cupboard mounted on the outside of the kitchen wall, she retrieved the pitcher. Moving quickly, she came inside and shut the door. "Look!" she said, as she poured the milk into mugs. "It's already frozen a little!"

"Oh, I love it when my milk is cold," Karaliene bubbled. She looked at Ellie, and then at Myra. "You two are my favorite people in the whole entire world."

Ellie and Myra exchanged glances over the meal.

"Myra," Ellie began, "I wonder if you could help me with something."

"What do you need, dear?" the cook responded.

"I thought it might be nice to take Karaliene on an outing tomorrow for her birthday," Ellie answered.

"Are we going to go to the place the man in light told you to go to?" Karaliene interrupted excitedly.

Startled, Ellie looked at the little girl. "W-what?" she stammered.

Karaliene spoke matter-of-factly, pulling bread and cheese apart, as she chewed; "the man who was in the Nursery this afternoon."

Myra's eyebrows raised; an apple slice in her hand. "There was a man in your room, Miss Ellie?"

Shaken by Karaliene's disclosure, Ellie hesitated. Suddenly, her face felt flushed. "It… it wasn't like that," she stuttered.

Every servant in the castle knew the penalty for unauthorized "liaisons" among members of the royal household. Without warning, Ellie's thoughts were racing. What would happen to her if Myra were to report Karaliene's words to the Queen?

Ellie didn't notice the smile beginning to break on Myra's face. The cook spoke softly. "Princess, may I ask you a question?"

"Yes, ma'am," Karaliene's voice was expectant.

"What did he look like?" Myra asked.

"Jophiel?" the little girl responded.

"Is that his name?"

"That's what *he* said it was."

Absorbing the conversation happening around her, Ellie was amazed. "Hold on," she interrupted. "Kara, were you just *pretending* to be asleep? What *did* you see?"

Karaliene looked across the table at Ellie, her eyes wide. "No ma'am. I was asleep on your lap. You sang to me. I love it when you sing. I love it when you play your lute too.

"Then, in my dream, a man in a robe with wings came into the Nursery. He had a gold belt on, and his wings went through the ceiling. His said his name was Jophiel. He told you there wasn't much time left. He said some other things that I didn't understand."

She paused. "Are we really going horse-back riding tomorrow? Are we going to the *town?*"

Ellie was stunned. What could she say, she queried silently, to explain things; to not get into trouble, or lose her station? What if Myra suspected her of treason in the Queen's absence? What should she do? Her mind was filled with whirling thoughts.

At first, she had doubted whether the encounter had been real. She had tried to push it to the back of her mind, going ahead with daily affairs as if nothing had occurred. But now, Karaliene's words had not only brought Jophiel's visitation to the forefront, but it had stirred the memory of the disturbing dream she had been trying not to think about for days.

It was Myra who broke the silence. "Sounds like a Light-Bearer to me," she said.

"Have *you* ever seen a Light-Bearer?" Karaliene wanted to know.

"I *have* seen them," Myra responded in a whisper.

"Really?" Ellie asked. "Where?"

Myra assessed the princess' nursemaid. "In many places," she said. "Didn't your own mother tell you they were always with you?"

Ellie didn't know what to say. She nodded.

Myra gazed at her. "How old *are* you, child?" she asked.

"I'm fourteen years," she answered. She paused, thinking. "How did you *know* that? Who *are* you?"

Myra didn't answer. She stood from the table. Putting her first finger up to her lips to indicate a need for silence, she looked toward the kitchen's outer door. "I need to make dinner for the guards now," she answered, her voice changing to a normal demeanor. "Is there anything else, your ladyship?"

At that moment, the door opened, allowing six of the Queen's guards entry. It was time for the watch to change. These were the first of many men who would invade the kitchen over the next hour.

Ellie had not realized until that moment, how many soldiers there actually were living on the castle grounds. How many, she wondered? She counted at least ten towers, between the inner castle, and the outside walls. Doing the math in her head, she estimated there must be at least a hundred armed men safeguarding little Karaliene all the time. That number did not include the rest of the household staff.....

How would she ever accomplish what Jophiel had told her to do?

"Gentlemen, please! Did you forget the Queen's command to knock before entering? Can't you see that her little majesty is still finishing her meal?" Myra spoke in a raised voice to the first man in line. "Go away! Please come back in a few moments. And don't stomp that mud on my clean floor!"

Startled by the cook's manner, the first guard answered. "Yes, ma'am." He looked at his companions. "Dinner's not ready yet, boys, let's go to the guardhouse." Grumbling and muttering came in response, amid complaints and statements of inconvenience. "You'd think they'd know a man's hungry after being outside all day." "Why do we have to go back to the guardhouse?" "My feet are cold…" the men's voices continued; trailing off as they moved in company away from the building towards the guardhouse.

When the door was finally closed, Myra let out a hearty laugh. Ellie couldn't help but giggle, with little Karaliene following suit. The cook moved to the fireplace. Taking the long tongs, she swung the largest of the pot brackets out from over the fire, to over the hearth. After stirring the pot, she tasted the soup. "It's ready," she said. Next, she removed two loaves of hot bread from the oven, and placed them on the counter to cool. "Now," she muttered, "where did I put that jam?"

A thousand miles away, in the western kingdom; in the lowest underground levels of the winter castle, Queen Souhaites stood in silence. She was angry. Those in her attendance could tell her audience with the Dark Prince had not produced the results she had asked for. It would take longer to achieve the status she was seeking.

His image had descended into the Pit, dissolving only moments before.

The room in which she stood had been set aside for such visitations; lit only by two candlesticks, and the eerie glow produced by the cauldron fire. In the center of the room, round steps led to a high, circular stone platform. On the top of the platform, a circle of benches surrounded the pool of black liquid, mysteriously fed by a source in the nether regions of the earth. It was into this pool, the Dark Prince's image had descended.

Queen Souhaites stood on the second step from the top, enraged. Even angry, her face was pale. Her long, black, straight hair added to her already ethereal appearance.

"I have done everything he has asked me to do," she muttered. "Still he refuses to give it to me."

Flipping her black cloak open, the Queen pulled out a large glowing crystal. Her long, claw-like nails were filed to razor-edged points. With the first finger of her right hand, she traced the outside of the crystal's edge with a red-tipped fingernail.

"No matter," she seethed. "*I* will *give* him *more*. I will *acquire*. *I* must have *more.* "

At these words, a black fire within the crystal pulsed, as though in response to her statements. She looked to her underlings, who filled the room with snarling sounds and guttural noises.

Stepping down from the dais, the Queen moved to the corner of the room where her books and scrolls rested on shelves, along with innumerable bottles with visible animal parts stored in liquid. Carefully setting the crystal on the table near her, Souhaites paused, and then made a dramatic turn to face her audience.

"He has *given* me the *black* fire," she shouted, "but he denies me the *purple!*" At these words, a moan emanated from the mass of hooded creatures cringing before her. "And....," she continued, punctuating her words with a dramatic pause; "And, he will give us the *gold* fire only if we bring him the soul of a Mortal who has turned!"

"That should be easy enough, my queen," hissed the subject closest to her. "There are *always* those who only keep up *appearances.*"

"Easy?! You think this will be *easy?*" she screamed. "He doesn't want just *any* Mortal soul who has turned! He wants a *warrior,* a *champion* who has turned! And it must be *fresh* blood; *young blood!*"

The Queen observed her underworld Court. Yes, with these who stood before her, she held great power! But even now, it was not enough.....

Yet, she considered, it would be the power of these that could undo the Great Divide! She would yet rule, as she had been *meant* to rule!

Momentarily, her thoughts flashed to the *Before.* They had *all,* Sausmas included, been magnificent beings then.

For a millisecond, she remembered what it had been like to have feathery wings....

How she hated Suzerain.

To turn a Mortal champion would take a great deal of intellect. She would need the help of the most powerful in her dominion.

"Muddlers! Gather closer!" she coaxed. Immediately, there was a stirring amidst the throng before her. Moving to the front of the horde were the tallest and largest creatures among the group. Many were wearing regal robes. Some were dressed in gold.

"What do you *want?*" the largest of those begrudged to her by Sausmas, spoke, as though he would run her through with his talon.

Undaunted by his arrogance, the Queen lowered her voice and whispered in his ear. *"Results, you idiot! That is all I care about. Just remember who you are talking to. I could skewer you right here, and you would be reduced to nothing; you are nothing!"* In fearful silence, her challenger diminished slightly in size, sulking away.

Raising her raspy voice once more, Souhaites continued. "If we are to turn a Mortal champion, we must use all of our resources of great knowledge and achievement. We must use opulence to lure. We must use this mortal's achievements as weapons for defeat, and discover which appetites will invite the most destruction. *Those* are the appetites we must enslave." Souhaites was reeling them in, and she knew it. "I will need the most intellectual of your kind for the mission. Come to me with strategies; methods of logic to defeat the Experience of their Encounters; Understand.... I want no trivialities or simple plans. We must find the right candidate! The Dark Prince has set terms for us."

She looked over the group of Muddlers in front of her before going on. "Go! Devise! And then bring me one of yourselves to accompany me back to the Surface. Whatever conflicts you encounter, deal with them! Fight these things out among yourselves."

She paced to the farthest corner, and looked out into the middle of the room.

"Weavers! I have work for you! Gather closer!"

A group of somewhat larger, somewhat hunched-over creatures, with multiple deformities, moved closer to the Queen. Where wings had once grown from their backs, humps now were evident. But this was not the most concerning of their appearance. Each Weaver had multiple mouths, positioned all over the body. Each mouth was filled with sharpened teeth. The mouths were all continually whispering, demanding to be fed.

"Yessssssss?" came the whining reply. All of the mouths on the body of one creature had voiced the answer together.

"Just listen, my lovely," the Queen crooned, stroking the top of the creature's head.

"As you know, the Muddler who attends my mission will be preparing the ground of the mortal's soul for the Weaver who attends my mission. In that same way, *you* will be preparing the ground for the Shade I shall choose.

"Weavers, I want strategies from *you* we can use to confuse and trap our mortal champion. We must explain away and distort all of our mortal's understandings of Suzerain's words and actions. We want every Light-Bearer in relationship with our mortal to become ineffective in giving instruction or protection. We must consider how to explain away the king's powers.

"So then, how shall we *squeeze*, in order to create an opening in the soul's armor of our mortal for the works of the Shades? I need the most skilled of your group to work in preparing an environment of Shadow Smoke and Self-Doubt. When I have chosen our subject, the assignment will be to discover the deepest source of Pain in that mortal, so that we may achieve a quick and solid turning to Sausmas' side."

Her statements were met with comments and whispers from every mouth in every Weaver groveling before her.

"Silence! I don't want to hear your words," the Queen shouted. Then, changing her tone to one of cajoling and gentleness, she continued. "Now be off! When you return, it must be with two of your most skilled manipulators."

Turning to pace back and forth, flipping her great black cloak as she went, she continued. Souhaites changed her focus of attention, and scanned the rest of the great room.

"Oh, Sha-a-des," she called in her sweetest voice, "it's time for *you* to gather closer now."

Materializing from the shadows; changing form from furniture to creature; seeming to make the very air itself move; the creatures known as Shades floated to stand before her. Shades were the most versatile of her minions. As a result, Souhaites was prepared to invest the most time and attention into developing her scheme with this element.

She stood in silence for a moment, waiting for the remnants of Muddlers and Weavers to dematerialize.

Yes, a Shade was a better assistant than any other of her subjects. She could ask a Shade to fulfill a task in visible *or* invisible form. A Shade could shift identity and appear to be what they were not. They could slip in and out of a room without notice. They could change into sand. A Shade could adapt to any environment and seem like a natural element within it. They were the most difficult for mortals to discern, and almost impossible to take out of power once played into a situation, because they drew Mortal Attachment.

"Come," she said with sugar-sweetness, "help me find the spells and potions we can use to get our way. We will need all of our resources if we are to succeed."

Moving to the shelf, the Queen reached for a small vial. "My recipe is almost complete," she announced. She then added thirteen drops of the vial's contents into the cauldron simmering over the coals.

"This will provide our entrance into Suzerain's Realm. Gather 'round and the Image will show us their weaknesses."

As the host of Shades gathered around her, billowy white smoke began to rise from the cauldron. Then, within in the smoke, a picture began to emerge. The figures in the image were standing still, as though a moment in time had frozen, captured for memory.

"What do you see, my beauties?" the Queen asked.

Clearly seen were wagon wheels, and the leggings of seven individuals. As the picture came into clearer view, suddenly a loud roaring, tempest-like wind, moved through the cavern, sweeping the room clean. Souhaites was hurled off her feet, onto the stone floor.

"What was *that*?" she stammered. Around her, even forms of the dimmest light had vanished. She sat up, rubbing her lower back in the inky blackness. After a moment, she lifted her hands to peel back an outer layer of skin from her eyes.

Emerging from beneath, her actual identity became evident; too evil for mortal imagination. After removing the veil from her genuine eyes, the Queen found it possible to see in the complete darkness.

Blinking, she looked around the immense cavern. As she appraised the effects of the roaring wind, she screamed out loud. All of the Shades subject to her rule had dematerialized from the room. Every flame, even to the remnants of the cauldron fire, had been extinguished. All of her spell dictionaries, recipe journals, and deep magic resources had been dislodged from the shelves. Loose pages had been scattered throughout the room. She could not even see where her ancient scrolls had landed.

No, wait. There was part of one scroll. She recognized the symbols along its edge….. How had it unrolled and torn in half in that amount of time?

Looking up, she saw the larger specimen bottles which still stood on the shelves, but the majority of the smaller ones were distributed across the floor; many shattered and unrecoverable.

In the middle of the stone floor where she sat, indented deep into the stone, was the giant image of a lion's head. Feeling the print of the image, Souhaites realized it was as though a great seal had been lowered quickly upon the room, somehow melting the stone.

Suddenly, she smelled something burning. Looking down, she saw smoke beginning to rise from her great black cloak. Abruptly, she jumped up, moving away from the intense heat.

The image was still so warm; her fingers had begun to burn.

In the western Kingdom, five house-wagons, accompanied by one rider on horseback, travelled on the trade route towards the east. They had been on the road for almost two weeks now. The days had quickly settled into a routine. They would stop in the early evening near a water source. Firewood was gathered; a fire-pit dug and lined with stones. An iron tripod with a hook at its center was then placed over the fire, and a large pot was hung from the hook attached to its apex. Water was drawn from the water source and heated.

As laundry was washed, or children were bathed, each wagon took turns hunting for food. So far, the fare had not been bad at all, Peyton considered. They had eaten rabbit twice, fish once. Last evening, he, Jaret, and Tividar had been hunting in the woods, and surprised a nide, or large group of pheasants. As the flock had scuttled into flight, three arrows had hit their marks.

When the hunters were unsuccessful, the menu included potatoes, cabbage, and other root vegetables capable of storage. Peyton's favorite cooks so far were Pythia, Galen and surprisingly, his father, Tvirtas.

After supper, the company would sit around the fire telling stories, or, playing music together. Strange, Peyton considered. He hadn't considered *using* his hand-drum on his journey. It had been a last minute addition, in case he might have time to modify its construction. He had been unaware that Tvirtas, his father, had brought his violin.

One night, after dinner, Shyla had pulled out her panpipes, weaving a lingering melody. After light conversation, Tvirtas left the circle to go to his wagon. Peyton thought his father had gone to bed, but then, the man returned, with violin and bow in hand. Sitting on the ground next to Shyla, he began to weave a counter strain; in and out, up and down, moving through her haunting melody. It was at that moment, Peyton remembered bringing his hand-drum. He retrieved it from the wagon he and Jaret were sharing. Sitting on the other side of his father, he began to beat out an accompanying rhythm.

It wasn't long before Tvirtas and Peyton took up a livelier tune, with strong rhythmic overtones. In response, Shyla switched her melody maker to a flute. Soon, Ramon and Damara began to dance, and Jayden soon joined in as well.

From behind him, Peyton heard a musical sound he had never heard before. He turned, and saw Galen, her face showing a wide, toothless smile, holding a small instrument, with one end in each hand. There were buttons on its ends, and a round sack with folds in its middle, holding the ends together. It appeared to be a sort of squeeze-box. The combination of the instruments was like nothing he had ever heard before! He wanted it to just keep going! The music was unbelievable, he realized. They were all playing together, and in the same key. They didn't know what song it was.... *And it was fun!*

That night became forever etched in Peyton's memory. It marked the beginning of his actual Discoveries in the King's Realm. As the musicians continued to play, the boy watched in astonishment as Galen began to transform. By the time the song had finished, her wrinkles were gone, her back was straight, and her hair and teeth had returned! Her body had also become slighter, and her cloak had lost its look of rags.

Unable to stop himself, he had said something. "Galen, what *happened* to you?"

She laughed. "You have never *seen* this before?" she asked.

"Never," he replied. "How? What does it mean?"

"I'm not quite sure, really," she answered. "I only know this phenomenon happens when two things occur in my life: When my heart plays my concertina, and when I am in the midst of a battle."

Peyton hadn't understood her meaning. "Your *heart* plays?"

She nodded. "Yes. I used to play with my mind and fingers on another instrument. I made lots of money in Hausse. Then, Kyriel taught me how to play with my heart, and he gave me the concertina. Now, every time I play, I feel younger, lighter.... Stronger somehow."

"And when you are in *battle*?" he asked. "Surely *you* have never been to *war*."

Galen's eyebrows went up. "So... much there is for you to learn... you will see." She had paused, as if thinking through whether to express her next thoughts. "I know I look very old, Peyton. But in my heart, I am no older than you are. I have seen many battles. In the King's Realm, I am known as a Chevaliesse. That means I am a female knight, trained in all aspects of warfare. My official title is (she lifted her hands, and made a motion of parentheses in the air)... "Knight of the First Order of the Dragon's Cross, Mistress of the Sword." It is my station to create unique weapons, for individual warfare situations. Even now, there are moments when I hear Suzerain's voice and I can communicate what he says to those in my company.

"For *this* mission, I am a medicine woman." She looked at him evenly. "But never fear, with all of the support the King has placed on this team, we will definitely be in a battle. I have no doubt of it."

"All of the *support*?" Peyton repeated. "What does that mean?"

Galen smiled. "Hasn't your father told you?"

"Told me? *Told me what*?"

"The military stations of those involved in this mission…. and *his position* in the King's Service."

"He has told me stories about things that happened when he was a soldier."

Galen nodded, and looked at him. "*Was* a soldier?" she questioned, clarifying.

"You mean, he still *is* a soldier?" he asked, his mouth dropping open.

"I don't think anyone *really* retires," she responded. "Look at me!"

They both laughed at that. She continued.

"Your father," she paused, lowering her voice, "is the retired Commander of *Prince Kyriel's* visible army. He carries the highest order of the Dragon's Cross and is Guardian of the Purple. His rank is that of Armor-Bearer to the King… Somehow I doubt the Suzerain will ever retire him *completely*. He has been too fruitful to just set aside."

"What are the stations of the others in the mission?" Payton asked. "Are there *other* knights here?"

Galen smiled. "What do *you* think?"

"You said there was a great deal of support on this mission…"

"Did I say that?" she teased.

"Come on!" Peyton prodded. "Tell me."

The medicine woman pointed towards Tividar, who was standing with Pythia and Panna, the sisters from Area Two. "Panna is twenty-four. Pythia is twenty-five. They are sisters whose grandparents came into Area One many years ago. Their father, who had grown up in a travelling circus in Hausse, trained them in acrobatics and trapeze from the moments of their first steps."

"They are really good," Peyton noted. "Is that all they do?"

"No," Galen replied, giggling. "They are both champions in knife throwing. Panna speaks four languages. Pythia can juggle up to eight items for long periods of time without even a hesitation. And…"

"That's amazing," Peyton said.

Galen put her finger up to signal him she still had more to say. "And… each is Chevaliesse in station. Panna holds the rank of Knight Second Class of the Dragon's Cross. Pythia is also of that rank, but she has the added title; Bearer of the Silver." She paused. "Haven't you fenced with Panna in sword drills?"

Stunned, Peyton didn't answer her. Was Galen saying he had been sparring with a knight, without being aware of it?

"Peyton?" Galen nudged his arm. "Are you awake?"

The young man shook his head. "Yes," he answered. "Sorry. I was just thinking…. What about Tividar?"

"As you know," she continued, "he is Knight Second Class, and is well skilled with the sword and in trap building. He grew up in the Protectorate, but hasn't allowed that to affect him. He has worked diligently to cultivate his skills for one so young."

She nodded toward the fire-pit, where Ramon and Shyla were kneeling with their children near the fire. Ramon had long sticks in his hand. Shyla had a bowl of a white substance she had been developing all day in their wagon.

Several days ago, they had come across a marsh area near woods. In the midst of the marsh, were several patches of wildflowers. Excitedly, Shyla had dug up all she could find of one variety. "These roots make a wonderful treat!" she had told Peyton. She had worked all day on the concoction; pounding the white roots into powder; adding just the right amounts of honey. When she was finished, a sticky, white mixture had emerged. Now, it appeared she and Ramon were loading the fire-sticks with it. As Galen and Peyton watched, they wrapped the end of one stick in the mixture, and held it over the fire.

Galen moved over to the family with Peyton following her. "What is that stuff?" she asked Shyla.

Pulling the stick in her hand away from the heat, Shyla answered, "Mallow." She pulled the brown casing produced by the fire, off the top of the stick, and popped it into her mouth. "There's nothing like it," she told Galen. "Here. Try some."

As he tasted it, Peyton didn't think he had ever had ever tasted anything so sweet... or so good!"

Shyla laughed, as she prepared a stick of mallow for herself to roast. "Just don't eat too much of it. The children ate their fill of it one time, and got really sick!" For some time that evening, Peyton sat with Galen, Ramon and Shyla and the children. There were so many things to learn, he realized, as he sat by the fire, roasting mallow and talking. In the course of conversation, he discovered Ramon and Shyla's military stations in King Suzerain's service.

Ramon was thirty years, and Shyla was twenty-seven. They had been married for ten years. Surprisingly, both were active officers who worked on special assignments for the king. Ramon was a reassigned Commander; a Knight of the First Order of the Dragon's Cross; Keeper of the Flame. Shyla was an armaments officer; skilled in archery, small swords and strategy. Her rank was Chevaliesse; Knight of the First Order of the Dragon's Cross; Strategy Architect.

"What does an Armaments Officer *do*?" Peyton asked her.

"It has to do with the music I play on the pipes. When there is damage to a knight's armor, or they have suffered injury in battle, the music from the pipes and flutes brings healing and repair."

"How does that happen?" Peyton wanted to know.

"I don't know, exactly," Shyla answered. "I can feel the power rushing through me when it is happening, but I know that I am not the source of the power."

"Where do you think it comes from, then?" the boy asked.

"Oh, all power *like that* comes from Suzerain," she answered.

Peyton sat by the fire for a long time that evening after everyone else had settled into their wagons. It was amazing to him. He had been chosen to participate in a mission, by the king, and to train with real Knights of the Dragon's Cross. Just how many were travelling in the group, he wondered? He began to count them: Tvirtas (his father), Galen, Panna and Pythia, Ramon and Shyla, and Tividar. All had finished Discovery Season Ten, or its equivalent, and had served in enough missions and battles to become distinguished in leadership.

Added to his astonishment was the realization that the collection gathered for this particular mission had been handpicked by King Suzerain. Moreover, it astonished him that he and Jaret had been included, when neither of them had completed even their *first* Discovery Season.

Not only that.... why were *children* included in this mission? Jayden and Damara he understood, since both of their parents were involved in the assignment, but still; wasn't this mission a dangerous one? Why were so *many* knights involved, with children also allowed? Having someone with a gift of Divine Sight was understandable, he reasoned.... even if that someone was a child.....

"You'll have to get some sleep if you are to be of use to the king tomorrow," a familiar voice spoke just behind his shoulder.

Peyton started. He had thought everyone in the camp was asleep. Turning his head, he stared at the man in the long cloak standing not two feet behind him. How had he come so close so silently, without startling the horses? And whose voice was this? Didn't he recognize the voice?

The cloaked man moved closer. "Can I sit down with you for a little while?"

As the hood on the cloak was lowered, the man stepped into the firelight. Peyton let out a deep breath in relief. It was Zynicker, his classmate and friend from Discovery Season One.

"Spider! What are you doing here? How did you get here?"

"Oh, I was just riding home, and saw your fire," his friend replied. "I wasn't sure who it could be, but I needed a place to rest for the night. Can I stay here?"

"Sure," Peyton responded. "Where is your horse?"

"Back in the woods a ways," came the reply. "I tied him to a tree. I was going to go back and get him once I found out if things were clear."

"Are you hungry?" Peyton asked.

"No, I'm fine." Zynicker sat down next to him. The two remained side by side for a short time in silence.

"How are classes going?" Peyton asked.

"Oh, I'm doing well," Zynicker answered. "I love school."

Something inside Peyton's brain felt a sudden concern; a twinge; a warning. Something about the Zynicker sitting next to him was out of sync with what he knew of his classmate.

Unprepared, he was startled by the sound of Elder Tallis' voice in inside his head.

This isn't really your friend. Move away from him.

Peyton stood up. "I think the fire needs another log." He moved to get a piece of firewood from the pile stacked a few feet away.

Zynicker spoke. "What are you thinking about, out here all alone?"

Don't tell him anything. Talk about trivial things. Don't tell him anything.

Peyton shook his head. "Oh, I was just thinking about things that happened today. You know, when there are so many of us, it's difficult to find a quiet moment. So, I grab a few minutes here and there when I can." He paused, and glanced sideways at Zynicker.

"Can I join you?" another voice spoke. Uriel stepped into the firelight, and sat down on the other side of the newcomer.

Don't call Uriel by his name. Don't say his name at all. Just be calm.

"This is my friend Zynicker," Peyton said to Uriel by way of introduction; putting a log on the fire. "He is in Discovery Season One with me."

Uriel looked at Spider. "You're a long way from home so late on such a remote road. And young too. Where are your parents?"

Zynicker looked at him with an even glare. "*You* are a Light-Bearer," he snarled, his voice low and guttural, growling with angry hatred.

"And *you* are *not* a fifteen year-old boy," Uriel responded, suddenly enlarging, transforming into his created design. At the unexpected appearance of the White Light shining from Uriel, the intruder screamed. "My *eyes*! You're hurting my eyes!"

Without warning, out of the shadows, a silver willowy figure, wielding two long-swords appeared. She moved in quick flexible movements. Before Peyton could assess who she was, what she was doing, or how she was doing it, the figure had somersaulted through the air from somewhere over their heads. Then, faster than his eyes could follow, she landed on her feet in front of Zynicker. With one sword, she ran him through the heart, and lifted him up over their heads. The second long-sword, she held to his throat.

Who is that strong, Peyton thought?

Watching, Peyton realized that Zynicker was still breathing. Strangely fascinated, he watched the chest moving in and out.

"By Prince Kyriel, who *are* you?" Galen, Mistress of the Sword, demanded, as she held her stance.

A high-pitched scream rushed out of the individual still hanging in the air. "I am sent to find an encampment of seven. The Dark Prince craves blood; *young blood*. The blood of a *champion*."

Uriel responded. "Sausmas is no prince. He is fallen, as are you. Besides, you are wasting your time. There are more than seven in our party."

The creature responded. "Then why attack me?"

Galen responded. "I don't tolerate Muddlers, in any form, especially when they seek to deceive me… *or* those in my care." She looked at Peyton. "We resist your deceptions."

At that moment, it was as though a bag had been emptied. The casing of Zynicker's appearance fell to the ground and turned to a chalky powder. What had been hiding inside that casing was now evident for all to see. Separated from the sack-like imitation of Zynicker's body, a Muddler remained, squirming and skewered on the sword. It was sputtering for breath.

Galen, young in form, clothed in silver, looked at Uriel. "What shall we do with him?"

"Banish him to the barren places," the Light-Bearer told her. "And forbid him to return until after our assignment is over."

Galen nodded, and spoke to the creature. "You heard him. You are banished to the Barrens, to the Borderlands; and you may not return to us, nor to anyone having to do with us, by the word of Kyriel."

At the sound of Kyriel's name, the Muddler began to scream once more, putting his hands over his ears. "Stop *saying* that! I don't want to *hear* that! Okay! *Okay! I'll go.* I'll go! Just stop."

Galen lowered her long-sword, bringing the creature to rest on the ground. She then placed her silver-armored foot on its head, and pushed, providing leverage to remove her sword.

"Here, let me help you," Uriel offered. Reaching down, he picked up the Muddler, who suddenly became quiet and shrank considerably in size. Rolling the creature up like a ball, Uriel pulled back his arm and pitched it into the atmosphere. A trace of fire from Galen's long-sword still burned from its center. In silence, the three of them watched the Muddler disappear into the distance.

After a moment, Uriel spoke. "I saw him when I was securing the horses for the night. He flew into the woods just over there." He nodded his head towards a denser, distant part of the forest.

"I was readying myself for sleep, and Lysandra alerted me." Galen responded. "She was watching the stars in the window and saw him as well."

"She *saw* him?" Peyton repeated. "What did she see?"

Uriel spoke. "Remember I told you she holds the gift of Divine Sight."

"Yes," the boy replied.

"She can sense Evil before it arrives, and can see the true identity of the Dark Forces underneath their disguise," the Light-Bearer explained.

Peyton was intrigued. "Was she watching for him?"

Uriel smiled. "Probably."

Galen nodded. "She climbed out of her sleeping berth, and tugged on my nightdress. It was just a matter of preparing myself after that," the Mistress of the Sword explained. She brushed her hands together as if she was removing debris.

"Well that was fun!" she laughed. "What's next?"

"I would suggest," Uriel whispered, "we *train* these children, now that a bear trap has been removed." Just as quickly as he had transformed into his created image, he returned to his normal Romani gypsy disguise.

Realizing Uriel was speaking of the Muddler, Galen smiled and nodded. "We will have to keep an eye out. Those things always travel in groups of two or more."

Uriel smiled at her. "You had better get some rest. You will be tired tomorrow, after all this exertion."

"Thank you," Galen spoke. "Come to think of it, I *am* a little weary."

Chapter Seven
A Different Way to Do Things

Morning began slowly for the Romani family the next day. Normally the one to make the morning coffee, Galen uncharacteristically slept in. By midday, the decision to delay travel for another twenty-four hours had been made. So, by the second day, travel began extra early.

After stopping at a village market to purchase vegetables, the wagon caravan passed through the town of Buway. On the outskirts was a small farmhouse. Tvirtas and Ramon noticed an old man sitting on his porch as the wagons drove by. In one hand, he held a large paintbrush. Sitting next to him on the step was a large bucket of whitewash.

Uriel shouted a greeting to the man, and he responded.

"Hey, any of you guys good at whitewashing?"

"I used to be," Tvirtas responded. "You need help?"

"Sure do," the man replied. "I was working on it, but my arm gave out… its being so blasted old….I can't pay ya' but I'd give ya' some meat fer yer family. Got plenty of chickens this year."

Tvirtas, Ramon, and Tividar whitewashed the small house in an afternoon. While they were busy, Peyton and Jaret spent the time teaching Jayden and

Damara how to hold a bow and arrow, and how to take aim. The women cooked their employer a meal, which they all shared that evening together. As they rode away to find a place to camp for the night, Tvirtas noted the man seemed happier for the company of the people who had come to help him, when it was all said and done, than he did for the help with his home. The fellow was a farmer, and, as he said, he had no money to pay them. However, he did offer ten chickens.

"I'd be mighty pleased if ye'd take 'em," he drawled.

"Thank you!" Uriel told him. "We'll put them to good use!"

That's night's meal had been wonderful, Peyton thought. The Romani family, with the farmer, had consumed *three whole chickens* for supper. Pythia saved the carcasses to cook down for soup the next day.

That had left seven chickens; six hens and a rooster, to be exact.

"What will we do with *seven* chickens?" Jaret asked. "If we kill them for the meat, it won't keep. If we travel with them, the rooster will create a stir every morning."

"A chicken alive is worth more than ten dead," Panna had told Peyton during sword drills that day. "Think about it. We could have eggs every morning."

As a result, Pythia and Panna had pleaded with Uriel and Tvirtas for the lives of the birds. "We will make sure they are fed," they implored. "And besides, it would be nice to have fresh eggs."

Laughing, Uriel had agreed. "Just be ready to eat them when their smell gets to you!" he warned good-naturedly.

And so, gathering the eggs became a part of the morning routine. That first day, Ramon and Tividar built a small pen for the birds to sleep in. From that point forward, when camp was set up each night, the pen was put together. The birds were placed in it somewhere within the campfire circle, inside the wagons' camp. Each morning, when it was once again time to travel, the little pen was broken down, and reconstructed and attached to the small porch which was part of the back of Pythia and Panna's wagon.

The next morning, they set out early.

By mid-morning, they had been on the road for more than three hours. It was time for lessons.

The last wagon in the column was pulled by a small burro. On any other day, the driver holding the reins would have been a terribly old woman, who looked as though she had been born "before time began." But today, Galen was elsewhere. Driving *her* wagon, was Uriel. The sight was quite comical, if we think about it. Imagine the tall, strapping hulk of a Light-Bearer holding the reins on a small little burro. In fact, Uriel had considered harnessing his stallion to pull the wagon, but then decided against it. The splendid onyx stallion he usually rode was following the wagon in front of him, tethered to a large hook in its back wall.

Normally, the hook held a lantern, but for today, Peyton had placed the lantern inside. He would be riding in the second wagon today with Jaret. Pythia was driving their wagon, fourth in the caravan. Tividar drove the third, with Panna keeping company, and Ramon drove the second.

In the first wagon, a grey-headed man in a fedora held the lead to a magnificent black charger. Somehow, Tvartis noted, he had developed an attachment to his new hat. Perhaps he *liked* being a gypsy, he considered. He would have to suggest the idea to Anbeter when he arrived home.

Inside the second wagon, the younger members of the Romani family were in the midst of an educational moment. Each of the children involved in the mission had lived in a Protectorate Area since birth. As a result, they were unfamiliar with many of the cultural differences between the home they had grown up in to this point, and the general Kingdom of Hausse. The focus today was to help the children grasp the difference between the economic base of King Suzerain's Realm, and the Protectorate Areas, from the Queen's domain, known as the Kingdom of Hausse.

In Suzerain's Realm, every citizen could say that *someone somewhere* in the history of their family line had defected *from* Hausse, barely escaping the Queen's control. The majority of *those* citizens, like Bibi, Peyton's grandmother, had *barely* eluded death from the Queen's clutches. Coming into a particular Protectorate Area, these refugees owned nothing, even clothing.

As a result, the king had developed a Design; a Design through which everything a person defecting from Hausse could possibly need was provided by his

Treasuries; housing, clothing, food…. even medical care.

In Suzerain's Design, a fugitive seeing Sanctuary in a Protectorate Area was also given the opportunity to learn a trade, or, to use a trade they already knew. When they already knew a trade, they could provide services and products for people living in Hausse. Since Hausse monies were not a means of exchange in the King's Realm, or in the Protectorate Areas either, monies received from citizens in Hausse were filtered through the King's Treasuries, many times mysteriously multiplying in value. As a result, every person living in The Beautiful Land; where Suzerain's Castle was located; or, those living in the Protectorate Areas, always had everything they really needed, and most of the time, more than enough.

In contrast, things were much different for those who lived in the Kingdom of Hausse. In the Queen's domain, citizens worked at an occupation, earning and receiving an hourly wage. With their wages, people bought items they needed, after taxes were paid to the Queen. The more a person earned an hour in their occupation, the more money they earned. Those with more money gained status and importance, and were given jurisdiction to rule over those with less.

Peyton and Jaret had joined the children for the lesson today, during the hours of travelling. In fifteen years of living, neither of them were sure they fully comprehended the culture of the country they were about to invade. They had experienced a few hours of instruction with Elder Tallis during Discovery Season

One, but to be truthful, Peyton had become bored with the lesson that day, and Jaret had fallen asleep in class.

Now, realizing they were unprepared, the boys had asked to hear the lesson as well. To help little Lysandra grasp what she was being taught, Galen had come to interpret the lesson into sign language.

As Shyla explained the differences between the Protectorate Area culture, and that of the Kingdom of Hausse, Jayden, Damara and Lysandra were amazed.

"You mean the Queen doesn't *provide* for them?" Damara asked, confused.

"No, everything they have they must *earn*," Shyla responded. "That is why we will be working in the villages and helping people. When we do, they will pay us for working."

"Why, Mama?" Jayden wanted to know.

"They pay us for the work to show us that our work has value. The more valuable it is to them, the more they pay," she answered.

"But King Suzerain doesn't do it that way," Lysandra signed, as Galen interpreted.

Galen signed back to her, and spoke to the group. "No, you're right, Lysandra. The King *doesn't* do it that way. In the Protectorates we work as hard as they do, but we also rest. We are paid in other ways."

"How are *we* paid?" Damara asked.

Shyla smiled. "We are paid with the things that fill us up inside. We don't do what we do for the king for money. We do what we do because we want to; because we love the king. Because the king gives freely, we don't work because we are *earning* something. We get to work at what we love to do."

"What fills *us* up? What do you mean, Mama?" Jayden inquired.

"Well," Shyla answered, "it can be something different for each person. For example, I am filled by having time with you and Damara. And, something inside of me is made new again when I listen to Prince Kyriel's stories. I love to listen to his stories."

Everyone nodded. "Ooh," Jayden said. "Could we listen to one of his stories right now?"

His mother laughed. "No, Jayden, not right now. This is a different time."

Disappointed, the boy responded. "Okay."

"I feel my heart fill up when I help people," Galen interjected. "Depending on what is needed, I can make them a medicine that will bring healing, or I can make them a weapon that will help them. Sometimes, I am filled up by just having time."

"I like *our* way better," Jayden observed. "It makes more sense."

"I agree with you," his mother answered. Reaching into a drawer built into the side of the wagon wall, she pulled out a pair of silver gloves, and a small, black velvet bag. As she put on the gloves, she spoke carefully. "Today's lesson is about economics. I want to show you what the money of Hausse looks like."

Opening a cupboard, in which could be seen swords and a quiver full of arrows, Shyla retrieved a silver cloth. As she sat back down with the children, she prepared the ground in the middle of their circle by laying the cloth out flat.

"Why are you doing *that*, Mama?" Jayden asked.

"Well, the money from Hausse is coated with a special powder," she explained. "It comes off on a person's hands."

"What kind of powder?" Damara wanted to know.

"It is poison," Shyla answered mysteriously, "and it kills very slowly." Lifting up the velvet bag, she emptied the money it contained onto the silver cloth.

The children, as well as Peyton and Jaret, leaned in for a closer look. Peyton now understood why she had needed to put on her gloves.

"You cannot touch these coins," Shyla warned the children. She began separating the coins into stacks of the same kind. "I have gloves on, and I still need to be careful. Do not get too close to the coins either. The dust can be breathed in and cause damage as well." She looked at each of the children.

"Why is the money poison, mama?" Jayden wanted to know.

"It is the substance the metal is made from, Jayden," his mother answered. "The coins with the smallest value are made from lead. Because they have the least amount of value, there are more of them in circulation. People save them, in order to be able to acquire the more valuable coins.

"Lead is a poisonous metal. When a person is exposed to it, even little traces are stored in the body, until one day, the poison becomes collected enough that the person gets sick, or even dies. Because there are more coins made from lead, than any other metal, the dust from the lead coins rubs off on the other metal coins. That makes *all* the coins in Hausse dangerous to hold, keep, or *even touch*."

Shyla picked up the smallest coin; a grey, round, metal disk. "This is a farthing," she told them. "This is the smallest coin. This is the one made of lead."

She held it up for the children to understand. "Can you see how this coin looks like a little dish?"

The children nodded in response.

"All of the coins in the Kingdom of Hausse have this shape. It is called a "scyphate." That means it is curved to fit a person's thumb. So, if a person has coins in their pockets, they will naturally want to rub their thumbs over the indention. That causes the metal residue to come off on their hands, going into the skin."

She held the coin up by its edges, between two gloved fingers, to enable the children to see its imprinting. "All of the coins in Hausse are imprinted with images. The image is stamped into the coin before the metal hardens. The farthing has this imprint."

The children pressed in to see the coin. In the center of the concave design was a rendering of a human skull, with a long snake curling out from the mouth and eyes. Along the top rim of the coin the words, "More for the Kingdom," were written. Along the bottom rim the words "One Farthing" could be read.

Shyla continued. "If a person has a farthing, they can buy a loaf of bread, or a large cup of soup in the marketplace. If they have ten farthings, then have enough money to buy a good steak at an Inn. If they want to stay the night at that Inn, they will need twenty-five farthings."

"That's a lot," Damara said.

"And it can get heavy," Shyla answered. "So, if you have twenty-five farthings, you can trade them in for just one of these." She picked up the copper coin.

"This is called a 'rupa.' It is worth twenty-five farthings, and it is a day's wage in Hausse for anyone who works in the fields, or does menial labor. People who work at a trade might earn a little more. But, for the most part, this represents a whole day of working."

She pointed to the imprint on the copper coin. "Do you see the imprint here? It was stamped with this design to honor those who work in the field to provide food."

"Oo-oh," the children responded.

Shyla moved the coin around so her students could get a good look at the three stalks of wheat and the scythe stamped into the metal. At the top rim of the coin, the words, "More for the Kingdom," were also inscribed, and along the bottom, "One Rupa."

"Now we come to the Lesser Ducat," she continued. Putting the penny down, she picked up a larger, silver coin. On its face were the images of a crown and the letter "S." To Peyton, the letter looked more like a snake than it did a letter, and he wondered whether anyone else might have thought the same thing. But he said nothing. He brought his mind back to what Shyla was teaching them.

"It takes thirty rupas to buy a Lesser, or Silver Ducat. If a rupa is a day's wage, you can see how much this coin might be worth. This coin says "More for the Kingdom" and "Lesser Ducat.""

"Do people in Hausse have a lot of money?" Jayden asked.

Shyla shook her head. "No," she replied. "Most of them are very poor, because no matter how much they might earn, or how hard they might work, the Queen requires the payment of taxes out of every farthing earned. Whenever a tax amount is less than a farthing, she rounds it up to the nearest farthing. It's very expensive to live in Hausse."

"In *many* ways," Galen interjected.

Lysandra pointed to the gold coin, and signed a question. "What is *that* coin, and why does *it* have printing on *both* sides?"

Shyla smiled at her and picked up the coin. "This is a *Golden* Ducat. On one side, you see the imprint of the Lion, which represents Suzerain the Lion-hearted, who is our King. This side of the coin is printed with 'Suzerain Lives Forever.' It takes one *hundred* Lesser Ducats to equal one golden, or Greater Ducat."

She flipped the gold coin over in her hand. "This is the only coin in the Kingdom of Hausse with imprinting on *both* sides. On the other side are two emblems; a ladder reaching up into the sky, and a dagger. The ladder and dagger are more accurate than the designers of these coins realized, when it comes to describing what life is like for the citizens of Hausse.

The words, 'More for the Kingdom' and 'Greater Ducat' are imprinted on this side."

Shyla reached into the drawer from which she had originally taken the velvet bag filled with coins. From the drawer, she pulled out six small velvet bags. As she continued speaking, she handed one to each of the children, and to Galen. When Peyton received his, he looked inside it. The outside of the bag was black velvet, while the inside was made of the same silver cloth Shyla had placed on the floor of the wagon before she had emptied out the coins.

"Why do we get these bags, Mama?" Jayden inquired.

His mother smiled at him. "Tomorrow, we will begin using the skills we have been developing, entertaining the people in the villages, as well as helping them as we pass through. People are going to want to pay us, and when they do, they will be paying us with these coins. It is important that the coins never touch your hands. When someone wants to pay you, open the bag, and let them drop their coins in as you hold it open for them. Then, pull the drawstrings shut. As we leave each village, please bring me the bag, and I will empty it and give it back to you."

She looked at each of them. "Do you understand why we have to do things this way?"

Around the wagon's interior, there were nods and verbal acknowledgments.

"Good then," Galen spoke up. "Now, what game shall we play? We will be riding for a while longer. There is still a long way to go before we reach the river."

The river Galen spoke of had been called the Mortal's Folly River for as long as anyone could remember. It was sort of an unofficial boundary marker between the eastern and western kingdoms. It was a mile wide body of water which ran the entire length of the Kingdom of Hausse, beginning in the mountains, then splitting into two branches, and flowing into the Great Sea, not far from the Queen's summer castle.

"Speaking of the river," Peyton spoke up, "can I ask a question?"

"Say on," Galen replied.

"Why is the sky so dark near the Borderlands?" he asked. "We have light of day in the Protectorate Area, but I noticed when we left the Protectorate the sky suddenly became filled with dark clouds. The further away we have travelled from the Borderlands, the more light there seems to be in the sky. Why is that? Will the sky continue to change after we cross the river as well?"

Galen smiled. "Wherever Suzerain dwells, there is light. The Dark Prince hates Suzerain, and wants nothing to do with *anything* that represents him in any way. As a result, his territories, the Dark Lands, have *no light* at all. The Borderlands, where dragons dwell, are the edge of his dominion. Out of all the Protectorate Areas, that region is closest to Protectorate Area One. It is in the western kingdom, not far from the Queen's winter castle. As we travel into the *eastern* kingdom, we will be approaching the King's Realm. You might even see some real sunlight!"

"When we lived in the Protectorate, we always had light," Peyton responded. "Is that because the Protectorate is under Suzerain's rule?"

Galen smiled. "Well, in truth, *all of the land* belongs to Suzerain. *But*, when Sausmas tricked the first mortals into giving *him* their loyalties, the areas where *he* lives stopped having light at all. Not only that, but the air became thick and heavy with Fear as well."

Peyton wasn't sure he understood what Galen was trying to say. "So, is that why it rains so much, and feels so gloomy? And why there is so much scary weather?"

Galen nodded. "I think it *must* be, but it is just my own opinion." She paused. "Remember that everything seen *and* unseen was made by Suzerain. And, since he made it all….. he is bigger than *it all*, even Sausmas, *and the* Queen."

"How many more days will we be riding, mama?" Damara asked.

Shyla stroked the child's hair. "I don't know exactly, dear," she said, "but we begin our entertaining tomorrow."

"Does that mean we get to dance to some music?" Jayden asked.

"Yes, it does!" Shyla laughed. "We get to sing as well; and Pythia and Panna will throw knives; and they will do their acrobatics; we will have archery contests; and Galen will make medicines…"

"We're going to be very busy, aren't we?" Jaret asked.

"Very," Galen responded. "You will want to get a good night's sleep tonight." She paused, and then rubbed her hands together. "Now, who wants to hear a story?"

"And who thinks it's time to eat a snack?" Shyla exclaimed, getting up to gather some fruit from a wagon cabinet.

"Ooo," came the children's responses. "Can we have mallow?"

Shyla laughed. "What about apples instead?"

In the darkness of the underground caverns of the Queen's summer castle, malevolent minions were scheming. Several Shades were meeting together. These had worked systematically to gain greater supremacy in their ability to manipulate the mortals of Hausse.

Additionally, these were unconvinced of Souhaites' professed levels of power.

"She *has* gained the black fire." The largest one said. "I don't see how she plans to use the crystal to depose Sausmas."

"The black fire gives her the power of death over the mortals. When she gains the purple, it will increase her in all aspects of intellect and magic. She will have greater Sight." He paused, and then added, "Or so she *says*."

"What is the gold fire, master?" one of the Muddlers seated in the circle asked.

The Shade sniggered. "When Souhaites has gold fire within the crystal, she will have the final piece of the combination she desires to take full Control. Gold fire will give her power and more wealth in the visible realm of the mortals. When those three fires are gathered together within the crystal, she will then only need mortal blood. If we can turn a mortal champion, and I say *if*, then we will bring him here to this cavern. She will then kill him with the sharp tip of the crystal, driving it through his heart. That will release the three fires, and their powers of destruction."

"And then what?" another Muddler asked.

"The boundaries of our darkness will be increased. Souhaites will become as strong as Sausmas. The eastern and western kingdoms will be as the Dark Lands, and together we will seize power from Suzerain."

"Oh, I get it," the first Muddler said.

There was silence in the great room for a moment.

"Didn't we try that once before?" a Weaver asked.

"Yes," replied the first Shade, "and the result was our gaining power over the mortals in the first place. I just wonder…"

"What if…?" several of his cohorts questioned. "What if we were to rally our comrades and seize power *from* the Queen, instead of *helping to make <u>her</u> stronger*? I'm sure Sausmas would reward us for exposing this trickery."

"Oo-ooh, and we wouldn't be *controlled* by her anymore," the first Muddler observed. What if Sausmas then sentenced her to *exile*? Or, if she was exiled to the torture chambers, or even the dragon fields?"

Two of the Shades in the center of the discussion cackled hideously. "Oh, we are working on grander schemes than *those*," one of them replied snidely. "Just *wait and see*."

In the top level of the principal tower of the summer castle, a Weaver crouched in an assigned dark corner, waiting for Ellie and Karaliene. They would be returning to the Nursery soon. Unseen by mortals, his job, with two others, was to patrol the castle grounds, listening for signs of infiltration from the enemy. He had hidden himself in the first group of castle guards entering the kitchen at dinnertime.

Apparently, a Light-Bearer had been lurking about.

They would have to work quickly to get rid of the nursemaid.

His Shade would join him soon.

Ellie and Karaliene were climbing the stairs up to the Nursery. They had spent several hours sitting by the fire, playing Dragons and Stepladders after dinner. It had been fun to listen to the conversations of the guards and sentries as they ate. Most important, however, had been the moment when Myra had removed the birthday cake from the oven.

"Can I have some *now*, Myra? Pl-ee-ase?" the princess had begged.

"Well, I don't know, your little majesty," Myra had teased. "If we cut into it now, there won't be anything to put icing on for tomorrow."

"Couldn't you just cut a piece from the middle, and then shove it together?" Karaliene pleaded. "I wouldn't tell. And the icing would cover it."

Myra had clucked her tongue. "I say it all the time, Princess. No one knows just how smart you really are." She pretended to be in deep thought. "No, I can't cut it yet. But here is something for you!" She reached into a crock on the counter and pulled out several small pastries she had baked earlier in the day.

"Now, I'll send one of the maids up with these on a tray with your bedtime tea in a little while. Would that be to your liking?" she asked.

Karliene hugged her legs. "I love you, Myra!" she squealed. She looked at Ellie. "Just think! I get *two* birthday cakes! One little cake *tonight*, and one in the morning!"

Myra patted the little girl on her head. "Now there, missy," she cooed. "I'll just put the finishing touches on your cake, and see if I can't round up some little candles for wishing on. But you need to listen to

Ellie, and get your bath and ready for bed without any complaining. What do you think about that?"

Karaliene had looked up at her with shining eyes. "Yes ma'am," she replied.

With that, she and Ellie had moved towards the door. Now, they were playing a skipping game on their way to the top of the tower. It was a game they often played when it was necessary to climb the stairs at night. The torches placed on the stone wall were far enough apart, that Karaliene hesitated in the darker shadows. Ellie had taken a lantern with her from the hallway, to provide them light as they made the long climb, but the child was still just a little afraid of the darkness.

Karaliene was full of chatter and excitement. She was thrilled in anticipation of being allowed to leave the castle grounds the next day.

"Did you see my birthday cake, Ellie?" she asked excitedly. "Myra said I could eat the *whole* thing *all by myself* if I wanted to."

Ellie stepped up four times and down once for her turn in the game, and replied, laughing. "You might have a stomach-ache if you eat it all at once, don't you think?"

Karaliene pursed her lips in a small pout. "I won't get sick. *Myra* made it!"

Ellie waited for the princess to complete her skipping turn, and then spoke softly to Karaliene.

"And aren't we going horse-back riding tomorrow too?" she prodded, whispering in the little girl's ear.

Karaliene clapped her hands. "Oh, I can't wait! It's going to be the best birthday anyone ever had!" She looked up at Ellie. "I think I like this year even better than last year!"

"I'm so glad, Kara," she replied. "I was hoping you would have a good day tomorrow."

On the fourth turn of the stairway, the lantern's light began to brighten. Immersed in their stepping and counting game, neither Ellie nor Karaliene noticed what was happening. With heads down, watching their feet, they continued counting, skipping, and talking about the next day, and all the fun they would have together.

On the fifth turn of the stairs, Ellie's head bumped into an obstacle. "Oh," she blurted, startled, "I'm sorry…. Excuse me."

"Hi Jophiel!" Karaliene announced.

Surprised, Ellie stepped back, and almost fell down the stairs. The Light-Bearer stretched his arm out and caught her. Chuckling, he spoke to her. "Are you all right?"

"Yes," she answered. "It's just that I wasn't expecting you right *now*….I mean *here*…. at this moment."

He smiled. "You'd probably be surprised how often I hear that very statement."

"Is something wrong?" Karliene asked.

Jophiel smiled at the little girl. "Well, sort of," he answered. "I was going to appear in your room, but we have a little interference. There is a Weaver waiting for you up there. So we'll have to talk here."

Involuntarily, Ellie gasped. "A Weaver? W-Wh-at's *he* waiting for?"

"What's a Weaver?" Karliene wanted to know.

Jophiel sat down on the stairs. As he did, the girls followed suit. Looking at Karaliene, he answered, speaking just above a murmur.

"All Weavers work for Sausmas. Some of them are in the service of Queen Souhaites as well. Mortals cannot see them, but they are there just the same. They used to be covered in light, but not now. If you could see one now, its entire body is covered with tiny mouths, which whisper and drool all the time."

"That's *nasty*," Karaliene declared.

"Yes they are," Jophiel agreed, "*very* nasty. The problem is this: A Weaver's undertakings are always aimed towards mortals. A Weaver's whispers cause a mortal to doubt, and to become afraid. Weavers love to cause confusion, because then a mortal becomes open prey to Deception. Whenever the king sends me on a mission, I always run into a Weaver, or a Muddler, or even a Shade, trying to stop the Mortals I am sent to help. Those creatures try to keep the mortals from listening to me. They work to prevent anyone from following through with the king's instructions."

Suddenly alerted, Ellie spoke. "And there is one of these things in the Nursery?"

"Yes," Jophiel told her. "I think he might be here because of your discussion with the cook earlier today."

"I told her about you," Karaliene said.

"I know you did, little one," the Light-Bearer answered. "It has caused us a little difficulty, and our

156

plans have changed. You must promise me to keep what you hear and see a secret until I tell you it is safe to talk about these things. You cannot afford to trust *anyone,* especially those in the castles.

"Do you remember what I told you about tomorrow? I think we might need to move the timetable up."

"To when?" Ellie asked.

Jophiel brought his voice down to an even lower volume. "To tonight," he answered. "There is scheming afoot in the palace, and from what I hear, the danger for both of you is about to increase. There are powers at work here beyond anything either of you have ever seen.

"Karaliene," he said, looking the little girl in the eyes, "It is very important that you do *exactly* what I am about to tell you, even if it makes you sad."

Surprised, the princess regarded him. The Light-Bearer continued. "Be careful who you trust. Not everything is the way it appears."

"What do we need to do?" Ellie responded.

"That is an *excellent* question!" Jophiel told her, with a wide smile. "You are to go upstairs, and get ready for bed as though it were a normal evening. When the castle is quiet, under the cover of the night, you are to get up, and pack your bags, without lighting a second candle. Take only what you can carry. Meet me here on the stairwell, and I will help you."

"Are we still going horse-back riding tomorrow?" Karaliene asked.

"We will see, little one," Jophiel answered. "It has become too dangerous for a joyride."

"Is that because I told about *you*?" the child wanted to know.

Jophiel did not answer her directly. "You didn't know then it was a secret. There are many inside this castle, who desire to see the Queen's plans for the Rebellion come to pass. She is at war with Suzerain; and with Sausmas as well. Anyone who is from the King's Realm automatically becomes an enemy. I am from the King's Realm."

"I'm sorry, Jophiel," the little girl said. "I was so excited. I won't say anything else."

"Good girl. Don't talk about this to *anyone*… except Ellie. And only talk to her when you are *sure* you are alone. I will be at work to protect you. But understand…. What we must do *together* will only work if it happens as a *secret*. We have to surprise our enemies. Now, remember what I have told you, and go on up to the Nursery. Keep your conversation *with everyone* to a minimum just to be safe."

Then, as quickly as he had appeared, Jophiel vanished. Ellie and Karaliene were left in the relative darkness of the tower stairway.

As the reality of what had just happened sank in, the girls exchanged sober glances. The game forgotten, they continued up the stairwell. Ellie put her finger to her lips, to indicate they should be quiet.

When they arrived back in the Nursery, Ellie prepared an uncharacteristically quiet Princess Karaliene for bed. Seeking to be as normal as possible,

Karaliene was bathed, dressed in pajamas, and her hair was brushed. Then, it was time for a story. Ellie perused the bookshelf for one of the princess' favorite tales. Sitting in Karaliene's bed with her, she began to read out loud.

Just then, a knock was heard on the door.

"Come in!" Ellie responded.

Myra poked her head around the door. "I sent the maids home. I thought I would bring up your tea and little cakes myself."

"Oh goody!" Karaliene cried. "We *do* get cakes!"

"I wouldn't forget *you,* little one!" Myra told her. She wiped her forehead. "But I tell you, I never saw so many stairs as there are in this tower! How do you climb them so many times each day?"

Ellie laughed. "I guess you get used to doing the things you have to do."

"That's very true, dearie," the cook responded, "and very wise."

You should let her know what's going on. She won't tell anyone. Subconsciously, Ellie shook her head. Suddenly, she felt confused. No, she shouldn't tell *anyone.* Hadn't Jophiel had just spoken to her with clear instructions? Maybe she *could* tell Myra later, but not now.

"Are you all right, Ellie?" Myra wanted to now.

"I'm just tired," the nursemaid responded. "It feels rather late to me."

"Well, all right then," Myra told her. "I was going to try to stay with you and talk a while, but I think now I should just let you go to sleep. I'll leave your tea and cakes here on the little table. Perhaps you should try to have a little something warm to drink. It would help you to rest."

"I will," Ellie promised. "I'm just getting Karaliene to sleep now."

"Good job, good job," Myra bubbled. "I'll be going then. Sleep well."

"You too," Ellie murmured. "And thank you."

"No worries, love," the cook answered. "Good night."

"Good night."

Karaliene waited until the door had closed. Then she turned and whispered to Ellie. "Can I have *one* little cake before I sleep?"

Ellie smiled at her. "How about just one *bite*? And then we will have to brush your teeth again!"

Thirty minutes later, not far from a sleeping child, Ellie was seated by the fire, sipping from her teacup. A little plate of dainty pastry morsels sat on the table. All the items Myra had brought upstairs had remained untouched, except for one. It had a child-sized bite missing. As she sipped her tea, Ellie went over the events of the past few days in her mind. How quickly everything had changed!

Finishing her drink, she rose and blew out the candlesticks. Then, using the dim light of the fireplace as her only light, she went to a nearby armoire, where she withdrew two satchels; one medium sized, and one larger. Working quickly, she chose the most simple of the princess's clothing, the sturdiest of shoes; in short, the most practical things she could find. She then chose the same type of items for herself.

We will have to dress like I used to when I lived in the village at home.

But what had that looked like?

Why was it suddenly so difficult to remember what she used to wear when she was Kara's age and living in a village with her family? Her head felt fuzzy. *Why was she unexpectedly so sleepy?*

In the corner of the room, huddled not far from where she was working, mouths from the invisible form of a Weaver were shouting vile obscenities and accusations. With each phrase uttered, the atmosphere of the room deepened in a sense of futility and weariness.

This will never work, you know. Why don't you just lie down and go to sleep for a moment?

Ellie yawned. All at once, she felt so tired.

What was the point? In fact, why was she participating in a plan she didn't completely understand?

The shadows seemed to be playing with her mind. *Was there someone standing over by the fire?* She took a hard look, and saw nothing. But two moments later, in her peripheral vision, she saw something small and inky dart across the room, just above her ankles. No, it couldn't be. And then it happened again.

A knock was heard at the door.

"Yes?" Unnaturally shaken, Ellie moved the satchels to the floor and answered.

Myra peeked her head in the door once again. "Are you done with your tea, milady?" she asked.

161

"Yes ma'am," Ellie responded. "I'm finished. You can take the tray if you like."

Myra moved to the table by the fireplace. "Oh, but you didn't eat the pastries!" she noted. "Are you feeling all right?"

"Yes," Ellie answered. For a fleeting moment, she was inclined to just pull her friend over by the fire and sit down with her. Perhaps it would help to just talk through with *someone* the strange happenings of the past few days. "I was just straightening up a few messes Kara and I have made before I get ready for bed myself," she lied.

"Oh, I see," the cook responded. "All right then."

Picking up the tray, Myra turned around. "Are you *sure* you're not ill, dear? To be honest, you just don't seem like yourself tonight."

Ellie looked at her blankly, unsure how to answer. "Yes, really, I'm fine."

Myra moved closer to the nursemaid, and looked into her eyes. "Are you *sure* there isn't anything you want to tell me? You know you can trust me...."

Instinctively, Ellie backed away. "Yes, I'm sure, Myra," she answered. "I think I'm just tired, that's all. The Princess has just been a handful the last few days, what with all the rain we've been having, and being trapped indoors. I think she must be bored, don't you?"

Myra smiled. "Yes, she *is* a bundle of energy, that's for sure." Looking down, she saw the half-packed satchel lying at Ellie's feet. She bent down and picked it up.

"Oh, what's this?" She looked in the bag. "Whose clothes are these?" She looked at Ellie for an answer, but the nursemaid said nothing.

Myra rummaged in the bag, continuing in her discovery. "These are *travelling* clothes! They are the little majesty's clothes!"

The cook looked into a corner and spoke into what seemed to Ellie like empty space.

"Get me some support! *Go now!*"

Somehow, her voice was different, Ellie noted; a little lower? Was it more hoarse sounding than it had been?

"Who are you talking to, Myra?" she asked. "There's no one here but the Princess and me."

"Who indeed!" The cook rasped angrily at her. As Ellie watched in horror, an alarming and speedy evolution took place in front of her eyes. Placing both hands on the sides of her own neck, Myra quickly pulled forward on her own skin. Ellie watched, frozen by the shock of what she was witnessing. The skin and hair that had been Myra's form were splitting down the center of her back. The cook's hands and arms were still pulling the skin apart, but *someone,* or *something* that had been hiding inside Myra's *form* was emerging, growing, then *towering* over her.

The looming specter bent over to inspect her. Its eyes were venomous and glowing an unearthly red. "Where are you *going*, Ellie?" it growled. "You *belong* to the Queen. You cannot leave without her permission."

"I – I..." Ellie began, faltering. "Who... *What...* *are* you?"

The creature brought its mouth close to her face as it answered. The jaws were lined with what appeared to be spiked razors, and the stench of its breath was worse than anything the girl had ever experienced. Involuntarily, she retched inside.

"*I* am the Shade in *control* of this castle!" it seethed. "I am more powerful than anything you can *even imagine.* Do not even *try* to play games with me, or resist me. I can turn you inside out with just one of my talons. I have *killed.* I *have eaten.*"

The Shade vaporized and swirled in a cloud around Ellie. As it did, she felt as though every nerve in her body had moved to the outside of her skin. It was as though a thousand tiny blades were raking across her, leaving her raw and bleeding, and yet, nothing physical was taking place.

In terror, she shrieked. "No! No! Stop it! You're hurting me!"

The Shade continued to torment her. "I will stop when you give me what I want. Tell me who is helping you."

Confused, Ellie screamed. "I don't know what you mean! Helping me *what?*"

The Shade sneered. "I will make this torment a physical reality," it threatened. "You will *die,* and no one will come. Where *is* Jophiel, the Light-Bearer?" It spat out the last two words, and Ellie felt the heat of its angry hatred.

Then, the creature raised its other-worldly arm, and Ellie saw a long, black knife in its clutches. Steeling herself, she prepared for the deadly wound that was inevitable.

"I'm sorry, Jophiel!" she cried out. "I tried!"

Suddenly, seeming to emanate from every corner in the room, a thunderous voice resonated. "Pick on someone your *own* size, Pimedus! I am *right here*!"

With that, the pointed flame of a mighty sword cut through the ceiling, swinging back and forth, slicing the room into two pieces. Stepping into the chamber, like an adult taking part in a child's tea party, was an immense Jophiel, his wings reaching far above the turrets of the tallest tower in the castle. He was accompanied by two other Light-Bearers, each of whom had longer hair, and a feminine appearance. Both of these were dressed in glowing robes similar to Jophiel, but with several major differences. These Light-Bearers each wore silver belts, and had four wings each instead of two. Also, *their* wings were smaller. In addition to their flaming swords, these two carried shields bearing the imprint of a Lion.

The three Light-Bearers touched down on the floor of the bedroom. With a hideous laugh, Pimedus threw his head back as though drawing in some sort of dark power. Almost instantly, he grew in size as well. Joining him from nowhere, were more Weavers, and another type of dark creature Ellie had not yet seen. These dark creatures were armed also; with axes, pitchforks, whips, and various other frightening implements which hung around their necks, or were held in their hands.

Looking up, she watched in fascination as the ceiling melted away. Suddenly, the sky was filled with light, with images of flaming swords cutting through the night. As the battle climbed higher and higher into the sky, the Nursery was once again filled with Jophiel's voice.

"Run, Ellie! Take the princess into the tunnel. We will meet you. If we are delayed, go to the location I gave you in the second dream."

Instantaneously, Ellie was once again aware of her surroundings. The room was no longer cut in two, and the sky was no longer visible. Fast asleep in the bed next to her was Princess Karaliene. Hastily, she gathered their belongings together, and finished packing each of their satchels.

Don't forget Kara's doll. You will need your lute as well.

Had Jophiel spoken again, she wondered, or had that voice been in her head? No matter. She would remember those items.

Waking Karaliene, she dressed the sleepy child in travelling clothes, a warm jacket, and boots. She had also created a sleeping roll for each of them to carry on their backs with the satchels. Thankfully, the child awakened enough to be able to walk, but was not alert enough to ask questions. Whispering in Kara's ear to "stay quiet and just walk with me," she led the child out into the hallway.

Strangely, the castle was empty as they made their way down the tower stairwell, into the lower levels of the castle. Torches had been lit in the halls on the way to the courtyard.

Where were the guards, she wondered?

Unlike the West winter castle's *secret* tunnel entrance, the tunnel escape route in the East summer castle was in the middle of the main courtyard. Between the two castles, there was a difference in the tunnel lengths as well. The winter castle's tunnel was just three or four hundred feet in length, and rose to the surface in nearby woods with an exit ladder. Comparably, the summer castle's tunnel had been a major undertaking to construct. It went deep into the earth, with entrance and exit *ramps* on each end.

In ancient days, the Queen had devised a way for her household staff to get loaded wagons to and from the town's market, without having to cross the drawbridge, or ride in a rowboat. Ellie wondered now whether it had also afforded the creatures under the Queen's dominion access to the castle, and townspeople, without too much effort.

The summer castle's tunnel was much larger as well. A person on horseback could easily ride the distance to the town; passing under the moat, leaving the island, and crossing under the small lake. Some two hundred feet from the shore of the lake, in a wooded area, the mainland entrance to the tunnel was hidden; inside an ancient, sculpted, hollowed out oak tree. From the outside, the tree looked real enough. However, once a person stepped inside it, the ramp descending into the lower regions of the earth was clearly visible. Width and height-wise, both ramps and tunnel were large enough to accommodate a rider or two on horseback. The entire tunnel was five miles long. Since both entrances had been graded with ramps, even small carts or wagons could be loaded, carrying goods to and from the castle during the harvest season.

Later, Ellie would say she didn't know how or why the idea came to her, except that Karaliene had been talking about riding horses for two days. On their way to the courtyard, she made two quick stops. The first was the kitchen, where she took the birthday cake, placing it in a small crate with a handle. Her second stop was the stables, where she saddled the horses she and Kara usually rode on clearer days. Strapping a still drowsy Karaliene into a saddle, Ellie took those reins and hooked them to the back of her own saddle; just as she had done when she had taught Kara to ride in the past. Then, after placing satchels and bedrolls behind packed saddlebags, she led her own mount, with the sleeping princess in tow, down the ramp and into the tunnel.

Light faded quickly as they moved further into the underpass entrance; down into the nether regions of the earth. The path seemed to go deeper and deeper. Was it becoming warmer as well, she thought? It was so dark here, and the only way she could make her way was by feeling the sides of the wall. Why had Jophiel told her not to light a second candle?

Had that meant only in the castle?

Should she have brought a candle with her?

What if this was the wrong way?

What if Jophiel had told her to go the wrong direction?

What would happen to her, or to Karaliene?

She did not know it, but two Weavers had followed her down into the tunnel.

"We will win by many means," Pimedus had told them. "Stay with the princess."

Chapter Eight

A Shade of Deeper Darkness

Standing still in the tunnel's darkness, Ellie wondered why she was suddenly so fearful of failing Jophiel's expectations. And why had dark doubts so multiplied since they had entered the tunnel?

"Someone, help me," she whispered. In response, the image of Jophiel's flaming sword cutting through the Nursery ceiling, and the subsequent air battle flashed through her mind, taking her consciousness back to what was real.

I wonder if those thoughts of doubt are part of a battle as well, she thought; oh well, no matter. It was a little late now to begin doubting a Light-Bearer. She now deliberated how long it would take to get to the end of the tunnel. She had never had to walk in total darkness before, much less with two horses and a child.

You are going to die down here. Soon you won't be able to breathe.

Ellie jumped as she felt something brush against her cheek. What was that? A wind wafted through the tunnel. Where had it come from?

We are all around you. Do you know how far underground you are?

Suddenly gasping for breath, Ellie stopped in her tracks, leaning against the cold stone wall of the tunnel.

This tunnel is as far down in the earth as a tomb. It will become your tomb as well.

Closing her eyes, she tried to recreate the image of Jophiel's sword cutting through the ceiling once more. As the memory surfaced again, her fear was minimized. She re-engaged her progression forward.

She spoke softly to her mare. "It's all right, girl." She stroked the mount's neck. We will get to the other end of this. Just keep moving with me."

In response, her horse gave a soft grunt, and nuzzled her cheek. Comforted by the slightest sense of tenderness, Ellie felt tears beginning to trickle down her cheeks.

You are only fourteen years, after all. Someone much older should be doing this.

For a moment, she felt a deep pull; something trying to magnetize her heart towards self-pity.

"No," she said out loud. "I'm not giving in to that. We do have a Light-Bearer to protect us. In fact, we have *three* Light-Bearers. I must keep moving forward."

Ahead of her, Ellie saw a tiny speck of light. At first, she thought it had to be her imagination, and then she realized it was growing. Was it moving towards her? Perhaps she was actually asleep, and this was a dream. She shook her head, as if to clear it, and continued moving; her back against the wall.

Looking down, she became aware of a new ability to see the dim outline of her own feet progressing across the floor of the tunnel. Looking backward, she noticed a second dot of light, also growing, moving towards her. Within seconds she was standing in the center of what felt like a whirlwind. What sounded like hundreds of voices spun around her head; screaming warnings of impending doom. Ellie shut her eyes and leaned against the wall, holding her breath; just waiting for the cyclone to end. Among many screams, she could make out just a few of them.

"Get away! Leave us alone!"

"This is our territory! Stop!"

"Don't send us to the Barrens!"

Suddenly, there was a loud crashing sound, with exceedingly more volume than anything she had ever heard before. Afraid of what she might see, Ellie opened her eyes.

She fully expected her life to end.

Instead, she found herself immersed in the midst of an unbelievable battle. Whirling around her, around

Karaliene and the horses, were two unbelievably ugly creatures, covered all over their bodies with mouths. From what Ellie could tell, the screams were all coming *from* the mouths. Why were they screaming? Why was she able to see them? And what were they fleeing from?

She looked down the tunnel for what had been the specks of light traveling her direction. Without warning, a brilliantly glowing figure, with a circular shield in one hand, and a sword in the other, winged in over the horses towards her. Intuitively, she ducked, as a large; flaming broadsword was wielded back and forth over her head. With each stroke of the blade, fragments and chunks of the unbelievably ugly creatures were flying in every direction. The place where she stood was filled with light now, and her ability to focus had returned.

Discerning, she realized. These were the two Light-Bearers who had accompanied Jophiel at the castle! Now, they were battling with two Weavers, just above her head.

Were these Life-Guardians, she wondered?

"Keep moving, Ellie!" one of them shouted. "Don't be distracted!" The Light-Bearer lifted her shield, holding it over Ellie, making a clear path for the two horses to pass, all the while swinging away to protect her. The other Light-Bearer continued warring with the second Weaver just behind Karaliene's horse.

It was strange, Ellie thought. Kara was still asleep, in spite of all this noise.

Then, unexpectedly, the top of the tunnel opened up. Jophiel stepped into the tunnel. Ellie watched as all of the Light-Bearers moved out of the passageway and up into the sky, finishing their battle with the Weavers.

Taking in the surroundings, Jophiel smiled. "So I see we are riding horses after all?"

"I don't know why I even took them," Ellie answered. "At the time, it seemed like the best way to get Kara all the way to town. She's gotten so big I can't carry her like I used to."

The Light-Bearer nodded. "I understand." He paused, looking at her. "Ellie, I have a question for you. There were precautions taken to keep your journey to the tunnel hidden from the Queen's followers. Did you bring *anything* with you that was given to you by the Queen?"

Ellie frowned. "I have been at the castle since I was nine years. Everything I own has been bestowed on me since then."

"That's not what I mean," he replied. "Is there any item that would have her touch or influence…. Something that could have been cursed with a spell before you left…. Perhaps not from the Queen, but from someone in her employ."

Ellie thought for a moment. "I can't think of anything… no wait. I took Kara's birthday cake from the kitchen when we left. She was looking forward to it, so I wanted her to get a chance to taste it. She loves Myra's cooking and baking."

"Myra is a *Shade* named *Pimedus*." Jophiel said it plainly. "Anything *she* made would have had a curse on it; either by physical poison, or by Deception. She might have even put something in the cake enabling her

173

to see where you are in her crystals and follow you. Where is the cake now?"

Ellie reached to the crate she had tied to the saddle. The Light-Bearer took the crate from her.

"This is probably how they found us," he told her. "Pimedus was probably watching from the castle. It isn't enough to stop you. He wants to gain power from the Queen."

Ellie's eyes became wide, as she realized what Jophiel was telling her. "A Shade can *do* that?" she asked, astonished.

"And more," was the grim reply. "Remember, Myra doesn't really exist. *She is only an image.* Pimedus disguised himself to gain your trust. She was a mask to hide the Queen's infiltrator." He took a vial of red liquid from his belt and emptied it on the wooden crate, which shriveled up into nothing and disappeared.

As awareness dawned on her, Ellie sprang into action. "Oh no.....NO! Oh, we have to do something." She moved towards Karaliene and began shaking the little girl, trying to wake her. "I thought it was strange she didn't move. She's usually such a light sleeper.... Jophiel, you've got to help me with the princess!"

Alerted, the Light-Bearer answered, "Why? What's wrong?"

Ellie continued. "Well, before Kara went to sleep this evening, Myra came upstairs with a plate of pastries. She said she had sent the maids home, and wanted to bring up our bedtime snack herself. She had never done that before; but I didn't think it was unusual, because of Kara's birthday tomorrow.

"I didn't eat anything, but I let Karaliene have *one* bite of *one* piece, just so she would settle down to rest. Then, when I woke her to travel from the castle, she never said a word. She was very drowsy. I thought she was just extremely tired. But now that you say what you did, I've been thinking. The entire time we have been in the tunnel, she has been on her horse, with her head down on the horse's mane, sound asleep. At least, I *thought* she was asleep. But she has slept through all of this commotion..."

She moved to check Kara's breathing and pulse. "She's not breathing! And I can't feel her pulse!"

Jophiel moved into action. From his belt, he drew a golden horn, which he blew into, although it made no sound that Ellie could hear. The nursemaid pulled the child from her horse, and laid her on the floor of the tunnel. Checking the child's mouth, she saw nothing visible which could be choking the child. Still, she decided, she should turn Kara onto her stomach and try to dislodge any foreign object. But the child's body was limp and lifeless. In fact, a sort of stiffness seemed to be taking taken over.

But then, before she could turn the little girl, a man appeared in the tunnel. He was dressed in everyday hunting clothes, and at first, Ellie thought she recognized him as one of the townspeople from the village. There certainly wasn't anything physically remarkable about him.

"What's happened here?" he asked.

"I'm not sure," Ellie told him. "I don't hear her breathing, and I can't find a pulse."

"She will be all right." The stranger answered. Ellie looked into his eyes, to make sure he wasn't just saying something to make her feel better. He gazed back at her for just a moment, and she was struck by the kindness and deep compassion in his eyes.

"She has too much living to do yet," was all he said. With that, the man reached under Karaliene's neck and knees, and picked her up, cradling her in his arms.

He looked at Ellie. "Don't be afraid," he said. Then, he kissed the child's forehead. As the nursemaid watched, a pulsing, white glow began to grow from the kiss's point of impact. It grew and grew in ripples, bathing the little girl and the man in a bright light. Amazed, Ellie watched, as the kiss continued to send out its powerful shockwaves until the entire chamber where they stood was warm with light.

Mysteriously, Ellie's panic had disappeared. Somehow, her heart was at peace.

The man smiled as he placed Karaliene into Ellie's arms. "All will be well," he said.

And then he was gone.

But the light remained.

In wonder and surprise, Ellie looked down at the little girl in her arms. Kara's eyes were fluttering as if she were awaking from a deep sleep. "Where are we, Ellie?" she asked.

But Ellie didn't hear her. She was stunned at what she had just experienced.

"Thank you," she murmured, hoping the man could still hear her.

In the village of Sorrettu, the town's watchmen had just completed their night-watch duties. Although it was still dark outside, replacement guardsmen were taking their posts for the early morning shift. In the marketplace, several shopkeepers had begun throwing wide their doors and shutters, setting up displays; preparing for that day's bargain hunters.

Unlike those who had slept through the night, and were now opening up for the day, Nathan the baker had been up most of the night. His busiest time of the day for sales began just before sunrise and extended into mid-morning. Usually, around mid-morning he would close his doors, and try to catch a few hours of sleep before reopening the store towards the dinner hour. Many customers who were unable to come by in the morning, stopped on their way home to buy bread, pastries, or even cakes for celebrations.

Nathan was a likeable man. He had lived in Sorrettu his entire life, and, as a result, was a good friend with just about everyone in the village. His wife of thirty-five years had died two winters ago. It had been then he had decided to put all of his energies into the bakery. Over the years, he had created several varied flavors of bread, most of which were now recommended favorites of the townspeople.

Nathan's two daughters and one son were now full-grown. His daughters were married. Ingrid and Karin were both mothers now, each one looking more and more like his departed wife every day. Between the two of them, Nathan had the joy of five grandchildren. Most days the children would come by to see him on their way to school in the morning or on their way home from classes in the afternoons.

After sweeping the entry way to his place of business, Nathan straightened the outdoor tables and benches, where customers rested to talk as they shared his pastries over mugs of varied warm teas. Assessing the state of his shop, he left it for a few moments to draw water from the town well. It was time to heat the water he would need to serve the teas. As he portioned out leaf mixtures, and warmed the honey, the baker's nose caught the first waft of the aroma of fresh baked bread from the batch of pastries currently in the oven. The smell always made him hungry.

The smell was the best part of being a baker, he decided.

He hoped Ingrid would stop by with some of her soup later today.

He had just finished pouring the last pitcher of well water into the great iron pot hanging over the fire, when he heard a voice behind him.

"Nathan!! Are we in time for breakfast?"

Startled, the baker turned, and saw Jophiel, dressed in everyday travelling clothes, standing in the center of the room. Just outside, were two horses with riders who looked weary and worn.

Laughing, Nathan moved to greet the Light-Bearer. "Jophiel! It is good to see you!" He lowered his voice. "How did your mission go?"

"We are ready for the second step. Are you prepared?"

Nathan smiled. "I am ready. Have we heard from the others?"

"Nothing yet," the Light-Bearer answered. "I am going to find them, and give Uriel any help he might need. The Life-Guardians of the two girls will be here with you, to provide them with safety."

"Thank you," Nathan replied. "I am sure I will need them."

Jophiel patted Nathan on the back, and smiled. "You *always* do well. Just keep your ears and your heart open, and you won't miss a thing." He paused. "Oh, there is one item that will help you in reaching the child. I had to destroy a birthday cake destined for the princess. The nursemaid had taken it from the castle and didn't know it had been prepared and poisoned by a Shade infiltrator. *Today* is the princess's birthday."

Hearing this, Nathan's eyes and face brightened. "I'm sure I will be able to find a cake here somewhere hereabouts." He paused to ponder. "How many years is she this day?" he asked.

"Five," Jophiel told him. "The nursemaid is not much older, at fourteen years."

The baker was surprised. "They are both so young to be involved in such a dangerous enterprise."

"Yes, they are." the Light-Bearer answered. "But there is no other way. Please take care to get them to the Refuge Site as soon as possible. They have witnessed a great deal in the past few hours." Jophiel moved towards the door, and Nathan walked with him. Reaching the outside, he stopped once more, and looked at the baker with a direct gaze.

"Nathan," he said.

The baker looked at him expecting further instructions. Instead, Jophiel reached into his robes and pulled out a small, golden bag. He placed it in Nathan's hands.

"Prince Kyriel sent this to help pay the expenses you will incur."

The shop owner was surprised. "I didn't expect anything, Jophiel. You know that."

"Yes," the Light-Bearer replied, "I know. But the Prince has foreseen circumstances you will encounter. He wants to provide for your safety. You and I both know he never does anything unnecessarily."

Humbled, Nathan took the purse from him, and looked into it. The bag was filled with golden ducats. He was amazed.

What could possibly occur that he would need such a fortune?

"I will keep it safe," he replied. "Thank you."

"Don't be afraid to use it when the need arises."

In the eastern kingdom; within the deepest cavern of Queen Souhaites' summer castle, Pimedus paced back and forth, fuming aloud. Around him, Weavers and Muddlers sat, rapt at attention, waiting for a fire-bolt or thunder-ball to descend upon them. Few of them had ever seen Pimedus in this level of rage.

"There is no telling what he will do to one of us if we try to leave," one Muddler whispered to his cohort. "We are all better off just waiting until we receive instructions."

In the center of the ring were two Weavers, who had, in some way, fueled the Shade's explosive condition. Both were badly burned, and displayed fresh battle wounds.

"They got into it with Light-Bearers," one of the Muddlers observed quietly. "It doesn't look like it went too well for them."

"It never does, *does* it?" his associate responded.

A Weaver crouching next to them overheard their comments. "Didn't you hear? Princess Karaliene escaped with her nursemaid, and right under Pidemus' snout too!"

An Entity standing behind them chuckled. "He thought he was so smart!" it sneered. "*I* would have done it differently. Everyone knows, you never manifest in a human form as long a period of time as he did *this* time."

Overhearing them, Pidemus stopped in his deliberations. He stepped into the center of the group, where the murmurings had been taking place. Reaching out his talons, he took the Muddler who had first spoken by the throat and pulled him up off the ground, making a face-to-face confrontation.

"Who says I didn't *plan* things to happen this way?" he taunted. "Who says the poison in the evening pastries wasn't the *first* line of attack? Without the princess, there is *nothing* for them to protect."

The group nodded, grumbling agreement. The raging Shade released the Muddler, throwing him down to the ground. The Muddler bounced like a ball, and landed in the far corner, huddling in fear; licking his wounds.

Pimedus continued his tirade. "Without the *princess*, the Queen has no options. It was *my* plan to get rid of her." Everyone in the room knew he was lying at this point, but they also knew no solution would come to them if Pimedus' anger was further aroused.

The Shade lowered his voice and leaned in towards them. "But I have one concern. I *saw* the child eat the pastry, and I *watched* them leave the castle. I sent *those two,*" he indicated the two battle-burned Weavers; "after them to make sure the child was dead. And did they follow through with their assignment?"

He looked at the two unfortunate creatures, sneering, "No! NO! They did NOT fulfill their assignment! They know *nothing*! They came back with *no information at ALL! AND WE MUST* KNOW!! Without knowing whether she is dead or alive, the agenda we have set in the Queen's absence will fail. Not only that, but these two miserable excuses for our prince's cause *lost* their little fight."

The larger of the two Weavers spoke up, defensively. "It was three against two, Pimedus! No one could have won that battle!"

"Bah!" scoffed the Shade, and fell silent.

The Entity who had spoken before, who had been watching from his perch on the wall, laughed out loud. It was a derisive, revolting sound, and all those in the room shuddered in response. It spoke.

"If that is all we are concerned with; a simple fact-finding mission; then we should follow the path they took and just find out. Surely some mortal in the town will be holding a funeral *somewhere*."

There was silence in the cavern. It was too workable of an idea to ignore. And yet, Pimedus was unwilling to admit that such a concept could have come from anyone but himself.

"I considered that," he said.

The Entity would not be relegated. "And," he prodded, mocking, "Oh Great One, what did you deduce?

Pimedus whirled around and flew to face his new competitor. "Don't toy with *me*! he warned, seething.

His adversary flew from the wall to face him, peering at him with unique red eyes which glowed bright with an angry light.

"Or *what*?" His opponent puffed himself up to appear larger, and looked at the crowd. "This Shade thinks he has outsmarted everyone, but it took *one* Light-Bearer, and a *little girl* to fell him. *Years* of plans laid, traps set and sprung; *months* of scheming; and it has all come to *this*. We are licking our wounds, still under Souhaites' thumb, and no closer to our goal!!"

He strutted out into the open, and removed the hood from his cloak. "Allow me to introduce myself," he began. "Many of you know me. *All* of you have *heard* of me. I am Enki; Sausmas' second-in-command. I have been sent by our Dark Prince to fix your little problem. And believe me when I tell you our lord is just a little upset by this latest fiasco; this botch of circumstances."

Throughout the cavern, the realization that a Python spirit was among them, drew fear from the largest of each of the Queen's minions, even the most experienced of the Shades.

With that, the Python raised his black tendril-twisted extremities up from the ground, levitating himself to hang in mid-air. Using all the barbs of his power, he pointed at Pimedus and the two Weavers who had initially followed the princess. Instantly, a line of black fire rocketed from his hands and feet, joining themselves into one colossal, onyx fire-bolt. Halfway through its rapid journey, the one bolt branched into three. Each of the three bolts had been timed to arrive at their marks in the same instant; each one shooting a gaping hole through the middle of its objective. Stunned, the horde watched in surprised terror. Immediately, moans emanated from the unfortunate targets, as they dropped onto the floor in pain, unable to move.

"Don't worry, you worthless *worms*," Enki continued, deriding them. "You *can't* die; but if you fail our prince again, you will *wish* you could. This little demonstration is just a *tiny* reminder of the reality of his power. *Don't* let this happen again."

He strutted over to his victims, using one of his long talons to skewer the three of them up, one at a time, like trash on the end of a pike. With a loud voice, he lifted them up over his head.

"Now go! You are banished to the Borderlands, until you can prove you are not an absolute disappointment and failure to me... *or to the Prince!*" As the mob watched, Enki pulled back his arm, shaking the three into the air. He then batted them with his hand, to send them a far distance. Suddenly the cavern's earthy roof opened up. The sky became visible. Everyone in the cave watched until the three disappeared over the horizon.

Many hoped they would not be back.

Enki looked around the room, at the rest of the minions, who were now huddled together, pulling away from him in disgust and fear. He changed his tone.

"Now, now, I am a reasonable creature. It isn't *hard* to please me. I just need a little cooperation. So... who wants to volunteer for our little fact-finding endeavor?"

No one in the cavern moved.

Enki continued. "Now relax. All of you. What gets Pimedus into trouble is the fact that he is power hungry. You all would agree with me, wouldn't you? There is no other way to handle a creature like that, right?"

Noises of assent began to filter all over the cavern. He continued.

"Now, I know none of *you* have that problem, so we will work well together. Agreed?"

Reluctantly, members of the horde began to approach the Python.

Enki rubbed his hands together.

"Here is what our Prince would like to see happen…. As you know, the Queen will be returning soon for the warmer months. She will be expecting the princess and her nursemaid to be in place, just as they were when she left for the winter castle. And so, they must be. All must appear as it did when the Queen departed months ago. If we cannot find the princess, or if she is dead, we must make Souhaites believe nothing has changed. If this should be the case, two of you Shades will have to take the forms of those mortal little girls."

"*Why?*" asked one Shade. "Why don't we just let her discover the princess has gone, and watch her go crazy?"

Enki growled. "Because, you fool, Souhaites' mortal body gave *birth* to Karaliene. The princess is her weak spot. Do I need to remind you she has been grooming the child for the past five years? We are still another *two* years from her Fifty-year Gala Celebration. That means….," he paused for dramatic impact, "*this is the year she will begin grooming the mortal princess to become her Host.*

"*If* you remember, the Queen must appear continually young. Every fifty years, she takes

186

habitation of a new Mortal body. If we can fool her for the next two years, Souhaites will fail in this regard, and the kingdom will fall to Sausmas. He has known for some time that she has been plotting his overthrow."

"He *knows?*" one of the Muddlers echoed.

Enki sneered. "Of course he knows. She thinks she can overthrow Sausmas; but she will fail. At the very least, she is planning to become second-in command. That would mean *my* demise."

He looked around the room. "I'm certain none of you were part of her plans. Am I correct?" he said. Then he added, "Giving *you* the opportunity to please me, I will not even mention to Sausmas that you knew what she was up to."

Around the room, voices were heard in response. "Oh, no, Enki; Not me, Enki; I have always been loyal to you, Enki," and so on.

"That's good, that's good," the Python replied. *"See to it you keep it that way."* His focus changed to the problem at hand.

"Now, who will volunteer to help me find the princess?"

Chapter Nine
The Queen's Rule

They were now in the village of Tournant. In front of a crowd of close to fifty townspeople, the Romani family was presenting their program of entertainment. Over the past few weeks, the troupe had performed in several villages. By sheer repetition, daily activities had developed into a loose type of schedule.

Since beginning the entertainment portion of their mission, the ensemble would arrive in a village on a day, and spend that afternoon setting up camp, meeting the townspeople, and letting the inhabitants know of the entertainment they would present the next day. Sometimes, in the midst of setting up camp, they would find someone in need of skills held by one of the troupe, and that individual would spend that afternoon in service in one way or another. The first evening, they would rehearse, eat, and sleep. The next day, Galen would offer free medical help to those in need, giving away medicines, as well as advice. On the second evening they would present their entertainment. On the morning of the third day, they would pack up, and head to the next village, getting an early start.

Peyton was enjoying being a part of a gypsy troupe. He had learned so many things in the past few months. Sometimes it was difficult to remember what life had been like back in Protectorate Area One. As he waited for the rest of the group to arrive, to begin the evening's entertainment with music, he found himself thinking about their journey together so far. He was amazed at how far they had all come. For a few moments, he considered the changes he had observed in those who were his old and new friends, also on the mission.

Several hidden giftings had become visible during this mission, not just in one, but in all involved.

For example, Jaret's gift for writing and sharing poetry had shown itself; something Peyton had never known about his friend. And it was really good stuff too, he realized. Why had Jaret had never shared with his peers? Yet now, it was necessary as a part of a cover for a greater purpose.

Tividar's father had been a fashioner of swords, and had passed related skills to his young son. From his earliest years, the young knight had practiced juggling with swords lit on fire. Peyton was surprised at how close the fire came to his friend's hair and skin when he maneuvered the swords in practice. And yet, he had never burned himself.

Damara had shown great skill as a dancer. The townspeople everywhere seemed to always love watching her ballet skills. Tvirtas had accompanied her on his violin, in duet with Shyla's panpipes. The piper's haunting melody held the attention of the audience, and brought calm in the middle of a busy season for most of the population.

Smiling, Peyton considered his father. For as long as Peyton could remember, his father had been able to produce a flower from his sleeve when meeting a pretty girl. It always drew a giggle from the object of his father's attention. Thinking about it now, he realized his father had worked to perfect such talents for clandestine missions such as these. When he was younger, Peyton had wanted to learn the skill himself. So, one afternoon Tvirtas spent time showing him how to complete the illusion, and several more. Since that day, Peyton had added a couple of other illusions and some riddles to his part of the show.

When he first began, the audiences had thought he was doing a comedy routine, he had failed so miserably. But with the "family's" encouragement and further instruction, as well as with the choice to laugh at his own mistakes, Peyton had kept trying. Now, after four weeks of presenting every day, he was actually believable!

Whenever the troupe arrived in a village, Galen was the first one to walk the streets, announcing their arrival.

"Gypsy doctor available! Free clinic at the gypsy camp! I have medicines for all kinds of ills! Come and see the show tomorrow!" As a result, she was usually busy continually after the Romani Family's arrival until well after dark.

Even Lucinda and Jayden got in on the act. Their part had happened by accident, if one was to tell the truth. In the midst of travel one day, Jayden had wanted to ask Lucinda a question, but didn't know her language. So, he had asked Galen to interpret for him.

"Why don't you tell her yourself?" the old woman had prodded.

"I can't. I don't know how," the boy responded.

"Sure you can!" came the reply. "You will just have to watch me, and make the signs I make. I want you to learn to communicate with her. After teaching him the alphabet, she helped the two children with two or three sentences. Then, the old woman patted the boy on his arm, and walked away.

"He's such a bright student!" she told Shyla. In subsequent days, the midst of learning sign language, Jayden had created a game to play with Lucinda. He would act out an animal, and she would tell him the sign for it. It proved to be quite hilarious, especially when Jayden couldn't think of anything for a certain animal other than getting on all fours. Lucinda would then run through names of animals so fast in sign language that even Galen couldn't keep up. Several nights, they played their game with the audience for everyone's enjoyment and merriment.

But Peyton's most favorite of all the acts was Pythia and Panna, who juggled knives, spun plates on sticks, and did tumbling to clapped rhythms. Peyton loved to see the blur of their colorful costumes when they were really moving fast.

Just yesterday, they had asked Uriel if they could add something to the presentations. When Uriel asked to see it, the entire camp had watched, amazed. Panna leaned against the side of a wagon, while Pythia stood some twelve feet away.

"What are you going to do?" Jayden had asked.

"We are knife *throwers* too!" Pythia had laughed.

"You just watch yourself!" Panna had chided her, kiddingly. "It's *my* life on the line here." She paused, and looked at her sister sideways. "You're not *mad* at me about anything, are you?"

"Don't worry! You're fine! Pythia responded. Then, she had taken aim with her throwing knives, and outlined her sister's form with them. Panna stayed perfectly still during the exercise. In the end, twelve identical knives were stuck into the wagon's side, their positions outlining a shape showing where Panna had been.

"How did you *do* that?" Peyton had asked her.

"Lots of practice with straw dolls when I was young," came the answer, with a good hearted laugh.

That evening the crowd was larger than usual for a normal village gathering. When the entertainment ended, the Romani family began to play lively music for a village dance. It began well enough, but several of the older men of the town brought a barrel of ale and a number of mugs with them. By the time the music had finished, people were tired of dancing. Three of this particular group had obviously taken in too much of the strong ale. Apparently, they weren't in the mood to go to their homes just yet, so they sat by the Romani family fire, and began to talk. It wasn't long before their conversation turned hostile, and they began to quarrel.

In the midst of the disturbance, Tvirtas sat near the fire the entire time, drawing in on his pipe, whittling away on yet another wooden chess piece. As the three men's argument rose and fell in volume, stances and postures would also rise and fall. In the midst of the conflict, Tvirtas remained; calmly whittling. As the argument escalated, its participants moved throughout the gypsy camp, tripping over benches, falling backward, and stumbling. Periodically, Tvirtas would lift up his tray to get out of their way; moving to a different location where he could continue to whittle. Finally, one of them turned to their attention his way.

"What duh y-*yoooo* think?" the fellow bellowed, his drunken breath blowing over the quiet whittler.

"About what?" Tvirtas replied, still whittling, never taking his eyes off his chess piece.

"Ab-ab-about our fight," the man replied.

"Oh, I wasn't sure what to call it. Thank you for telling me."

A second man joined the first. He leaned into Tvirtas' face and shook his finger. "Y-you don't even *look* like a gypsy. I kn-know what gypsies look like."

Nonplussed, the former commander took his pipe from his mouth and held it. He looked at the man speaking, and replied. "And just what *do* gypsies look like, exactly?"

"Well, you know," he spoke and then stopped to think. "Well, they're *stupid* for one thing. I mean, who would rather live in a *wagon* than in a house?"

"I see what you mean. But aren't *we* living in wagons? Doesn't *that* tell you that *we* are gypsies?" Tvirtas answered, without looking up, continuing his whittling. "You don't *like* gypsies either, do you?"

The drunkard nodded, and leaned against Tvirtas, pointing his finger into the whittler's chest for emphasis. His hand moved up and down, probing the same spot on the older man's chest, in rhythm with his words.

"I don't like *anyone* who tells me what to do," he taunted.

The third man in their circle spoke. Although less drunk than his comrades, he was still antagonistic. His voice was tinged with anger.

"So, tell us, *Gypsy*," he inquired with a sneer, "who are you and your family loyal to? King Suzerain or Queen Souhaites?"

Tvirtas was a little taken back by the question. "I don't understand your meaning," he said truthfully. "Isn't the Queen supposed to be loyal to the King?"

The second man spoke up. "That's what she *wants* us to believe. But we all *know* it isn't that way at all."

Having overheard the increasingly loud encounter, Ramon had come outside his family's wagon, to join Tvirtas, as had Tividar. Quietly observing, the two younger men sat down on the back step of the wagon nearest the former commander.

The whittler put his project down and looked at three villagers. "Who are *you* loyal to?" he asked.

The second man leaned closer to Tvirtas, threatening. "Answer the question, old man!" he demanded.

The older man smiled at him, disarming. "Why are you so angry, friend? We are the Romani family, and we are *all* loyal to Suzerain. So now, why don't *you* answer *my* question? Who are *you* loyal to?"

The three men looked at each other, and then at the Tvirtas. "Why, the *king*," they said, "Of course, the king."

"What did you *think* was happening here?" the older man asked them.

The first man responded. "Well, I know what Suzerain says about how people are *supposed* to live, but that stuff doesn't seem to be a part of how life *really* is."

The older man put out his hand. "I'm Tvirtas, by the way," he said.

The first man spoke. "I am R-R-Reginald." He introduced the second man, who was still unsteady on his feet. "This is Valerian, and this is Tadd."

Tvirtas shook their hands, one by one. "It's good to meet men in Hausse."

Reginald laughed derisively. "I'm not sure what you mean by that," he said.

"Just what I said," Tvirtas responded. "As you know, there are many more women than men in this kingdom. It's good to meet *three* men of Hausse, in one place, who are *friends* with each other."

Tadd smiled. "Well, my father served in the summer castle as a boy, and he has told me the horror stories," he said. "Reginald's grandfather was exiled to the Borderlands by the Queen when he was a young man, and he made his way back in secret."

"And I have always lived in this village, but my parents paid the price for having a boy," Valerian interjected. "I married my wife ten years ago, but we have never really been happy. Now we have two daughters and one son, and the sorrow in his eyes is unbelievable."

Tvirtas spoke carefully. "My mother-in-law was once a dragon."

Amazed, the three men reacted to the whittler's words. Reginald broke the silence. "*Was a dragon?*" he repeated. "I thought once that happened life was over."

The former commander lowered his voice, and leaned into the circle to whisper his response. "Well, I did too. But to be truthful, things in Hausse are not currently going the way King Suzerain would have them."

"What do you mean?" Tadd wanted to know.

Tvirtas paused, weighing his question before he asked it.

"Have any of you ever been to a Power Portal?" he said.

"My mother used to take me to one," Valerian offered, "but when I got older I stopped going with her. It never made me feel better."

Both Reginald and Tadd shook their heads in agreement.

"Yep. Same thing here."

"That's what I think, too."

Tvirtas moved closer to the wagon step where Ramon was sitting. The three men followed him. He regarded Valerian. "Tell me about your son."

Valerian looked at the former commander. Fear showed itself in his eyes. It was clear he was struggling with whether to trust the whittler he had never met before.

Tvirtas nodded to Ramon. "Why don't we show him?" he said. "That way…." He stopped and looked at Valerian.

"Why don't you go and get your son?"

The man was surprised. "Why?" he asked. "*Why* do you want to see my son?"

"I'd just like to meet him, that's all." Tvirtas shrugged. He looked Valerian in the eyes. "Would you just go get him, please?"

For some reason, Valerian felt an urge to do what the strange gypsy was asking him to do. "All right. I'll be right back," he answered.

Tvirtas and Ramon looked at each other. What would happen when these men discovered the truth?

Inside the wagon, Shyla had just tucked Jayden and Damara into their cots for the night.

"Mama, can we hear a story?"

So, the young mother had told them a story.

"Mama, can we have a drink?"

So, the young mother had poured small glasses of water.

"That's enough now, children," she told them. "Go to sleep. I will be just outside the wagon if you need me." Slipping out through the side door, Shyla found a quiet place to sit under a small tree close to the family wagon. She looked up at the stars. How beautiful they were this time of night, she thought.

She hadn't been sitting for long, when a voice spoke behind her. "May I join you?" Uriel said, as he approached the place where she was sitting.

Surprised, Shyla looked over at him. "Sure," she said.

The Light-Bearer sat down next to her. "We had a good day, didn't we?" he asked.

"Yes, we did," she answered. "I think I like living like this."

"Are the children sleeping?" he asked.

"I surely hope so," she laughed. "They had more than their usual quota of stories, and drinks of water this evening. Some days I find myself so tired at the end of the day."

Both of them were silent for a few moments. It was finally Uriel who spoke first.

"The King says 'it's time, Shyla,'" he said.

"Time?" she echoed.

"Look into your heart," came the reply. "You know what I am referring to."

"Oh," she said. "Really? I'm not sure I'm ready."

"You will be," he said quietly. "Prepare your soul."

On the other side of the wagon, Tvirtas and Ramon were waiting for Valerian to return to the gypsy camp with his son. As Tvirtas observed his approach, the former commander signaled such to Ramon.

Walking with Valerian was a ten-year old boy.

Tvirtas noted the boy's appearance. He looked just like any other ten-year old young man in Hausse. He was taller than some. But the trademarks signs of almost every boy raised in the Queen's kingdom were easy to note.

Valerian had reached the wagon. "This is my son, Jowan," he said, putting his son in front of him. "He's very smart."

"I'm sure he is," Tvirtas answered. He crouched down in front of the boy. "It's good to meet you, Jowan. Did you like the Gypsy show tonight?"

Jowan nodded his head. He looked at Tvirtas with wide eyes.

The former commander patted the boy's shoulders. "Now, don't be afraid, son. It's all right. Everything is going to be all right."

Reginald and Tadd had gone back to their homes for the night. The former commander looked at Ramon.

Ramon looked at Valerian. "Would you like to meet *my* son?"

Jowan nodded.

"You have a son too?" Valerian asked Ramon.

"Shyla and I have two children," Ramon answered. "Twins; a girl *and* a boy."

Ramon ducked quickly into the wagon, where he moved to Jayden's cot. "Are you sleeping, Jay?" he whispered to his son.

"No, Papa," Jayden whispered. "I can't sleep. Can I come outside with you?"

"Sure, let's go!" Ramon answered.

Jayden bounded out of bed, and moved towards the back door of the wagon.

"Jay!" his father whispered his name abruptly, so as to not awakened Damara. "Wait a minute! You need to be ready to go out there!"

Jay stopped and turned around. "What? *Who's* out there?" Without stopping, the boy opened the door and moved into the night air.

Tvirtas greeted him. "Hi, Jayden! Can I introduce you to a new friend?"

From inside the wagon, Ramon could hear his son answer, "Sure!"

"This is Jowan. He lives here in the village," Tvirtas continued.

"Hi!" Jayden spoke.

There was silence. What was happening, Ramon wondered?

Before he could get to the door, his son bolted back into the wagon. Silently, with large eyes, he grabbed his father's hand, and pulled Ramon back outside. In the innocence of childhood, Jayden spoke the most obvious thing out loud. As they once again reached the outside, the boy pointed at Jowan.

"Papa, why doesn't he have a mouth?"

Alerted and aware, Tvirtas and Ramon glanced quickly at each other. It had been inevitable that this point of disclosure would come. Inevitably, Jayden would have learned the truths he was about to encounter at some juncture during their mission.

Apparently, the boy was in for the lesson of his life. And it would come tonight.

For their part, Valerian and Jowan were equally surprised. Almost at the same moment of Jayden's words, Valerian also voiced the obvious.

"Your son has a *mouth! And* he has the ability to *speak*!" the man blurted out, much louder than was wise, given the situation.

Startled, Ramon looked around quickly, making sure no one had heard. "Shhh!" he warned. "Come inside the wagon, and we'll talk."

"B-but *how*…" Valerian began, stepping forward towards the wagon.

Tvirtas motioned for him to wait. "We will answer all of your questions. Just come inside and sit with us."

"You are the Queen's spies," the man accused, as he entered. "I *knew* it! The only man-child allowed to speak in the entire kingdom, is the one whose family is in the Queen's employ!"

Stepping into the wagon, Valerian and his son stood just inside the door. Ramon reached took the lantern from outside, and brought it in to provide light. As he did so, he checked on his daughter, Damara, still sleeping soundly.

"I don't want to wake her," he whispered. "I'm sure my wife had a difficult time getting her to sleep. Travelling is so exciting for her. Damara is afraid she will miss something if she goes to sleep, even for a moment."

Valerian smiled. "Both of our children are the same way, and we are not living on the road."

Tvirtas motioned for them to sit. Jayden moved to sit next to Jowan. Valerian sat on the edge of one of the benches, noticeably wary.

"If you are *not* in the Queen's employ, then you must be something far worse," he reiterated.

"Why can't we just be gypsies, travelling to avoid the Queen's politics?" Ramon offered.

"Because it would take more than wagons to avoid the Queen's spies," Valerian replied. "They're everywhere."

"Not really," Tvirtas chuckled. "They just work very hard to make sure everyone *believes* they are. They keep everyone in fear. When mortals are afraid, we give more power to those things we don't understand than is necessary."

"I *am* afraid," Jowan's father replied. "That's true. I don't want to lose my son."

"How could you *lose* him, sir?" Jayden asked.

Surprised to once again hear Jayden speak, Valerian answered, addressing his answer to the little boy.

"Years ago, I was a Regent for the Queen's court in this village. You might not know this, but boys born in Hausse are immediately marked for death, unless their family agrees to bring them up according to the Queen's Rule. That means they are not allowed to do anything without permission, or to pursue their curiosity in learning. If they do, they are beaten. If a family does not agree to the Queen's rule, they are punished. Many families just allow the Queen to execute their sons, because they are afraid of what will happen if they let them live."

"Why does she do that?" Jayden wanted to know.

Tvirtas spoke. "She is afraid a male leader will rise; one who will show people the truth about who she is; how she has twisted what her subjects believe about Suzerain."

"If she can kill all the boys before they become men, or if she can control them," Ramon interjected, "then no leader can step forward."

"But what happened to Jowan's mouth?" Jayden asked.

Valerian continued. "I'll come to it. As I was saying, the Queen rewards families with gifts when they have a girl; or, when they agree "The Queen Rule" in regard to raising their sons. At first, when Jowan was born, we tried to do what we had been told, but there came a day when I just couldn't hurt him any longer. I am afraid he overheard me speak words of anger against the Queen. When he repeated my words, as most children do, the Queen demanded I beat him into compliance. Most boys who receive a beating like that end up dead, or worse. So I refused.

"As a result, I lost my position and my title. Most of our belongings were taken away. The Queen summoned us to the winter castle, where she sealed my son's mouth until the day he turns twelve.

"You see, boys are expected to join the Queen's army at the age of twelve. If a boy expresses disagreement or criticism of the Queen, she will take away his ability to speak. She seals his mouth."

"How does he eat or drink, then?" A small voice spoke from the cot in the corner. A sleepy Damara was sitting up on the edge of her cot.

"He doesn't do either one," Valerian answered. "He has become very thin over the past year. I know it is only a matter of time until he dies. If he *does* live, he will be required to join the Queen's service at the winter palace when he turns twelve. Even then, he will still be unable to eat or drink until he proves himself loyal to the Queen. The only way to rise in power is to never argue, or question the Queen."

In the town of Sorrettu, Ellie and Karaliene were resting in front of a warm fire. Upon being welcomed into Nathan's store, they had enjoyed a breakfast of warm bread, fruit and cheeses, with steaming berried tea, sweetened with honey.

Even though Jophiel had assured them beforehand of Nathan's loyalty and safety as a host, both girls had found it difficult to trust him immediately. But now, several hours later, after a meal, a bath, and a nap, both Ellie and Kara were relaxing; experiencing the first real respite they had known in a long time.

"I don't know why I'm still sleepy," Ellie had told the princess an hour after waking. "I slept all day long."

"I did too," Karaliene replied, "and I want to go back to sleep. And I *never* want to do that."

Ellie laughed. "Aren't we a pair?"

Karaliene giggled. "Where are we, Ellie?"

"I think we are in a town called Sorrettu. Jophiel brought us here," the nursemaid answered. "This is the town on the other side of the lake from the castle."

"That's right," the princess answered. "We went through the tunnel last night." She paused.

"Ellie?"

"Yes."

"What happened in the Nursery?"

"You mean, last night?"

"I ate a little cake and got sick."

"Yes, you did. And I thought you were sleeping."

Karaliene nodded. "I wasn't though. I just couldn't move my arms. And then after you dressed me, I could move my legs a little."

"I'm sorry. I didn't know you had been poisoned, Kara. You could have died."

There was silence in the room, as they sat together on the large fluffy bed, nestled in the soft pillows Nathan's daughter, Ingrid, had given them.

The princess spoke softly. "I think I *did* die, Ellie. But there was a man who came into the tunnel and kissed my forehead."

Ellie was amazed. "You remember that?"

Karaliene spoke like one much older than her five years. "I think I will be able to recognize a Shade from now on. I shouldn't have given Myra any part of my heart."

"Nor should I, little one," Ellie answered. "Nor should I. I wondered how I was going to tell you."

Silence reigned in the room for a few more moments. Once again, the princess broke it.

"Where is Jophiel?" she asked.

"I don't know," Ellie told her. "He mentioned something to Nathan about having to meet someone. And we are to follow Nathan's instructions."

"Is he a Light-Bearer too?"

Ellie giggled. "No, silly, he has children. Light-Bearers don't get married!"

"Oh," the child said. "I just remember the two girl Light-Bearers who were with us last night."

"And here I thought you were sleeping."

Ellie looked at her. "I was, sort of," she said. "I was looking down at you at first, and could see everything happening. There were two of them, with silver belts and they had shields."

"Yes, they did," Ellie told her. "Jophiel said we each have had one with us our entire lives. They are our Life-Guardians. The King asked them to protect us."

"Then it *was* real," the child said.

"Yes, dear one, it was *very* real."

Part Three

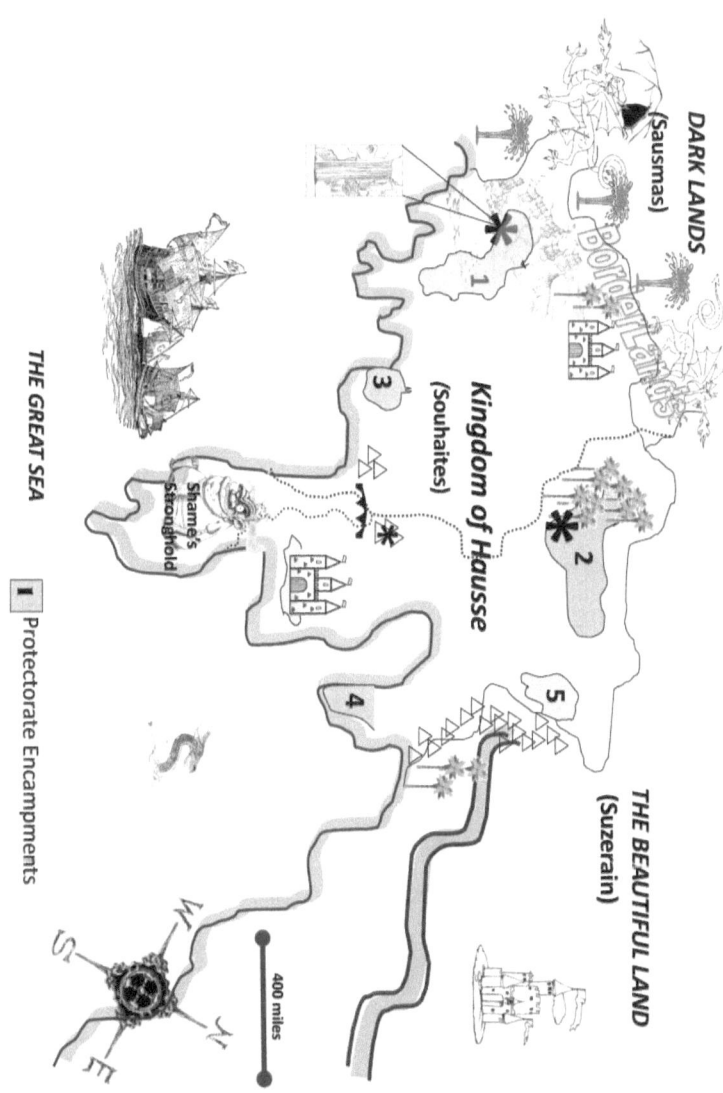

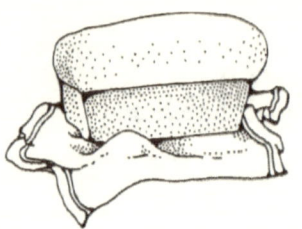

Chapter Ten
Dark Discovery

North of the western kingdom, just a hundred miles within the Borderlands, Pimedus the Shade and two Muddlers crouched next to a black geyser. It had been days since they had arrived in the Barrens. In the minds of all those who inhabited Sausmas' territories, "Barrens" was a much more accurate description of the region of the Dark Lands. They were huddled in a larger group of underlings to the Dark Prince.

"I can't even *tell* them," one Muddler complained. "The knight forbade me to, and the Light-Bearer with her told me I would have to stay here until their mission is over. The Queen will skewer me when my mistake is discovered. I will pay dearly when it is all found out. I will pay."

"I hate it when they do that," another one moaned. Then he mocked in a screeching voice, "by the word of Kyriel! Get away!" His voice lowered back to its normal level. "Who do they think they are?"

The first Muddler answered. "I am so tired of being cut up into little pieces. I'd like to take a sword and run them all through; the lot of them."

Until this moment, Pimedus had stayed aloof from the others who were experiencing exile. At the mention of a Light-Bearer, however, his hearing skills had re-engaged. He spoke to the complaining Muddler.

"What Light-Bearer?" he demanded.

The Muddler whined in response. "I don't know," he answered. "He was one of those who can change his size. I didn't get a good look at him, because he showed his light."

"Where were you?" Pimedus wanted to know.

"Why is it important?" The Muddler complained.

Pimedus snarled. "Don't try my skills. I will rip you in pieces myself!"

The Muddler backed away, as did the others around him. "I don't remember *exactly*," the creature moaned. "The Queen conjured an image, but its reception was interrupted. Instead of a moving picture of what was actually happening, we saw a *still* picture; a wagon, and seven pairs of legs. Then the wind blew."

"But *where were you?*" Pimedus' tone became inflammatory.

"In the woods somewhere close to the winter castle."

"What did you see?" the Shade probed.

"I saw a boy from Protectorate Area One, named Peyton. I covered myself in the form of his friend Zynicker. It seemed strange to me that he had left his schooling this time of year, and was traveling with a gypsy family. He told me nothing. Then, out of nowhere a Chevaliesse flew in and impaled me. She was skillful, and commanded me here. Then, the Light-Bearer came. And the whole time, they were instructing Peyton. It was like they were on a mission or something."

Pimedus fell silent. A gypsy family? There were hundreds of them traveling through Hausse this time of year. What had happened? What was Suzerain up to? Had they been sent covertly to meet the princess? Had that Light-Bearer been Jophiel? Why else would a female knight and a Light-Bearer be traveling together with a young boy in his first Discovery Season?

He growled at the Muddler. "Did they mention a plan? Or the king's business? What language did they use?"

The Muddler threw up his arms. "What is it with you Shades? There always has to be more to the story. But there isn't. There *isn't*. And I don't know anything else. And even if I did, it wouldn't make a difference. The Light-Bearer said I have to stay here until their mission is over." Rising to walk away from the group, he once again used his high-pitched, mocking tone. "By the word of *Kyriel*. By the word of *Kyriel*. By the word of *Kyriel*."

Pimedus pounced. "Mission? You're sure he said 'mission?'" But the Muddler had walked away. With his back to Pimedus, he waved his arms in the air. "Yeah, yeah, yeah. He said 'mission.' So what? They're *all* on a mission. Isn't *everybody*?"

Pimedus stood and walked away from the group, to think and strategize. The two Muddlers exiled with him followed.

"Master," one of them wheedled, "we could return now. We have information that will ensure you are not a failure or a disappointment to Enki, or to the Prince."

Hearing the banishment decree quoted verbatim rankled Pimedus. He grabbed the Muddler by the throat and drew the creature up into his line of sight. "Don't ever quote that monster, Enki, to me again! Or you will wish you hadn't!"

Tersely, he hurled the Muddler to the ground. "I think we can return now. I have the beginnings of a plan." The Weavers watched as he flew up into the air.

"Where are you going, Master?"

"Just keep up, and don't ask stupid questions."

As the wagons left Tournant, Jayden sat inside his family's wagon with his new friend, Jowan. Damara and Lysandra sat on Damara's cot, while the boys sat on Jayden's. For the moment, all four were playing a guessing game with their new friend.

Tvirtas and Ramon had convinced Valerian and his wife to allow Jowan to travel with them to a Protectorate Area, where their son could receive care to heal his voice and throat. Badly malnourished, the boy would also receive medical attention to rebuild his frail body.

At one point that night, Uriel and Shyla had joined the discussion taking place within the wagon. Talking into the wee hours of the morning, Valerian had requested Sanctuary in a Protectorate Area for the rest of his family as well.

Uriel and Tvirtas knew they would not be able to take on a rescue project in the midst of the current mission. However, Jowan's health demanded immediate attention. In the end, it had been decided that Jowan would travel with the Romani family, who would eventually transfer him into the care of one of the Protectorate Areas. Then, at a future date, still undetermined, a Rescue Party would come for Valerian, his wife and daughter, and reunite them with Jowan at a to-be-disclosed-later site.

"Take care to prepare yourselves," Uriel told them. "Use this time to get rid of everything you don't need, and be ready to go at a moment's notice."

He had then set up a series of code words, to indicate the identity of any contact sent from one of the Protectorate Areas. Their goodbyes with Jowan had been bittersweet, filled with tears, but also with hope.

Unable to speak or make a sound, Jowan had motioned in his own private form of communication with his mother, and had hugged his father and sister.

Now, travelling in the wagon caravan, his eyes were bright with excitement. Jayden, for his part was overjoyed. To this point in the journey, the boy had felt outnumbered by Damara and Lysandra, who had developed a fast friendship.

"It's hard to be the only boy," he had whispered secretly to Shyla, his mother. "I wish we had another boy with us."

Shyla had comforted him, rubbing her hand over the top of his head. "I know you do, Jay," she had responded. "Perhaps it would help you to stay closer to your father and Tvirtas."

Jayden had been thoughtful. "Or Uriel," he suggested. "Uriel's awesome!"

Shyla had laughed. "Or Uriel!" she agreed.

Now, he had a friend! Jayden was overjoyed.

Today, plans for the children's lessons had changed. Today, Galen and Lysandra were going to help Jowan learn sign language.

"You've been unable to tell anyone anything more than 'yes' or 'no' for too long!" Galen had told him. "Tomorrow, we are going to teach you how to speak with your hands."

Jowan was excited. Explicably, he found himself watching Jayden's mouth every time his new friend would talk. Would he ever be able to again talk like that, he wondered?

Outside, on the driver's bench, Ramon and Shyla sat together. Ramon held the reins, and Shyla held a large sweetened mug of strong espresso. Periodically, they would trade; his reins for her mug, as they shared sips of the brew. Uriel rode his stallion, keeping pace with the wagon. The three of them were in the midst of a discussion.

"How far is it to the river?" Ramon asked.

"We should get there by afternoon," Uriel answered.

Observing the landscape, Ramon noticed the change in the terrain over the past few days. The road had been gradually climbing the farther east they were travelling.

"We will have to rest the horses more today," Ramon told Uriel. "They can't travel all day with this incline, without a break."

Uriel nodded. "We have several scheduled stops today. As we move farther east, the view as we travel will be much different than it has been up until now."

Shyla smiled and sighed. "I can't believe how beautiful everything is becoming!" she exclaimed. "The closer we get to the eastern kingdom, there is so much color! Everything is so green!"

Uriel nodded. "It's true. And, it will continue to surprise you, the closer we come to the border between Hausse and The Beautiful Land."

"What is that sound we hear now each morning?" she asked.

"You mean, besides that pesky rooster?" Ramon interjected.

She playfully poked her husband. "Not the rooster," she told him. "That beautiful song we hear every morning from the trees." She looked at Uriel. "Are the trees *singing*?" she asked.

The Light-Bearer laughed out loud. "No, dear girl, not here. Although, in the King's Realm, the trees *do sing!*"

Shyla was surprised. "Really?"

The Light-Bearer smiled. "Really," he answered. "But what you have been hearing in the mornings here, is the sound of birds singing."

"Birds singing?" she echoed.

"They are flying creatures the King has filled his Kingdom with."

"Like chickens?"

"Yes, a chicken is a bird. But a chicken cannot fly, except to rise into the air and fall once more. These creatures are made to ride the winds."

"What is their purpose?" Shyla was intrigued, having spent her entire life in the western kingdom, where the Queen's loyalty to Sausmas filled even the atmosphere with shadow and darkness. The only creatures she had ever seen fly were dragons. Oh, and the occasional bat.

"Purpose?" Uriel asked.

"Yes. Why do they exist?" she asked.

"To bring joy and beauty to the Realm," he answered simply.

For a short time, Shyla fell silent. The idea of something's purpose having only to do with joy and appreciation had occurred to her before, but she had never added experience to her mental information. She found herself in deep thought. She had *thought* she understood….. *but*…. how different it must be to truly live in the King's Realm!

Her reverie was broken by the sound of a giant rustling of wings over her head. Startled, she looked up, but could see nothing but the normal gray cloud cover. The sky was empty. Looking around, into the trees, she still could find nothing amiss.

"Did you hear that?" she asked her husband, beside her.

"Hear what?" Ramon answered.

"That noise like huge wings," she answered.

Ramon chuckled. "Do you have those bird things on the brain? I didn't hear anything unusual."

But Shyla's warrior senses had been aroused. Tucking into the wagon, she checked on the children and Galen, who were deep into sign language lessons.

"What's wrong, Mama?" Damara asked.

"I'm not sure," she answered, glancing at Galen. "I thought I heard something."

Opening the storage cupboard, she retrieved her quiver and bow, as well as a smaller sword. Ducking through the hinged opening in the front of the wagon, she returned to her seat with Ramon.

"Do you know where we are headed?" Shyla asked, as she once more took her place next to her husband.

Ramon looked at her. "Uriel said we were to head towards the Mortal's Folly River, and then cross over to follow the river twelve miles upstream, toward Protectorate Area Two. Twelve miles from the Great Bridge, we will come to some sort of Portal. Uriel has not disclosed everything to us, but we will know when we get there."

It wasn't very long before the sound of the river, Mortal's Folly, began to make its addition to the sounds of the journey. The roar of the waters grew in volume as the distance reduced. Arriving just short of the Great Bridge, Tvirtas pulled the caravan into a protected area between two giant boulders.

After pulling the horses to a stop, he stepped down, and began walking down the wagon line, checking the horses and the status of the rest of the travelers. When he arrived at the last wagon, what he saw surprised him.

As usual, when Galen was teaching the children, Uriel had strapped his stallion's reins to the lantern hook on Pythia's wagon. He had driven Galen's medical wagon. But today, instead of Uriel sitting by himself on the driver's bench, another man Tvirtas didn't recognize had joined him.

How had that happened, he wondered? They hadn't stopped to take on a passenger. No riders had approached them that he remembered.

"Uriel!" he called the Light-Bearer's name in greeting.

"Tvirtas, I want you to meet someone," came the reply.

"I don't remember taking on a passenger," the former commander said. "This must be someone from the King's Realm."

The man on the bench laughed. "You're right," he said to Uriel, "he's very perceptive."

At that moment, Shyla came into view of the last wagon. "Uriel," did you notice a rustling sound overhead as we travelled? I have checked the wagons, and no one has been harmed. What do you think…" she stopped mid-sentence as she saw the man on the bench.

"My name is Jophiel," the second Light-Bearer told them, as he stepped down from Galen's wagon. He looked up at Uriel, still seated. "I am glad these two are on our side." Reaching his hand out towards Tvirtas, he said, "I believe we fought together for Prince Kyriel awhile back."

Tvirtas looked at him with squinted eyes. "I *do* remember you – you just look a little different at the moment."

Jophiel smiled. "Yes, just a little." He brushed the dust off of his trousers. "I came to find your team, and be of assistance if needed."

The former commander nodded. "I wondered about that. Do you think we will encounter resistance?"

"It will depend on what the enemy knows, and where they are when they make their discoveries." Uriel responded.

"Pimedus came after us as we left the summer castle," Jophiel told them. "He poisoned the princess, but she was brought back."

"Where are they now?" Shyla asked, concerned.

"We have agents in the process of taking both of them to the Refuge Site. All have skilled Guardians to ensure they arrive safely," came the answer. "So I am here. It is vital we arrive there before nightfall."

Inside the winter castle, Queen Souhaites was holding an audience in her throne room. Cowering before her were two Weavers, still showing signs of a recent battle with Light-Bearers. They had fallen from the sky into the center courtyard as she had been speaking with castle guards, giving them instructions regarding doomed "guests" who would be arriving the next day.

The last twenty-four hours had not been pleasant. Only one day remained before her self-imposed deadline. Her season in the winter castle was ending. Tomorrow, she and her entourage would dematerialize. They would then appear just before the Great Bridge, in full pomp and procession. It was time to return to the summer castle. There, little Karaliene would be almost ready to begin her days of preparation.

But these two…. Somehow their stories did not match. Something was amiss. She threatened them once more.

"I will give you one more chance to tell me the entire account. If you continue to try to deceive me, you will suffer more than you can even imagine." She flipped her cloak open and drew out a long sabre. "Perhaps I should skewer you both right here, and send you to roast for a thousand years on a spit in the Dark Land caves."

She looked over at her advisor, a tall, faceless, thin Specter who floated behind her. "What do you think, Betruger? Should I send them to the tormentors?"

The place she referred to was a cavern deeper still in the earth than the caves Peyton had seen in his dream with Uriel. Even her most resentful minions would do anything to avoid being sent to that place.

"Do whatever you deem necessary, my Queen," Betruger responded, in a guttural, menacing growl.

"No," whined the smaller of the two Weavers. "This entire situation has gone wrong for me from the very start."

"For *you*?" his partner complained. "*I* was the one who was diced into *pieces* by Guardians."

"You forget that *I* took the first hit," retorted his cohort.

"But *I* warned you of the Guardians," wailed the other.

Annoyed by their conflict, the Queen paced back and forth. Finally, she interrupted them, shouting, "You BOTH were *told* to remain at the summer castle with Pimedus. *He* was left in charge there. How is it you have arrived *here?*"

"W-*we*...," began the smaller one.

"Yes? Don't even *try* to deceive me," she repeated. "This is your last opportunity." With that, she reached out with her claws, grabbed the throat of the larger Weaver, and held him over the fire.

"St-o----p!" he screamed. "Okay! Okay! I'll tell you what I know, but it isn't very much."

Holding him in place, she pierced him through with a talon. "Consider this a foretaste of what will happen if you hide anything from me; *anything at all!*" she threatened.

Alarmed, the smaller one blurted out phrases all at once. "Pimedus did away with the castle cook, and took her form. Then he gained the trust of the princess and the nursemaid."

"He killed Myra?" the Queen asked.

"Yes," they both answered, in unison.

"Then he gained the trust of the princess and the nursemaid," the larger one repeated.

"Yes, he did. He did," the little one echoed. "The day before her birthday, Karaliene told him, or Myra really, that there had been a Light-Bearer in the Nursery."

The Queen's face turned black as she listened. "What?" she screamed. "What did you say?"

The larger Weaver coughed. "A Light-Bearer was in the Nursery."

"Where were the sentries, and the guards?" she demanded. "Why was this allowed to happen?"

"And then…," began the little one.

"There's *more?*" she bellowed.

The larger one sighed. He had no opportunity for secrecy now. "There is *so much more*," he whined.

She squeezed his neck. "Do *tell* me," she ordered.

"Myra…. Pimedus made … he made pastries with poison in them, and gave them to the princess and Ellie."

"Did they eat them?"

"Ye—e—s, your majesty-ship," the smaller one stuttered. "The princess did. The Nursemaid didn't have anything but tea."

"What happened?"

"Pimedus went to the Nursery, but it was too late. The Light-Bearer, Jophiel, helped them get away. Their Life-Guardians fought us in the tunnel."

"Get *away?*" It was almost as though the Queen could not absorb what she was hearing. *"Did* they get away?"

"They did, on horses," the larger one answered. "But the princess didn't move. I was lying on the tunnel floor in pieces when I saw lots of light. It was too bright to see *anything*. I don't know what happened after that. I had to get out of there."

"Me too," the little one repeated, "Me too. It was too bright to stay."

Stunned, the Queen pulled her hand, and the larger Weaver from the fire. Setting him on the floor, she asked, "Is there more?"

The larger Weaver nodded. "Yes, my Queen. Pimedus called all of us to a meeting. He was enraged. He ordered us to help him find the princess before you got back to the summer castle."

"And then a Python came and exiled him and the two of us to the Barrens," the smaller one added.

Alerted, Souhaites responded. "*A Python,*" she repeated. "He *exiled* you. Who was he?"

The two Weavers looked at each other. What would she do when she heard who it had been, they questioned silently?

"I'll tell you, but promise you won't get hurt me again," the smaller one answered. "It was Enki."

Souhaites eyes widened. "*Enki* banished you to the Barrens?"

"With Pimedus."

"Why was *he* at the castle?" she asked.

"Sausmas knows why you want the fire," the larger one uttered.

Souhaites looked at them. Her face broke into a sinister smirk.

"He knows *nothing*. I am actually helping him, to achieve both our goals. *Enki* lies."

She paused. "What was his condition for your return?"

The little one took a deep breath. "He said we had to stay in the Barrens until we had found a way not to be such a failure to him or the Prince."

"What happened that you are *back here,* then?" she asked.

He continued. "There was a Muddler in the Barrens, who had been banished there by a Light-Bearer *and* a Chevaliesse, who were together in one place. They were traveling together. They were part of a gypsy camp close to here."

The Queen snorted. "That doesn't mean they are automatically part of something dangerous to our plans. They could be in the kingdom for any number of reasons. The King is always sending them into my territory."

"Y-yes," the larger one groveled. "That is true your worship, but there were two things about them that pointed towards Pimedus' conclusion. First, there was also a boy with them from Protectorate Area One. I have seen him before. He has always been able to speak, and his father was a commander under Kyriel."

"So, this is dead commander Tvirtas' son," she answered. "Go on."

"The second thing, is that when they banished him, the Light-Bearer told him he had to stay in the Barrens until their *mission* was over…." He paused, letting his words sink in.

"Oh, he used *those words*….that *does* mean something…..What *mission*?" she questioned out loud. She looked at them. "With Karaliene *dead*, Enki thinks he has postponed my realization of taking a new Host," she said.

"Was that it?" She paused. "No, it *couldn't* be that simple…because if the princess *is* dead, they would not still be searching for her….. unless….. they are not sure she is *really* dead."

She stood once more and again began pacing.

"We need a plan to catch Enki at his own game. He has overstepped himself this time." She stopped and glared at them with great intensity. "And both of you are going to help me, or I will see you roasting on spits in the caverns for a thousand years."

In the lower caverns of the same winter castle, not even five hundred feet from this exchange, Pimedus was covertly creating a mixture he could use to find the location of Princess Karaliene and her nursemaid. Unaware of the Weavers' betrayal taking place two stories above his head, he worked quickly to avoid discovery. To bring back his standing, not only with the Queen, but also with Enki, he would need to return both escapees to the summer castle, by any means possible, before Souhaites returned to the eastern kingdom.

That would be tomorrow, he realized. He could feel the time closing in around him.

After measuring and mixing, the Shade found the reference he was seeking in one of the Queen's ancient scrolls. An hour later, he poured the mixture he had created into a small pot over the fire. As he did, he read aloud the poem from the scroll he had found.

As he reached the end of the poem, a giant puff of smoke billowed up. Spurred on by these tangible results, Pimedus repeated the process a second time, and then a third and fourth. Each time, there was a giant puff of smoke in response to the spell he read.

The fifth time, Pimedus waited. He double-checked his recipe, making certain he had added all the needed ingredients to reach his desired goal.

As he finished reading the spell out loud, Pimedus poured the bottle into the cauldron, and then stepped back, bracing himself for what was sure to follow.

As the fifth cloud of smoke arose, it filled the room. From its center emanated a strangely musical sound.

"Here, to my forearm, Shadow," Pimedus ordered.

Suddenly, the smoke began to billow in and out, pulsating under the beating of great wings. From its center, an intimidatingly huge image began to emerge. With its wingspan of almost eight feet, the immense bird somewhat dwarfed even the Shade.

Lighting on his arm, the speckled gray owl pulled its feathers in, all the while observing its surroundings.

"What is your pleasure, my lord?" it asked.

Enjoying the title, Pimedus spoke. "You will travel with me into the Kingdom of Hausse. Together, we will find Princess Karaliene and her nursemaid.

They must be captured and returned to the summer castle before day's end tomorrow."

"Yes, my lord," the owl replied. "We will do as you tell us for a period of days, because you are the one who summoned us. After that, we will do as we please. Understood?"

Although the Shade had been aware of this information before that moment, Pimedus had not considered the long-term implications of his actions until the possibilities presented themselves.

He wondered; what did the owl mean, *"After that we will do as we please?"*

"Who will you *become* after that period of days?" Pimedus asked, his hand experiencing a slight tremor.

"Our name is Legion," the owl answered, "for we are many."

Chapter Eleven
The Next Step

Seated on the grass next to the road, Tvirtas and Peyton had been waiting for almost an hour. Father and son were in deep in the midst of a learning exercise.

"There are dragons you *fight*, and dragons you *rescue*," Tvirtas continued. "A seasoned warrior can tell the difference."

Peyton was fascinated. "But I thought you said that *mortals* turn into dragons."

His father smiled. "Only *some* do. If and when a mortal has given oneself over to the Queen's Rule *completely,* then that mortal will come to a place of choosing. Those who make the wrong choice, many times do become dragons." He looked at his son. "And then there are those....."

"How do you tell the difference?" the boy wanted to know.

"It's not easy at first," the former commander told him. "It takes practice, *and* a willingness to admit your mistakes. I misidentified several when I was in training, and in my early days in Suzerain's militia. For me, the key is to look into their eyes, and not be distracted by anything else they do or say."

For a moment, the dream Peyton had experienced of the Borderlands emerged in the boy's memory. "In my dream, a giant dragon talked to me," he said.

"Tell me about it," his father urged.

"About the dream; or about the dragon?"

"Both, if you wish; but more about the dragon, I think," his father replied.

Peyton closed his eyes. Yes, the image of the hot air coming up behind him was still there. "He blew fire at me that went over my shoulder. When I turned around, he was breathing in my face. He said, 'what are you doing here, *boy*?' And he was pulling young mortals apart. He was eating them. Some he threw into a cave that led underground."

"What else did you see?" Tvirtas asked.

"Uriel took me into an underground cavern. As I think about it now, it must have been some sort of torture chamber."

"The Hollow of Tormented Souls," his father answered. "I have seen it many times. You will see it again."

"How?"

"I am almost sure we are headed there on this mission. There is still much to discover before we are ready to complete our assignment," came the reply. "Suzerain always sends Light-Bearers to assist us in an assigned mission, but we never know or grasp all there is to know about our project at the beginning. Understanding begins to unfold whenever we take the next step."

"The next step?" Peyton repeated.

"In my experience with King Suzerain, I have never fully understood any of my assignments when I have received them. In fact, many times, they have been somewhat cryptic in nature. Then, when I began to follow the instructions I received, whether through a Light-Bearer, or directly, I began to see a pattern show itself.

"Even now....but I never seem to get more than one instruction at a time; perhaps because he knows me so well. I would try to take control of my efforts. When I let go of my desire to do that, I gain the understanding

I need." Tvirtas spoke this last part of his disclosure with softness in his voice.

"So... does being successful in this kind of thing come down to just trusting what I am told?" Peyton observed.

"Yes," his father responded. "I suppose it does; but there is a little more perhaps.... a perceptiveness that comes from practice?"

"What do you mean?"

"You will have to discover that for yourself, my son."

The two of them sat quietly for a few moments. It was Peyton who broke the silence.

"Papa?" he asked.

"Yes, son?" came the reply.

"What did you mean when you said, *'and then there are those?'* You didn't finish. And what do the eyes of a dragon that must be *killed* look like?"

Tvirtas took a deep breath. "Well, there are *mortals* who are overtaken by dragon *logic*. Their minds become clouded and resistant. Those are the mortals in danger of turning *into* dragons.

"Then, there are dragons that have always *been* dragons. Some are the counterparts to Suzerain's Life-Guardians. They seek to shadow *mortals* and lure them with promises of false power.

These dragons are those who must be killed, because the mortal they lure and trap becomes their rider. However, the mortal is deceived into believing they are in control and the dragon is giving them power."

Peyton listened intently. "Deceived...but what really happens?" he asked.

His father continued. "In the end, the dragon shortens the mortal's life span, and rides into the life of every *other* mortal they know. The dragon then destroys the rider's relationships, and stalls their ability to feel anything at all. Everything those dragons touch becomes tainted with death. That is why they must be killed."

"How are those dragons different? How can I tell?"

"You will learn to read their eyes," his father said. Tvirtas gazed into the horizon, remembering days long past. For a moment, he chewed on the blade of grass he had been holding between his fingers.

"So.... you want to see one, eh?" he said, redirecting the conversation. "You think you want to go to battle with a dragon?"

Peyton answered, his voice tinged with excitement. "I really do, Papa. Do you think *I* could ever be a Dragon-*slayer*?"

His father chuckled. "You remind me so much of myself, Peyton. Just remember, if you go into battle with the desire to *kill* something, you will have the wrong focus, and will probably kill the *wrong* thing. Guard your heart. A champion goes into battle with the desire to *protect*."

The older man fell silent as the back door of the wagon next to them opened. Panna emerged with a small pan of seed, and began to feed the chickens. From inside, Pythia's voice was heard, calling to her sister.

"Is there a water source nearby?" the older sister asked.

Peyton laughed to himself, as he watched Panna roll her eyes and reply. "You're kidding, right? Don't you hear the river?"

"Can you get me some water for washing?" the voice responded.

Panna looked over at Tvirtas, who shook his head. "We are hiding here in the blind, so we don't disclose ourselves to the enemy. We have to wait for Uriel and Jophiel to return," he told her.

"No, I can't," Panna told her sister, without elaborating.

"Come on, Panna! You know what it looks like in here!" Pythia's head poked out of the door. "Why can't you?"

Smugly, Panna pointed at Tvirtas. "*He* said we have to stay hidden."

Pythia looked over at the commander. "Oh well, then. I see how things are." She looked around at the wagons, which stood in caravan readiness to cross the Great Bridge. In the trees overhead, several birds sang. "I guess I'll just have to do the dishes later," she said brightly, emerging from the wagon. "I just don't know what I'll do with all this time!" She moved past her sister, and came to sit with Tvirtas and Peyton in the grass.

"Where is everyone?" she wanted to know.

"I think Jaret and Ramon went deeper into these woods to find some food for supper," Peyton told her. "Ramon said he thought we might be too tired to hunt after we cross the river. I didn't understand his reasoning."

Panna interjected from their wagon's porch. "Shyla and the children are napping in their wagon. Jowan is with Galen and Lysandra. I think Galen was going to put another treatment of ointment on his neck while we were resting the horses."

Peyton looked at his father. "Where did Uriel and Jophiel go?" he asked.

"They will be back soon. I think they went to seek reinforcements. We will need all of our strength and more if we are to cross the Great Bridge," Tvirtas answered. "We need our number to be a surprise to the enemy when we do cross, so we thought it best if just the two of them went; just in case."

He looked up at the sky, assessing the sun's journey across it. "We will be heading towards dusk soon," he told them. "We had best ready our weapons."

The Mortal's Folly River was the dividing boundary between the eastern and western kingdoms in the land of Hausse. Beginning in the mountains with melted snow and natural springs, it was much narrower at its source than it became further into the land. By the time the river reached the middle kingdom, it was over three miles wide and more than twenty feet deep. It rushed and tumbled along in violent white waters, down the entire length of the nation to the Great Sea. Just north of the Great Bridge, its waters divided into two smaller rivers, known as the Stream of Fear and the Way of Pride. Between the two smaller rivers was land uninhabitable by mortals; filled with marshes, swamps, bogs and lowlands.

Some ten miles from the waters' division point, moving seaward, anyone who travelled would reach the Great Bridge. Built in the time of the Ancients, it was constructed of three arches, two of which each spanned one of the smaller rivers. The central arch marked the beginning of an independent territory, marked on either side by the watery offshoots of the Mortal's Folly River.

The bridge was more than one hundred miles long, guarded on one side by Shades, Weavers, and Muddlers. It was the only way to reach the eastern kingdom. Many mortals who had tried to escape the western kingdom had lost their lives on the Bridge. Many had been captured and forced into servitude. Still others had been severely wounded, spending the rest of their lives in misery in the east.

The independent territory between the two smaller rivers spanned all the way to the Great Sea, and was called "Shame's Stronghold, and was ruled by Trolls."

Now, since the territory was ruled by trolls, no mortal had set foot on the land and remained free for centuries. Also, for centuries, no mortal had avoided servitude to the trolls after setting foot in the Stronghold territory.

Strange creatures, the trolls wanted nothing to do with mortals, the Queen, or King Suzerain. They fiercely guarded their independence, claiming the Great Bridge as part of their territory. Consequently, the Trolls took captive anyone seeking to cross the Great

Bridge. Those captives were put into positions of slavery, having to earn their passage into the eastern kingdom.

The trolls who ruled Shame's Stronghold were fierce by reputation. They held to tribal rule, with a chief and his advisors ruling in any given situation; the strongest and largest holding positions of dominance.

In the same way that Souhaites professed outward loyalty to the Suzerain, so did the Trolls. At the present time, the Troll Chieftain's name was Jotnar, an immense and grotesque giant, whose temper matched his size.

Jotnar's skin was a deep gray, as was the skin of all the Trolls under his domain. He was round, with folds of membrane overlapping his belly and legs. He covered his deformities, brown lesions and body warts with elegant robes of gold and silver.

However deceiving his looks might have been, no one could contest him for his inordinate strength. From the time of the Ancients, he had defended his title as warlord. His height alone was intimidating at twenty feet. He had grown one half-inch for each century he had ruled the Stronghold.

As a whole, Trolls were extremely unconventional in their fighting methods. Even at their earliest ages, the group had earned a reputation for ferocity in combat. Young trolls were known to use weapons occasionally, but more often spat out a substance to impede their opponent's movement, rendering them vulnerable to capture. Adolescent trolls played tricks on their opponents, using illusion to confuse them into standing still in midst of a conflict. Most dangerous, however, were the adult trolls. Their large teeth were coated with a highly poisonous substance. One bite would paralyze a mortal. A second bite ushered in brain damage, or certain death.

In the Tribal Center of Shame's Stronghold, Chief Jotnar was seated, his feet warming in the fire. Nearby, a smaller troll entered with a tray of pineapples.

"There are visitors outside, to see you, your Greatness," he said, placing the tray on the ground next to the overlord.

"Who are they, Wartall?" the chief asked, popping two complete pineapples in his mouth, chewing vigorously. With two fingers, Jotnar reached into his throat and pulled out the leafy tops of the fruits and threw them into a pile of additional discarded tops in the corner. Burping loudly, he looked at his attendant, waiting for an answer.

"They look like mortals," the subordinate troll answered. "But it doesn't seem likely they would get through to this part of the Stronghold avoiding capture, much less alive."

Jotnar was silent for a moment. "Show them in," he ordered. "They are probably here from the Suzerain. Let's see what they have to say." Popping two more pineapples into his mouth, he gulped to finish them before his visitors made their entrance. Digging out the remaining fruit tops, he tossed them towards the corner.

On its way to the corner, the second fruit top hit Jophiel in the face.

The Light-Bearer spoke. "Good afternoon, Jotnar," he said, wiping pineapple juice from his nose.

Jotnar looked down. "Oh, I thought it might be you," he said. "Sorry about the pineapple."

Jophiel had dealt with trolls before. He had learned how to bypass their angry tribal instincts. "It smells good," he answered. "Would you share?"

Standing just behind Jophiel, Uriel chuckled as he spoke. "Greetings, Jotnar. How have you been?"

"Fine, fine. Just fine," Jotnar replied. "I'm not sure I'm important enough for a visit from two such powerful warriors. The king must have something afoot, for a worthless creature like me to be receiving the likes of you two."

Jophiel smiled. The only way to deal with a troll was to appeal to their insecurity and sense of insignificance. He and Uriel knew this chieftain only too well.

"I brought you a gift from the King," he said.

"A present?" the Troll exclaimed. "For me?" The chieftain began clapping his hands like a small child.

Drawing a bag of golden ducats from his pocket, Jophiel placed it in Jotnar's hand. "This is to repay you for any trouble we might cause you this evening. We are completing a rescue mission for the King, and must use your Great Bridge."

Jotnar's chest puffed just a little with pride when he heard the term "*your* Great Bridge." He responded.

"Yes, too bad the Queen and Sausmas don't see it that way. I'm sure they will seek to stop you. How many are in your party?"

Uriel answered. "We have five wagons and several children in our party.

"How many Knights?" the troll chieftain asked suspiciously.

Jophiel smiled. "Probably not enough to get through the Queen's Shades and Weavers. Could you help us? We know how well your army can fight."

"What is in it for me, if I help you?" Jotnar wanted to know. "Somehow, I think a sack of golden ducats won't begin to cover the price my men will have to pay if a group this important to the king makes it over my bridge."

"*If?*" Uriel repeated, laughing. "You yourself have warred against us. Do you want to fight *with* us, or *against* us?"

Jotnar was silent.

Uriel continued. "The King says that I should offer you his assistance and protection the next time you are in conflict with Queen Souhaites or Sausmas. He asks only that you recognize him as your King, and say the same to those in your realm."

"He is asking for what he already has," Jotnar replied. "Of course, we are loyal to Suzerain." He called for his attendant. "Of course we will help you tonight. You will have safe passage across the Great Bridge. And, in addition, as a show of goodwill towards the King, I will assign a company of my men to ambush your enemy."

237

"Thank you," Jophiel reached his hand out in agreement. The chieftain took his hand and smiled his toothy grin.

A half-hour later, Jophiel and Uriel materialized at the wagon camp.

Approximately fifty miles from the town of Sorrettu, four hooded riders were headed due west. They had slipped out of town under cover of darkness the night before. Through the darkest hours of the night, progress had been made across the landscape. As morning dawned, they had stopped at a small cottage in the woods for breakfast.

Three days prior, Nathan the baker had hidden Ellie and Princess Karaliene in the spare room of his daughter, Ingrid's home. Ingrid and her family ran a small farm just outside the Sorrettu city gates. Ingrid's husband, Jamison, was out of town at the moment, servicing fruit and vegetable suppliers in the market stands of several local villages.

In his absence, Ingrid had made Ellie and Karaliene very comfortable. She had fed them, and had taken care to help them rest. Both girls had stayed inside the house to ensure their safety, sleeping more hours at a time than they had ever done before.

On the day they were to leave for the Refuge Site, Nathan had arrived at Ingrid's home in the late afternoon, carrying bread and pastries as he usually did in the midweek. Close to dusk, Nathan's son, Daniel, also arrived for a weekly dinner. It had been a wonderfully enjoyable evening for all of them. The grandchildren looked forward to Nathan's visits each week. For them, a few extra guests meant dinner had become a party. Adding to the festivities, Nathan had brought a birthday cake for Karaliene.

"Surprise!" everyone had shouted.

"For me?" the little girl had exclaimed, jumping up and down, in excitement. "I thought I wasn't getting a party! Thank you! Thank you!"

Earlier that day, Ingrid had purchased several gifts for Karaliene when finishing her shopping in town. It was tremendous, she realized; Jamison had set up a bartering system with the merchants they serviced, trading farm-grown foods for what they needed. In this way, they avoided the lead-based sickness inflicting many in the town of Sorrettu.

Nathan and Ingrid had loaded food and water to take them through the next day. Nathan had laughed out loud packing the saddlebags. He had made it a point to also leave room for what was left of the birthday cake.

"Outdoor riding makes me more hungry than usual," he told the girls.

"Is all of this for *you*, then?" Ingrid had teased him.

"It most certainly is," her father had answered, with a twinkle in his eye. He had looked at Karaliene. "I might even eat *all* the birthday cake!"

Karaliene had never been exposed to teasing in a loving relationship before. Something inside of her told her it was safe to laugh. For a moment, she stood still, unsure of what to say or do. Then, suddenly, she joined in.

"But it's *my* cake!" she pointed out. "I don't think *you* should have *any*."

Nathan laughed good-naturedly and looked at her with a fake pout. "Oh, princess, please," he begged. "I *love* cake. Just look at me!"

At that the entire party burst into laughter.

As they had departed from Ingrid's home, Nathan pulled his daughter aside. "Here," he said, placing two golden ducats in her hand.

His daughter's eyes grew wide. "Father, where....?" she began.

Nathan touched his finger to his lips. "Shh, now," he whispered. "The King knows and sent provisions for us. Pay your taxes."

Tears filled Ingrid's eyes as she considered the miracle she was experiencing. Her hand went to her mouth. "Oh..." was all she could say.

"And get something for the little ones from me," her father said.

"I will," his daughter replied. "Jamison will be so relieved."

"Be safe, and be well." Nathan had repeated the traditional family parting statement as he mounted his horse for the long ride.

"Be safe and be well," She had responded.

Karaliene had never observed such behavior.

Why are they so nice to each other, she wondered?

Carrying the warmth of the prior evening in her memory, Princess Karaliene found herself nodding off. Finally, giving in, she rested her head against her mare's mane. Beside her, Nathan's horse kept stride.

Behind them, Daniel and Ellie rode side by side.

Looking over at Karaliene, the baker assessed her condition, and raised his right hand, signifying a stop was in order. A few moments later, they had all dismounted.

"What is it?" Ellie asked, concerned. "Is something wrong?"

"Not in the manner you might think," Nathan responded, standing next to Karaliene's horse to help the child down. "It's the little princess."

"Did I do something wrong?" the child asked. "I'm sorry."

Nathan stroked her hair, smiling. "No, little one," he said. "But you look very tired once more."

"I couldn't sleep at all last night," she answered. "I was falling asleep on my horse."

"That's what I thought was happening," he said quietly. Then, like a grandfather, he bent down to Karaliene's level, his voice brightening. "I tell you what..."

"What?" Ellie responded.

"Let's rest the horses here, in case we need them for a hard ride later. Let's eat a little something to keep our strength up, and then, if Karaliene is still tired, she can ride with me, and I will tether her mare to mine. That way we will continue on."

"Come to think of it, I'm a little tired myself," Daniel rejoined. "I think that is a splendid idea."

So, after an early lunch of fruit, bread, cheese and fresh well water drawn from Ingrid's well, they readied themselves to ride once more. Just before mounting, Nathan cut an apple in four pieces. Moving from one horse to another, he gave each one a quarter he had cut, placing the apple piece in his open hand, cupping the horse's mouth.

"What are you doing?" Karaliene asked as she watched each animal draw the treat into its mouth with its lips, and then chew it well.

"I'm rewarding them for being good horses," Nathan told her. "*We* can drink from our water-skins, but they have *no* water here. A little taste of something sweet tells them we care about them. It also encourages them."

This was a new concept for Karaliene. She had always tried to behave well in order to avoid her mother's anger, or Myra's criticism, or worse.

"You're nice, Nathan," she said directly. "I like you."

"Thank you, your majesty," he replied, brushing his hands on his pants. "I like you too."

With that, he scooped the little girl up and set her on his stallion. He unlatched his bedroll from behind the saddle, and tied it to the front of the saddle, using his stallion's belly-strap for connection. Then, after tethering her mare behind his own, he then prepped to ride behind her.

"Nathan?" she asked, as they settled into the saddle. "The next time we stop, can I have birthday cake?"

"Absolutely, little one," he answered gently. "We could have it now, but if we do, the sweetness will make you thirsty. There is only so much water to go around on our journey."

"Then I can wait," she told him with a yawn.

"Good girl," he said. "Why don't you take this time to rest, now?"

Rubbing her eyes, the child nodded and once again rested her head. This time, however, her head rested against Nathan's bedroll. "This is a good pillow," she told him. "Thank you ever so much."

Riding on his horse behind Nathan, Daniel looked up at the sun, evaluating the time and distance remaining in their voyage.

"What are you doing?" Ellie asked.

"I'm looking at the sun's journey across the sky, to see how much time we have left before we must be at the Refuge Site," he told her.

"How do you do that?" she wanted to know.

And so began a discussion about how to tell time without a sundial. Ellie was captivated by what she was learning. They talked for some time.

Approaching late afternoon, they came to a fork in the road they were travelling on. Just in front of an immense oak tree, the path divided, going into two different directions.

"Where do these roads go?" Ellie asked Daniel.

"The road to the left will take a traveler to the Great Bridge, which crosses over the territory of Shame's Stronghold. The one on the right is our road. It will take us into the woods." He looked up at the sky once more. "We have another couple of hours at the most," he said to himself.

"Pater?" he called to his father, using a childhood nickname. "We need to hurry."

Ahead of him, Nathan nodded.

"Why do we need to hurry, Daniel?" Ellie asked.

"It is easier to protect you both during the day than it is at night," Daniel explained as a matter-of-fact. "We must get you girls to the Refuge Site before nightfall."

"What will happen if we don't make it?" she inquired.

"Oh, we will make it," came the reply, "even if we have to ride at a hard gallop."

Silently, Ellie considered this. The memory of the battle in the castle's tunnel just a few nights prior was still very vivid in her mind. Could these men protect her and the princess from *Shades*, or *Weavers?* Could m*ortals* do battle, warring like Jophiel or the Life-Guardians? She doubted it. And what if there were *more* Shades and Weavers than even their Guardians could fend off? What would happen then?

"Are you afraid, Daniel?" she asked.

"Me?" he responded. "Perhaps a little. But I have learned over time not to let it rule me. A *little* fear reminds me be careful and take wiser steps." He looked at the young nursemaid.

"I know you have seen a lot happen in the past few days," he continued. "Please don't worry, Ellie. The King has given us specific instructions. He has foreseen *everything* we will face."

"Oh," was all Ellie could say.

Almost immediately after taking the fork in the road to the right, the foursome changed in formation from two by two, to single file. The road had become a path, and was much narrower. Nathan took the lead, with Karaliene's horse tethered behind him. Ellie followed the unoccupied mare, with Daniel bringing up the rear.

Almost one mile into the forest, after multiple unexpected twists and turns in the path, they came to a clearing. In the center of the clearing was a charming cottage, covered with ivy. If she hadn't been looking for it, Ellie decided, she would never have seen it. It blended in so well with its setting, a person could be standing in front of it, and never realize what they were looking at.

"How clever!" she said to Daniel. "What place is this?"

"Welcome to my home!" he replied.

"Really?" she asked, amazed.

Jumping off his horse, Daniel landed on his feet, and came towards her. "Come on in and see it!" he invited. "We have to change our horses here."

"I have to leave Blackie?" she asked. "But she's my favorite horse of all time. She's been my *only* horse!"

"I'm sorry, Ellie," he answered. "I should have told you. If you, or Kara, keep either one of the horses, it will make it easier for the Queen to find you. Someone could recognize the horse as belonging to the Castle stables."

Her feet on the ground, Ellie looked up at this kind man who had helped to rescue her. So much had happened in the last week. Suddenly, she felt overwhelmed. Tears began to trickle down her cheeks.

"I understand," she said. Reaching out to touch the strong muscles in her horse's neck, she ran her hand along the smoothness of the mare's skin. She took the reins and drew Blackie's head down close to her own. "You've always been a good girl," she said to the horse. "I will miss you."

She looked up at Daniel. "Will she be safe?"

He smiled. "It's what we do. She will be *very* safe," he said. "I am sure of that."

Behind her, Nathan was dismounting his horse, and helping Karaliene down from her resting place.

"It will be all right, Ellie," he told her. "And who knows, you might meet up with her again. We told King Suzerain we would keep you safe, and we intend to keep that promise."

"I do appreciate that," Ellie told him. "It's just that Blackie was the first gift I received when I came to the summer castle. I needed a mount to ride next to the baby's wagon, coming through the western kingdom. I remember when the Queen gave her to me. Blackie was only a yearling then."

Nathan stood beside her, and began unloading the saddle bags. "Saying goodbye to something we wish we could onto is very hard indeed," he said.

After unstrapping the saddle from her mare, the older man used the saddle blanket to rub the horse's back down. As he did, he continued his conversation. "Can you understand why it is dangerous to keep her?" he asked.

"I can," Ellie answered. "And I have decided these past two days that I don't really want anything that will tie me to Souhaites. She is an evil woman."

Nathan's eyebrows went up. "She is more than that," he answered. "And you are very wise to discern what you have."

"I don't know," she said. "I just never understood why she didn't want to spend time with Karaliene. Kara's such a sweet little thing. And there was something in her eyes that scared me sometimes. But I never knew why I was afraid, or what it was exactly."

"You *will* know in time," Nathan told her. "All lessons will unfold themselves. Just stay on the path you are on now."

Ellie thought about what he was saying for a moment. Silence sat between them. "What path has Daniel been on?" she wanted to know. "Is he married?"

Nathan chuckled. "You are very perceptive for someone so young, Ellie," he said. "Be careful lest your curiosity and awareness get you into deeper trouble than you are ready to handle."

"I didn't mean to pry," she said. "He's just been so kind to me."

"He is almost thirty years old," Nathan replied. "He *was* married, but the Queen sent his wife into exile to the Borderlands. They had two sons, who starved to death when their mouths were sealed."

"Mouths were sealed?" Ellie repeated, inquiring.

"Yes," Nathan told her. "There are laws about raising boys in Hausse. Souhaites does not want to be contradicted by anyone, especially by a man. So, when a boy is born, she requires the family to agree to enter their son into what she calls 'leadership training.' She tells parents that their sons need to experience abandonment and rejection in order to become leaders. Fathers are told to be harsh, and punish their boys for crying, or for asking questions. Mothers are told to ignore their sons, and treat them unkindly. She says this will toughen boys into leaders."

"Does it work?" Ellie asked.

"No, it doesn't work at all," Nathan answered. "By the time a boy reaches five or six here in Hausse, his parents have blamed the Queen for causing distance in their relationship with their son. Those who tell the boy the truth, cause the boy to repeat what has been said in the home about the Queen. She has agents everywhere, who reinforce her rule in the villages. She calls them 'regents.'

"She used to just execute everyone who disagreed with her, and then she discovered she needed slaves to do her dirty work. Now, when her authority is questioned, she summons the boy and his family to the winter castle. No one who has gone through her punishment there is allowed to talk about it, but when a family returns from their audience with her, the wife has become bitter and hard. The husband is angry, and loses his temper easily. The son's mouth has been sealed. He cannot eat, drink, or speak."

"But what do the little boys *do*? Aren't they thirsty?" Ellie exclaimed.

"I'm sure they are, little one. Apparently, she gives each one a special medicine before she closes their lips, to slow the digestive system, and the progression of starvation."

"I wonder if that is why the Queen wouldn't allow us to leave the island," the nursemaid said. "She would never allow Kara to ask questions."

Nathan smiled at her use of the child's nickname. "I don't know why that would have been, child," he answered. "All I know is what happened to my grandsons, and to my daughter-in-law."

"The boys starved to death?"

Nathan stopped rubbing the horse down to look at her. For a fleeting moment, a shadow of sadness moved across his face.

"They did. We watched them waste away. And there was nothing we could do. I had never realized how evil she was until the day I held my grandson in my arms and watched him breathe his last breath."

Ellie's eyes grew wide. "You did?"

"Yes, I did," Nathan replied grimly.

"What did you do?" she wanted to know.

"Well, Ingrid is my oldest *daughter*. She is just a few years younger than Daniel," he told her. Remember, you stayed at her house?"

Ellie nodded.

"Well, her husband's name is Jamison. To help you understand, I need to tell you a little of *his* story."

He took a deep breath.

"When Jamison was little, his family took asylum in one of King Suzerain's Protectorate Areas. As he grew, Jamison completed all of the Discovery Seasons to ready him for development as a knight. When he graduated, he wanted to leave the Protectorate Area he was in, and begin to work in rescuing those dying in the Kingdom of Hausse. It is very dangerous work. If Queen Souhaites discovers what he is doing, he can be imprisoned or executed.

"Jamison had just *met* Ingrid back then. They weren't married yet, but he trusted us. He was part of a group called a Hidden Well Community. They helped us escape from Hausse, and hide in a Protectorate. It was several years before we were ready to, or even wanted to, come back and help Jamison in his work.

"Daniel has found great joy helping other families to save the lives of their sons. As far as the Queen knows, he was dead long ago; by the hands of one of her Shades. So it is vital that he remains hidden. Keeping the secret helps keep what he is doing in rescue work to be successful."

"I see," Ellie answered. "Is he a knight too?"

"You cannot serve as an agent for Suzerain without becoming at least a Knight Second Class," Nathan explained. "We all are."

"Are there *girl* knights?" she wanted to know.

"Absolutely," the baker responded. "They are called 'Chevaliesse.'"

At that moment, Daniel poked his head out the front door of the cottage. "Are you coming in?" he asked. "Karaliene and I have decided we need to finish eating the birthday cake before we finish our journey."

Little Karaliene stepped out onto the cottage porch. "Yes, you'd better come now," she teased, with her hands on her hips. "I might just eat the whole thing all by myself!"

"Okay, okay!" Nathan told her. "We'll be right there!"

To Ellie he said, "Let us put the horses in the back."

Questioningly, she looked at him. "In the back?"

"Follow me," he said.

Taking two of the horses by their reins, he handed them to Ellie. Taking the other two horses himself, he walked towards one of the cottage walls covered with ivy. From his pocket, he drew a large skeleton key. Then, feeling along the wall, he found a door, which he unlocked. Leading Ellie through the door, he closed it behind them.

"I'll be right back," he told her.

Ducking out the door once again to the front of the cottage, Nathan retrieved the saddle and blanket he had removed from Blackie's back earlier. He then relocked the gate.

Looking around, Ellie was amazed. Inside what appeared to be the walls of a large cottage was a vast compound. All around its perimeter were stone walls, covered with ivy. Inside the walls three buildings existed: a stable, a house, and a greenhouse. In the center of the courtyard, a private well yielded a bucket attached to a long rope. Next to the well was an outdoor oven and fire-pit for cooking.

"Let's take them into the stable," Nathan instructed.

Ellie followed him into the low-roofed structure, and discovered eight stalls. Working quickly, she settled Blackie into a stall, filling her water trough, and refreshing her alfalfa hay. Then she did the same for Karaliene's mare.

As she finished, Nathan came out of another stall. "You're quick, lass," he declared. "If I didn't know better, I'd think you'd kept horses for a living."

Ellie laughed. "Kara and I spent a lot of time riding, and helping take care of the castle horses. I love these animals."

"Me too," the baker told her. He paused. "Why don't we go in and have some cake? We will have to get going again soon."

"Sounds good to me!" Ellie replied, closing the stall doors.

Together, they walked into the cottage.

Chapter Twelve
Stirring of the Pot

Pimedus stood on the parapet of the tallest tower in the summer castle. He stood with his arm bent at the elbow, in a somewhat enlarged state. An owl called Legion perched on his elbow.

"The princess and her nursemaid must be returned here before Souhaites returns," the Shade was instructing the bird. "They escaped through the tunnel, so look for them in the town, Sorrettu, just over the water. If they get to the King's Realm, there will be no chance of my stabilizing my status with the Queen."

"I am aware," replied the owl, in a throaty tone. "*If* the princess is alive, and I find them, whom should I return; the princess or the nursemaid? I will only be able to carry one at a time."

Pimedus growled. "If she is dead, I want proof. Either way, you must bring be some sign of your discovery."

The owl dug its talons into his arm. "And if she is alive?"

His fears triggered, the Shade shouted back at Legion. "What do *you* think, *imbecile?* Everything must be as it was when the Queen returns! It will not be enough to have just *one* of them." He paused. "But, if you must choose, bring the princess back first."

"I will do as you bid me for only a short season more of days," the owl replied. "And then...." Moving its giant wings back and forth, the bird rose into the air, disappearing into the dark night sky.

Pimedus shuddered a little, watching the great bird ascend out of sight. As he did so, he muttered to himself under his breath. "I will have to find the spell I need to control that creature."

As he thought about the owl, the Shade was unaware of a recently materialized presence behind him, waiting and watching him in the shadows. When a deep bass voice spoke, it startled him.

"What *adventures* have you been pursuing in the Queen's absence, that you have gained the assistance of Legion?"

Shaking, Pimedus turned around to face Betruger, another Python, who was Souhaites current spirit advisor.

"I-I summoned him," he admitted. "I am working on something for the Queen."

"*Really,* now," cooed Betruger. "That's strange, Pimedus, because she sent me to *find* you."

Nervously, the Shade faked a laugh. "I can't imagine why."

The Specter's voice became even colder in tone.

"It might have *something* to do with reports she has received. Or, the fact that you are *not maintaining your station* at the summer castle in her absence."

"Oh, there is that," Pimedus shrugged, in a manner he hoped was nonchalant.

"Let's go and see her now, shall we?" Betruger hissed, placing his large claws on the Shade's shoulders and lifting him up off the ground. Together the two of them dematerialized, in transport to Queen Souhaites' audience chamber.

Upon re-entry, the Specter threw Pimedus to the stone floor, as his claws released their hold. The Shade rolled head over heels, stopping with no little force against the foot of Souhaites' throne.

Humiliated, Pimedus realized where he was. Standing quickly, seeking to regain his composure, he straightened his black sheath. But as he looked around the room, he realized there would be nothing he could do to appeal his fate, or explain his position.

Seated next to Souhaites, was the Python who had banished him to the Borderlands. *Seated* in the Queen's presence, was Enki.

Just outside the courtyard of Daniel's cottage in the midst of the forest, four horses stood still, waiting for the cottage owner to secure the gate. As he did so, Nathan was speaking to the girls.

"We have just two hours to go," the baker told them. "Once we get to the Refuge Site, you will be safe. However, it is possible we will encounter some opposition on our way. It is important we all keep our hoods up over our heads, so that we are not recognized. If we *do* have to ride hard, do you feel secure to do so?"

Ellie looked at Karaliene. "Do you remember how to gallop?"

The princess nodded excitedly. "I love to!"

The nursemaid smiled. "Can you keep stride with me?"

"I think so," the little girl replied.

Daniel stepped up into his stirrup, and took the saddle. "Well, let's go then," he said.

Leaving the cottage, the path was still narrow, and very dark. They rode in single file, with Daniel in the lead. At the end of the forest, the path opened out into a clearing and became wide once more. The light of a full moon lit up the sky, as well as the ground.

"How is it the sky is *clear* tonight?" Nathan noted out loud.

It was true, Ellie thought. The sky was hardly ever clear in Hausse, and yet, tonight, there were no clouds at all. Had they been back at the summer castle, she would have spent the night outdoors on the balcony, looking at the stars.

Nathan was speaking again. She shook her head. *I must pay attention.*

Speaking to the girls, he spoke softly. "Stay close, and keep your heads down. *Do NOT* look up at the sky, even if you think you hear something."

"Like what?" Karaliene wanted to know.

"Anything at all," Nathan told her intently. "If you hear noises above you, ignore them, and just ride hard to the place Daniel told you about. Don't stop for either one of us. Do you understand?"

"I do," the little princess answered. "Will you be all right?"

Nathan chuckled. "We've both made it this far! I don't *plan* to see something happen now."

Above them, a great gray shadow was criss-crossing the countryside. Alerted by the sound of horses' hooves in the cover of the forest, the owl had returned a second and third time, searching for riders exiting from the woods. At first, when *four* riders entered the clearing, the creature had decided the riders must not be his target. But then, finding no other riders, or even slightly suspicious movements coming from and around Sorrettu, he had returned to find them once more.

It would be necessary to discover whether the princess and her nursemaid were part of the party, he decided.

He would flush them out.

Just to be sure, Legion maintained a safe enough distance in his flight path, so as to be able to hear their discussions, but not be observed.

Don't talk now. Just ride silently.

Ellie and Karaliene both felt the same words being spoken inside their minds. Instinctively, they looked at each other, and then at Nathan and Daniel. The men too, were sensing something afoot. Daniel touched his forefinger to his lips; just to be sure they were all on the same page.

In the western kingdom, in the audience chamber of the winter castle, Souhaites stood from her throne, and moved to a cowering Pimedus. "So, you decided to take things into your own hands, did you?" she demanded. "What were you thinking?"

Pimedus wasn't willing to yield ground just yet. He put on the most subservient tone he could muster. "My Queen," he began. "I don't believe you have the entire picture of my efforts. Everything I have done, I have done to serve you."

Souhaites flicked her new black robe, and laughed. "Really?" she asked, throwing her head back. "Do you know the *damage* you have done?"

"Me?" the Shade was visibly amazed. "What have *I* done?" He pointed at Enki. "Why don't you ask *him* what *he* has plotted against you in your absence?"

Enki nodded solemnly. "The Queen *knows*, Pimedus. I'm afraid I had to *tell* her of your plans."

Pimedus couldn't believe what he was hearing. "Your majesty," he blurted out, "Enki is the one who has plotted to overthrow you. He is the one who has told all of your minions that Sausmas has sent him to destroy your plans. He is the one who banished me and two of your most loyal Weavers to the Borderlands. I didn't do *anything*!"

The Queen moved to Enki. "Is that true?" she demanded. *"Are* you plotting against me?"

Enki smiled at her, and spoke in a soothing voice. "Souhaites, we have known each other since before time began in this miserable little kingdom. Why would I want to cause trouble with you? I *have* power. Sausmas gives me *all* I desire." He rose and came to stand by Pimedus. He pulled out a talon, and ran it through the Shade's arm.

As he continued speaking, he began twisting, and a popping sound was heard.

"*Ask* this one what he was doing in your cavern downstairs with a spell book. *Ask* him why he summoned Legion to the surface. *Ask* him where the owl is now. *Ask* him...."

The Queen's face was black with rage. "Is this true?" she pressed. "And is it true you posed as a mortal in order to poison my child?"

As his arm was twisting, Pimedus looked around the room. In the corner, Betruger sat, watching; smiling. Next to him were the two Weavers who had been banished to the Borderlands by Enki; who had followed him back.

Enki spoke. "We have *all* of you now, and we have the whole story. Don't even try to deny it, Pimedus."

He let go of the unfortunate Shade.

Lying on the ground at the Queen's feet, Pimedus gasped for breath. "My Queen," he started to say.

She placed her foot on his head, and answered. "Yes, Pimedus?"

"*Believe* me when I say that I took Myra's form to find out about the nursemaid. I wanted to gain the princess's trust in order to help strengthen your ability to gain her body as a host."

"Why should I believe you?" the Queen wanted to know.

"Because I have nothing to gain here," the Shade spoke. "But *Enki* has everything to gain. He told all of us; the Shades, the Weavers and the Muddlers, here in this castle; that we were going to replace the princess with a decoy, and deceive you for two years until your Gala Celebration. Enki said that way you would *have* no Host, and he could take your position as ruler of Hausse."

Souhaites reached out a tendril of an arm; stretching it towards Enki like a long, looping rope. Taking him by the neck, she lifted him off the ground, and brought her to face her within an inch of her face.

"*You* did this?" she screamed at him. "*You* planned this?"

In spite of his predicament, Enki smiled at her. "You have no idea, do you?" he spat at her. "You cannot hold control *forever*."

"Oh, *really*?" She hissed back. "Sausmas has full knowledge of my plans. We are in league together. We have a pact that benefits us both. You...... *you have been tested*.....and you have failed MISERABLY! Sausmas knows all about your desire to replace even *him*. So, unless you want me to *tell* him that you designed this entire plan; *and* that you are planning to sell him out to King Suzerain...."

"But that's not true!" Enki protested. "That's a lie! I might have planned revolt against *you,* but I would *never even think* of leading resistance against the Dark Prince."

"It doesn't matter what's true," the Queen threatened. "It only matters what he *believes* when I tell him."

Looking smugly around the room, she continued. "So, let me tell you what you *are all* going to do."

Not far from the Great Bridge, swampland marked the beginning of Shame's Stronghold. Paddling furiously, two tightly harnessed crocodiles pulled a small boat towards the Stream of Fear River. Holding the reins to the two reptiles was the High Assistant to the Troll Chieftain, Lord Wartall.

"Can't you pull any faster?" he demanded. "I have to get there before sunset."

The larger of the two crocodiles grunted in response. "We are pulling as fast as we can, your lordship," he grumbled. "We could go a lot faster if you weighed a little less."

Wartall sighed. He never seemed to get respect. Well, maybe it would be different after tonight.

The message had said to come alone.

As they approached the western branch of the Mortal's Folly River, Lord Wartall squinted against the sun. He scanned the far riverbank for his rendezvous point. He spoke to the crocodiles.

"We have to move further upstream before we cross," he told them. "The waters will then carry us downstream to the meeting place."

Grumbling to each other, the two reptiles made a hard right turn, and moved further north. Close to a quarter mile up, they made a hard left turn, and began to cross the river's waters. As Wartall had predicted, the quickly moving torrent carried them downstream.

"Keep paddling! Go faster!" He shouted to the crocodiles.

The two crocodiles looked at each other. "If I didn't have this harness around my snout, I think I would make *him* swim for it," the smaller one muttered.

"Mm-mm," the other one grumbled. "Let's just get this over with. We still have to take him home."

As the boat neared the water's edge, Wartall's prediction proved to be true. They were at the trysting place the message had described.

The little scroll had arrived at Jotnar's Lair some hours after the two Light-Bearers had departed. Wartall snorted to himself. He had known who they were. There had been no need for secrecy.

He was tired of feeling second class.

The crocodiles pulled the boat up onto the shore. Wartall stepped over the bow of the boat, onto the backs of the reptiles until he could stand on dry land.

As he did so, the animals grunted under his substantial weight.

Not far from where he disembarked, a shadowy figure stood waiting for him.

Looking ahead, Wartall waved.

There was no response.

No matter, the troll decided. They would discover how useful he could be. Yes, yes; that would show itself in time. He would *still* become someone important; even if he *was* a troll.

"Greetings, Lord Wartall!" the specter intoned. "I see you received my message."

Wartall was surprised. "How did you know *I* would be the one to meet you?" he asked.

"We have ways of becoming informed of everything that happens in your Stronghold," came the answer.

"Everything?" the Troll wanted to know.

"Yes, everything," the image snapped back.

"Then why am *I* here?" Wartall spoke more to himself than to his counterpart. In his simple mind, the question was an obvious one; one which he spoke before considering how it might cause him to appear to the fearsome entity he had come to meet.

The Shade snarled back at him. "Listen, you insignificant speck of slime! You will give me the information I ask for, or I will raise one talon, and send a fire-bolt through your miserable hide!"

Wartall withdrew. This was not what he expected at all. He blustered back. "Why would you treat me this way? I came to meet you in respectable confidence, and this is your response? Why, I'm tempted to just turn around and go back to Jotnar, and tell him exactly what the Queen's agents do when you trust them!"

His bluff called, Pimedus stopped in his tracks. He considered. It would not do at all for Souhaites and Enki to hear of yet another area where he had sabotaged an opportunity for their advancement. In that event, they would exile him for sure. However, his prideful nature could not simply ask this mere troll for the information. He had to gain the facts while maintaining his personal sense of superiority.

As a result, silence hung between the two of them for several extended moments.

Wartall broke the silence by turning to leave. He called for the crocodiles. "Come! We're leaving!"

Pimedus saw the opportunity to improve his situation slipping from his hands. "Your Lordship, now don't be like that," he soothed. "We can work this out!"

Wartall looked at him evenly. "I may be a troll, but I am not stupid. You need me, and you need what I know. If you kill me, I am of no use to you. Now, do you want to continue playing your game of cat and mouse, or do you want to do business?"

The troll's response was so unexpected; Pimedus was caught off-guard. He burst into a cackling screech. "You are someone to be reckoned with Wartall," he said, slapping the creature on his back. "All right then. The Queen and her consort, Enki, need to know of any unusual movements made by the Suzerain or his agents over the next few days."

Wartall's eyes widened. "Does *today* count?"

The Shade's interest piqued. "Something happened today?"

The Troll rolled his eyes. The next time he spoke, his words dripped with sarcasm. "No, I just said it because I was trying to make conversation. Of course, something happened today!"

"Don't try me," Pimedus warned. "Go on."

"Today, Chief Jotnar received two guests who looked like mortals, but they weren't mortals. No mortals ever make it far enough into the Stronghold to get to the Chieftain's Lair. They are captured first."

"So where *did* they come from?" Pimedus inquired.

"I'm not sure," Wartall explained. "I think they were Light-Bearers. Jotnar knew one of them for sure, and the other thought he had fought with the Chieftain at some point."

"What did they want?" the Shade pressed.

"Safe passage over the Bridge," Wartall shrugged. "I didn't hear when it would be, but it will be in the next day or so."

"Why do they need safe passage? What is their mission?"

Wartall looked at him. "I don't know, actually."

Pimedus patted him. "Okay then," he said soothingly. "Just keep your eyes open, and we will get in contact again. You can send a messenger to me if you discover anything new."

Wartall nodded, and turned. Moving slowly in the dimness of dusk, he made his way back to the boat.

"Did everything go well, milord?" the larger crocodile asked.

"Oh, yes, yes," the troll babbled. "Just as I expected."

"We heard you call us," the smaller one spoke up.

"Oh, it was nothing; nothing at all," Wartall answered somewhat absent-mindedly. "Let's go back home, now."

Boarding his small boat, he sat down as the reptiles pushed out into deeper water, once more crossing the Stream of Fear.

Standing on the riverbank, watching him pull away, Pimedus was deep in thought.

The Light-Bearers were working together now, were they? What party of mortals could possibly need safe passage over the Bridge, and require the support of the trolls?

It must be an important mission indeed.....

Raising his sheath around his head, he dematerialized. This piece of the puzzle was something the Queen would want to know immediately.

On the other side of the Mortal's Folly River, some twenty miles upstream, Nathan's party of four riders had emerged from the woods.

"It's beginning to get dark, now," Nathan spoke over his shoulder. "We need to get a move on."

"How far away are we?" Ellie asked.

"Where are we going?" Karaliene wanted to know.

Nathan smiled. "We are going to a safe place. It is about ten or fifteen miles from here; perhaps a little less."

"How will we know when we get there?" Karaliene asked.

"Just stay close to me," Nathan whispered. "We need to be quiet now."

But it was too late for silence.

Above them, the owl named Legion had overheard their conversation. Just as Nathan finished his last sentence, the enormous bird swooped in over them, just missing the top of Daniel's head with his talons.

Surprised, Karaliene shrieked in fear.

"Quickly," Daniel shouted, "keep your hoods up. And let's ride!"

Spurring the sides of his horse, Daniel took the lead, as all four of the riders broke into a gallop.

"We will need to make a run for it now," he told them. "Hang on tight!"

Realizing he had failed in his attempt to discover the riders' identities, Legion rose up into the sky. He spiraled up and up, gaining altitude. He would need the height in order to gain speed. As the bird reached its apex, it let out a deafening scream, the sound of which sent chills up and down Ellie's spine.

The four stiffened themselves against a second aerial attack. But none came. At least not right away.

But then, without warning, the second wave began.

Out of the woods behind them, came a swirling cloud of bats. Suddenly, Nathan, Daniel, Ellie, and Karaliene were engulfed inside the movement of hundreds of bats. As they galloped ahead, the bats pursued them; each one making unearthly sounds. As the cloud enveloped the four of them, it became clear all of the bats had the same task in mind.

"Hold your hoods on!" Daniel yelled, as two bats landed on his head, and began biting at his cloak's hood to pull it back from his face.

"Go away!" Karaliene screamed at the four perching on her shoulders, also working to pull her hood back. "Ellie, help me!"

But Ellie was in the midst of a skirmish of her own. Not only were there bats working to remove her hood from her face as she rode, but there were also bats opening her saddle bags.

"What are they looking for?" she asked Daniel.

"They are on a mission of sorts, I think," he responded, as he swatted at a bat too near his face, sending it flying up into the hemisphere.

Watching his response to the little creatures, Ellie began swatting at those attacking her as well. She also experienced success in whacking a few away.

Then, just as suddenly as the attack had begun, it lessened. The bats began to withdraw, as if on cue, all at once; leaving the four to continue their ride. As the last bat lifted from Nathan's head, Daniel pulled the horses to a stop.

"Are you all right?" he asked, first Karaliene and then Ellie.

Breathless, they nodded.

"I've never been in anything like that before," Ellie stated. "What was it?"

As soon as they came to a halt, Nathan dismounted, and checked the horse's hooves. Coming around the back of her horse, he touched Ellie on her leg to get her attention. He then pointed behind them.

Silently, they all turned to look where he was pointing. And there, not fifteen feet from where they were, was an immense gray owl. Looking at it, Ellie noted there was nothing particularly distinguishing about it, other than its size... and perhaps.... perhaps its eyes.

Yes, its eyes. They glowed red, as though some strange fire had lit them from within.

Without a sound, the great gray bird opened its wings. Then moving them back and forth, it rose into the sky, and turned to cross the river. Unconsciously, the four of them watched until it disappeared into the far horizon.

It was Daniel who broke the silence. "Let's get going now," he said, "before it comes back."

"What was that?" Karaliene asked.

"Did the bats come from the owl?" Ellie wondered out loud.

"I think so," Nathan responded. "Whatever it was, it was on a mission for the Queen, and it has seen our faces." He rose into his mount, and clicked to his stallion to get a move on.

Daniel followed suit, as did Ellie and Karaliene. Before long, they were once again in the midst of a galloping ride to the Refuge Site.

"Is it much farther?" Karaliene asked.

"We are only a few more minutes closer than the last time you asked me," Nathan laughed out loud. "Don't worry. We'll be there soon."

In the audience room of the winter castle, Souhaites paced back and forth. Enki had just returned from the lower caverns of the fortress.

"Did they know anything?" she asked him.

Enki muttered in disgusted response. "No… Pimedus was very clever. He kept his plans hidden, even from these two Weavers here. I'm not even sure, listening to all of them, that he even had a plan to begin with."

"I see," the Queen replied.

At that moment, the movement of great wings was heard on the balcony. Souhaites stepped outside to investigate. She was met by a great gray owl.

"Good evening, my Queen," the owl spoke. "We are glad to see you once more."

"Good evening, Legion," she replied with austere reserve. "What is your mission?"

"Your Shade, Pimedus, summoned me from the netherworld," the owl answered. "It is my mission to find your princess and her nursemaid. I am to return them to the summer castle before your return there."

Souhaites laughed. "I have *heard* that was your mission. However," she spoke conspiratorially, "when your period of servitude is completed, I have a new mission to suggest to you." She straightened. "What did you discover?"

"I have returned to report to Pimedus that I have found them. They are in the company of two men, on the other side of Mortal's Folly. They are near the three hills."

Souhaites was pensive. "So she *is* alive.... She had help, that little one. They are headed to Suzerain's Refuge Site."

"Do you know where it is?" the owl asked.

"I have an idea, but I have never been able to discover its pinpointed location. It has been hidden from us since Time began," she answered. "Legion, they must be stopped. If they reach the Refuge Site, I will never have access to either of those girls again. There is too much time invested for this to fall apart."

She moved back inside, followed by the owl. She spoke to Enki.

"We must rally what troops we can assemble immediately, and materialize by the Great Bridge."

She looked at Enki. "It is time for our plan to be put to use. It appears we are about to lose a princess."

She called for a sentry and passed the news. They would leave within the hour.

When Pimedus returned to the castle, materializing just inside the gate, he noted the hustle and bustle within the castle grounds. "What is going on?" he asked one of the sentries.

"The Queen has decided to leave for the summer castle tonight. We are to travel within the hour."

The owl must have found them, Pimedus concluded. He headed to the audience chamber.

"My Queen," he greeted Souhaites as he entered the room. "I have news. We now have an alliance within the Troll Stronghold; one I hope to draw upon the future."

The Queen sat down once more and looked at Pimedus. "So you had success then. What did you ascertain?"

Pimedus paused for effect. "The troll with whom I have an understanding with is Lord Wartall, High Assistant to Chief Jotnar. He says that Jotnar received two Light-Bearers as guests just this afternoon. They were disguised as mortals, but he could tell who they were."

Souhaites smiled tightly. "Interesting…. What did they want with Jotnar?"

"You will find this thought-provoking indeed, my Queen. They paid for troll protection and assistance in getting over the Great Bridge," the Shade responded.

Souhaites looked at Enki.

Enki looked at Souhaites.

"Didn't the owl tell us that Karaliene and Ellie were on the *other* side of the Mortal's Folly River? Then *who* is with the Light-Bearers? Why do *they* need more than one Light-Bearer? Is this the gypsy caravan the Weavers mentioned?"

Pimedus interjected. "Your majesty, if I may be so bold…" he began.

"Yes, yes, Pimedus," Souhaites motioned with her hand. "Out with it."

"What if there are actually *two missions*? What *if* they are to combine into one greater purpose *after* the wagons cross the Great Bridge?"

Enki had been sitting silently, taking in the spoken disclosures of the recent moments. Now he stood, and began to speak.

"Souhaites, do you remember the day you gave birth to the princess?"

The Queen nodded.

"Do you remember giving birth to twins?"

"Yes. Yes," she answered, impatience surfacing in her answers. "What is your point?"

"Is it possible……." Enki paused, contemplating what he was about to suggest.

"Didn't you instruct Elda to destroy the man-child?"

"Yes, I did. And yes, *she* did," the Queen answered. "That was why I trusted her with Karaliene. She was young enough to do exactly what I asked her to do without question."

"But let's say… What *if*….." Enki paused. "What if she *didn't* destroy the man-child? What if she conspired in some way to help him *live?* The winter castle is close enough to a Protectorate Area…." He let his voice trail off.

Souhaites' face began to pale. "You mean *you* think the *man*-child is still alive? Are you thinking he might be in the *gypsy* wagons? Are they intending to meet at the Refuge Site with *both* of them? *Together?*"

Enki shrugged. "It makes sense to me."

"Then we must leave at once!" came the reply. "If they reach Suzerain's Realm …. They have to be stopped!" She stood to her feet.

The Python smiled. "Let me suggest that we also set up an ambush against them, in case this stage might fail?"

The Queen flicked her black cloak, considering his suggestion. "We *won't* fail!" She looked at him. "But if couldn't hurt to be prepared."

"Then I will go and make those preparations," Enki declared.

"No, you won't," Souhaites countered. "I need you with me. *Remember?*"

Pimedus spoke up. "I will go for you, my Queen," he offered.

Souhaites smiled. "Yes, Pimedus, I think you will do nicely. You will take Betruger with you, to ensure your success."

Betruger emerged from the shadows. "I will see to it, your Majesty."

Chapter Thirteen
Time for a Shield

Emerging from the trees, Tividar and Peyton approached the Romani wagon camp with their third set of sticks and firewood for the fire. They then went to work digging a small fire-pit, preparing to set a cooking fire.

It had been less than an hour since Jaret and Ramon had returned from hunting, with several rabbits. The two of them had also discovered a small stream of water. It flowed through the forest, well hidden from anyone's sight, near the Mortal's Folly River's edge.

Seeing the rabbits, Pythia and Shyla had immediately gone to work cleaning them, preparing a stew for dinner. Panna and Galen had taken the children to draw water for cooking, as well as to forage for berries, or other wild fruits that might be available in the forest as well.

"We still have a few potatoes, and a little cabbage," Pythia told them. "There is also a little bread left from yesterday. We should be able to feed everyone one good meal before we cross the bridge."

Hearing her, Uriel nodded.

"We all should probably eat a good meal before we deploy," Uriel agreed. "Each of you will need all of your strength, as well as all of your senses, to be alert, and ready for the journey."

Upon their return from meeting with Troll Chieftain Jotnar in Shame's Stronghold, Jophiel, Uriel and Tvirtas had taken a walk in the woods. They were devising strategy for the Romani family's crossing a little later that day. Not far from where the children were foraging for berries, Jophiel discovered a crop of giant morel mushrooms. Cutting one down at its base, he called Jayden and Jowan to where he was standing.

"Wow!" Jayden exclaimed. "What is that? It's awesome!"

Jophiel smiled. "It's a morel mushroom. It will take both of you to carry it. Would you boys take this back to Pythia, please, and tell her that I suggested she cut it into slices for dinner? She can steam this, and use the slices for plates this afternoon, instead of using dishes."

"Great idea!" Jayden responded. The boys took eagerly to the task.

Adjacent to the wild mushroom crop, were several large boulders, lodged in the ground. "Let's sit here to talk," Uriel suggested. "We'll be out of earshot."

Back at the camp, Ramon was taking time to prepare the three younger boys for what they might encounter during the Bridge crossing in a few hours.

"You will need to have your swords at the ready," he told them.

Tividar nodded. "I have my armor, and have completed my training," he responded. "I am concerned for Peyton and Jaret, though. Will they have enough protection, still being new students in Discovery Season One?

Ramon smiled in response. "Don't worry, Tividar. It's honorable you are concerned for them. Tvirtas and I will be are arming each of them before we deploy for action." He looked at Peyton and Jaret. "We will be drilling with swords in the woods today. And Uriel has asked us to outfit you with shields as well."

At this, Peyton and Jaret brightened. How they had come to be included in the mission, they didn't know, but both were eager for the opportunity and the experience.

"What kind of shields, Ramon?" Peyton wanted to know. "Will they be like the one in the painting in Initiate's Hall?"

Ramon considered him. "You mean the Knight's shield with the four images and the wheel of eyes?"

"Yes, that one! Do we get shields like that?" the cadet inquired.

The older knight smiled at him. "The emblems on a knight's shield are added through his or her experiences. The shield in the painting is the shield of the highest order of the Dragon's Cross. Your father carries a shield like that one into battle, I believe."

"He does?" Peyton asked.

"Haven't you ever seen it?" Jaret asked.

"I've never been in a battle with him before," Peyton answered. "In fact, I'm not sure that he ever needed to use it while I was growing up in Area One."

Ramon smiled. "He probably *did* use it, when he was away from home on missions like this one. You have not been old enough to understand what was happening until now." He paused. "This is your first mission, isn't it?"

Peyton and Jaret looked at each other. "Well," Jaret replied, "there *was one time* five years ago or so, when we completed a mission for Commander Carel."

"When you were *boys*?" Ramon asked, surprised.

"Each of us was ten," Peyton began.

"My birthday came before his did. I was almost eleven years when we did the mission," Jaret interjected.

"What was the assignment?" the older knight inquired.

"I went into the Queen's winter castle," Peyton answered. "I took a package from the castle to the Commander."

"At ten…. You took a package from the Queen's winter castle to the Commander." Ramon stopped and looked at the boys. "What was your part in this mission, Jaret?"

"I waited in the woods and provided cover. We were told not to tell anyone of the mission."

"Did your father know?" this question was directed at Peyton.

"I don't know," he responded. "He must have known, or I wouldn't have been allowed to do what I did."

"Did you encounter any Shades, or Weavers, or Muddlers during your mission?"

Peyton shook his head.

"And you were *inside* the *winter* castle? You're *sure*?"

Peyton looked at him and nodded. "Is that so hard to believe?"

Ramon paused, as though weighing what he would say next.

"Peyton," he began, "did you know what was *in* the package?"

"No, not at first," Peyton answered truthfully. "I was told to go to a certain room in the castle and wait for a contact. When I got there, the room was dark. I waited a long time. I almost fell asleep, and then a girl who was a little younger than me came into the room. She said the code words I was told to wait for. And she handed me the package."

"Do you remember her name?" Ramon asked.

"Esmer.... No, that's not it." The boy racked his brain. "Eggl... no.... *Elda*! That's it! Her name was Elda!"

"How did you get *out* of the castle?" Ramon asked.

"There was a trap door in that room. It led down into a tunnel. The tunnel let out into a small covey of woods. Near where the tunnel let out there was an abandoned guard house. When I went into the guard house, there was a large basket, and a crate full of scrolls and bottles and things. I put the package in the basket, and then put as much as would fit in the basket in on top of it. Then, I got on Goliath and held the basket in front of me to ride.

"About half way to where Jaret was, I remembered Elda had told me to be very careful with the package. So, I stopped and repacked the basket, so the package would not be crushed by the contents from the crate that I had added to the basket."

Ramon was silent. "I see," he said. "When did you discover what was inside?"

"When I reached Commander Carel's Encampment, I watched him unwrap the package. He already knew what was inside."

"What *was* inside?" Jaret asked.

Peyton's voice became a whisper. "It was a baby boy. He had been born in the castle that day. The Commander couldn't tell me who the baby belonged to, but now that I know what happens to boys who live in Hausse, I understand why he was given away. They saved his life..... *we* saved his life."

"Yes, you did," Ramon replied. He motioned for the boys to sit down, and as he did, he joined them. "It is extremely important you keep what I am about to tell you a secret. It is something you are only to discuss with those of us who are also on this mission. Tonight marks the first step in our mission, and it must be seen through to the end."

Ramon paused, and waited until Peyton was looking at him. He looked the young man in the eyes and held his gaze. He continued.

"Peyton, the baby boy you rescued is my little Jayden."

Peyton's eyes grew wide. "But I thought he and Damara were twins. They look alike, at least to me."

"Yes, I know they do," Ramon answered. "I think that was part of the Suzerain's design. That day, when you brought the "package" to Carel's Encampment, I was away on a mission for the King, in one of the Coastal Protectorate Areas. I received word Shyla had given birth to twins, and I wondered about it, because she had not seemed large enough in her pregnancy to deliver twins. But, I passed it off, and accepted Jayden as my own.

"It wasn't until *this* mission, when Uriel told me to ask Shyla about my son's birth, and how it came about. She had been ordered not to tell me. But now I know, and I understand why she hid the truth from me. We would have been tempted to discuss it, and could have been overheard. It would have endangered Jayden.

"Anyway, our mission is to deliver Jayden to the Refuge Site on the other side of the River. We apparently have another mission which will be awaiting us there.

"Your task this evening is to protect the children. We are not sure how much the Queen knows of our mission, or how much has been deciphered of our purpose. You may encounter a battle, and you might not. But whatever happens, you are to protect Jayden, Jowan, Damara, and Lysandra with your own lives. We will hide them in Galen's wagon tonight.

"Tividar, it will be your assignment to protect the wagon, and fend off all attackers. *All* of us will be warring tonight."

Straightening his back from his seated position, Ramon patted his knees as he rose. "Now, let's see what's next. Are your swords strapped to you? Good. Good. Stand in a square now, and let's spar as though we are each fighting off more than one opponent. I want to show you a few things."

For the next hour or so, the two knights and two cadets practiced their sword skills. Peyton discovered his skills were close in development to Ramon, and Jaret learned several new skills with his foil. As the drills came to an end, Jayden came running into their circle.

"Mama and Pythia say dinner is ready, and to come while it's hot!" he announced.

Ramon scooped him up. "So-o, how's my son doing?" he asked.

"I'm good, Papa," the boy answered. "How're *you* doin'?"

"I'm good too." Ramon responded.

Listening to their exchange, Peyton found himself wondering what would happen to the relationship between father and son when the mission was completed.

Exiting the woods to the right of the four of them, were Uriel, Jophiel and Tvirtas. Seeing his son, the former commander made his way to Peyton.

"Come and eat with me, son," he invited. "I missed spending time with you this afternoon."

Peyton put his arm around his father. "I missed you too, Papa," he said. "I have so many more questions to ask you."

"Would you like to eat inside my wagon, where we can talk?" Tvirtas offered.

Peyton was relieved. "Yes, sir, I would."

As the Romani family prepared their plates, which tonight were made from large slabs of morel mushrooms; Peyton observed the relationship between Jayden and Damara, and between Jayden and his mother. What would the little boy do when he learned his real identity? He tried to imagine what it would be like if the situation were happening to himself. What would he think? What would he feel?

Later, in his father's wagon, Peyton found himself noticing more about his father than he ever had before. Somehow, it was as though his mind had become more aware of their situation, and surroundings.

Somehow, he felt more thankful to have been given the life he had experienced so far.

"Did your day go as it should have gone, son?" Tvirtas asked, seeking to open conversation.

"I think so," Peyton responded. "I'm not sure."

He paused. "Papa," he began, "did *you* know about Jayden's real identity?"

Tvirtas nodded.

"Why didn't you tell me?" his son asked.

"That you had rescued the Queen's son, you mean?" his father responded.

Peyton's jaw dropped open. "I didn't have that part of the story," he said.

"Well, who did you *think* had given birth in the castle, son?"

"I don't know," the boy answered. "I guess I didn't think about it until now." He thought for a second. "Why didn't you tell me?"

"Timing is everything in life, Peyton," Tvirtas responded. "If I had told you at the wrong time, it could have done damage to your soul. Now is the right time."

"Oh, I see," Peyton responded. "So then, why are there so many of us to rescue this one boy?"

"Well," his father began slowly, "we don't know how much the Queen actually knows about him. She commanded his death on the day he was born, but the informer inside the castle saved his life."

"Elda, you mean," Peyton offered.

"Yes, Elda." His father began packing his pipe.

"But she is younger than I am. How is she able to be an agent for Suzerain?"

"She is young, that is true," Tvirtas answered. "But her parents instilled an understanding of love and loyalty into her before the Queen stole her away."

"How did the Queen steal her away?" Peyton asked. "What does that *mean*?"

The former commander lit his pipe and puffed it once or twice before he answered the question.

"The best way to begin her story would be to tell you that Queen Souhaites realized that Elda's parents were loyal to Suzerain. They did not have any boys as children, and she wanted to teach them a lesson. So, she instructed the people in the town where they lived to stop hiring either one of the parents. That made it impossible for them to pay their bills, or to buy food. In addition to that, Elda's little sisters needed their mother's care during the day, and no one would help take care of them. The Queen waited until they were desperate and hungry. Elda was only about eight years old, when the Queen made an offer to give her a position serving in the castle kitchen."

"Why did they let her go?" Peyton asked.

"There wasn't another way," his father answered. "The Queen would have taken her against her will had they refused. Our Hidden Well Community in their town tried to help them as much as we could, but they refused asylum. They kept thinking things would improve."

"What happened?"

Tvirtas drew in again on his pipe. "Elda went to work in the castle kitchen. The king's agent who worked in the castle, just happened to be the Queen's head cook. He took her under his care, and had her do menial things like dishes and peel potatoes. Each night when she went home, he sent her with food for her family.

"But then, during the Queen's pregnancy, Souhaites became ill. She sent for Elda to help her. It must have been a great comfort, even for a creature like Souhaites, to have a child waiting on her needs. The Queen gave birth to twins. When Souhaites discovered there was a boy *and* a girl, she immediately ordered Elda to kill the boy.

"Can you imagine being eight years old, and being told to kill a baby? The little girl was deeply upset by the order she was given, and she went running to the cook to confide her struggle.

"The cook had been instructed that such a moment might occur. So, arrangements had been set in motion before the Queen went into labor. Commander Carel was told to stay in position until the plan was completed. We felt it would be a simpler task if a child was trusted to do the mission. And you had already developed to rapier status in your sword skills. We knew Jaret would be trustworthy, because of his responses to the disclosures of his grandfather's Dragon Rescue.

"Your Life-Guardian and Jaret's were prepared by the Suzerain himself for your mission. Additionally, Prince Kyriel assured me that he would be with you throughout your entire mission. It happened at a time when the Queen was incapacitated through labor, and Enki had been summoned by Sausmas to the BorderLands. Betruger, the Queen's spirit advisor, had been also summoned by Sausmas. So, the Queen was guarded only by her mortal army that evening.

Peyton was amazed. "So *that* is why the castle was so empty that night."

"Yes," his father answered. "We wouldn't have put you in mortal danger. There was a *slight* chance something could have gone wrong. But, we knew the tunnel would be left untended that night, and that all of Souhaites minions were off exploring their own pursuits. The cook helped Elda arrange her connection with you."

Peyton looked at his father with wide-eyed discovery. "And, if anyone had stopped me, they would have assumed I was a lost little boy, with a package... that I was on my way home."

His father smiled. "Something like that." He looked at his son. "You'll never know how proud I have been of you for your entire life. But that night you completed a mission many of our brave fighting men were even hesitant to volunteer for."

"Wow," Peyton answered. "Can I ask you something else?"

"Anything, son," his father responded, as he drew in once again on his pipe.

"Why are we rescuing Jayden? Why now?"

Tvirtas drew in on his pipe once more, and stopped to think about how to explain what he wanted to say.

"The original mission was just to rescue the princess," he said.

"The princess?"

"Princess Karaliene," came the answer. "She is Jayden's twin. The Queen's fifty-year Gala Celebration is just two years away. Each time she has a Gala, she emerges from the Celebration using a fresh mortal body as a host."

"A host?" Peyton wanted to know.

"Souhaites is not really mortal. She only appears to be so, because she takes the form of a mortal woman. She changes her host every fifty years, so she can appear to have eternal youth and beauty."

"Was she going to take Elda for that purpose?" Peyton asked.

"We thought so," Tvirtas answered. "And then, she was pregnant."

"How did *that* happen?" Peyton asked. "How does a being like that become pregnant?"

"I will tell you more when the time is right. Some of this, you will learn in future Discovery Seasons."

"So where is Elda now?"

"She is Karaliene's nursemaid. Jophiel has been helping them to escape from the summer castle. They will meet us at the Refuge Site."

"Why are we rescuing Jayden? I don't understand why we don't just keep him hidden."

His father smiled. "You are a strategic thinker. But think about this. If Souhaites learns about him, she can work to use him as a host as well. It would give her the means to deceive the citizens of Hausse to an even greater degree than she has done already. Her efforts to control the mortals must be kept in check, until Suzerain's time."

A knock was heard on the wagon door.

"Come in!" Tvirtas invited.

Ramon stuck his head in the door. "Hey there," he said. "Uriel says we will be pulling out in within the hour. Do you want to provide Peyton his shield, and armor, or should I instruct him?"

Tvirtas' face brightened. "Is Jaret equipped?"

Ramon smiled. "Done!"

"I would *love* to arm my son!" the older man answered. "I'll signal you when we are ready."

"I'll let Uriel know," Ramon answered.

After the door had been pulled to, Peyton looked expectantly at his father. "What does he mean; 'shield and armor?'"

Tvirtas stood up, and moved to a compartment above the wagon window. As Peyton watched, the older man pulled out several large pieces of supple, sectioned silver, as well as a large square box, two feet by two feet.

"What is all of that, Papa?"

"It's your armor for this mission, Peyton."

"But I haven't drilled in it."

"I know," his father answered. "This is armor for a specific purpose. Your personal battle armor is something you will acquire as you complete your Discovery Seasons. However, the armor you will wear from this point forward in *this* mission will fit you the same way the *Seasoned Armor* you receive in your Fifth Season will also fit you."

"And the shield?" the son asked.

"Your shield is an Initiate Cadet's shield. However, after this mission, your shield will automatically change to reflect your experiences on this mission." Tvirtas tossed the box at Peyton. "Here, you can open this."

Standing up, the boy looked for a knife to open the box. Inside, he found a circular shield with the imprint of a lion's head on it.

"That is the image of the Suzerain the Lion-Hearted. He is your king. He is also your shield. There is a transponder inside your shield with a direct link to not only your Life-Guardian, but also Prince Kyriel and the Suzerain himself. Whenever you are in a dangerous situation beyond your abilities to resist, and you are holding your shield to protect yourself, their help will come.

"Now, let's put your armor on." He raised the first piece of sectioned silver. As he placed each piece over its designed position, the silver formed snugly to Peyton's skin. Raising his arm, the boy realized that somehow the metal was lightweight and flexible. Additionally, it allowed air to travel through it.

"That's surprising," he told his father. "I thought it would be heavy and cumbersome."

"No, it's *made* to fit you. One a piece of the king's silver is fit to you, it shifts with you, and changes as you grow. It will move with you, and conform to any movement your body makes. This silver is more flexible, and stronger than any substance in our sphere. It comes from Suzerain's Realm. Now, let's strap your sword to you as well."

Peyton was fascinated with the elasticity of his armor. He practiced moving about in it, while his father donned his own silver. When Tvirtas moved to gather his shield, the boy moved in for a closer look.

"I've never seen your shield before," he told his father. "Why didn't you tell me you were Commander of Prince Kyriel's visible army? Why didn't you tell me of your title?"

"Who *told* you?" Tvirtas wanted to know.

"Galen told me, close to the beginning of the mission," Peyton answered.

"I see." His father smiled. "My titles are not what is important to me, son. I could have all the titles in Hausse, and be miserable. *But* when my relationships with your mother and you children are secure, then I know I have done better than any mission I might have completed."

"It just would have been something good to know," Peyton replied. "It helps me understand you more."

"I wanted us to know each other without some kind of image being in the way," his father told him. "Now, where are the tools Lord Tallis gave you before you left home?"

"You know about them?" Peyton was surprised.

"Yes, I do," Tvirtas answered. "Have you looked at them since leaving home?"

"I have *looked* at them," his son answered, "but I'm not sure how to *use* them, or *when* to use them."

"Stay close, and I will teach you," his father told him. "Where are they?"

"In the wagon I share with Tividar and Jaret," he said. "Do you want me to go and get them?"

"Please," came the answer.

Peyton stepped out of the wagon, and walked across the camp, to the wagon he shared with Jaret and Tividar. Moving inside, he found the tools Lord Tallis had given him, inside his leather knapsack. Picking up the satchel, he remembered the night he had left on this mission, and how his knapsack had grown a pocket all at once.

"You will always have what you need..." Peyton smiled as he remembered Lord Tallis' visit that evening. Going through the knapsack, he counted the five tools. As he left, he also picked up his quiver and hunting bow. He then headed back into Tvirtas' wagon.

Shutting the door, he noticed his father had begun polishing the large shield.

"What do you think will happen tonight, Papa?" he asked.

"I'm never sure, Peyton, when we approach the unknown. It will depend on what the Queen knows."

He pulled a medium sized velvet bag from a drawer in his wagon. "This is for you to put your tools in, since you don't want to carry your knapsack with you into battle."

Peyton took the bag. "Thank you, Papa," he said. "I might be able to carry the bag in my quiver."

"That's what I was thinking, too. You might find it easier to use them if you have them with you all the time."

"How did you *know* that? That is what Lord Tallis told me when he gave them to me."

"Because it's what I remember of what he said to me when he gave my tools to me as well," his father answered.

"He taught *you?* How old *is he?*" Peyton asked.

"I have no idea," Tvirtas answered, chuckling. "It's strange, isn't it; to think we have each had the same teacher? Here. Put your tools down on the table."

Peyton did as his father bade him. Tvirtas stood, and assessed the implements Lord Tallis had given his son.

"I know Tallis gave these to you in a hurry, so I want to give you a quick hands-on lesson of how to use them." He picked up the compass and the quadrant.

"Let's go outside for a moment. Bring the map."

As they moved outside, Peyton noticed Jaret with Ramon and Tividar just across the compound. He was exercising the usage of his shield. Peyton realized he had no idea of his friend's level of development in sword skills. Would he need to protect Jaret when the battle came? Or would his childhood friend be able to fend for himself?

Tvirtas took them away from the wagon, into the shelter of the trees. Checking the environment around them, he gave instruction.

"Lay your map out here, flat on the ground."

Peyton did so, smoothing out the edges where the leather parchment wanted to curl up.

"Now, take your quadrant and your compass in hand. Now, step onto the map."

Peyton looked over at his father.

"Don't worry, son. I'll do it with you. Let's go on three. One. Two. Three."

On the count of three, father and son stepped together onto the map. There was barely enough room for the two of them to fit their feet within its borders, but they managed.

"Now," Tvirtas instructed, "open your compass and tell me what you see."

Peyton obediently opened his compass. The arrow pointed towards the north.

"Turn your body to face the direction of the arrow."

Peyton did so.

"What do you see?"

Looking around, Peyton noticed his surroundings had changed. No longer was he in a forest, next to a gypsy wagon. Now, he stood on a large globe. He could see the Great Sea to his right, and the mountains to his left. Behind him were the BorderLands.

"Look up, Peyton," his father continued. "Do you see the north star?"

"I'm not sure I do," the boy responded. "How can I tell?"

"It is just above Suzerain's Castle. Do you see the Castle?"

"Is it made of gold?"

"It is," came the reply. "Look directly above it."

"Oh," Peyton replied. "Now I see the star."

"The North Star is always directly above Suzerain's Castle. Whenever you are lost, head towards it. Two things will happen as a result. You will find your way, and help will come to you," his father explained. "When you gaze at the North Star through the quadrant, you will be looking at a reflection, so remember to turn it right side out in your mind, before you plot your pathway, or you could be headed in the wrong direction. Remember; things in Suzerain's

Realm function in the opposite manner of our sphere. When you see the reflection, reverse it to find your way.

"Also, if you cannot remember your mission, open your letter from the King while you are standing on this map, and things will be made plain to you. Its message will change to address the situation you are in, telling you what to do." He paused. "Do you still have your flask?"

Peyton reached into his armor, and pulled out the flask from against his chest, to show his father.

"Lord Tallis told me to keep it on my person all the time," he said. "But I'm not sure what to do with it."

His father smiled. "You can drink from the flask when you are thirsty. If you are tired, it will refresh you. If you share its water with others, always pour it out.

"You are right in thinking you should keep it on you at all times," Tvirtas continued, pulling out a similar flask from inside his own armor. "It will always have what you need, and it will never be empty, unless you violate the provisions Lord Tallis explained to you. Do you remember them?"

"Yes," Peyton answered. "If I let someone else drink out of it, or let what they say or do flavor it, or if I don't pour it out before I share it, the nature of it will change, and it will stop flowing, and the color of the fire in my sword will change." He paused to remember.

"Oh, and the water in the flask is always full. It comes directly from Suzerain's Realm. If I begin to use it in the wrong way, it will become empty."

"There is one other thing, Peyton," Tvirtas told him. "In the event you are lost, or discouraged, and you step on this map; just think of your home, and it will appear before you. You will instantly receive a sense of what is happening at that very moment with your mother, me, and your siblings.

"Now, let's talk about what you see."

Peyton glanced at his father. "Can't you see what I see?" he asked, surprised.

"No," his father answered. "This is your map, and it is for your own understanding. There are some things which I would also see if I stood in my own map, but these disclosures are yours and yours alone, from the Suzerain."

Still standing on the map, Peyton turned to view what the map was disclosing to him. He could see the BorderLands, and the dragons fighting there. He could see the Queen's winter castle, and a caravan being prepared for travel. He could see the gypsy camp, and the nature of the surrounding landscape. He could see Protectorate Area One, and his classmates as they were dismissed to go home to their families. He could see Lord Tallis standing at the window. Looking more closely, he could see his mother, working on a project as she sat by the fire, his siblings playing close by.

He also saw the summer castle, on the other side of the river. Wait. There was a dark figure standing on the river's edge, and a creature in a boat, being drawn by two crocodiles. What did that mean?

Then he saw a grouping of hills in the landscape, some miles up from the Great Bridge. Four riders were riding furiously on horseback towards them. Behind them, a large gray owl was flying with a speed faster than anything he had ever seen, towards the winter castle.

And over everything he saw, a golden mist had settled. Somehow, he knew this mist had something to do with the Suzerain. Funny, he considered. Stepping into the map, a person could see their individual place within a larger plan. His own struggles to understand didn't seem so big, in light of the events the Map was giving him Sight into.

Next to him, Tvirtas was speaking.

"Come now, son. Tell me what you see."

Peyton was surprised. "And you're sure you can't see what I see, even though you are standing on my map with me?"

Tvirtas answered. "I could, if I were standing in my *own* Map. But you are standing in yours. You are the only one who can see what you see. If I go to get my Map, I could tell you what I see, and we could compare what we observe. When we do that, we will gain a bigger picture of what the Suzerain is doing at any present time. You see, the map allows you to see only what is necessary for you to know for the next step."

"Oh, I get it," Peyton answered. "Well, I see several things. Up by the winter castle, there is a caravan preparing for travel."

"That means the Queen will be moving towards the summer castle tonight."

"I see Miemi," the boy continued. "She is working on something by the fire, and the house looks like it did when we left."

"Good. Good," his father replied.

"I see a dark figure, and a strange, funny-looking creature in a boat drawn by crocodiles, not far from here," Peyton told him.

"Oh," Tvirtas replied. "That would be one of the trolls. It most probably means he has made a pact of some kind with the Queen's agents. Uriel will want to know that information. Anything else?"

"Yes. There are four riders on horseback on the other side of the river. They are riding fast. For some reason, there was a huge gray bird following them, and then it flew to the winter castle."

Tvirtas listened, his brow furrowed. "Everything you see when you step into the Map will be important. So, when you don't understand what something means, bring it to whoever you are with from the Suzerain's Realm, and ask them. Don't pass off *anything* you don't understand. Battles have been lost because the warrior didn't ask questions in order to understand the Sight they had been given."

He looked at his son. "Do you know what the gray bird means?"

"Not really," Peyton replied. "I thought it was just a bird.

"That *would* be an acceptable conclusion, were it *not* one of the elements you saw in the Map," his father answered. "It means something, and I'm not sure I know. We will have to ask Uriel or Jophiel."

Tvirtas' focus changed from teaching to the mission at hand.

"Very good, son. Let's step off the Map now." The two of them stepped back onto the forest grass. Tvirtas bent down to pick up the map. After rolling it up, he handed it to Peyton.

"You can see why it is important to take good care of this. Always put it back in a safe place each time you use it. It will appear to be just a hand-printed map to everyone else. But to you, it will come to mean so much more than that. Whenever you step into it, your eyes will be opened to what is really important. Come with me now."

Moving back into the center of the wagon compound, the two of them walked to Galen's wagon, where Uriel was instructing the children regarding their part in the mission. Jophiel stood outside the wagon, in readiness.

As they approached Jophiel, Tvirtas spoke. "Here is Jophiel. Let's ask him what it means."

"Ask me what?" the Light-Bearer inquired.

"I stepped into my Map," Peyton began. "And I saw several things."

Tvirtas interjected. "I think what he has seen might be pertinent to the mission. We might have to adjust our strategy."

His interest piqued, Jophiel looked intently at Peyton. "What did you see?"

"Up by the winter castle, there is a caravan preparing for travel. I saw my mother working by the fire on a needlework project. I saw a dark figure, and a strange, funny-looking creature in a boat drawn by crocodiles, not far from here. That creature was meeting with a dark figure. I saw four riders on horseback on the other side of the river, riding fast. For some reason, there was a huge gray bird following them, and then it flew to the winter castle."

Jophiel's eyebrows went up, and he looked at Tvirtas. "Legion has been summoned by someone on the Queen's side."

"Legion?"

"A covey of evil Shades, who all work in tandem to bring destruction. They were banished by Kyriel years ago, but have gained access to more fragile mortals over time. They gain right of entry by deception. This particular group has learned to work together to achieve a common goal, and they operate very closely with Sausmas. When they appear in the owl form, it is a warning of something soon to come.

"In the past, the owl appeared in order to wreak havoc against those loyal to Suzerain. It will be important we stop the owl before he disseminates into individual Shades. As long as they remain in the owl's form, they are limited. But after the assignment the owl has been summoned to complete, the Shades will leave that form, and will spread out. It has always been their goal to network together to control the entire Realm."

Chapter Fourteen
No Time for Fear

In the courtyard of the winter castle, an immense army of Shades, Weavers and Muddlers was assembling. The center of the courtyard was marked with a raised stone dais, or platform. From the middle of the dais rose a small stone pillar. At the top of the pillar, an unearthly-colored purple flame burned, flooding the entire area with a strange sort of purple light. The firelight changed the colors of the items it touched, pulling the crystal particles within the stones, turning them into neon orbs.

Standing on the platform was Queen Souhaites, readying herself to address the forces that stood before her. Behind her, Enki spread his cloak, and enlarged his size to create the illusion of great bat wings.

Souhaites raised her voice. "Hear me, O evil horde," she began. "I am calling on you to fight tonight! We must prevent the gypsy caravan from crossing the Great Bridge. We have been betrayed by spies, and agents the Suzerain has sent among us. We stand to lose all that is rightfully ours by the forfeit of the Ancients. We must win at all costs. I charge you to use whatever arms you must in order to prevent the crossing. We must also recapture our child, our beloved princess Karaliene, from those who have stolen her away from us. Will you fight for your Queen?"

"We will *fight!*" the throng shouted in chorus.

"Will you fight for your future?"

"We will *fight*!" the answer came once more.

"Will you fight for Sausmas?"

"We will *fight!* We will *fight*! We *will* PREVAIL!!" they shouted once again. The answer became a repeated rhythm, coupled with the stamping of monstrous feet, and the clapping of terrible claw-like hands.

"Then let us embark! To *war*!" With a flourish, the Queen mounted her chariot, with Enki standing behind her. She tugged on the reins, which were harnessed to six giant wolves, each one as large as the chariot itself. As she flicked the reins, the wolves lunged forward, straining against them. The Queen's chariot took the lead, with wagons of weapons behind her. With a great reverberation, the multitude of dark specters fell into marching rank behind her.

It wasn't far to the Portal. They would dematerialize there, and be at the Great Bridge within the hour.

In the forest near the Great Bridge, the Romani family was in formation, beginning to move towards the first branch of the Mortal's Folly River, known as the Stream of Fear. In the lead, Uriel rode his black stallion. Tividar and Galen drove the final wagon, bringing up the rear. Jaret and Peyton were inside

Galen's wagon with Jayden, Damara, Jowan and Lysandra. Jophiel was nowhere to be seen, although the team members were aware he was close-by.

It was almost three hundred feet to the water's edge. Uriel led the wagons out from behind the covey of huge boulders which had served as their shield from sight.

From inside the wagon, Peyton kept watch through the side window. As soon as all of the wagons were out in the open, the boy noticed a large ship moored to the pylons of the Great Bridge.
The vessel was fashioned in a different shape than he had ever seen before. It appeared to be a galley ship, with multiple oar ports on each side. The craft itself looked more like a barge than a sailing vessel. On its deck were a collection of strange-looking gray-skinned creatures. Round and fleshy, they had short stubby legs with feet that resembled chicken feet. Their hands were similar mortal hands, but each hand had six fingers.

But it was their faces that struck Peyton. Each one had a wide mouth, with a protruding lower jaw, and two rows of jagged teeth. In the center of each face was a nose covering more than half of the distance between the enormously bulging ears. Two wide nostrils spread almost flat against the face. Just above the nose, eyes receded under an overlapping forehead.

Even from this distance, the boy could see that most had bellies bulging over their belts. Each belt had a sword. Some had additional weapons. The creatures were of differing sizes, and Peyton found himself wondering why the smaller ones had been allowed to come.

Moving towards the front of the wagon, he opened the small door that led to the riding bench.

"Galen," he asked. "What are the creatures there?"

Smiling, she responded. "Those creatures are called Trolls. They inhabit the entire territory from the beginning here under the Great Bridge, from one shoreline to the other of the two branches of the Mortal's Folly river, all the way to the Sea. Their land is called 'Shame's Stronghold.'"

"Why did they let their little ones come?"

Galen laughed. "Trolls live for thousands, sometimes tens of thousands of years. As trolls rise in status and responsibility, they begin to grow a little each century they are alive. The largest troll of all is Jotnar, their Chieftain. He is over twenty feet tall."

"Will he be fighting with us?" Peyton asked.

"I doubt it," the Chevaliesse responded. "He has sent his generals to help us fight, should we encounter any problems. But it looks as though he isn't expecting us to meet much resistance. He has apparently sent just a small party tonight."

"Do you think we will have to fight tonight?" the boy asked.

"It seems likely to me," Galen answered. "There are too many indicators for us to just ride across the bridge without any resistance at all."

"Indicators?"

"When you stepped into your Map, Tvirtas explained that what you saw were situations affecting your position, remember? You saw what was happening in different parts of Hausse. You didn't understand *why* you were seeing them, or what they *meant*. As you grow, and become more and more used to battle, you will also learn to interpret what you see in the Map. *Everything* you saw was an indicator. *That means it indicates your position in the situation you are in.* Since you are *with us*, and we all have the *same* mission, those indicators affect all of us as well."

"What indicators?" Peyton was amazed.

"Well, you saw a caravan readying to leave the winter castle. You saw a troll in a secret meeting with a Shade. You saw the princess and her nursemaid riding hard with two agents to get to the Refuge Site. And, you saw Legion chasing them."

"I did see all those things!" the boy exclaimed.

"Yes," replied Galen. "And as you grow, you will learn what to do with the information you see. That is called application. When you *apply* actions to *what* you know, *responding* to the information, you learn to *perceive*."

"What does that mean: 'perceive'?"

"Well, to perceive means to 'know inwardly.' It is the first step in developing Inner Sight. When you are seasoned in perception, the Map becomes part of you. You can receive information anytime without physically stepping into it."

"That would be awesome to know how to do!"

"But, you need to know that it is possible for mortals to receive *false* information as well. Sausmas is always looking for a way to deceive and entice mortals into his dominion. If you ever receive information you think might be false, check it by stepping into your Map."

"Okay," Peyton responded.

His mind was swimming; trying to actualize the images he had seen just an hour before. How would someone apply the information he and his father had received standing in the Map, he wondered?

Silently, the boy drew back into the wagon, and went once more to the window, where he now had to share space with Jayden.

"Hey Peyton," Jayden greeted him. "Do you know what these weird looking creatures are in the river?"

Peyton smiled. "Galen says they are Trolls."

"Did she tell you why they look like that?"

For the next several minutes, Peyton found himself answering the questions of an extremely curious five-year-old boy. Across the room, Lysandra and Jowan were in the middle of a lively sign language discussion. Jaret had been reading a book to Damara as she sat on his lap. Now they were both asleep.

Abruptly, Lysandra stood up and moved over to where Peyton and Jayden were talking. Peyton looked up, knowing the child couldn't speak.

"What is it, Lysandra?" he asked.

In response, the child pointed outside.

"You want to see outside?"

Frustrated, she shook her head. She made the sign for "wings" from her shoulders, and pointed outside once again.

"Where is Uriel?" Peyton guessed.

Nodding, she smiled excitedly.

The boy moved to the front trap door to the wagon and opened it. "Galen?" he said.

"Yes, you have another question?" the Chevaliesse responded.

"No," Peyton laughed. "Thank you for showing me another area where I have so far to go. No, Lysandra wants to see Uriel."

Quickly, Tividar raised the flag on the side of his wagon. This was the signal that a Light-Bearer was needed.

"What is it Tividar?" Uriel asked.

"Lysandra wanted to see you," the young knight told him.

At that very moment, the sound of whizzing arrows was heard. Three hit the wagon, sending a shockwave through the little room. The arrows had struck with such force, the wagon shook on its wheels.

"Shut the door, Peyton, and wake Jaret. It's time to stand your post." Somewhat instantaneously, Uriel rose into the air, changing into his true form as he did so. Bright white light burst forth from him, changing the murky darkness of the approaching night once more into light.

"And so it begins!" he shouted. Making a quick turn in the air, the Light-Bearer made a flying pass in front of the Trolls, many of whom responded with surprise.

All of the drivers in the gypsy caravan had predetermined their response. In unison, they shouted as well:

"With Suzerain and for Kyriel!"

Although it was a delayed response, a unified chorus, shouting agreement came from the Trolls, who immediately began disembarking from their flat-topped galley ship. Peyton chuckled as he watched them.

"Why are you laughing?" Jayden asked.

"They just seem funny to me," came the response. "Take a look!"

Indeed, the scene was a little comical if one had never seen a troll before. To be troll-shaped was to be round, with short legs. Therefore, trolls didn't walk; they waddled; their entire body moving back and forth like a clock pendulum as they moved.

"I would think they would be quicker just *rolling* along," Jayden blurted out.

The two boys looked at each other, and began to laugh.

Outside, the scene was less humorous.

From his aerial view, Uriel noted the horde of Shades, Weavers and Muddlers approaching from the west. Those in their front lines had released the first barrage of arrows. He noted the trolls had taken positions in the swamp, under the bridge, and along the river's edge.

The caravan was fully onto the Great Bridge, almost a half mile across. There could be no seeking cover now. They *had* to proceed.

"Life-Guardians!" Uriel thundered with a loud voice. "Take your places!"

Immediately, more beings filled with Suzerain's Light rose from the caravan. Corresponding in gender to the mortal warrior each one defended, they materialized into the visible realm.

Transfixed, the children watched from the wagon windows, as Shades from the Queen's army also rose into the air, also taking their true form. Black and grotesque, each one also had wings. But, Peyton noted, the wings on the backs of the Dark Forces were leathery and veined, and somewhat transparent, almost like a duck's feet. They too, maneuvered the sky with dexterity.

All at once, fighting exploded above all of the onlookers.

It was then that Peyton noticed the hoods each member of the Queen's army wore. Similar to a mask, they allowed the wearer to see through it.

He would have to ask one of the warriors the masks' purposes later, he decided.

"Look!" Damara pointed to the flat-topped ship, where the trolls had once stood. Now, a sort of giant crossbow stood on its deck. Two of the smaller creatures were loading a cylindrical wooden container made of staves of wood hooped together. At the end the children could see, was a circle of holes. Into these holes, the trolls were loading arrows. After the cylinder was full, they would light the arrows, and proceed to turn a crank handle. The crossbow then released a series of showering fiery missiles into the ranks of the enemy.

Next to the crossbow, was a metal bucket filled with purplish-blue fire. This was the source from which the arrows were set ablaze.

Next to the bucket, a trebuchet had been installed. More of the smaller trolls stood in line next to it, waiting to be catapulted into the midst of the approaching enemy. As each one left the trebuchet's sling, beginning their short flight, a loud high-pitched squeal was heard. As each troll passed over the wagons, the sound faded and then ended with a loud crash that shook the very ground beneath them.

"That looks like fun!" Jayden exclaimed. "I'd like to fly through the air like that!"

"I would too," Jaret answered him. "It's what could be waiting on the ground when I would land that concerns me."

Responding to a felt a tug on the leg of his armor, Jaret looked down. Jowan was motioning for him to join him.

On the other side of the wagon, Jowan stood at the corresponding window. He had been watching the trolls as they landed. Some landed on top of the Weavers and Muddlers still in route to the bridge, crushing them under their tremendous weight. Others, surprisingly, landed on their little feet, and ran into the crowd with mouths open and weapons drawn. Jowan watched in fascination as one troll ran a Weaver through with its sword, and then bit off its head. Making a face, as though it had tasted something with a nasty flavor, the troll spit out the head and moved on in the lines. Each one continued through the crowd, snapping and biting and spitting, leaving a trail behind him.

"Those things are fierce!" Jaret noted. "I'm glad they're on our side. I wonder what kills *them*?"

Peyton said nothing. Flashing across his mind was the image of a Shade's secret meeting with a Troll.

"I want to fight too!" Jayden proclaimed. "I want to stop those ugly things! They need to *go away*!!"

Looking up, Peyton noted the mid-air battle taking place above them. Guardians and Light-Bearers were slicing away at Shades and Muddlers with swords blazing with white fire. Chunks of those elements of the Queen's forces were showering down all around. The Dark Forces battling against the Light-Bearers did so with miscellaneous weapons; all of which were lit with the dark purple fire, which blazed continually. And, while the Suzerain's troops carried sword which blazed with brilliant white fire, the swords carried by the Dark Forces blazed sporadically, emitting a tainted yellow fire.

As the Shades fought, they continually changed form; disappearing from one spot, and then appearing in another. They also filled the air with whispers, which joined in rhythm and rhyme, repeating once spoken, gaining in volume, never fading.

"You cannot defeat us!"

"There are more of us than you can imagine!"

311

"Give up your fight now!"

"You have no power to change things!"

"Stop and consider how bad things are now!"

"This is all there is to life!"

"You are deceived. Suzerain doesn't really exist at all!"

"Why try?"

The sounds continued to grow, until the whispers became almost deafening. Instinctively, each of the children put their hands to their ears, to drown out the sound.

"That's hurting my ears!" Damara said. "I'm afraid!"

"Come here and sit by me," Jaret told her. "I'll hold you safe until it stops."

Suddenly, the front door leading to the riding bench opened, and Galen stepped into the wagon's room.

"I've had enough of this!" she told the children. "It's a knight's battle now as well." Moving to the bench where Peyton and Jayden were sitting, she motioned for them to move. "Excuse me, boys," she said.

As they stood, shifting positions, Galen lifted the bench lid, and looked into the storage box inside. Reaching in, she drew out a long tube, with what looked like a pointed roof on one end, and a fuse on the other. She looked around the wagon, her eyes coming to light on what she was searching for.

"Damara, pass me that long stick leaning against the wall behind you," she requested.

Damara looked around and saw the stick the old woman was asking for. She handed it to her. Galen then reached into the box once more and removed some twine, which she used to wrap around the rocket and the stick, tying them together. As the box was open, Peyton noticed a stack of folded blankets which were also stored there. Each one was a deep brownish-burgundy, with the word "Kyriel" embroidered in the corner.

"Thank you children," she said, as she once more exited and shut the door behind her.

"What is she going to do?" Jaret asked.

Peyton's eyes were wide. "I don't know," he answered.

Arriving outside, Galen had transformed into her younger self. Drawing her sword, it burst into white flame. Holding the stick, she used her sword to light the rocket's fuse. She then stood, waiting until the rocket had launched into the sky.

"There!" she told Tividar. "That should take care of it!"

"What was that?" Tividar asked.

"Just watch," she responded, as she put her sword back in its sheath.

Above them, the rocket exploded into bright white and red blossoms of fire. As each blossom detonated, it seemed to set off a chain reaction of its own, developing more and more blossoms of white and red. The effect continued for several minutes. When it was completed, the sky was silent.

"I'd had just had enough of that nonsense," she declared to Tividar.

The shy young man smiled. "I like you, Galen," he told her. "I want to learn what you know."

Surprised, she looked at him. "All right then," was all she said.

On the other side of the Bridge, Nathan and Daniel were still riding furiously, with Ellie and Karaliene in company. It had been almost thirty minutes since the great gray owl had left them; almost forty-five since they had been invaded by bats.

"Where are we, Nathan?" the princess asked.

"We aren't far now, little one," the baker answered. "Do you see those hills in the distance?"

Karaliene squinted. "It's hard to see in the dark," she answered.

Nathan smiled. "Especially when you've never been here before," he noted.

"Exactly," she responded.

"Well," the older man explained, "just ahead are the land of Three Hills. The Refuge Site is close by."

"*Really now?*"

The voice reverberated all around them. In response, all four riders began to slow down.

Nathan's horse slowed and then reared up.

Nathan looked around him to Daniel and Ellie. "Who said that?"

Daniel was also looking. "Not me."

The two men looked at each other grimly, and drew swords. They would not give up the girls without a fight.

"Karaliene, you belong to me!" The Queen's voice echoed around them. "Elda! What have you done!"

At the sound of their names being spoken, each of the girls experienced a sense of feeling fearful and overwhelmed.

Ellie looked at Nathan, her eyes wide. "It's the *Queen!*"

Nathan nodded, and put his finger to his lips. "Don't say anything, Ellie. Try not to give in to those fears. Doing so gives her power over you."

Ellie nodded in response, and moved back into formation to ride next to Princess Karaliene. The little girl's voice and hands were shaking as she spoke to her nursemaid. "Ellie, I d-don't want to g-go back there!" she cried tearfully. "I want to get out of here!"

Instinctively, the nursemaid pulled Karaliene from her horse, and placed the child in front of herself. "Is that better?" she asked. "Do you feel safer?"

The five-year old nodded, and snuggled next to Ellie. "Please keep me safe, Ellie. I'm afraid!"

Because her head was lowered to tend to the child, Ellie had not witnessed the cause of the rising shadow which had seemed to form from the very dust of the ground. It was now looming over them.

"Ellie!" Nathan shouted, startling her, "Ride hard! Now! Get to safety!"

Looking up, Ellie was astonished to see a giant dragon, with unique red eyes glaring at all of them. Mounted on its back was Queen Souhaites. In her hand, she held a black wand, which had at crystal orb at its top. The Queen pointed her wand at Karaliene. From the crystal's tip came a beam of black fire.

Ellie put her cloak over the little girl, and dug her heels into the side of the mare she rode. But the black beam had been poorly aimed. It sailed just above her head, and hit a nearby oak tree, burning into its bark.

Ellie turned her horse around. As she did so, the dragon's claws came down towards her shoulders.

"Where are you going?" it growled in a low and menacing tone. "You didn't ask permission to leave the castle!"

Ellie breathed in a sharp breath, waiting for the strike that was sure to come.

But she needn't have worried. As the dragon moved closer, breathing spark and fire, it was thwarted by an invisible shield. As it bounced, reflecting its power back to wreak its damage on the dragon and its rider, two Life-Guardians materialized, swords flaming with white light.

Behind the dragon, Jophiel materialized.

"Where did that thing come from?" Nathan asked Daniel. "Did you see it?"

"It seemed like it was part of the earth itself," Daniel responded. "It was as though both the Queen and the dragon rose up from nowhere."

Jophiel looked at the two Guardians. "Stay with the girls," he instructed. "Get them to the Refuge Site. I will take care of this."

The two Life-Guardians moved to follow Ellie and Karaliene, staying visible.

As the girls moved away on horseback, Souhaites screamed at the dragon, "Follow them, Enki! Follow them *now!*"

With huge wings, the dragon moved to rise in the air, but two male Life-Guardians materialized just above him. With a growl, the dragon breathed in and exhaled a shower of fire and ash towards them. In response, the Guardians lifted their shields, and waited for the fire to pass, but did not move out of the way.

Nathan and Daniel watched in wonder, then discovered they were being rained on by molten ash and fire. Watching them, Jophiel shouted, "Ride!" We will take care of this distraction!"

Realizing this particular battle had moved beyond their capabilities, Nathan and Daniel spurred their horses into a run once more.

As the two men pulled away, Jophiel raised his sword and moved in to strike at Enki. As the dragon extended its neck, preparing to blow out his destruction fire at the departing riders, the Light-Bearer moved in behind Souhaites, seating himself on the dragon's massive back, just above its tail. This was an area of the dragon's body which neither Souhaites or the dragon could reach, or even see from their current positions.

Trying to find his opponent, Enki began turning in circles. As he did so, the Queen began to scream at him. "Stop it, you idiot! You are going to make me fall off!"

"Don't tell me what to do again!" the dragon growled. "You have more to lose in this battle than I do!"

Looking at the male two Life-Guardians, Jophiel nodded. At the same time, each of them took action. Sitting on the dragon's back, Jophiel drew his flaming sword and plunged it deep into the creature's hind quarters. At the same time the two Life-Guardians dove down upon Souhaites, piercing her through with their swords.

All at once, two earth shattering screams emanated from both the Queen and her dragon. From the place where Jophiel's sword had dug into the dragon, a light began to spread, burning away the shell of its body. As the dragon dissolved away, the Queen fell to the ground, her host body mortally wounded. For his part, Enki emerged from the changing configuration; from dragon back into Python.

"Oh..." the Python groaned. A large portion of his backside had been cut away. Standing, he limped over to where Souhaites was lying.

"Look what you have done, you *irresponsible imbecile*!!" she heaved. Her body was bleeding, and the strength to move was gone. Disgusted, she growled at Enki. "You have destroyed *everything!*"

With a great effort, the entity inside of the Queen's human host split the frame in half, and began to crawl out, as though it were stepping out of a pea pod. As it did, it grumbled bitterly at Enki.

"You will pay for this, you stupid moron! If it takes a thousand years, you will pay dearly!"

Enki, the Python looked at his superior with anger. "I am too spent to argue with you further, Leviathan! I don't care about the Princess, or your *stupid Gala*. I am going to the BorderLands for a rest!"

His energies spent; his plans foiled; Leviathan snarled at Enki. "This is far from over! Don't forget that you *owe me!*"

But the Shade was long gone.

Leviathan looked around for someone to blame; someone with whom to fight.

But he was alone.

Jophiel and the two male Life-Guardians had only stayed around long enough to be assured of their victory.

There were more important matters to attend to.

Jophiel had been called to another Realm.

The two male Life-Guardians were needed with their assigned Mortals. The mission was not yet completed.

At the Great Bridge, the gypsy wagons were almost to the other side. As the battle raged, they had crossed over the Stream of Fear, the Marshes and most of the Way of Pride, the second distributary of the Mortal's Folly River.

In the midst of the battle, Galen had released a second rocket, and the trolls had significantly reduced the number of Weavers and Muddlers. Now, as they neared the bridge's end, the attack seemed to intensify. At the end of the bridge, a gang of Weavers and Muddlers blocked the path for the wagons to proceed. Behind Galen's wagon, another collection of these same dark forces had gathered. As the wagons slowed, those entities behind Galen's wagon began creeping forward, looking for a way into the children's hiding place. They knew the one of them responsible for bringing the Queen's son back would be given special recognition.

As the wagons came to a halt, the knights stepped down from their riding benches, with weapons drawn, ready to protect their assigned charges. Above them, the battle between the Shades, Light-Bearers and Guardians had intensified.

Looking down, in the midst of battle, Uriel noted the surprise attack taking place at the Bridge's end. He also observed that the trolls had retreated back into the Marshes.

Their ship had also disappeared.

So, that had been the Shade's strategy.

What had the Queen given the Trolls in exchange?

No matter. That would soon show itself. He was sure.

"Galen!" he shouted. "Cover the children!"

Hearing him, Galen ducked into her wagon. "Hello, children," she panted.

"This is so cool!" Jayden declared. "Can I fight now?"

"Not this time," the Chevaliesse answered softly. Looking at the children, she spoke calmly and carefully. "Listen to me, all of you. I want you to go to the back corner of the wagon. You are to stay inside and be completely still. I am going to give you each a blanket, and I want you to wrap yourself in it. Then, I want you to wait until one of us comes for you."

Outside, the sound of Shyla's pan pipes had begun a soothing melody. As the notes rose, moans and groans from the Dark Forces outside the wagon could also be heard.

"Why are they moaning?" Jaret asked.

"The music hurts their ears. It reminds them of where they came from, and what they have lost," Galen replied, as she once more opened the storage box.

"Quickly!" she said, as she threw the brownish-burgundy blankets to them, one at a time. "Wrap up and sit still."

As she handed the last two blankets to Peyton and Jaret, she gave them instructions. "You two are to use these as mantles on your armor. Fasten your mantles to the *focale points* made for them on your shoulders. Your assignment is to keep the children safe. Guard these little ones. They cannot defend themselves. It would be a good idea to draw your swords now, and get your shields at the ready. Stand in front of these little ones."

Peyton drew his rapier and looked down at it. Astonished, he realized it had begun to blaze with the same white fire as the older warriors' blades.

"Look!" Jaret exclaimed as he drew his training foil. It had also been set aflame.

As Galen turned to leave the wagon, two Weavers broke through the side door. One gained entrance due to the element of surprise. He stepped towards the children. All the mouths on his grotesque body were shouting, "Where are you, son of the Queen?"

It was Jaret who first moved towards the children, reaching for his shield as he did so. Using it to bang the Weaver in its head, he stepped between it and the children. As he did so, his mantle touched the Weaver. The creature recoiled as though it had been burned. "Ow!" it screeched. "That's not fair!! I gained access the right way! I didn't violate any of the rules!! The mortal prince belongs to *us*!"

Galen laughed. "I don't think so!" she replied, drawing her long swords, which burst into flame as they left their sheaths. Reaching through the door, she skewered the second Weaver, who was just stepping into the wagon's door.

She looked at Peyton. "Remove their hoods!" she told him.

Using his rapier, Peyton cut through the masking fabric over the first Weaver's face. As the bright white light of his sword cut through the cloaking materials, the Weaver shouted in Fear. "No! Don't! The Light hurts my eyes!"

Peyton could feel the words he had heard Galen say to a Muddler during a similar encounter flashing across his mind.

Galen glanced at Peyton, anticipating his words. "Was there something you wanted to say, Peyton?"

Smiling, he looked at her. "Yes, there is!" He looked at the two Weavers. "By the word of Kyriel, begone to the Barren Places, and don't return here! Ever!"

At the same moment Kyriel's name was spoken, a pair of earth-shattering screams were felt and heard by all involved in the battle. Suddenly, the air was still. The Weavers inside the wagon vanished.

Galen, Peyton and Jaret looked at each other in surprise. Could it be? They stepped outside the wagon.

All around them, the sky which had been filled with Shades had emptied. The masses of Weavers and Muddlers had also disappeared. Above them, the cloud cover had begun to lift, and the stars were beginning to show themselves.

Uriel and the Life-Guardians touched down on the ground next to the Great Bridge. Uriel nodded to the Guardians.

"Thank you," he told them.

As the Life-Guardians once more departed the visible realm, Uriel took on his appearance as a mortal. "Is everyone all right?" he asked.

"All are safe and accounted for," Tvirtas replied.

"And the children?" the Light-Bearer wanted to know.

Galen answered. "A little shaken, but all are safe."

Uriel nodded. "Good. Let's head to the Refuge Site," he said.

Almost twelve miles away, four riders had entered the land of the Three Hills. The night had fully descended now, and each of them was occupied with their own thoughts.

Rounding the second hill, they came to an immeasurably old tree, with its limbs twisted and its roots exposed. Daniel raised his hand. The rest of the party followed his lead. From his shirt pocket, the younger man removed a small scroll.

"I always think I have this memorized, and then when I get here, I doubt myself," he told them. "Does anyone have a torch?"

"I have an oil lamp," Nathan answered. Dismounting, he reached into his saddlebag, and drew out the small lamp in question. Reaching into the bag a second time, he pulled out a flint and steel.

As he was doing so, Daniel dismounted and began looking around for some dried grass, to serve as kindling. After several tries, the kindling was lit, and Nathan took a lighting stick from his pocket and touched it to the lamp. Picking up the lamp by the handle, he looked at Daniel.

"Now where is that latch?" Daniel spoke more to himself than to anyone. Putting his hand inside the twisted trunk of the tree, he felt around until he found what he was looking for. "There it is!" he muttered.

In response to his actions, the sound of stone pushing against stone was heard, as though a great wall were being moved out of its place.

"Look!" Karaliene pointed to the tree. As the sound progressed, the tree was untwisting, straightening in front of their eyes, to reveal a closed door within its center.

"It's a door! Where does it go?" Karaliene asked excitedly.

"We will discover that in a few moments," Daniel told her. "It would be good to dismount now."

But the mission was not quite over. The battles were not over. One more barrier remained before they could enter the Refuge Site.

Reaching up, Nathan lifted Karaliene from her horse. At the same time, Ellie dismounted. As Nathan placed Karaliene on the ground, a low growling sound was heard from the surrounding shadows. Picking up his lamp from the ground once more, Nathan lifted it and stepped out into the darkness.

"Who is it?" he called.

"We came for the child," a low, growling voice responded. "If you give her to us, we will let you live."

Nathan drew his sword, as did Daniel, both of which immediately burst into white light. The men put their backs to each other, and the two girls between them. Their swords faced outward, and they began to move cautiously in a circular motion.

"Who are you?" the baker repeated, to the voice speaking to him from the glooms.

"We are the Chanticleers of the Moon, and we serve the Queen," came the answer.

Daniel muttered the word "wolves" to his father, just loud enough for the other three to hear. Then, silently, he dug in his pocket for the key to the door in front of them.

"The child means nothing now," Daniel told them. "The Queen is dead."

A howling laughter came back at him in reply. "Her *host* is dead, you mean to say. The child means *everything.*"

Ever so slowly, Daniel made a move towards the door, holding his sword out in front of him. Nathan lifted his lamp, and made out the silhouette of a rather large wolf. In his other hand, the man held his sword, which pulsed with white flame. Nathan lowered his sword in the direction the voice was coming from.

"Be careful you don't burn yourself," the wolf taunted. "You know you're afraid."

"I know nothing of the sort," Nathan answered him. "And by the way, the Suzerain's fire cannot hurt me. But I think perhaps you might be worried about yourself. *Here!*" On the word "here," the baker lunged with his sword towards the silhouette he had seen. Hopefully, he thought, I will cut into *something*...."

His thrust was met with a yelp and a scream. "Hey!" the wolf accused. "You didn't say you were going to do that!"

"Do I need to do it again?" Nathan threatened.

Behind him, the five additional wolves pressed inward. The largest one crouched, and then sprang toward the baker, landing on Nathan's back. The baker could hear snarling just behind his ear, as the wolf dug its claws in to gain a more advantageous footing. The man knew an inch or two closer, and the wolf would be in a place to dig its teeth into his neck.

Another wolf ran into the circle, while both men were distracted, snapping at the girls. "You belong to us," it growled at Karaliene.

In size, the wolf's head was eye-level with the child. Muscles rippled under its fur. Its mouth opened and closed, seeking to gain a hold on Karaliene. She pulled away and screamed.

Ellie grabbed her satchel and began hitting the wolf on the top of its head, trying to fend it off.

For his part, Daniel was having trouble getting the key into the door lock. Flustered, he dropped the key.

Concentrating on his own battle with the wolves, Nathan was unaware of his son's difficulty. "I could use a little help 'ere, son" the baker intoned. "You got a hole in yer pocket there?"

Crouching down to pick up the key once more, Daniel answered. "No, I'm having trouble seeing the lock. I'm working on it."

Suddenly, the sky filled with light. The two male Life-Guardians arrived. As the light grew, the ability to see around them also grew. Squinting into the light, Daniel counted six giant wolves, almost the size of his horse.

"Sorry to disappoint you," he said, directing his words to the largest one. "We hate to meet and run," as he spoke he turned the key in the lock, and opened the door. "We are expected somewhere else right about now."

Nathan turned around, and gave the girls a push towards the door within the tree. "Go now!" he said. "I will see you again in the future."

Realizing he was saying goodbye, Ellie reached out and hugged him. "Goodbye Nathan," she said.

"I'll see you soon," he promised.

"I love you, Mr. Nathan," Karaliene said, as she was tugged through the door.

As the girls entered the Portal, Daniel quickly shut the door behind them and leaned against it, as he turned the key in the lock once more.

"His Life-Guardian will help him," he told the girls.

Outside, the sound of swords striking targets was heard, and then yelping and whining. Then all was silent.

"They are dealt with. And he is headed home," Daniel told them.

"Back to Sorrettu?" Karaliene wanted to know.

"Yes, back to Sorrettu," the younger man nodded. "Now, let's see what we are to do next."

Turning around, the girls saw four closed doors.

"We must choose wisely," Daniel told them, "or we will end up in a worse situation than the one we came from. Now that we are here, we must wait."

"Wait?" Ellie asked. "What for?"

"We are to be joined by another party," Daniel answered. "That is all I know."

It was another two hours before the wagons arrived. Uriel was the first to enter the Refuge Site Door. He was quickly followed by Ramon and Shyla, who carried their sleeping children. Peyton and Jaret entered. Jaret was carrying Jowan. Then Tividar entered, followed by Pythia and Panna. Last was Galen, who held a sleeping Lysandra in her arms.

It had been a long, long day for all of them. Exhausted, each one fell to the floor inside the Site, and went to sleep, none caring for a pillow, or for comfort.

Sleep was all that was necessary.

Chapter Fifteen

Portals to New Beginnings

No one really knew what time it was when they began waking up. The first one to open their eyes was Pythia. Usually an early riser, she looked around, trying to figure out where she was. Then she remembered the events of the night before. Panna, her sister had settled not too far away, so she whispered her name, to see if she was also awake.

"Panna, are you awake?"

There was no answer.

"Panna," she whispered. "Can you hear me?"

"Sh-h!" came her sister's reply. "I don't want to get up yet."

"Where are we?" a child's sleepy voice asked.

"We are inside the Portal," Panna answered.

"What's a portal?" the child asked.

"A door to someplace new," Panna replied.

"Who are you?" came the inevitable second question.

"My name is Panna. What's yours?"

"I'm Karaliene, and my nursemaid Ellie is here too, but she's sleeping."

Silence returned to the room, as mortals continue to receive rest inside one of the Suzerain's Refuges.

After a few moments, Panna rose and stretched. It had been late when they had arrived the night before. Now she was sure it was morning, but could not tell the time, since they were inside the Portal's Vestibule. Assessing her surroundings, she noted four doors on the far wall.

On the left wall, were shelves filled with books, scrolls and boxes. From floor to ceiling, the shelves were filled. Along the outside of the shelves, a wheeled ladder served as a means of retrieving things stored in the highest locations.

On the right wall, was a table set with silver platters filled with food. "Someone has been here during the night," she murmured to herself. Realizing she was thirsty, she stood and moved over to look at the offerings left for them by the undisclosed night visitor.

"Oh my," she said, perhaps louder than she should have. "Chicken, and beef, and bread…. and.. oh…." She exclaimed as she discovered a fresh orange. It had been a long time since she had eaten an orange.

"I wonder if they would mind if I…" she murmured as she reached for the orange.

Just then, Tvirtas snored. It was a sudden noise which woke him up as well. Panna pulled her hand back instinctively, and then giggled.

So Tvirtas snored. Who knew?

Behind her, Panna heard a noise. Turning she saw a young man a little older than herself. "Were you wanting to eat that orange?" Daniel asked.

Not sure who she was speaking to, Panna put out her hand. "I'm Panna," she said. "Part of the rescue mission."

The young man shook her hand. "Daniel," he introduced himself. "I am responsible for the maintenance of this Site, and for delivering those seeking asylum to their contact point."

"Nice to meet you," she said. "And yes, come to think of it, I was hoping for an orange."

Daniel smiled. "Help yourself. It's all here for everyone. Don't be shy."

"For me that's easier said than done," she replied. "Can I ask you a question?"

"Surely," he answered.

"Is there anything to drink?"

"Oh, yes," he told her. "There is a well in the corner over there."

"Thank you," Panna said. She made her way to the corner, where she found the well, and drew water into a cup for a drink. She also used some of the water to wash her face and hands.

Thinking about the battle the day before, she rubbed her neck. No wonder her joints were tired this morning, she decided.

One by one the members of the two groups began to stir. One by one they discovered the well and the prepared plates of food. After everyone had awakened and eaten breakfast, Daniel pulled them all together.

"Can I get your attention, please?" he asked in a loud voice. "I know we all had a long day yesterday. I know you all have a ways to go in completing your mission. Have you all rested sufficiently?"

Most everyone in the group responded affirmatively. Daniel continued. "Uriel will be here within the hour, so I want to give you the opportunity to refresh yourselves. Behind the bookshelves is a room where you will find fresh clothing for designed to fit each of you, as well as a station to wash and cleanse your body. Please take turns, and I will bring the wagons inside."

With that being said, the women in the group began to discuss who would go first. Galen suggested they each take a child in with them when they readied for the day. Ramon interjected the conversation with an offer to help Jayden. Jaret offered to help Jowan. After that, everyone waited their turn.

Going outside, Daniel opened a great cellar door disguised in the earth. Leading the horses down the ramp, he unharnessed each one, and stabled them. He parked the wagons in horizontal stations, where they would wait until they were needed once again. He was sure the knights involved in the mission would need to retrieve a few items before they went through the Portal, but for now, he would leave things as they were. His chore completed, Daniel went again to the surface, and shut the cellar door. He re-entered the Refuge Vestibule through the door in the tree.

Entering the Vestibule, he heard Uriel's voice in conversation with Tvirtas and Galen.

"There are four Doors here," Uriel was saying. "Each one leads to a different Destination. For those of us who know which door leads where, we can choose wisely. But if anyone should come into the Vestibule by accident, or trickery, they have no way of determining which door leads where."

"What do the signs on the Doors mean?" Peyton asked.

The Light-Bearer smiled. "If we begin on the left, and move to the right, I will explain each door as we go," he told them.

He moved to the first Door. "The sign on this door says, '*The Grandest Souls Are Not Ruled by Appetite.*' Behind this Door is a Portal to the BorderLands. It opens just outside the cave entrance to the Hollow of Tortured Souls. As is the case with all of the Doors, this outer Door, is not the actual Portal. The anti-room is filled with delicacies and luxuries beyond compare. The room is guarded by a Fat Fox, who very rarely halts anyone from entering the Portal."

"What does the anti-room *mean*, Uriel?" Jaret wanted to know.

Uriel regarded him. "That is a very good question, Jaret. It is Sausmas' treachery to use a mortal's appetite to pull that mortal into torment. The mortal becomes so focused upon satisfying their own appetite, they cannot hear or see anything else. At that point, the appetite begins to rule them. The Fox represents the trickery that deceives a mortal into believing he or she needs no help. Such mortals are Urge Driven."

Moving to the second door, Uriel continued. "The sign on this door says, '*The Purest Souls Prefer the*

Process.' Behind this door is a Portal leading to the "Cavern of Darkness and Confusion" within Sausmas' Underground Lair. The anti-room is guarded by two Beings. They are called "Passivity" and "Discontent." A mortal who enters this door will only escape if he or she refuses to hear their words, or come under their logic. Such mortals are Fear-Driven, and have become unable to Choose."

Looking at Jaret, he disclosed the meaning behind the room's symbols.

"It is Sausmas' strategy to use a mortal's unhappiness against him or her, igniting discontentment. However, at the same time, Dark Forces convince a person they can do nothing to change their situation. The deeper into this anti-room a mortal goes; they will soon decide they have no need to open a second Door to discover a Portal. In that way, Sausmas has stolen away their desire to Choose. Rather, they find their feet on a slippery slide where there is no footing at all. That slide ends in Sausmas' Lair."

Moving to the third Door, Uriel pointed to the words engraved there: *'The Wisest Souls Seek No Fame.'* He continued.

"Behind this Door is a Portal to the Community Circle in the center of Protectorate Area Five. The anti-room is guarded by two lions, each of which is chained to the wall. If a mortal enters this Door, they must keep to the middle of the pathway, and no harm will come their way. The farther they progress into this anti-room, the lighter the room becomes, and the more the Mortal conquers the Giant of Fear."

At the fourth and last Door, Uriel stopped and looked at each person. "This Door leads to a Portal into Suzerain's Castle."

Peyton read the words engraved on the Door out loud. "*The Richest Souls Are Souls Outpoured.*"

The Light-Bearer continued. "The way to this Portal is not guarded. However, as a Mortal passes through the Portal, the white fire that courses through your swords, and all Beings of Suzerain's Realm, also makes up the substance of the Portal. If, in your heart, you are loyal to the Suzerain, then the White Fire will make you stronger. If, in your heart, you are loyal only to yourself, then the White Fire will consume you."

"What if you don't know *what* you are?" Jaret asked.

Uriel smiled at him. "The Portal will show you, and help you to Choose wisely."

He turned his attention to Ramon and Shyla. "Ramon, this Portal is offered to you and those in your care. Today, Suzerain invites you and Shyla to a private audience. He specifically wanted me to invite Jayden and Damara as well to come with you."

Hearing the invitation, Damara began jumping up and down with excitement. "Oh Mama, I've always wanted to go there!! Can we pl-e-e-ease go there?"

Ramon bent down. "Of course we are going!" He looked up at Uriel. "Are we *done* serving in the Visible realm?" he asked.

Uriel chuckled. "No, I hardly think so," he answered. "There are many who come and go from the throne room, and serve in this realm." He paused, and

336

spoke in a whisper. "Honestly, I think he actually has another assignment for you."

The Light-Bearer looked at the children. "Are you ready?"

"Oh, *yes*."

"Please."

"Are you coming with us?"

"Is it a long trip?"

Uriel smiled at them, and then looked at Shyla and Ramon. "Are you ready?" he asked.

Both adult Mortals nodded in response.

Stepping out of the way, the Light-Bearer indicated the Door should be opened. Moving forward, Ramon tentatively reached out his hand, and turned the Door's handle. As he opened the Door, Light from the Portal radiated through the opening and filled the Vestibule. Accompanying the Light was Music. It was an atmosphere one could breathe in, Peyton considered. As he took a deep breath, he felt the atmosphere on the other side of the Portal fill his entire being. The Music was more of a Substance than notes hanging in the air.

"Oh," Shyla said. "Should I...?" Hesitating, she looked at her husband.

"What is it?" Ramon asked.

In his gentlest voice, Uriel spoke. "Shyla, you won't need your pipes. They will be here for you when you return. Suzerain has some you can use while you are there."

"Oh," Shyla said once more, relief filling her face. Immediately, she brightened. "Come on children," she called. "Let's hold hands!"

And just like that, the rest of the Romani family watched a third of their party walked through the Portal and disappear. As their silhouettes disappeared from sight, the fourth Door closed on its own.

Uriel looked at those who remained.

"Can you guess which Door you have been asked to travel through?"

Peyton looked at the Light-Bearer. "I first met you in a dream. You took me to the BorderLands."

"Yes," Uriel nodded. "I remember."

"Are we going through the First Door?" the boy asked.

"Yes, we are!" Uriel beamed, and rubbed his hands together.

A small hand tugged on his pants leg. "Uriel?"

Looking down, Uriel saw and felt Karaliene standing with her arms around his leg. Tears were streaming down her cheeks.

Bending down, the Light-Bearer spoke gently. "What is it, little one?"

"Why doesn't Suzerain want *me?*"

The Light-Bearer picked her up. "Oh, Karaliene, what has caused you to think that?"

The child's voice broke as she answered, "Because I didn't get to go to his house too!"

Touching his finger to her face, Uriel brushed away her tears. "O, but you *do* get to go, too! We have one more special job that *only you* can do, and then I can *take* you there!"

Her eyes brightened. "I get to go there with you?" Really?"

"Yes, really," he replied. Then, rubbing the head of the boy standing next to him, he said, "And Jowan too!"

Continuing to carry Karaliene, Uriel's words returned to his disclosure of the mission ahead.

"What lies in the future may possibly be more dangerous than anything we have done together so far," he told them. "If you are unsure, or if you have any doubts of our victory, you are free to return to your homes, and I will accompany the children. All but two of you have been to war before, and know what to expect. After recent encounters, I would consider each of you to be a true champion."

He looked each one squarely in the eyes, assessing their resolve. One by one, each member of the team gazed back unflinching.

"Tvirtas," the Light-Bearer declared, "You have a fine team of Mortal Warriors here."

"I agree," the older man nodded.

"That being said," Uriel continued, "let me explain our mission. As I mentioned before, we are heading through the First Door. The other end of the Portal opens in the Borderlands, very close to the cave entrance to the Hollow of Tortured Souls."

Abruptly, Peyton's mind was drawn back once again to the dream of the BorderLands. At the mention of the mammoth cavern in question, night-images of torment he had witnessed in the nether regions of the earth held his attention. It was these images he considered as Uriel went on to describe the group's upcoming assignment.

"When we emerge from the Portal; Galen, Tvirtas, Panna, Pythia, Tividar and their Life-Guardians will provide cover for those of us entering the cave."

"Us?" Jaret echoed.

Uriel smiled at him. "Do you remember the last time you were there, Jaret?" he asked.

"Yes," Jaret answered. "I was ten. I went with another Light-Bearer to the Hollow, to defend my cousin's soul." That was when I discovered how much I want to become a knight."

Peyton had had no idea his friend had been to the BorderLands. Surprised, he looked at Jaret with new eyes.

"Do you remember the caverns underground? And the Hollow?" Uriel asked.

"Yes, sir," Jaret answered.

"That is where we will be heading together," the Light-Bearer told him. "For this mission, I want you to stay with Jowan. Your assignment is to help him defend his own soul. You are to be his shadow. Don't leave him, no matter what."

Uriel turned to Peyton. "Your assignment is Karaliene. You are to do the same for her. Her soul is also captive in the Hollow. I believe you saw her in your dream when we began this exercise." He paused, allowing Peyton's memory to recall the image of a little girl being tormented by a three-headed being in the cavern below.

"You mean the…." the boy asked.

"That's the one," the Light-Bearer responded, smiling.

"Is there anything I can do to help?" Ellie asked.

Uriel looked at her. "You are with me," he answered. "You have an assignment of your own to complete."

Surprised, Ellie looked at him. "I do?"

"Yes, you do," came the answer. "I'll explain as we go."

Opening the Door, Uriel was the first to step into the anti-room filled with delicacies and luxuries. "Ignore the baits placed in this compartment," he instructed them. "*Thinking* about them will *distract* you from our mission. *Eating* them will *destroy* your sensitivities."

As Galen, Tividar and Tvirtas entered the anti-room, Uriel gave them one more piece of advice. "Be ready for anything, and keep your shields up."

With eyebrows raised, Galen looked at him, inquiring.

Uriel smiled at her with a mischievous grin. "There are more than the normal number of dragons, lurking about today."

Galen flashed a bright smile, still in her younger form. "Let's go, then!" she replied.

All three knights laughed in response as they passed through the Portal to the BorderLands. Following them, three sets of two entered the Threshold together: Jaret and Jowan, Peyton and Karaliene, with Uriel and Ellie bringing up the rear.

Progressing through the Portal, it occurred to Peyton that the actual Portal was more like a hallway than an actual transportation device. As they approached the end of the hallway the entryway into the Borderlands opened on its own. A gust of sweltering air blew over the travelers. As they passed through the Door into the territory, each one was struck by the scorching heat.

Instinctively, Peyton reached for his water flask. Surprisingly, he found it was cold. Uncorking the lid, he took a drink, and then another. He hadn't realized how thirsty he had become. Pulling the flask away from his mouth, he checked how much water was left.

How was it possible, he wondered?

His flask was still full.

Looking around, he assessed their surroundings. Funny, he considered. He had never been here before, but it all looked familiar.

Gradually, Awareness came upon him. He *had* been here before!

The dream had been real.

Emerging from the Door, he turned to look back, curious to see where the Portal was hidden. But there was nothing visible but sky.

"Where did the Door go?" he asked Uriel.

The Light-Bearer touched his finger to his lips, as a signal for silence. Peyton understood. They would talk later.

Taking the lead, Uriel led them to the entrance of the cave. Looking inside, Peyton recognized the stairs leading down into the earth, and the flames of fire rushing in streams along the ceiling.

Silently, Uriel signaled to Pythia, and indicated where the most strategic place was for her to stand. He then signaled Tvirtas and Panna, sending them closer to the cliff ledges. Galen and Tividar were stationed at the door of the cavern. Amazed, Peyton once again noted the contrast in the white fire filling their swords, and the auburn color of the fire in Sausmas' Lair.

Uriel motioned for the remaining five of them to come closer to him: Ellie, Peyton, Karaliene, Jaret and Jowan. As each one neared him, the Light-Bearer extended his hand over them, bathing them in a bright light.

"Stay close to me," he whispered to them all, just loud enough for them to hear. "Hold on now!" he told them.

Peyton took Karaliene's hand. The brave little girl closed her eyes. Suddenly, Uriel lifted himself up from the ground. As he rose, so did those who stood with him. When they were about five feet from the ground, the Light-Bearer, and those bathed in his light dematerialized from sight. Seconds later, they appeared in the Hollow of Tortured Souls.

Uriel leaned down to speak to Karaliene. "I want you to walk around and find the little child who looks like you do. Peyton has seen her, and he can help you. When you find her, you need to help her get away from the Monster who is hurting her. Peyton will help you.

Here is what I want you to say, '*I don't belong to you anymore, and you have to leave me alone, and let me go by the word of Prince Kyriel.*' Can you do that?"

With wide eyes, Karaliene nodded. "This room is what I feel like inside when I am with the Queen," she said.

"I know, sweetheart," the Light-Bearer told her. "That is why we are here. Suzerain wants us to help you. Do you remember what to say?"

The little girl repeated the words he had instructed her to say. As she did, Uriel helped her remember.

When the Light Bearer was confident the words were secured in her memory, he released them to move about. As Karaliene walked away, holding Peyton's hand, Uriel turned his attention to Jowan.

"Hey Jowan," he said, rubbing the top of the boy's head.

The little boy looked at him with bright eyes. The salve Galen had been applying to his neck over the past days, had been absorbed into his skin, restoring his strength. Resting in the wagon had been good for him as well.

"Are you ready?" Uriel asked him.

Jowan nodded.

"I want you to hold Jaret's hand, and walk through this cavern. Somewhere in here, there is a group of souls being tormented. Those souls will look like you feel. Something will have been done to their mouths, to stop them from speaking. When you find the one that looks like you, here is what I want you to do. Over the past few days, the salve Galen has been rubbing into your throat muscles has done a healing work in your vocal chords. Inside your throat, have you tried to make noises over the past couple of days?"

Jowan's eyes widened with surprise. He nodded.

"I just guessed, little one," Uriel told him. "Now, I want you to say something inside your throat, even though your lips have not been restored, and you cannot form words with your mouth. Do you think you can do that?"

The boy clapped his hands and then signed "yes" in a large, dramatic movement. Sign language communicated in this way expressed intensity and emotion.

Yes, Uriel considered. This little guy was absolutely invested in his own growth.

"All right," he said. "Here is what I want you to say, in the best way you can: '*I don't belong to you anymore, and you have to leave me alone, and let me go by the word of Prince Kyriel.*' Can you do that?"

"I will help you remember, Jowan," Jaret told him. "We can do it together."

Uriel looked at Jaret. "I know you want to help him. But please understand. He has to be the one to do this. If you do it for him, he will never be strong enough to stand alone when we leave here."

"Understood," Jaret responded. "I just want to help him."

"That is worthwhile," Uriel told him. "It is good to have that desire. Just allow him to exercise the muscles of his soul, so he will stay free and grow strong."

"Yes, sir," the boy answered, as Jowan tugged on his arm.

"Remember," Uriel instructed, as they moved away, "there will be a group of them all together. Look for the boy who looks like he does."

After they had moved away, the Light-Bearer leaned down to speak to Ellie. "Now it is our turn, dear girl."

The nursemaid had not said much in the past few hours. She had taken care of Karaliene for the past five years. She had thought her life was settled. She had become resigned to being the property of the Queen, and having to work as a slave in her service. But over the past few days, her heart and mind had become filled with memory of and hunger for her own family. Would she ever see them again, she wondered?

"Let's go find the part of you that has been locked away," Uriel said gently. "I will help you. Your soul will be with those who torment themselves. They hold whips, and similar weapons. The Creatures in this cavern see to it that they continue to punish themselves. You have been doing that for a long, long time, haven't you?"

For the first time in more than five years, Ellie felt a flood-rush of hot tears well up in her eyes. She had been strong, by necessity, for as long as she could remember. But somehow, it felt good to be able to sense her own emotions.

"It will get better, little one," Uriel told her. "Let's get you free. Come on." Taking her by the hand, they began to move through the cavern, searching for the soul of a young mortal girl, who could not seem to stop blaming herself, hating herself, or hurting herself.

Not far from the cave entrance, two Weavers sat nursing their wounds. Every mouth on both bodies was muttering curses.

"Did you hear him say *'ever?'*" one moaned to the other. "I *hate* it here!"

"Go to the Barrens and *'don't come back!'*" the other replied, quoting Peyton. "That's just not fair!!"

"That means we'll *both* end up in the caverns, doing the dirty work!" the first one stated.

Not far from the Weavers, Tividar and Galen had become the focus of attention for three rather large dragons. The Chevaliesse had not yet drawn their swords, so they appeared to be unarmed mortals, ready for the picking.

"Look at this one!" the first dragon declared. "He's mine! I haven't had a tasty mortal meal in quite a while!"

"No, Abraxas," the second one spoke. "It's *my* turn to choose. You can have the old woman."

Abraxas snorted and breathed fire. He spoke to the third dragon. "Jonas," he sniffed, "you will have to learn how to eat your own kind if you are to survive."

The third dragon said nothing, but looked at Tividar and Galen with sad eyes. He spoke to Abraxas. "If I had known what listening to your words would do to me, I would have sent you away at the beginning."

Abraxas laughed at him. "You chose, you chose, you chose," he chanted, mocking the mortal named Jonas, who was now trapped in a dragon's form.

"I don't *want* to be here anymore!" Jonas shouted, breathing fire and sparks as he spoke.

Abraxas nipped at the unfortunate young dragon, and penetrated him with piercing red eyes. He addressed the second dragon once more. "Whiro, it seems our apprentice has lost his sense of appreciation for all we have done for him," he seethed.

"Yess-ss," hissed the second dragon. "He thought he wanted *all that power*. Poor man; now look at him!"

Taunting Jonas, Abraxas continued speaking. "What *shall* we *do* to him for resisting us?" he asked. "What lesson shall we teach him today? Shall we find his children in the caves? Or better yet, his wife?"

Whiro moved around so that he was behind the smaller non-dragon, named Jonas. He lifted his great head up, and opened his mouth wide. "I think we should take a bite out of his tail, since he has chosen to create a conflict instead of allowing us to enjoy our dinner!" With that, the great dragon brought down his mouth, filled with sharp fang-like teeth, into Jonas' tail, tearing away a large chunk of meat. This piece he tossed to Abraxas, who caught it, and then returned it to him.

And so began their game.

Hopeless and afraid, the younger non-dragon slouched down on the ground. There would be no escaping them. He had tried that.

There would be no defending himself. He was not strong enough.

"I wish I had listened to those who tried to help me," he muttered.

Hearing his statement, Tividar and Galen moved a little closer to him. Galen spoke first. "Is your name Jonas?" she asked.

"Yes," he moaned in answer. "Who's asking?"

"We are," Tividar told him. "What did you mean, 'I wish I would have listened to those who tried to help me?'"

"Nothing," the non-dragon replied. "It's too late. It doesn't matter now."

"Oh, but it *does*," Galen stated. "If it means what I think it means, we might be able to help you."

The dragon sighed. "All I meant was: I should have made better choices. I didn't know what I was doing to the other mortals in my life. I didn't know I was losing myself." His voice trailed off. "I didn't know...."

At that, Galen drew her long swords from the sheaths strapped to her back. As she pulled them out, they burst into white flame. At the same time, her silver armor began to appear, covering her; beginning at her head, and ending with her feet.

Taking his cue from Galen, Tividar drew his broadsword from behind his head, which also burst into flame. As he did so, his armor also appeared.

As armor appeared, so did the Life-Guardians of the two knights.

"Do you want to be free, Jonas?" Tividar challenged. "*Really* free?"

"More than anything," the dragon whimpered. "I just don't know what to do."

Looking into the trapped man's green eyes, she spoke one word, clearly and distinctly.

"Trust."

"What?" Jonas asked her.

"Trust." She repeated. "Just trust. Us. Right now."

"Can *you* help me?" the non-dragon wanted to know.

"Do you *want* to be helped?" she countered.

"Can you *help* me?" he asked again.

"Do you want to be *helped?*" she repeated.

Sighing, the non-dragon answered. "Yes."

"Then *trust* us."

"I trust you," he answered.

In that moment, a slight change took place in the dragon's eyes. The cold green color took on a lighter shade. The fins lining his back began to soften.

Unexpectedly, Abraxas and Whiro became aware of what was happening to their protégé. They turned angry red eyes towards Tividar.

"So," Abraxas stated, "what have we here?"

Without a word two Life-Guardians flew between their charges and the dragons. As Jonas watched, they grew in size, until their sizes were proportionate to the dragons threatening to strike.

Each of them lifted a shield, preventing the dragon's fire from reaching their mortals. As the fire brands hit the Guardian shields, they seemed to increase in momentum and heat, deflecting back to the source from which they came.

Tividar's Guardian looked back at him. "Take your trophy now!"

Realizing what was being said, the young knight ran around the Life-Guardians to the back of the two nether-worldly dragons. With a mighty heave, he sprang up onto Abraxas' back, landing just behind the dragon's head. There, he lifted his broadsword and drove it straight down into the creature's neck. Immediately, the great monster began writhing back and forth, its wings flapping involuntarily.

Surprised, Whiro moved to observe his companion. At that moment, Galen catapaulted through the air, as his fire stream was still being exhaled. Her feet landed flat on the smaller dragon's head, where she crouched down and brought her long swords together in one scissor-like motion, slicing off the being's head.

As the two dragons died, another flew in above them. The two Life-Guardians headed up to stop its progress.

Galen stood next to the young dragon called Jonas. "Are you ready?" she asked.

"Ready?" the dragon echoed.

"Yes," she said. "Listen, we could do this a whole lot faster if you would stop repeating everything I say…. Are you ready to be free from this place?"

"Oh, yes," Jonas replied. "More than anything."

From the hill just beyond the cave door, a man stepped towards them. He was dressed in everyday hunting clothes, and at first, Tividar thought he recognized him as one of the townspeople from the village. There certainly wasn't anything physically remarkable about him.

"What's happened here?" he asked.

"This is Jonas, who wants to be free," Galen answered. "He has been injured."

"He will be fine." The man answered. Tividar looked into his eyes, to make sure he wasn't just making an empty promise, or was one of Sausmas' agents. The man gazed back at the young man for just a moment. Tividar decided he had never seen such a depth of kindness.

The man knelt down by the injured dragon. "Do you want to be free?" he asked.

Jonas looked into the man's eyes. "Please, if you can help me."

"I can help you," the man answered. He looked at Tividar and Galen. "I will take things from here. You still have others to tend to."

Galen nodded and tugged on Tividar's arm. The young man was watching the dragon's interaction with the stranger with fascination.

"Come on," she urged. "Let's give them a little privacy."

"But, shouldn't we be here to help?" the knight asked.

"Are you kidding?" she replied. "He doesn't need *help.*"

"Why not?" the young man wanted to know.

"That's Crown Prince Kyriel," she told him. "And we just rescued a dragon."

In the cavern, Peyton and Karaliene had found a little girl in chains. Her back and face were scarred from years of torment. She looked up at them with hollow eyes. When she saw the princess, her eyes widened.

"Why are *you* here?" she asked.

Peyton answered. "We came to free you from this place," he told her.

"How?" she asked. "Why? Don't you know there is nothing you can do?"

Peyton looked at Karaliene. "What do you think?"

Karaliene looked at the child in chains. "I want you to be free from here. I want you to come with me."

Unexpectedly, the ring through which the chains was threaded, popped out from the wall, and landed at Karaliene's feet. The sound echoed through the cavern, and was heard over the moans of those in torment. Those monstrous creatures that had been inflicting pain elsewhere in the cavern, turned towards the sound.

"Hey! You there! You can't do that!" Two of them came running to where Peyton and Karaliene were standing.

"Where are your chains, mortal?" one of them asked Peyton.

"I need no chains," the boy responded, lifting his sword, its white light shining into the creature's red eyes.

"Put it away! I won't fight you!" it declared. "Just get out of here!"

"Not without what we came for," the boy answered. "Tell him, Karaliene."

The little girl stood up straight, and looked at the torturer.

"I don't *belong* to you anymore," she shouted. "You have to leave me alone, and let me go by the word of Prince Kyriel."

"Oh no," the creature screamed. The response was echoed by every torturer close by. "Don't say that again!! Leave us alone! Get out! *Get out!*"

As Peyton watched, the iron chains on the captive child's wrists and ankles dissolved into sand. Quietly, the child stood up and stepped *towards* Karaliene. *No*, he observed. She had stepped *through* her. No, that wasn't quite right either. Had the captive child become *part* of the princess? As he watched, the bruises and injuries which had shown themselves on the captive little girl became visible on Karaliene's body as well.

What did it mean, he wondered?

"Let's get out of here," she said. Grabbing Peyton's hand she literally pulled him forward to find Uriel.

In another chamber, just off a corner of the cavern, Jaret and Jowan had discovered a little boy. In fact, they had discovered a hundred or more little boys. Each one was chained to the wall, and had a large black, iron band of metal fastened into his skull. Every boy Jaret saw looked like a skeleton with skin stretched across the bones. Many appeared dead already. Just out of reach was a table, laden with rich foods. The aroma of tasty meat filled the chamber with a torturous smell. At each boy's feet, also out of reach, was a pitcher of water.

"Do you want to be free?" Jaret asked the little boy.

The boy nodded, fervently.

"Do you want to come with us?" he inquired.

Again, the boy nodded.

Without realizing what he was doing, Jowan reached up to the black iron band and touched the screws which secured it into the boy's skull.

"Do you want this to come off of you?" he asked.

The boy nodded.

As he did, the band popped off. What was revealed under the band was a face filled with bruises and scars.

"Thank you," the boy told Jaret.

At that moment, Jowan began making noises in his throat. For a second or two, Jaret thought perhaps there was something wrong, and then he remembered hearing Uriel's instructions to the boy. As Jowan came to the end of his inward speaking, the captive boy looked down, as his chains dissolved into sand. He moved towards Jowan, and his form combined into Jowan's form. Jaret observed in amazement as the two frames of the two identical boys merged together. As they did so, the mouth of the captive boy became visible on Jowan's face, as did his bruises and injuries.

Astonished, Jowan put his hands to his own face. He began opening and closing his mouth, and touching his jaw.

"Oh.." he said, looking at Jaret. "I forgot what it felt like to open my mouth! I can speak!!"

Suddenly, the boy became aware of the table laden with food, and the pitcher of water on the floor. Eagerly, he reached down and picked up the pitcher.

"I am *so thirsty*!" he exclaimed.

Impulsively, Jaret used his foil to knock the pitcher out of Jowan's hands.

Jowan reacted with a scowl. "What'd you do *that* for?" he asked.

"Are you crazy?" Jaret demanded. "Don't *touch* that! Don't eat *anything* that comes from here!

"Why not?" the ten-year old wanted to know.

"Because it will *keep you here,*" was the reply. Taking the boy by the arm, he pulled him towards the greater cavern. "We already know this isn't what you really want. Let's go. There are grander things ahead in your life than *this*."

On the nearby cliff's ledge, Tvirtas and Panna crouched behind a large rock, eavesdropping on a discussion taking place between several entities less than twenty feet away.

"We *still* need to ambush them as they come from the Portal," Pimedus was saying.

"Shut up!" replied Enki. "I am not doing anything else until I can walk again!"

"I know what you mean," one of the Weavers complained. "I wish I had known I would be dying over and over again when Sausmas first started his whispering."

Enki reproached him. "Don't you start in again! I'm warning you! When I can fly once more, I will kill you myself!"

The Weaver snorted. "Oh, I know. You'll roast me on a pit for a thousand years. You'll send me into oblivion. You'll boot-kick me into outer space. The least you could do is show a little imagination."

Another voice was heard. "All of you have all ruined my plans. Sausmas himself will deal with you. I had things perfectly set for the future, and you senseless idiots ruined it!"

The group together looked at Leviathan. Enki spoke for all of them.

"You don't have any leverage over us now. Don't forget, you don't even have a hope of a host. You are on the same level as I am now. So just shut up, and stop talking about your former glory."

Leviathan answered. "I have a plan."

Pimedus spoke up. "You *always* have a plan. I'm tired of your plans."

Leviathan repeated his statement. "I have a plan. I will yet have a Gala Celebration, and I will still be Queen."

With an arrogance he could not support, the Weaver spoke up, "Yes, we know. Blah. Blah. Blah. We have heard it all before."

Leviathan reached over and grabbed the Weaver by the throat. He lifted him off the ground. As the creature hung in mid-air, its feet kicking back and forth, the Python spoke with rage.

"You are an insignificant speck! You are a meal-worm! When Sausmas puts me back in power, you will be the first one I come after. Don't you *ever* even think about speaking to me, or about me, like that again!"

Letting go, he pitched the Weaver through the air. The creature flew over the rocks, and landed next to the listening Tvirtas and Panna. A few moments later, the Weaver sat up after crash-landing, its eyes focused on the two knights.

Tvirtas and Panna drew their swords, initiating their armor installation, and bright white fire.

Surprised the Weaver began screaming, from every mouth on its body. "They're here! Pimedus! They're *right here*!"

Pimedus stood, and flew over to the source of the screams. "*Who* is here, you irritating little retard! *What is* it?" But then, seeing the two warriors, he also began to yell.

"Leviathan, you will want to see this!"

As the Shade was speaking, two Life-Guardians rose to the air to defend their mortals.

As the Life-Guardians rose, a cloud of innumerable bats also rose from the cavern entrance. These began to torment Tvirtas and Panna, putting them on the defensive, digging into their skin.

From her stationed post, Pythia saw the Weaver fly as it was tossed through the air. She observed the Life-Guardians and their light rising in the sky. She also saw the responses on the faces of those in the dark circle.

Pulling silver arrows from her quiver, she mounted the first one in her bow. As had occurred with the others upon drawing their swords, so it occurred with Pythia whenever she drew any of her unusual weapons. The arrows and bow all burst into white hot flame. With incredible accuracy, she lanced Pimedus in the eye, and then shot the Weaver with two more arrows.

Unaware his forces were under attack, Leviathan flew to see what the commotion had been about. He was greeted by Tvirtas' Life-Guardian, filled and beaming with bright brilliance. Stunned, he halted in his advance.

"I *know* you," he stated carefully. "We have fought before."

The Life-Guardian nodded.

"Have you been re-assigned?"

The Life-Guardian shook his head.

Leviathan slowly moved beyond the cliff's ledge. Looking down, he saw the two knights, who were now standing and ready for battle. He also discovered the states of Pimedus and the unfortunate Weaver.

"Tvirtas?" he exclaimed. "I thought you were dead."

"As you can see," the former commander replied. "I am very much *alive*."

"How is that possible?" the Python demanded. "I *killed* you."

"I will give you a one word answer," Tvirtas said. "Kyriel."

Leviathan began screaming, spewing his rage in every direction.

"I *hate* that name! Don't say that name! Just shut up already!" The Creature put his hands over his ears, and looked down. "And there's no need to bully me with that light either!"

"No one is bullying you," a Voice spoke, filling the skies.

Leviathan shrank down into a huddle next to Pimedus.

Tvirtas, Panna and Pythia walked towards the dark circle of creatures, with their swords in front of them. All the while, they were repeating the name, "Kyriel."

Each time the name was spoken, the dark forces retreated, until they were at the opening to the underground caverns.

When they reached the door, Tvirtas pointed his great Broadsword at all of them, giving a little push. As a result, everyone in the group of dark forces lost their balance, and fell backwards into the cavern below.

"How did that Shade know you?" Pythia asked.

"I was an officer in the Prince's Military years ago. It was our assignment was to stop the diversion of materials which were being stolen, and get them into the right hands. Leviathan was the one leading Sausmas' forces. In the process of the mission, I received a mortal wound, and would have bled to death had it not been for Kyriel. It was then that Anbeter and I entered into a rest period with our family. It was then that we brought ourselves and the children into safe keeping in Protectorate Area One."

"Amazing," Pythia replied. "The more I learn about you, Commander, the more I respect you."

Tvirtas smiled. "That's very kind of you to say," he responded quietly.

"Where did Galen and Tividar go to?" Panna questioned. "Do you see them?"

"Don't worry so, Panna," Pythia admonished. "We are almost at the appointed meeting time."

In the cavern below, Uriel and Ellie had discovered a young woman who had been held captive for some time. She had been locked in a tiny iron cage. The cage had been hung from ceiling by a long chain. The chain was attached to the top of the cage, then run through a pulley in the ceiling. The end of the chain was hooked to a far wall.

Alone in the suspended device, the child was alone, with barely enough room to move about. Periodically, when her captivity became more than she could bear, the little girl would gain enough courage to move to the door, and shake it, seeking escape.

Each time she shook the door, the vibration released a series of images which projected on the walls around her. The images showed pictures of the girl in various happy situations and relationships. When the images appeared, the girl would begin to weep. In her weeping, she would bang her head against the iron bars of her cage, as though in punishment. Many times, she would seek to hurt herself in other ways. When she tired of those actions, she would be exhausted, and would sit still. Then, the images ceased their portrayal.

"How do we get her down, Uriel?" Ellie asked.

"Do you remember what I told you needed to be said?" the Light-Bearer asked.

Ellie nodded.

Bravely, she stepped into the room. Moving alone, she stood just under the cage, and spoke up to the child above her.

"Excuse me," she shouted.

"What is it?" came the response, in somewhat of a moan.

"Can I ask you a question?" Ellie inquired.

"You just did," the captive replied.

"No, seriously," the nursemaid persisted. "Can I ask you a question?"

The girl in the cage sighed. "What do you want?"

"Do you want to be free?" she asked.

"What does that mean?" the child wanted to know.

"Real freedom. Out of that cage. Out of here. Do you want it?" Ellie persisted.

The captive was silent for so long, even Uriel thought she might have gone to sleep. Finally, a quiet voice answered.

"It is all I have wanted for as long as I can remember, but it is no use. There is no way out."

Ellie looked at Uriel, who nodded.

In a loud voice, as loud as she could muster, she shouted at the cage, and the purveyor of the images.

"I want to be free from this place, from this cage."

Abruptly, the ceiling hook popped out from the wall, dropping the cage to the floor. As the cage hit the floor, the locked door popped open.

But still the girl sat inside.

"Come on out!" Ellie told her.

"I can't move," the girl replied.

"Why not?"

"Because even if I think things are going to be better, they never are," the child answered.

In response, Ellie asked her first question again.

"Do you want to be free?"

The captive responded. "More than anything else I can think of."

The words had no sooner left her mouth, than two monstrous creatures appeared from the shadows. Laughing hideously, and pointing fingers, they began working to reattach the hook into the ceiling.

Horrified, Ellie looked at Uriel. "What do I do?" she asked.

"Speak up!" he answered.

Closing her eyes, to muster courage, Ellie shouted once more.

"NO! I will not stay! I want to be free from this place forever!"

Her words echoed off the walls, filling the room with sound. As the sounds echoed, they grew in volume until the sounds themselves became a whirlwind. As the whirlwind grew in power, it consumed the walls of the room, destroying the images. As the images dissolved into mist and vapor, the two monstrous creatures became smaller and smaller.

Over the sound of the whirlwind, Uriel was heard giving Ellie instruction.

"Now, Ellie! Don't stop! You're almost there!"

Once more Ellie raised her voice to a shouting volume. "I don't want to be here anymore. I don't belong to you. I am loyal to Suzerain. You have to let me go by the word of Kyriel!"

Immediately, a bright white light broke into the room. The cage door was opened wider and wider, until its door was bigger than the original cage had been.

Moving forward, Ellie stepped to the door of the cage and extended her hand. The captive child stood and walked towards her, then into her, then merging with her. When the two parts of the one child had converged, the cage, the room, and its entities all disappeared.

Ellie stood with Uriel in a field of long grass, just outside the cave entrance on the surface. Within seconds Jared and Jowan joined them. A few seconds later, Peyton and Karaliene were added.

Uriel chuckled to himself. What a wonderful adventure this had been! Hearing his joy, Karaliene began to giggle. It felt so good to be finally free. Soon, all of them were laughing.

Five weary but fulfilled Knights of the Dragon's Cross emerged into the field from battle, along with their Life-Guardians.

Uriel gathered them all together. When there was a silent moment in the conversation, he spoke.

"Stand close to me now. This field is the Suzerain's Portal."

"Where are we going?" Jaret asked.

The Light-Bearer smiled. "We are all headed to *greater* adventures," he responded. "The first stop is Suzerain's Castle. Are you ready?"

Peyton and Karaliene, Jaret and Jowan, Tvirtas, Galen, Pythia, Panna, Tividar, and Ellie all kept their eyes wide open.

No one wanted to miss a thing.

The adventure continues in "The Chronicles of Hausse; Book Two; The Trouble with Tyrants."

Debbye Graafsma is an author, counselor, and songwriter who lives in North Carolina with her husband and daughters. She is a pastoral counselor, with a heart to help hurting people.

Other books by Debbye include, "Journey – A Novel," which is an historical fiction based on the life events of Mary Magdalene; "Elements of Identity Formation;" "How to Pray Prayers that Make a Difference," as well as the "G.E.M.S. Personal Discovery Assessment Tool." These are available through our ministry offices, or can be ordered online at amazon.com or lulu.com.

Debbye also has several instrumental (keyboard) and vocal worship projects available on iTunes and Amazon.com.

To make inquiries, or to book Debbye for a seminar, retreat, or worship endeavor, please contact our ministry offices at the website listed below.

Awakened to Grow Ministries
awakenedtogrow.com

www.ingramcontent.com/pod-product-compliance
Lightning Source LLC
Chambersburg PA
CBHW031101030726
47496CB00002BA/325

9 780985 268091